# Deadly Choices

Shelly L. Foster

Royal Peacock Publications
P.O. Box 931
Dayton, NJ 08810-0931

www.Royal-Peacock-Publications.com

Published by:

**Royal Peacock Publications**
P.O. Box 931
Dayton, NJ 08810-0931

Copyright @2005 by Shelly L. Foster

This book is the work of fiction. Characters, places, names and incidents are the product of the author's imagination or used fictionally. Any resemblance to actual persons, living or dead, business establishments or events is entirely coincidental.

Without limiting the rights under copyright, no part of this book may be reproduced, stored in or introduced into a retrieval system, or transmitted, in any form, or by means, electronic, photocopied, mechanical, recording or otherwise, without the written permission of both the copyright owner and the above publisher of the book.

Printed in Canada

ISBN, paperback – 0-9764930-8-X

Open Casket

A big polished
cherry oak model
trimmed in brass
awaits...

A plush satin
cushioned interior
promises a comfortable
resting place...

The casket anticipates
that moment of glory
happening soon...
Therefore in full groom
will this cherry oak model
be...
Standing front and center
during the wake...
For the WHOLE Evans family to see...

The knife of the fast life
can cut deeply...
Cheaply are the excuses iterated
harrowing
is the experience when sanity
is obliterated...

To rest, Cynthia's mate was laid
subsequently warranting
self-satisfying sexcapades
with lies and charades
making official

a life that's now superficial...
Shopping sprees spawned
via self-pity spells
kick in just in time as
hell arrives from earth's
center, to keep lives
downtrodden in simmer mode...
Truth remains untold
as mayhem besets the premises
deceit and chaos
are among the many blemishes
that tarnish a former pure life...

What's so becoming
is that Chris witnesses
every shortcoming
in her mother...
all that makes Cynthia a fool
...Chris sees as bein' cool...
as the Evans' household
becomes more tragic,
The door of the casket
opens slowly,
like magic...
Patiently awaiting
another statistic...
which...it can begin
permanently dating...

Marc Lacy, author of The Looking Heart: Poetry from Within, 2005

## Dedication
### My mother and "Aunt Lou"

I dedicate this book to my mother, Billie Gene Foster and my late, Great Aunt, Louise Lee. Thank you for your strength, your guidance and your leadership. It is only because of the qualities you instilled in me, that I am the woman I am today.

I thank you, Mom, for grooming me into a confident, secure woman.

Thanks, Mom.

Aunt Louise...Although you are no longer with us, I know that you are part of everything I do. I know you are watching over me, and still guiding and directing my path. I wish you were still here, but I keep you with me in my heart. I miss you.

With all my love,

Shelly

## Acknowledgments

Thanks to my Lord and Savior Jesus Christ!

Thanks to all of my loyal friends and family, who supported me throughout this endeavor. Thanks for your words of encouragement and daily prodding to keep me focused. I would have never completed this journey without all of you.

In loving memory of Mary Ann Holland (Family Friend) and Louise Lee.

| | |
|---|---|
| Crystalyn Foster (Daughter) | Billie Gene Foster (Mother) |
| Donald & Deb Green | Maurice & Donnetta Foster |
| Norma J. Collins | Crystal Holoman |
| Lucille Holoman | Candace R. Collins |
| Curtis & Eileen Minnis | John & Debby Faherty |
| Bennett & Samantha Ruiz | Mary McNamara |
| Pauletta Ashby | Ron & Dottie Cavil |
| Sam & Linda Martin | Evan Kane |
| Wayne & Cynthia Hines | Patricia Burley |

PCG Literary Marketing – Anita Peterson

Cover Design - Pittershawn Palmer

# Prologue

Cynthia and Chris are mother and daughter, both struggling to find themselves. The main character, Cynthia, finds herself struggling with her new found freedom, and makes many choices that are detrimental to her and Chris' life. After repeated mistakes, her choices cost them in a big way. By the time she realized the consequences for her choices, it was too late. Chris struggles emotionally to deal with the changes in her mother. Cynthia's irresponsible, reckless behavior caused their lives to unravel at the seams.

Many lose their lives...Did someone love her or hate her so much that they would kill because of her?

# 1

"STOP, PLEASE STOP! You son of a bitch, if you hit me one more time, I swear I'll kill you." Something registered in his brain, or the look in her eyes, revealed she was serious. He lowered his fists, turned and strolled out the room, as if he had just done something great.

She pulled herself up onto the bed, and turned to face the doorway, seeing a picture more horrifying than the beating. Her daughter stood with a puddle of tears in her eyes jolting Cynthia's heart, more pain than any mother could endure. Cynthia beckoned for her daughter. Witnessing baby steps as if her teenaged daughter were afraid, she watched her daughter approach her. They hugged and cried until they both fell asleep.After several hours of sleep, Cynthia awoke in a rage. She must have been dreaming that she was being beaten again. Luckily her activity didn't wake her daughter. Slowly slipping out of bed, inching her way to the bathroom, she needed to see what she must look like. Her body throbbed with pain, so she knew it must have looked as ugly as it felt. She closed the bathroom door, peeling off her

## Deadly Choices

clothes. It shouldn't have taken much effort, but, needless to say, she could hardly raise her arms. Even removing a piece of cloth with dried blood from her skin was so painful it stung. Looking in the full-length mirror on the back of the bathroom door, a snowball of emotions went through Cynthia's mind. *Why did he do this to me? What did I do to deserve this? Should I stop working so much, and pay more attention to him?* She closed her eyes tightly to shake the thoughts away. Her body was clad in only her panties by now, and as she viewed her body, she flinched. Her complexion was blotched with dark, bloody bruises. Her first thought was that she'd better hurry to adjust her appearance before her child appeared. After running her bath water and stepping in, she began gently swabbing the bruises with a soft cloth. Finally, she stepped out of the tub and put on her thick, terrycloth robe that covered her up to her chin.

    Chris lay awake gazing intently at her "Are you okay, Mom?" she responded, as softly as she could. "Sure honey, I'm fine." Before Chris could start asking her usual fifty million questions, Cynthia quickly told her, "Go to your room, and get dressed, we're going shopping." Shopping was a pick up for Cynthia, and Chris as well.

    Suddenly Jordan, her battering husband, appeared in the hallway. He opened his mouth looking pitiful, but before he could speak, Cynthia threw up her hand, indicating he was not to say a word. Usually when Jordan beat or cursed Cynthia unmercifully, he was able to calm her, and reconcile with her. But this time was different. He noticed it almost instantaneously. He stood dead in his tracks, trying to figure out what was going on in that pretty head of hers. He began to have flashbacks about how good things were in the beginning. He could strongly recollect how she captivated him when they first met. She was five foot two, one hundred and five pounds, neat as a pin, physically and domestically, and always impeccably dressed, matching from head to toe. Cynthia always conducted herself like a lady. Through wear and tear, physical and emotional, she never lost her touch. In every area of her life she put all she had into what she did. As a mate, a friend or a lover, she was flawless and protected from criticism. She valued her relationships. He replayed their love making, over and over, recalling how nurturing she had always been as a mother. Her friendships were endearing, and he had to remind himself how she would move heaven and earth to please him. At that moment, still unable to move, he tried to figure out and understand why, if she were all those good things, he treated her the way he did.

Jordan's usual mode of communication, rather than sit down or even laying down for that matter and rationally talking, was to beat, holler and scream to be "The MAN." A few seconds later, as if a light bulb went off inside his head, he went racing down the stairs, swiftly dashing past their bedroom, through the living room, down yet another flight of stairs into the den. He grabbed his keys and his wallet from the coffee table where he had set them when he first got home. A few moments later he was pulling out of the garage in his black utility vehicle, preoccupied with his thoughts. He hadn't even turned on the radio, which was one of the first things he did when he got into his vehicle. Realizing suddenly his routine, he pulled one of his oldies but goodies CD from the glove compartment, appropriate for his mood. The CD was a thirteen song, one-hour pack of the smoothest, most mellow love songs from the seventies one could imagine. Lighting a cigarette, he continued his journey. This was going to be the beginning of a new Jordan. The first day of the rest of their lives….. or so he thought.

Thirty minutes passed and Cynthia was nearly dressed. Chris,

## Deadly Choices

sitting on her mother's bed, was anxiously awaiting her mothers' completion of her dressing routine. Cynthia had to use excessive make-up all over her body to cover the bruises therefore, it took her a little longer than usual. Whether Chris realized that or not, she was extremely patient and never questioned how much longer it would be until her mother was ready. About twenty minutes later, Cynthia told her gorgeous four-foot eight little lady, "It's time to boogie."

Whenever Cynthia was feeling out of sorts, as she was this day, everything really had to be perfectly engineered. She was smartly dressed in a red, silk sun dress with six straps that crisscrossed in the back, a pair of red, patent leather, semi-flat sandals, and a red, patent trimmed handbag. Chris had on a red, jean jumper with red, leather sneakers. Both matched the red, BMW convertible, transporting them to their shopping spree. Three-fourths of the way to their destination, Cynthia had an urge to eat. When she asked Chris about eating, Chris's response was very mature for a teenager.

"Whatever you feel up to Mom. If you don't feel like eating I can wait until we get back home." Nearly one o'clock on a beautiful, sunny, Saturday afternoon, Cynthia opted to stop at a nearby restaurant to eat a meal before they shopped. Anxious to shop, they gobbled down their food.

Chris, more anxious than Cynthia, ate more quickly. Cynthia shopped as therapy. Her mind cluttered and unfocused, reeling with anger and frustration. Leaving the restaurant, Cynthia dropped her purse, scattering all the contents about the floor. As she bent to pick them up, her eyes zeroed in on a big pair of feet standing next to her purse. A really good-looking man was picking her things up, hoarding them in his hands. Chris reached down and slid the purse closer for him to drop the contents back into it. Cynthia thanked him and smiled as she and Chris walked out.

They practically shopped 'til they damn near dropped. Laughing in the car on their way home, trying to determine, if they were about to drop due to the time it took them, or from the weight of the packages. As they slowly pulled into the garage, Chris immediately noticed that her dad still hadn't returned home. Before Cynthia could bring the car to a full stop, Chris was opening her door to grab her packages, rushing straight to her room to ooh and ah over her new things. Cynthia couldn't quite move as fast, now beginning to feel the aches and pains of the beating.

Dropping her packages on the bed, she sat on the edge to catch her breath. As her body started to relax, she looked around the room, tastefully decorated in dark cherry furniture, with burgundy and evergreen floral drapes and bedding. A smile came across her face, thinking about how nice a home she had. Before the smile became complete, it turned into a frown. She stood, walked to the mirror and focused on a very unhappy woman. *What a mess I have made of my life. What do I do?* Slamming her fist on the top of the dresser, she said aloud, "I've had enough, I'm out of here!" Before the thought could set in place, Jordan came home. He burst into the house screaming, singing and obviously overwhelmed with delight. He came in their bedroom dancing and swinging packages. He tossed them on the floor grabbed Cynthia, spun her around and hugged her so tight, she felt like she could throw up. "What's all this about?" Looking, sounding, and talking in ways she had never heard before, he said "I've got a new lease on life. I've come to realize how much I've taken you for granted, and starting tonight, you, Chris and I are going out. The movies, dinner and a horse and carriage ride. Then he said more softly and sensually "We'll come home and make love, just like the first time." Cynthia pushed away from him so fast she almost fell.

"You Bastard, how dare you come bouncing in here pretending to be Prince Charming. Did your brain go on leave or something? Did you forget several hours ago you beat me like I was a rabid dog, tossed me around like a stuffed animal, and now out of the blue we're painting the town red! You have more gall than I gave you credit for."

"Cynthia, I know you're upset with me, and you have every right to be, but please just hear me out."

"Just hear you out? When have you ever bothered to just hear me out?"

"But baby, I've decided to put all the past behind us and start fresh."

"Oh! You've decided to put the past behind you. Help me to understand why I should bother. I've decided to put my well being in the forefront."

"What's that supposed to mean?"

"I don't really know just yet what I mean. All I know is something needs to change."

"That's exactly what I'm talking about, a new beginning."

"Well I don't know if I want my new beginning to include you."

"What would make you think I'll let you take my child, and just walk out of here?"

"One thing I do know is, if you beat me one more time, it had better be a good one, because it'll be your last."

Jordan had the same feeling come over him that he had a few hours before, which was that she meant what she said. She had that same commanding look in her eyes, and a staunch demeanor. It was clear to him this wasn't the time to call her bluff.

They muddled through the rest of the weekend with plenty of tension in the air. Monday morning came, but before the alarm could go off, Cynthia was up stirring around. All she could seem to concentrate on was what her strategy would be to get out of that house and start a new life. She wanted a life free of an abusive husband, and constant, negative energy. She sat at the kitchen table with her coffee, cigarette, a pad and pen. She reached to remove the phone from the wall. Her first call was to her boss' voicemail. "Maurice" she said, with her dry deep morning voice. "I won't be in the office today or tomorrow. Friday I wrapped up the Ferguson deal, and the Swanson deal is due to close on Thursday. There should not be any accounts that will require my attention today. Should you need my assistance, don't hesitate to page me or call me on the cell. Have a great day and I'll see you on Wednesday." Disconnecting that call, she dialed into her voicemail, and changed her message to indicate that she was out of the office, not returning calls until Wednesday. Next, she sat quietly, jotting down a list of things to be accomplished. She was more determined than she'd ever been about anything.

Ten years of wondering if today would be the day Jordan would beat her to death had finally come to an end. Cynthia told herself that she wasn't going to live that way anymore. This time she had to put action behind her thoughts. She had to execute a plan before Jordan had a chance to get next to her. Out of the blue, tears came streaming down her face. With the back of her hand she wiped them away and sauntered to the sink to rinse out her coffee cup. Before she could turn on the faucet, her eyes filled up with tears again, blurring her sight. It was almost as if she had cut an artery and couldn't stop the bleeding. The more she became angry with how unhappy she was with her life, the more tears fell. She stomped her foot so hard she felt as though she may have sprained her ankle. She swiftly turned and headed upstairs. She went into Chris's room, leaned over, kissed her on her cheek and softly whispered in her ear, "It's time to rise and shine, sweetie." They both dressed and left while Jordan slept. She stopped at a fast food restaurant to get Chris something for breakfast. Cynthia usually cooked breakfast but this time she didn't want to take any chances that Jordan would disrupt her plan for the day. She ran several errands and made some phone calls. The day quickly passed. It was nearly three o'clock and she had to pick Chris up from school by four. She had one last thing on her list to do. As usual, Cynthia had everything prioritized geographically so she didn't travel from one end of town to the other. Her last stop was at the moving company, only three blocks from the school. The movers wanted specific information about the number of pounds, the dimensions of the rooms, and other details.

"I don't have the answers to those questions and I'm sure this is standard procedure, but all I want to know is, the next available day I can get on your books."

Her disappointment heightened as she heard, "Ma'am, we need this information in order to quote you the correct price."

Cynthia stared at the tall, odd-looking man behind the counter for a moment. She kept a cool composure, but she said in an accelerated and agitated tone, "I have approximately four rooms of furniture: two complete bedroom suites, one king and one full; a completely furnished living room, sofa, loveseat, two chairs, coffee table, sofa table, two end tables, grandfather clock, some office furniture, an oak desk, entertainment center, three chairs, a computer and printer. There are also odds and ends, clothes, and everything in the kitchen cabinets. Cost is not a factor, time is, as well as what day can you come, and what time you will be there." The odd looking man hesitated for a moment, finally answering, "We had a cancellation for tomorrow. Would ten a.m. work for you?" Cynthia smiled slightly. "Yes, ten will be fine." She pulled a pen and paper from her purse, and wrote down both addresses. "Here's my address." She pointed to the other and said, "This is the delivery address. Here's my credit card." The man processed the credit card, got an approval number and told Cynthia they'd see her at ten sharp.

Cynthia picked Chris up at three-fifty. Chris chattered the entire way home, not much of what she said registering, because Cynthia was trying to get a handle on her own feelings. Partly she was sad, knowing that the last ten years of her life were coming to an end, partly, a feeling of triumph and victory. Cynthia and Chris pulled into the garage to find Jordan at home. Cynthia couldn't quite remember the last time he'd been home at four thirty in the afternoon. Seemingly, he lay awake in the same spot he was in when they left. He hadn't showered or shaved all day. For a short moment Cynthia felt sorry for him. That faded fast, as she had flashbacks. After all, she'd been in bed all day before. She stood at the foot of the bed staring at the sorry bastard. She knew that she needed to get him in good spirits, so he would be unsuspecting of her plans. She needed to make him feel comfortable about their relationship, or she'd catch hell trying to move. He had to be at work tomorrow so she could leave in peace. She slowly walked over to him, leaned over and kissed him on his forehead. Then she slipped out of her clothes, down to her sexy lace underwear, lay on top of him, on top of the covers, gently stroking his face, and the contour of his body. She whispered in his ear that she'd fix a bite to eat, get Chris to go to bed then make him feel better. Since she'd never tried to leave him before, he didn't have a clue what she was up to. Time seemed to pass so quickly. Eight-thirty, after dinner, Chris did her homework and started drifting off to sleep.

Cynthia ran a hot, bubble bath, inviting Jordan to join her, which he very willingly did. She made love to him better than she ever had, only this time it was a performance. He had no idea that within twenty-four hours he'd be alone.

# 2

Five a.m. couldn't come fast enough. Cynthia rolled over and slid her hands down Jordan's legs to arouse him. She figured one more round could only secure his confidence. After a while she started wondering if this was such a good idea. His lovemaking was so good, she was having second thoughts. One thing their relationship never lacked was great sex. Suddenly a thought crossed her mind. Maybe he knew her plans and he was performing this time. She quickly stored that thought to keep everything in perspective she realized it was too good to stop. She got back into it, and enjoyed every minute. When they finished, Jordan looked Cynthia directly in her eyes and told her he loved her. At one time Cynthia would have fallen for that, and from that moment it would have been business as usual. But she knew after ten years of heartache it wouldn't last. The plans she had made were best for her and Chris. She softly brushed his face, kissed him on his cheek, and told him they needed to get up and get goin'. Jordan reached for her arm and slowly pulled her back close to him. "Let's stay home and be together all day." Her eyes almost bulged from her head, as she thought *Shit, what do I do now?* Smooth and soft-spoken she cooed, "Honey, you know missing you turns me on. Let's savor this time and look forward to being together later." Looking at her, Jordan agreed. Cynthia felt so relieved. They both got out of bed, and while Jordan showered, Cynthia changed the sheets and tidied up the bedroom. She would never leave her house unpresentable, plus she knew the movers were coming, and she was much too private to let someone see what her night was like with her mate. Nevertheless she wouldn't be spending any more nights with him.

Jordan came out of the bathroom, towel draped loosely and partially open around his waist. God, he was lookin' good! His skin gleamed liked the sunrays bouncing off the ocean. Cynthia felt weak in the knees just looking at him. She had to shake her head to come to her senses. This was a mean, selfish, pompous bastard, who's only reason for doing anything was for his own benefit and his benefit only. Even though she had known this for some years, he was still so irresistible. She turned, and went upstairs to Chris' room. She and Chris did their normal, daily routine.

Jordan appeared in the doorway of their daughter's room, smiling as though the world belonged to him. Cynthia looked up and smiled back, only her smile didn't have the same meaning. Jordan asked Chris if she wanted him to take her to school. She jumped up from the bed, grabbed her dad and said with great delight, "Yes, Daddy." They all hugged and kissed, and off the two went. Cynthia couldn't believe how well things were going. She wondered, *Could this really go off without a hitch?*

After Jordan and Chris left, Cynthia sat on the sofa, anxiously awaiting the movers.

It was nine fifty-seven a.m. when the doorbell rang. Cynthia suddenly felt scared and couldn't seem to move from the spot where she was sitting. She finally rose and headed for the door. There stood this incredibly tall, handsome man and several men looking like henchmen behind him.

"Ma'am, we're from the moving company. Would you like for us to get started?"

"The quicker the better! What room would you like to start in?"

"We'll start downstairs first."

As the men began preparing for the move, Cynthia went upstairs and sat on her bed. Her eyes began to tear as she reflected on her memories. For a brief moment, she thought she might be making a huge mistake. Immediately, the beatings and the mental abuse brought her back to her senses. A call to the office, to see if there were any messages, would take her mind off her personal problems. The first message definitely did the trick. The President of Swanson & Swanson Co. previously scheduled to close on Thursday, was ready to sign the contract today. Cynthia listened to the other messages then instantly called Mr. Swanson to see what time he wanted her to come to his office. After the third ring his secretary answered, "Swanson & Swanson, how may I direct your call?"

"Rose, this is Cynthia Evans with Robinson, Cavil & Lee Architects. I need to speak with Mr. Swanson, please."

"Hi Cynthia, I'll connect you. Please hold."

"Phil Swanson"

"Mr. Swanson, Cynthia Evans, Robinson, Cavil & Lee Architects. I just picked up your message."

"Yes, Mrs. Evans. I'd like to schedule a meeting with you. I've read over your proposal and I have a few questions. Once I'm satisfied with your answers, we can do business. Your voicemail message says you're out of the office today, so later this week would be fine."

"Oh, no, Mr. Swanson, I can be there at two o'clock if that works in your schedule."

"Two o'clock it is. Since my brother has been the only one you've been dealing with, it will be a pleasure to finally meet you."

"Good day, Mr. Swanson, I'll see you at two."

Cynthia couldn't believe things were going so well. This was a 1.3 million-dollar project she'd been working on for several months. She went downstairs to check the progress of the movers. She asked the man in charge how much longer he thought they would be. He told her about an hour or so. It was eleven-thirty a.m. and he expected them to be pulling out at about twelve-thirty.

"Perfect," Cynthia replied to the man. "I have some business to take care of therefore, I'll have someone at my new place to show you where everything needs to go."

Cynthia went back upstairs, and called her girlfriend Ardelia, with whom she had been friends for twenty years. She trusted Ardelia's judgment.

"Ardelia, what are your plans for the day? I need a huge favor."

"What do you need me to do?"

"I'm moving today, but I have an unexpected business meeting at two o'clock. I need for you to meet me at my new place so I can show you where I want my things to be placed when the movers arrive."

"You're doing what today?!!"

"Moving. I'll fill you in later. Can you meet me at 1603 Pine

St. at 1:00?"

"1603 Pine St. Is that the new development near downtown?"

"Yes. Can I count on you to be there at one?"

"Of course. I'll see you shortly."

Cynthia looked in her closet to decide what to wear to this meeting. It had to be tasteful, not too flashy, not too short, but not boring. She pressed the button to rotate the rack, but before she went too far, the perfect outfit jumped out. A pale, yellow, silk suit. The jacket was long and covered her hips, which was a must. It buttoned at the neckline and didn't require a blouse. The pants were loose and slightly flared.

Since Nick Swanson was the one she'd always worked with, she knew to wear pants because he was such a flirt, and married with three children. Even though he had family pictures on his desk, he was always propositioning her to spend time with him. Cynthia preferred not to wear pants to a business meeting, but after the first visit with Nick Swanson, she felt it absolutely necessary. Hopefully, Phil Swanson won't attempt to mix business with pleasure. If he did, hopefully he won't be married, or use it as a condition to close the deal. However, if he did for a 1.3 million dollar deal, she could possibly go out with him.

Cynthia dressed and headed downstairs to speak with the movers once more.

"Sir? I need to go to my new place and meet my friend that will give you instructions when you arrive. Are you ready to leave, or do I need for you to lock up here when you're finished?"

"No ma'am. We're ready when you are."

"You do know where 1603 Pine St. is, don't you?"

"Yes. We'll see you there in twenty minutes."

# 3

When Cynthia pulled into the parking lot, she saw Ardelia sitting in her car. Cynthia waved out the window for Ardelia to follow her toward the garage. Ardelia was jumping out of the car before she could park.

"Are you Okay? What is going on?"
Cynthia responded with only these words, "I've had enough."

"I've been praying for this day. I've been worried about you."

"Once I get settled in, we'll get together and I'll explain. Right now I need to show you how I want my things arranged. I need to be at Swanson & Swanson in forty-five minutes."

"Swanson & Swanson, that's the big contract you've been trying to land for months, isn't it?"

"Yes. Hopefully I'll get signed contracts in hand today!"
Cynthia was showing Ardelia how she wanted her furniture arranged when the doorbell rang.

"Are those the movers already?"
"Must be."

Cynthia introduced Ardelia to the movers, and told them that in her absence she would be giving them their instructions.

"I'm headed out. If you need to reach me, leave me a message at my office. I'll check my messages as soon as the meeting is over. But whatever you do, don't call the house."

"I'll make sure everything gets done. Good luck on your meeting."

Cynthia arrived at the Swanson & Swanson office towers, but once parked, she began to get nervous. She hadn't had time to deal with her feelings, considering everything else that was going on. As she walked toward the elevators, there was this tall, dark, handsome man approaching at the same time. He was five-foot eleven inches tall, bald, with very broad shoulders. They made eye contact and, as usual, if Cynthia made eye contact she smiled and spoke. The two entered the elevator, and ironically they were going to the same floor. When Cynthia reached the secretaries pool, she told Rose she had a two o'clock appointment with Phillip Swanson.

"That was Mr. Swanson that got off the elevator with you."

"It was?"

"He is anxious to meet you."

"Mr. Swanson, I'm Cynthia Stark-Evans with Robinson, Cavil & Lee."

Phil Swanson rose from his desk to greet Cynthia. "It is indeed a pleasure Ms. or Mrs. Evans?"

"Just call me Cynthia"

"Have a seat, Cynthia."

Naturally her thoughts echoed, *I hope this hasn't started off too personal and he gets fresh like his brother.* She glanced at his hands, scanning for a wedding ring. *Hmmm, no ring!* That really didn't mean much. She knew a lot of men who were married and didn't wear a ring.

"Cynthia, why don't we start by addressing the concerns that I have from your proposal."

"By all means, Phil."

"My primary concern is the estimated time of completion. The time line isn't conducive for our company plans."

"What completion date would it take?"

"No later than September 20$^{th}$."

"We have a crew working on another large project and I would need to speak with the foreman to see where we are on the completion of that project before I could make a commitment for that date. I'll call him from here as soon as we have all of your concerns on the table. I'm almost positive that date could work."

"The other issues are small, and I'm sure we can work through them after I sign."

"Let me make the call to my construction foreman and get an answer on the completion date."

When Cynthia was on the phone, a big smile lit up her face, and predictably, Phil figured that the foreman was able to meet his completion timeframe. Cynthia hung up the phone, announcing, "Your timeframe for completion is not a problem. I'll have my secretary type up an addendum to the contract and fax it over. The original will be sent to you overnight mail. Are you ready to sign?"

"Cynthia, we have a deal."

Cynthia left Swanson & Swanson and dialed Ardelia from the car phone. "Ardelia, how is everything going?"

"Girl, the movers are finished and long gone. I've been unpacking boxes and putting things away in the cabinets."

"I didn't expect you to do that. I'll be there as soon as I pick up Chris from school. Is that a problem?"

"Not at all, I have the entire day free. Take your time, I'll see you soon."

During the drive, she was trying to figure out how to explain to her daughter what was going on. This wasn't going to be easy, since Chris adored her father. Being away from him would take getting used to. All she could hope for was that this wouldn't have a drastic effect on her emotionally. As soon as Chris saw her mother, she asked, "Mom, what's wrong?" As hard as she was trying to hide her emotions, this child could see right through her. "We'll talk about it in the car, sweetheart."

Later in the car, Chris continued, "Well Mom, we're in the car."

"Mom has made some decisions that will make our lives very different. I've found us a new place to live and..."

"A new place to live? Where?"

"We'll be living in a big, three-bedroom condo near downtown. It has lots of space, big rooms, and you don't have to change schools."

"Ooh, it sounds good, Mom."

"It sounds good, Mom? I didn't expect that kind of reaction."

"I know that you and Dad aren't happy. I can tell. I want him to stop being mean to you, but I want us to be together."

"Well, sweetie, he doesn't know that we've moved yet. I don't think he'll be too nice when he finds out."

The two pulled into the garage of their new home and Ardelia met them at the bottom of the steps. Chris ran up the steps asking, "Where is my room?" Ardelia led her to her new room. Everything was in place. Curtains were hung, bed made, stereo and television hooked up, and all her video "stuff" in place.

"This is great! I'm going to like it here."

## Deadly Choices

Ardelia stayed upstairs with Chris for a while to give Cynthia some time to absorb it all. When Ardelia appeared in the hallway, Cynthia was sitting in the middle of the living room floor with tears streaming down her face. Quietly, Ardelia sat next to her to provide comfort. Cynthia slowly turned and looked at her. "You know Ardelia, I've been waiting to close this deal with Swanson & Swanson for months, and this should be one of the happiest days of my career. But I can't even enjoy it like I should. Thank you so much for being here for me. How is Chris?"

"She's fine. She seems as though it is no big deal. That worries me."

"Give her a few days for it all to soak in and we'll be able to tell if she really is fine. What really worries me is how to handle Jordan. He is going to explode when he gets home and finds us gone."

The doorbell rang and Ardelia got up to answer it. It was Sharon, bringing some paperwork to Cynthia.

"Hi Sharon, come in. I completely forgot you were coming by."

"Your place is really nice, Cynthia. May I look around?"

"Sure, Ardelia will you show Sharon around? I'm not feeling much like doing that right now."

Out of earshot from Cynthia, Sharon asked Ardelia how Cynthia was really doing.

"You know Cynthia. You never know unless she comes right out and tells you."

"She appears to be on top of everything in the office, but that asshole comes around quite a bit bothering her."

"Cynthia is a strong lady, she'll do just fine."

Before either of them could say another word, Cynthia's cell phone rang. They looked at each other with wonder in their eyes.

"Hello."

"What the hell do you think you're doing, Cynthia?!!"

"Jordan! Would you calm down?"

"Calm down! I come home to a partially empty house and you tell me to calm down!!"

"Jordan, what will screaming solve?"

"Cynthia, I'm so angry I could kill you!!"

"I wouldn't get that crazy if I were you. I knew you wouldn't let me leave in peace, but it was time for me to go. You had to know that one day it would have to end."

"I won't give you any peace. I will take a leave of absence from my job, just to have time to make you miserable."

"You may as well take a leave of absence from your job, since your brain has taken a leave. I won't continue to talk to you while you're in such a rage. Call me when you can talk like you have sense. Cynthia hung up the phone before Jordan could respond. Cynthia gazed at Ardelia. "How did I ever love him, and why did I stay so long?"

"It is long past due for you to focus on you, your child and your career. He held you back from accomplishing all that you could have up to now. Move on, and don't look back. I have kept my mouth closed for years, supporting your decision to be with him, but I have to speak my piece. He doesn't deserve you or your love. He isn't good enough for you."

"I've been telling myself that for years, and you know I finally believe it. I'm determined not to go back."

"I sure hope not. You're free, go for it."

Cynthia, Sharon and Ardelia sat and chatted for about an hour. Chris raced down the steps, requiring attention from her Mom.

# Deadly Choices

Cynthia, informing Chris that she would be upstairs as soon as she showed her company out, encouraged Ardelia and Sharon to gather their things and they soon left. When the three went outside, Cynthia's next door neighbor was pulling into his driveway. He stopped before pulling into his garage.

"Cynthia. Cynthia Evans?"

"Yes."

"Frank. Frank Carter."

"Hi Frank. It's been a long time since I've seen you."

They conversed across the driveway while Sharon and Ardelia drove away.

Cynthia really wasn't feeling much like small talk, so she politely cut the conversation short.

"It was good seeing you Frank. I need to go inside. My daughter is waiting to talk to me."

Cynthia and Chris had a bite to eat and began preparing for the next day. Chris wasn't in bed fifteen minutes before she was fast asleep. Cynthia sauntered into her bedroom feeling confused and alone. She showered, and lay across the bed. Just as she started to drift off to sleep, the phone rang. When she answered, this voice came roaring through the line, with a riveting message. "BITCH! I won't let you do this to me!"

Cynthia hung up the phone, but before she could remove her hand from the receiver it rang again. She instantly picked it up and quickly hung up. Before it could ring again, she turned it off. The only comfort she had was that Jordan wouldn't show up at the door. She remembered that a month prior she'd bought some sleeping pills. She rose and went to the medicine cabinet. Emptying three tablets into her hands, she tossed all three into her mouth. She chased them with water, and went back to bed. Considering her tolerance to any drug was extremely high, she dozed off rather quickly.

# 4

Wednesday morning came much too fast. When the alarm went off, Cynthia reluctantly got out of the bed feeling drugged. She staggered to the bathroom, splashed water on her face, attempting to quickly wake up. Slowly she made her way to the kitchen for her morning cup of coffee and a cigarette. The kitchen was huge, with long windows on two adjacent walls. Normally, she would welcome the sunlight, but this morning the sunrays made her feel like melting. She sat at the table dealing with so many thoughts and emotions. At the same time, she began to look around her new home, and felt accomplished. "I did this by myself. It's pretty nice."

When Cynthia was nearly dressed, she awakened Chris. She didn't feel much like cooking breakfast, but her daughter wouldn't mind. Like most kids her age, Chris loved fast food.

When Cynthia arrived at her office, and immediately noticed the door was open, automatic nervousness quipped her, wondering if that idiot Jordan had secretly made a key, or had sweet-talked the secretary into letting him in. The open door made her wonder what this crazed person would do? Her secretary was nowhere in sight, and she couldn't see in before entering. She cautiously proceeded through the door to find Maurice Robinson, Paulie Cavil and Billie Lee.

"Good morning. What brings you to my place?"

As usual Maurice Robinson took the lead. "Close the door Cynthia we have some important business to discuss."

"Do I need to box up my things?"

In a very low, yet commanding tone Maurice said, "They'll be boxed for you."

The events of the last twenty-four hours culminated in a flash of weakness, and exhaustion, as Cynthia let herself drop into her chair. Billie waited for her to look up, before speaking in her strong demanding voice. "Cynthia we received a phone call this morning that caused us to reevaluate your position with our firm. We're going to move you to the corner office on the West Side of the floor." Cynthia sat quietly, wanting to ask questions, but knowing it was best to listen first. Paulie, the junior member of the team spoke up. "Mr. Swanson called from Swanson & Swanson to inform us that he was anxious to do business with our firm. He was very impressed with the way you took care of his company needs. You've done a great job here, and we think it is time to offer you a more solid position. Would you be interested in becoming a partner of the firm?"

"I'm speechless. Are you saying Robinson, Cavil, Lee & Evans?"

The senior partner, Maurice, stood up. "Will you consider our offer to become a partner?"

"There isn't anything to consider. I accept with great pleasure. Oh, by the way, here are the signed contracts. I need your signatures to get the ball rolling." Cynthia sat still in disbelief, as Maurice, Paulie and Billie stood to leave. Even before she could absorb what had just

## Deadly Choices

happened, the phone rang. On the other end of the line was the last person she wanted to talk to, Jordan. His timing couldn't have been worse.

"Yes Jordan, what can I do for you?"

"What the hell do you mean, what can you do for me? I'm not one of your clients."

"Jordan, I'm extremely busy right now. Whatever this is about, can we discuss it later?"

"No! You're not going to put me off!"

"I'm working and I need to keep things in the right perspective, Jordan. You need to understand that I'm not putting you first anymore."

"How dare you speak to me this way?!"

Dial tone.

"Cynthia? No she didn't hang up on me!"

Jordan redialed Cynthia's number. On the first ring she pushed the send calls button, sending the call to her voicemail. He tried repeatedly, but continuously got her voicemail. Cynthia couldn't help wondering though, what her hanging up on him might provoke him to do. Perhaps he would come to her office and make a scene. This prompted her to quickly tidy up some loose ends, change her voicemail, and tell her secretary she'd be working from home. Several blocks down the street on the other side of the median she spotted Jordan, just as he saw her. The median prevented him from making a U turn, allowing Cynthia to get ahead of him. It gave her more of an edge that he didn't know where she was living. She looked in her rearview mirror, but he was only several cars back. She accelerated and made the light. It was one of the busiest intersections in town and he couldn't run the light to catch her. She made it home without him on her tail, and stretched out on the bed to try to relax. Relaxing wasn't easy to do. Her thoughts kept whirling.

"How did I get to this place in my life? Why in the world have I allowed things to get this far?"

Mentally, Cynthia beat herself up for so long, that finally, she was able to drift off to sleep. After about an hour the ringing of the phone woke her. Once again, it was Jordan on the other end.

"B  I  T  C  H! What is your problem?!! Why won't you let me talk to you?!!"

"Jordan I need some time alone. Some time to think and gather my thoughts. Why can't you understand that?"

"What the hell do you mean gather your thoughts?"

"I really don't know how to explain. It's pretty simple. I need for you to leave me alone for a while. Just give me some space."

"How much time do you need?"

"I don't know. I can't put a timeframe on it."

"I can't take much more of this Cynthia. I need you and Chris to come home."

"I can't guarantee that we will come home, Jordan."

"Don't talk to me that way."

"Jordan, didn't you think that I'd ever get tired of being beaten constantly and called out of my name? Did it ever dawn on you that might get old?"

"I don't mean it when I do those things. I just lose control sometime."

"Well Jordan, it's time for me to take control of my and Chris', life. If we could just take time out to deal with our emotions, maybe we'll find our way back to each other. But in the meantime, I think you need to get some help taking control of your anger."

Deadly Choices

"Okay Cynthia, I will get some help. Would you help me find the right place to go?"

"I don't think I should be a part of that process. This is something you need to do alone. You've always relied on me to do everything. You have no idea how that has drained me. I need to do for me now."

"All right, I'll do it. I'll call you and let you know."

"Jordan, don't call for a while. Let's both get the medicine we need and in several weeks let's see how things are going."

"Several weeks!"

"See there you go already. You lose your temper so quickly."

"Fine, I'll do it."

# 5

After several Jordan-free days, Cynthia and Chris got accustomed to being by themselves. Cynthia had more exciting projects come her way. She was very focused on bringing these new clients on with her company, and was caught off-guard when she entered the hallway to her office and sitting in the waiting area was Mr. Jordan. She felt a lump in her stomach that knotted up tightly. Now, more than ever, she had to maintain her composure and professionalism. Glancing briefly at her secretary to get a feel of what she was thinking, Cynthia immediately greeted Jordan.

"Jordan, how are you?"

"Doing fine, Cynthia. I just wanted to talk with you for a bit."

"Come into my office. I have a few moments before I have to visit with a client."

As Cynthia closed the door behind them, he started cursing her in a very low tone.

"Jordan, what is this all about?"

"You think you can just sweep me under a rug like I don't exist, don't you?"

"Jordan, that hasn't been my intent. I thought we had come to an agreement that we would give this separation some time?"

"Cynthia, I don't mind the separation as much as I do not having any contact with you, and especially my daughter."

"I will be happy to make arrangements with you to spend time with your child."

"MAKE ARRANGEMENTS?"

"Jordan, please keep your voice down. There is no need to shout."

"Don't you tell me what to do."

"This isn't going anywhere. You are very defensive. Please go, and let's discuss this later."

"I'M NOT GOING ANYWHERE!"

"I prefer not to, but I will call security and have you removed."

"Cynthia, I didn't really come here to make trouble. I'll leave. Can I call you and talk?"

"Yes. I'll be home about seven o'clock."

Cynthia sat at her desk wondering how to best deal with this. Jordan was acting very different. His state of mind appeared to be almost suicidal. How would she handle the emotions that they all would have to deal with?

Sharon knocked on Cynthia's door, who was so into her thoughts, she didn't hear the knock the first two times. Sharon, a little nervous when she didn't get a response, put her hand on the doorknob to open and go in, when Cynthia said, "Come in."

"I just wanted to check in on you."

"Everything's fine, Sharon."

"Do you need me to do anything?"

"No, thank you."

"Well, if you need anything let me know."

"I will."

Cynthia gathered up her files and headed home to work, where she felt she could concentrate better. Before she knew it, it was time to pick Chris up from school. Time flew by even more rapidly after she picked her up. Before she could think about it, the phone rang. As soon as it did, she glanced at the clock. Seven sharp. It had to be Jordan. For a moment she hesitated, and thought about not picking it up. But if she didn't, that would only make matters worse. Expecting that their communication would definitely be a shouting match, she raised the receiver on the third ring. Jordan's deep sultry voice spoke from the other end.

"Hey, Babe."

"Hello."

"Is this a good time?"

"As good as any. You know I always have something to do."

"I won't keep you long. I just wanted to touch base with you, talk with Chris and make some plans."

"Make plans?"

"With Chris. I need to spend time with her."

"She's right here, I'll let you talk to her."

"Hey sweetheart. How's daddy's girl?"

"Fine."

"How's everything going?"

"Fine."

"Tell me what you've been doing."

"Not a lot. Just going to school."

"You don't have much to say. What's wrong?"

## Deadly Choices

"Nothing."

"I'd like to come get you and take you to the movies or something."

"Okay."

Chris had never been so cool with her dad. She was acting as if she really didn't want to be bothered. Jordan noticed how she was acting and told her to decide where she wanted to go and he would call her back tomorrow. He was so hurt that he didn't even ask to speak to Cynthia; he just hung up. That bothered Cynthia a little, and she wondered how it was going to affect him. Being concerned about his feelings should have been her last worry, but as always, she was considerate of the other person.

More than a week passed and Jordan hadn't called Chris back, nor bothered Cynthia. Cynthia began to wonder if Jordan would just go away, but she knew it wouldn't be that easy. Jordan was too arrogant to go away in peace. He had to call the shots. She sat at her desk, deep in thought. So much so, that the phone was ringing and she didn't hear it. By the time she picked it up, it had gone to her voicemail. She waited for the light to come on to check the message. When she did, the message was from another new client ready to close a deal.

"Damn! Sitting here thinking about Jordan I missed this call. I hope I can get her."

She immediately returned the call to Marla Duncan at Tiffany and Tony's, one of the largest diamond dealers in town, who were currently building a small strip mall downtown.

"Ms. Duncan. Sorry I missed your call."

"Ms. Evans. I'd like to see you. We've made a decision to use your company for our strip mall. When would be a good time for us to get together and discuss the layout?"

"My schedule is free all afternoon; would this afternoon be a good time?"

"Yes. I'll be near your office, so I'll stop by there about two-thirty."

"Two-thirty it is."

As soon as she hung up the phone, Maurice rang her on the intercom.

"Cynthia, I'd like to see you in my office."

"Surely, I'll be right there, Maurice."

Cynthia headed toward Maurice's office, when out of the corner of her eye she noticed the elevator doors had just opened. Slightly turning her head, she saw Jordan stepping out. She picked up her pace hoping he wouldn't see her, and went into Maurice's office. Once again she felt that scary feeling in the pit of her stomach, as she noticed Paulie and Billie sitting there. It must have shown on her face because Billie said, "Cynthia, what's that look for?"

"Nothing, Billie, I just know that when we all meet this way, it's about something big."

"You're absolutely right, Cynthia." Maurice promptly remarked.

We've been contacted by the Mayor's office in the city of Denver to do a proposal for a new development they are planning. We want you to take the lead with this. Since we don't have the staff to handle a project of this magnitude, you need to hire about three or four new architects to assist you. Whatever you need, or however many you need is not an issue. We have to respond to the Mayor's office within six weeks.

"Six weeks! To interview, hire and propose a plan?"

"Keep your cool, Cynthia."

## Deadly Choices

"I'm sorry, Maurice, that's going to require such diligence, and I'm wondering if it's possible."

"We realize how tough this is going to be, but we thought this would be good for you, particularly since your name is new to the business."

"Believe me I know the importance of my name associated with a deal of this size."

Paulie, who rarely says much about anything, chimed in to offer her opinion.

"Cynthia, this is an opportunity of a lifetime. Bottom line is, we've been in this business for generations and it's time to put a fresh new face in the spotlight. You're young, attractive and one hell of an architect."

Maurice asked, "So Cynthia, do you want to do this?"

"Well of course. I guess I'd better get started."

As Cynthia strolled down the hallway back to her office, she had such an accomplished feeling. She was on top of the world. In fact, her thoughts were very positive. *How in the world could things be so right? My life feels like it's coming together.*

So into the good things that were happening, she forgot all about Jordan getting off the elevator forty five minutes ago. When she looked up, he was sitting in the reception area right outside her office. She glanced over at her secretary, finding Sharon shrugging her shoulders as if to say, *There was nothing I could do.* Sharon was a wonderful person, and an outstanding employee. There was no way Cynthia could be upset with her because she couldn't get rid of Jordan. He was so aggressive she couldn't have gotten rid of him without the aid of security, anyway.

"Jordan, what brings you by?"

"Could we go in your office and talk?"

Cynthia, not wanting to tick him off, politely said, "Sure, come on in."

"What's going on, Jordan?"

"I want to talk about getting my family back."

"Jordan, I can't deal with that right now."

"I don't mean right this minute. I'd like to get together this evening for dinner."

"Okay, Jordan, what time do you want to pick us up?"

"Well, actually I was hoping to come over to your place and have some privacy."

"Jordan, how can you ask me to dinner and then expect me to cook?"

"You don't have to cook, I'll bring the food. I just want your undivided attention."

"Fine, Jordan. What time are you talking about?"

"Around seven o'clock tonight."

"Seven is fine, but don't expect to stay too late. I have some preparation for an early meeting in the morning."

"How can you put a limit on our time together?"

"Jordan, I have a responsibility to my job. I can't just brush it off because you want to spend time with me. Things have really changed for me, and I've worked too hard to get here to allow it all to go up in smoke for you or anyone else. Do you want to keep it at seven o'clock or make it for another day?"

"My, aren't you curt?"

"I don't mean to be short I've just got a million things on my mind. I'll see you at seven o'clock."

As they made their way to the threshold, Jordan turned to

## Deadly Choices

Cynthia and pointed out that he didn't know the address. Cynthia rattled off 1603 Pine Street.

"Do I need to write it down?"

"No, that won't be necessary. I'll see you at seven."

*Hmmm doesn't have the address. If he got the phone number, he got the address, too. What an asshole.*

Cynthia went back into her office to get all the contracts and layout plans for her two-thirty meeting. She rang Sharon on the intercom and asked her to step into her office.

"Sharon, I need for you to call the employment agency. I need to hire three, new architects and one clerical person."

"What's happening that we're hiring these people?"

"I've been assigned a potential multi-million dollar project in Colorado. We have six weeks to visit the site and develop a proposal for the Mayor's office in the city of Denver."

"Cynthia, I'd like to assist on this special project."

"I don't have a problem with that, but you'd have to train the new person on your current responsibilities."

"Would I be able to travel with you?"

"If we're able to get the bid, I could arrange for you to come on some of the visits."

"I'll call the employment agency right now. I need your planner to block some time the next two weeks for interviews."

Sharon returned to her desk, just as Marla Duncan arrived for their meeting. Sharon showed her to Cynthia's office and returned to make her calls to the employment agency.

Cynthia and Marla finalized the contracts and shook on the deal. By the end of the day, Sharon had the next two weeks of Cynthia's calendar filled with interviews.

Cynthia, so enthralled with her business, had forgotten about her seven o'clock "date" with Jordan. It was five forty-five, so she gathered up her things and raced off to pick up Chris. She knew she would need some down time to be ready to deal with Jordan, but she didn't have much time.

The two got home, began their usual routine and prepared for the next day, so that as soon as Jordan left they would be ready to retire for the night. Jordan rang the doorbell about seven-ten.

"Hey, what's cookin' good lookin'?"

"What's cookin'? You're supposed to bring the food."

"Calm down, honey, I brought the food."

"Come on in, Jordan."

Chris came into the room to greet her dad. She wasn't her usual happy go lucky self. In fact, she spoke to her dad in a very low, dry tone.

"Hi, Daddy."

"Hi, sweetheart! How's Daddy's little girl?"

"I'm okay, Dad, but I'm not a little girl anymore."

To get this night over with as soon as possible, Cynthia walked to the kitchen, and began setting the table. Moments later, Sharon arrived with contracts Cynthia had left at the office. At Cynthia's invitation, Sharon agreed to stay for a while.

"Come on in here you two. Let's eat, I'm starving."

"God, Cynthia, why are you rushing?"

"I'm tired, hungry, and I have to be up earlier than usual in the morning. Can we just eat?"

"Let's try to have a nice evening, Cynthia."

Cynthia figured if she could put on her happy face long enough to make it through the night, everything should turn out all right. She

## Deadly Choices

painted on her smile and started making small talk. After a while, they all became comfortable and actually started having fun. Before they knew it, it was nine o'clock.

"Chris, go up and get ready for bed."

"Awe, Mom, couldn't I stay down here just a little longer?"

"No. We have an early day. Say bye to your dad."

"Cynthia, we've had a lovely evening. Let the girl stay a while longer."

Cynthia shot him a glance so fierce she didn't need to say a word. He could tell from the not so endearing look he had no say in the matter. Cynthia repeated that it was bedtime, and she meant it. How the times had changed from a few months ago. She would have never contradicted what Jordan said. After Chris went to bed for the night Cynthia walked slowly down the hallway, dreading the company of Jordan, all the time wishing she could go downstairs, say goodnight and he would leave peacefully. She knew she was dreaming, but was extremely hopeful. She noticed the night lamp on in her bedroom. She hadn't turned it on.

"Jordan! What are you doing in there?"

When Jordan didn't respond she stuck her head in the doorway and heard the shower running in the adjoining bathroom. *No he didn't have the nerve to take up residency in my place.* Cynthia stepped into the bathroom, where candles were lit, music was playing, and glasses and cognac were placed on a TV tray next to the tub. She banged on the shower door as hard as she could, shouting and swearing for him to come out. Moments later, the water stopped, and the doors began to slowly open. He stepped out looking, absolutely like a perfectly carved sculpture. For a few seconds she felt weak. It had been several weeks since they had been together sexually. Never mind the fact that she hadn't been with anyone. But she knew it would be the worst thing in the world to let him bed her.

"What the hell do you think you're doing Jordan?"

"Come here, baby. Let me hold you... let me stay a while... This could be an incredible night. Let's finish it off right."

"You dirty dog! Stay away from me! Get out of my house!"

"Oh, now you want to pull rank?!!!"

"All I want is for you to leave."

"Well I'm not, so you might as well get in the mood!"

Cynthia let out a big sigh then marched out of the room. She went downstairs to clean up her kitchen. As she was finishing up, she turned around, and there he stood in the doorway.

"I should have never believed you! I should have known that you couldn't be trusted. Get out!"

Jordan had an ugly look on his face. She had seen that look before, and she knew it meant trouble. He walked over to her and slapped her face so hard, she lost her balance. She held her face, as she hunkered over against the cabinet. She shouted and screamed until her eye started to twitch. He dropped his head, turned and walked out of the kitchen. She knew the asshole couldn't feel bad about what he'd done because it was second nature for him to hit her. Cynthia grabbed hold of the counter top and pulled herself up. She slowly walked up the steps, thinking she should check on Chris to make sure she was asleep. Chris slept so soundly that she wouldn't have heard a thing. Just as she thought Chris was sound asleep. When Cynthia attempted to smile at her child she felt a sharp pain in her eye. She swiftly turned and raced to her bathroom to see what her face looked like. One half of her face was bruised and puffy. There were red fingerprints from her ear to her nose. She grabbed a face towel and wet it with cold water.

## Deadly Choices

She held it against her face for a few minutes, but when she removed it, her eye was blood red. All she could think about at that moment were the clients she had to see. How could she face her business partners, or anyone in public, looking this way? Thinking about how far she had come professionally, letting this son-of-a-bitch ruin it was out of the question. At one time, her emotions were those of a sad pitiful woman, but no more!! She got angry and stepped to the doorway to peer at him. There he lay across the bed watching television. He must have caught a glimpse of her from the corner of his eye. He raised up, looked at her, and said, with that deep, dry voice, "Fix me a drink! The glasses and the cognac are in there with you, in case you can't see them with one eye."

*"No he didn't say that, the insensitive pompous ass. Yeah, I'll fix him a drink all right."* She started looking through the medicine cabinet to find something toxic to put in his drink, but after a few minutes she came to her senses and decided that he wasn't worth any trouble with the law. While she was in the cabinet, she happened upon her eye drops. She placed the eye drops on the vanity then walked over to get his glass and the cognac. She sat the glass down on the vanity and decided that her eye was more important than fixing him a drink, so she picked up the eye drops, and started performing first aid. Since her eye was so puffy, and her nails were fairly long, it was difficult to get the eye drops in. Nervous and slightly shaky, she accidentally dropped the eye drops into Jordan's glass. Normally, she would have either gotten another glass, or cleaned that one, but tonight she didn't feel like doing right by him. *I should pee in his glass first! Maybe spit in it.* While she stood there pondering over what to do, the asshole yelled from the bedroom.

"Where the hell is my drink?!!"

## Shelly L. Foster

With no time to think, she hurriedly poured the cognac, on top of the spilled eye drops, and took it to him. She walked out of the room and went downstairs. She sat at the kitchen table smoking, while having a drink. She sat gazing out the patio doors as the rain pounded on the glass. Watching rain fall was more exciting than being with Jordan. Actually, watching paint dry was more fun, too. Thirty minutes later when she returned Jordan had passed out. Cynthia lay there, staring at him while he slept, *Things would be so much better in my life, if he weren't in it. I wish this bastard would die and be out of my life. His death is the only thing that will put me out of my misery.*

As the night grew, the weather got worse. The wind was blowing at forty miles and hour and the thunder was clapping so loudly the windows shook. The breeze was blowing through the screens, circulating a breeze that relaxed her. The pain in her face began to let up and she finally drifted off to sleep. About an hour or two later she was awakened by the loud siren of the security alarm. She jumped to her feet to go downstairs and turn it off. She noticed when she got downstairs, that her patio door was partially opened. She couldn't remember whether she closed it when she and Sharon came back in earlier that evening. The alarm company called to confirm if it was a false alarm. She laid back down, still puzzled about the patio door having been opened. She didn't know the neighborhood, or the place that well, which made her a little uncomfortable. She shook Jordan to see if he would go downstairs to check the entire place. She shook him a number of times but couldn't get a response from him. She knew he could handle more than the one drink she had fixed him, but she didn't understand why he wouldn't wake up. She got up and clicked on the light. He lay there extremely still. At this point she was scared. She attempted once more, but when there was no reaction, she called 911.

## Deadly Choices

When the paramedics arrived, she ushered them upstairs. One of the paramedics told her they would do everything they could.

"What do you mean everything you can? What's wrong?"

"We don't know at this moment, but we will notify you as soon as we have one of the doctors check him out."

Cynthia escorted them to the door then returned to bed.

# 6

As dawn was breaking, the phone rang. After it rang several times, Cynthia finally heard it. On the other end of the phone was this soft, squeaky voice. "Mrs. Evans?"

"Yes, this is she."

"Mrs. Evans, this is Dr. Randall from Memorial. I have some unpleasant news for you."

"What is it?"

"Mrs. Evans, your husband didn't make it. He expired about twenty minutes ago."

"What did you just say?"

"I know this is a shock, but there was nothing else we could do."

"What was the cause?"

"We're not sure. An autopsy is scheduled for the morning."

"Will someone let me know?"

"Yes, we will."

## Deadly Choices

After she hung up the phone, it dawned on her that she had to contact his family, and she had to make the funeral arrangements. For a brief moment, instead of the sadness she should have felt, she felt relieved, realizing she didn't have to put up with his ugliness anymore. She sat on the side of the bed trying to figure out how to tell her child that her dad was dead. She went into Chris' room and sat next to her on the bed, looking at her daughter so peaceful as she lay there sound asleep. Even though he hadn't been around for a while, she loved him a great deal, and Cynthia decided not to tell her until she came home from school. Cynthia needed time to deal with her own emotions, make the arrangements, and deal with his family's nasty ass attitudes.

Cynthia called her office to change her voicemail, then called her partners and left each of them a message, after which she called Sharon to let her know what had happened. Sharon needed to reschedule her appointments to accommodate her attendance at the services. This was going to really put a strain on the project she had just been given. The timeframe was already tight, and with this, it was going to put her a week behind schedule. Business seemed to be all she could think about. Jordan's death didn't seem to matter, for it was that maybe she was glad she wouldn't have to be beaten again. Maybe she was just tired of all the years of his shit.

After the hustle and bustle of the day, Cynthia came home to make time for her daughter, who would need extra care and time that only Cynthia could give to her. By six thirty that night the news was out. The phone and the doorbell were ringing continuously. The house filled up with family and people Cynthia hadn't seen in years. She really didn't want to be bothered, but she knew they were there to lend what they called support. Everyone was consoling her, something she really didn't want. She didn't feel a loss, in fact, she felt triumphant.

She couldn't fake the feeling at all. Neither a tear, nor a sign of remorse, were part of her being. When Ardelia arrived, she noticed almost immediately that Cynthia appeared much too in control.

"Cynthia, what's going on with you?"

"What do you mean?"

"You are too calm for a time like this."

"A time like what?"

"Come upstairs. Tell me what you're feeling."

"Nothing. Nothing at all."

"Don't you think that's a little odd, considering the "love" you felt for him? You have a child by this man, for God's sake."

"I can't pretend that I feel like crying, because I don't. Maybe I'm numb, or maybe I'm relieved that I don't have to deal with him anymore."

"I can understand all that, but you shared a child with the man. You know I didn't like him, but even I feel a loss."

"You didn't get hit on just last night by him, either."

"I noticed that your face is slightly puffy, and your eyes are a little swollen, but I figured you had been crying earlier."

"I do feel like crying, but not in mourning for him. I'm too glad that I won't be getting my ass whipped anymore."

They hugged and headed back downstairs. Ardelia stood in a corner watching Cynthia's every move. There were so many people in the house it seemed as though they were having a party. Cynthia kept up the façade as the guests continued to pour in. To her surprise, her next door neighbor Frank came over and sat in the kitchen conversing about Jordan. Ardelia noticed that Cynthia was very comfortable with Frank, so she went in to join in their discussion. Unfortunately, all Frank wanted to talk about was how low down Jordan was, which

## Deadly Choices

Ardelia didn't feel was appropriate at the time, so she interjected and tried to steer the conversation in a different direction. She wasn't very successful because those two were so involved in bashing poor old Jordan they both ignored everything Ardelia had to say. Frank made some comments that aroused Ardelia's curiosity, "I could have killed him for all the things he's done to you. He didn't die soon enough. He should have died a long ago." What would make someone say those kinds of things about someone who just died? It made Ardelia very suspicious of him, prompting her to feel it best to stay nearby and monitor him. Sharon came into the kitchen and took a seat. She too chimed right into their "Jordan bashing" conversation. Sharon made as many suspicious statements as Frank. Ardelia didn't like Jordan either, but would never say the kinds of things they had about a dead man. Ardelia focused on why these two were so intent on keeping the negatives about Jordan on Cynthia's mind. Something about the whole conversation didn't add up. Ardelia started to wonder if Jordan's death was an accident, or if these two may have had something to do with it. Inconspicuously, Ardelia took Cynthia to the side and told her they needed to talk some more. She needed to know the details of what was going on prior to Jordan's death.

"Ardelia, why all the questions? Why can't you just accept that this was just his time?"

"Something in me says there's more to this, Cynthia."

"Well, it's being investigated, so we'll have some answers soon. I'll let you know as soon as I have something to share."

"I still want to talk to you. I'll be by tomorrow and I want to know in detail what took place around here. Investigation or no investigation something's not right."

Cynthia mingled with her guests the rest of the evening,

wanting desperately for everyone to go. After about an hour the crowd started to thin out. The last two to leave were Sharon and Frank. Their offer to help tidy up was rejected by Cynthia, who said she could do it alone.

When they left, Cynthia went upstairs just as Chris came in Cynthia's bedroom, and asked if she could sleep with her.

"Of course honey, come on in."

"Ma, what caused Dad to die?"

"I can't answer that question right now, because I'm not sure myself how or why. Just try to get some sleep and we'll deal with this from day to day, okay?"

Before Cynthia could think of something else to say, Chris was sound asleep. Cynthia got out of bed to fix a drink. She lit candles all around the room, turned off the lights, lit a cigarette, and sat on the side of the bed. All she could think about was the life she'd once had with Jordan. All the nights he'd beat her then expect her to make passionate love to him. The days he'd come home with an attitude, and would not talk to her for days, without her knowing why. As her thoughts started to fade, she became tired and sleepy, blew out the candles and went to sleep.

Several days passed and the hospital still hadn't called to inform Cynthia of the cause of Jordan's death. She decided not to initiate a call to them, although she really wanted to know, to bring some closure. She didn't really want to open a can of worms. Cynthia buzzed Sharon on the intercom and asked her to come into her office.

"Have a seat, Sharon, and bring me up to speed on what's going on around here. I need you to contact the agency and get those interviews set up for the architects and clerical support. What is the travel itinerary for the Colorado trip?"

## Deadly Choices

"You have several messages from Swanson & Swanson. The interviews are set up for tomorrow at nine o'clock and ten-thirty a.m., one-thirty and three o'clock p.m. You leave for Colorado Thursday morning."

"I surely hope these interviewees can cut it. Leaving for Colorado in three days won't allow much time for more interviews."

"I have resumes from each of them, and I spoke with the representative at the agency who recommends them highly."

"They'd better be good. An incompetent team could cost us this account. Hold all my calls. I need to respond to these messages."

Before Sharon could get completely out of Cynthia's office, the phone rang. It was Phil Swanson.

"Hello, Cynthia."

"Mr. Swanson. I was just about to call you."

"I called to offer my condolences."

"Thanks, but I'm doing fine."

"How about lunch this afternoon?"

"Lunch sounds fine. What time?"

"Whatever time works for you."

"Eleven thirty will be a good time. Where?"

"The Country Club Café, the downtown location."

"I'll be there."

As soon as she hung up the phone, Cynthia realized she hadn't talked to the partners. She rose from her desk and headed down the hallway. When she entered Maurice's office, he immediately stood and approached her to give a hearty embrace. Maurice then buzzed Sharon asking her to get the other partners and have them come into his office. They all talked briefly about her circumstances. Maurice offered her time off, if she felt she needed it. Cynthia refused to give in to any of this. She quickly replied, "No, that's not necessary. I need to keep busy."

Billie instantly jumped in to say, "You really should consider taking some time off, spend some time with your daughter or take a vacation."

"I have too much responsibility to my clients to take a vacation. I'm leaving for Colorado Thursday. Maybe after this Colorado account is closed."

Maurice, Billie and Paulie looked at each other in amazement. Paulie asked Cynthia, "How can you just blow this off?"

"Blow this off. I have been tortured by this son of a bitch for too many years to allow him to control my life after he's gone!!!"

"Calm down. It's just not normal for a widow to act this way so soon after the death of her current husband."

"Normal? Who the hell defines normal, Paulie?"

Maurice, who always has a level head, interjected.

"This isn't necessary. If Cynthia doesn't want time off, so be it. Let's end this now before things get out of hand."

They all rose and headed off to their offices. As Cynthia approached the reception area and reached the point where a tall, male frame stood, she looked up and was surprised to find Frank.

"Frank! What are you doing here?"

"I'm working here."

"Who do you work for?"

"The telephone company."

"Really? How long have you been with them?"

"Twenty years. I've worked this area for the last ten."

"I've never seen you down here before. What brings you to my neck of the woods?"

## Deadly Choices

"Due to the storm the other night, lines are down and service has been interrupted all over the place."

"It was good to see you, Frank."

Frank stood there gazing at her strut back into her office, wondering if anyone knew he had been in Cynthia's office earlier when Sharon stepped away. He was also wondering, since Cynthia had never seen him in the building, if anyone else had. Frank had his eye on Cynthia long before she moved next door. Cynthia could have never known that Frank had had a thing for her since high school. He kept up with everything going on in her life. He went as far as keeping a log of her comings and goings for the past two years. Frank stood there so long staring into space Sharon finally asked him if there was anything else he wanted. Frank only smiled and walked away. Sharon sat there puzzled, wondering what Frank's real intentions were. Sharon was Cynthia's secretary, but she was also her friend, very protective of her, and would do anything to protect her from any kind of danger. Cynthia appeared at Sharon's desk to inform her she was going to lunch.

Phil and Cynthia had an enjoyable lunch. Although Phil was a client, she felt quite comfortable with him. Looking at him was like eye candy...all the sweets she needed at lunch. They discussed a little about their current business, but Phil didn't want to focus much on business. He felt Cynthia needed some "down time". Cynthia, on the other hand, wanted to stay focused on business, to take her mind off of her personal life. He made her laugh, telling her about this outrageous outfit his secretary had on today. They snickered at some of the clientele, who looked as though they should have been ticketed by the fashion police.

They were still laughing as they walked out the door as Phil walked Cynthia to her car and they parted. When Phil stepped off the elevator and rounded the corner to his office, he bumped into his secretary. He thought about what he and Cynthia had said about her, and as he excused himself for bumping into her, he smiled and chuckled to himself, went into his office and closed the door. He sat for a good fifteen minutes staring into space, thinking about Cynthia. He found himself far more fond of her than he expected, and surely more than he normally would a business partner.

Cynthia, on the other hand, was back into the groove as soon as she stepped into her office. She didn't have time to think about Phil or anyone else. She met with two more clients and had a conference call before leaving for the day. Chris and Cynthia went through their usual evening routine, going to bed a bit earlier than usual.

As morning drew near, Cynthia awakened shortly before dawn. She lay in bed mentally preparing for her trip. At four forty-five a.m., the phone rang.

"Good morning, Cynthia. How are you?"

Cynthia, totally shocked that Phil would be calling her at home, especially this early, pretended not to recognize his voice.

"I'm fine. Who may I ask is this?"

"Phil Swanson."

"Phil, what's the problem?"

"No problem. I just wanted to hear your voice and check to see how you are."

"I'm doing okay. I'm leaving for Colorado later this morning."

"Oh really? I have some friends there. As a matter of fact one of my buddies from college is the Mayor of Denver."

Cynthia sat straight up in the bed.

"You have got to be kidding me. I'm meeting with his staff

today for a project that they're proposing for the city."

"Yeah, Ole' W."

"Wayne Washington?"

"That's right."

Her phone in the bedroom was cordless, allowing her to get out of bed and start her morning routine without interrupting Phil's conversation. Her mind really started working, completely tuning Phil out. *Could this be the perfect opportunity to get this deal? Would Phil be willing to speak to Wayne on behalf of Robinson, Cavil, Lee & Evans? I really don't need him to speak for the firm or me. We have a solid reputation. Maybe I shouldn't have told him where I was going, or with whom I was meeting.* "Cynthia?" she continued thinking, *Maybe he'll use this as some type of leverage. Why in the world am I going out on this limb? This man has given me no indication that he has any motives. He's just being nice by calling and checking on me. Phil is nothing like his brother Nick.*

"Cynthia?"

"I'm sorry Phil, my mind was somewhere else. I'm just fixing my first cup of coffee."

"We were discussing Wayne Washington."

"Wayne and I went to college together. He's a good man."

"My initial meeting isn't with him. I will be meeting with some of his staff. I will try to meet him if his calendar is open, though."

"I can make a call to him, if you'd like."

"No, I think I'll just wait. I know once the proposal is complete, I'll meet with him."

"It's not a problem."

"I appreciate the offer, but I think it's best I wait."

Cynthia quickly ended the call, as she had so many things to do before leaving town. She didn't seem to be the least bit concerned about Jordan's death. But even stranger, Chris didn't either. Chris was handling her father's death a little too well. Cynthia called Chris to her bedroom.

"Hey, do you want to talk?"

"Talk about what?"

"Anything. You've been really quiet lately, and I want to know what is on your mind before I leave for this trip. If there's anything you want to discuss you know you can talk to me, don't you?"

"Yeah, I know that. There's nothing I want to say though. I'm just chillin' in my own world, but I'm okay."

"All right, if you say so. I'll be back tomorrow, and the number where I'll be is in the kitchen. I asked Ardelia to come and stay here with you for the night. She has a key, so she may be here when you get home."

"That's cool. Are you taking me to school, or should I walk to Dominique's and catch a ride with her?"

"The limo is picking me up. We can drop you off, if you'd like."

"Yeah. Dropped off at school in a stretch, without it being the prom or something, who wouldn't want to do that? I'll be ready in a minute."

Once they dropped Chris at school, the limo headed to the airport. The traffic was a "bitch." Seemed like there was construction going on everywhere they turned. At the curb, she checked in and proceeded to the gate. The flight wasn't long enough to go to sleep, so she ended up catching up on e-mail. There was a limo driver awaiting her arrival, near baggage claim, holding a sign with Evans written on it. She approached him making him aware that she was Cynthia Evans, after which he took her luggage and briefcase, and escorted her to the car.

# 7

"Hi. I'm Cynthia Evans. I'm here to see Bill Garcia and Mary Collins."

"We've been expecting you. Come this way, I'll seat you in the conference room. Would you like some coffee?"

"No, thanks, I'm good for now."

"I'll get Bill and Mary. They'll be with you shortly."

A few moments later Bill and Mary entered the room. Mary, a short, stout little woman with a booming voice, sounded like a drill sergeant. Bill, on the other hand, was this six-foot, muscle-bound, handsome man! He was so incredibly good looking, Cynthia was almost speechless. She rose from her chair, extending her arm to shake their hands. The closer her fingertips got to Bill's, the weaker her legs began to feel. It was like a magnetic force pulling them together and draining the life out of her legs. They made their introductions, sat and began their meeting.

After several hours of reviewing the plans, Bill suggested they take a break for lunch. Mary chimed in indicating that she had other plans. Bill turned to Cynthia saying, "I guess it's just you and me." He

## Deadly Choices

had this beautiful smile that lit up the room.

In the parking garage, they arrived at Bill's car. Cynthia realized it would be elegant. He drove an all white BMW 740, white body with white leather interior. When the doors opened, a sweet aroma hit Cynthia in the face. "Um, what a nice fragrance."

Cynthia kept a chiffon scarf in her purse at all times, to keep her hair in place. She tied the scarf on her head and draped it around her neck. "Nice look!" Cynthia smiled and they sped off up the ramp to the street.

"So where are we having lunch?"

"I thought we'd go to Mile High. It's a quaint little place that serves the best food."

"What kind of food? I'm asking because I have finicky eating habits."

"Oh I'm sure Mile High can accommodate your eating habits, and satisfy your taste buds."

"Okay, I'm trusting your opinion."

"Mr. Garcia, it's nice to see you. We haven't seen you in quite some time. Who's the lovely lady?"

"This is Cynthia Evans. She's visiting from Chicago."

"It's a pleasure to have you. Please come with me."

"Enjoy your lunch. Your waiter will be with you momentarily."

"So Bill, what are your thoughts about what you've seen of the proposal? Give me some idea of what you think the outcome will be."

"Actually, what I've seen so far is great. You seem to really know your business."

Cynthia and Bill had really good karma between them. It was

obvious they were attracted to each other, so they flirted slightly over their meal. They finished eating and flirting, then decided to go back to work, not a moment too soon.

Back at the office, Bill and Cynthia were greeted by Bill's secretary at the elevator. In an excited voice, Rosetta expressed to Bill that his wife had been admitted to the hospital. Bill told Cynthia he'd call her at her hotel later that night. He immediately left for the hospital.

When Cynthia returned to the conference room to gather her belongings, Mary entered telling Cynthia that they could finish up in her hotel suite if she wanted. Cynthia gladly took her up on her offer, wrote down where she was staying, and told Mary she'd see her there around seven.

Shortly before seven, the phone rang. It was Bill informing Cynthia that things weren't so good with his wife, and he would need to finish up in the morning.

"Oh, Mary offered to come by this evening and work on her piece of the project. This way, when you and I meet in the morning, we'll have covered some serious ground."

"With Mary you may get more ground covered than you want," Bill offered.

He hurriedly ended the conversation before Cynthia could raise any questions, "Cynthia, there's no need to come to the office, I'll just drop by there as well, and once you check out, you can go straight to the airport."

At seven o'clock sharp there was a knock at the door. Cynthia was surprised to see Mary all spiffed up, fresh and smelling good. She'd changed out of her corporate blue suit into some really nice khaki's, a yellow oxford blouse, yellow trouser socks and brown Italian loafers.

## Deadly Choices

She really looked nice. *Why in the world did she take the time to go home and change when they would just be working in a hotel room? Oh shit! Is that what Bill was talking about? Hmmm, two bottles of wine and appetizers. What is this evening going to be like? I'm dressed in a silk bathrobe, thinking I'm hanging out with one of the girls, and we'd work like we did when we were kids studying for a test... stretched out on the floor, or papers all over the table. Now, for some reason, I feel like I need to be on guard. Bill has planted a seed, and now I'm allowing it to grow.*

"So Mary, where do we start? You know which piece of this project is your area of expertise better than I do. Bill called, and we'll complete his portion in the morning."

"Girl, I am the numbers person. I only want to talk about the financials. Let's take a look at the long-range plans verses a year over year forecast. While you get those folders together, I'll pour us a glass of wine and get the finger food laid out."

Cynthia happened to glance over at the clock. "Nine thirty! Where the hell did the time go?"

"I don't know, but we seem to finally be finished. Now it's time to wind down. Can I pour you another glass of wine?"

"Sure. I need to relax. I've been going non-stop since very early this morning."

"Here girl, sit back and relax."

Mary sat on the floor at Cynthia's feet. "Here put your feet on my lap. You could use a massage. Once you get rid of the tension in your feet, the rest of the body relaxes along with them."

Twenty minutes went by very quickly. Cynthia was so relaxed she slouched down deeper into the sofa. Mary continued the massage and began working her way up her legs. Surprising to Mary, Cynthia began to moan. Soft, slow and steady……mmm……mmm…..mmm. Cynthia reached for Mary to move closer to her. Mary softly kissed her on the lips. Cynthia looked at Mary with a questioning look, but she didn't ask her to stop. The moment became more and more intense. Mary gently removed Cynthia's silk robe revealing her black, lace undergarments. Her thoughts were clear. *Gosh this woman is sexy.* The kisses became more aggressive, and the touches more sensual. The two were intertwined on the sofa as if they were one. The sex was incredible. Hours later, Mary whispered to Cynthia that she needed to leave. Cynthia saw her to the door and headed straight for the shower. While she stood in the shower, she questioned what had just happened. She'd never been intimate with another woman before. *How and why did I allow that to happen? Men have always treated me like a dog, but I've never desired a woman before.*

  Finally in the bed, she replayed the evening over and over in her head until sleep took over. Ring…….Ring…….Ring. Slowly, realizing the phone was ringing, Cynthia opened her eyes and reached for the phone.

  "Cynthia? Cynthia?"

  "Yes."

  "This is Bill. I thought I'd give you a heads up that I was on my way over. Are you still sleeping?"

  "I was, but I'll be dressed by the time you get here."

  At eight o'clock, there was a knock at the door.

  "Good morning, Cynthia."

  With this dry, raspy voice, Cynthia responded. "Good morning. Come in, Bill."

  "You seem to be dragging this morning."

  "I am. Mary and I worked late, but we got her portion

## Deadly Choices

completed."

Bill stood there with a wondering look in his eyes. Since he'd planted that seed the day before about Mary, he wanted to know if something had happened between the two of them. They didn't know each other well enough and, she wasn't about to tell him. She wondered, however, if Mary would tell him. At any rate, she was feeling so good that she didn't care.

"Let's get to it."

"Cynthia, this is really good work. I'm almost positive we're going to do business with your company. Of course, at this juncture I can't make any promises, but I sure will be making a strong recommendation on your behalf."

"That's really good to hear, Bill. When does the Mayor expect to make a final decision?"

"He has other proposals to review, so I would say approximately two to three weeks. We will give you a call and let you know what the next steps are."

Ring……..ring……..ring……….ring. The phone rang incessantly, as they stood looking at one another.

"Cynthia, you're not going to answer the phone?"

She figured it might be Mary, and she didn't want Bill to be able to pick up on any vibes.

"It's probably my office. They'll leave a message and I'll call them back."

"So, I guess this is where I say it was a pleasure meeting you and I look forward to doing business with you."

"It was my pleasure as well. Oh, by the way…how's everything with your wife?"

"She's fine now. The doctor plans to release her later today."

"That's good. Are you holding up okay?"

"I'm doing as well as expected at a time like this, but there are some issues that I'll have to tell you about another time. When might you be coming back this way?"

"Probably not before we're ready to sign paperwork and begin the project."

"That's too bad. I would love to take you out and show you our city."

"That's possible even during the final stages of the project, isn't it? You said it would be only two or three weeks, right?"

"Yes, but that time will be so hectic for you that you won't have a lot of time to relax."

"Actually, I was thinking that I would stay in our corporate apartment here during that time. It will be much too taxing to travel back and forth. I expect the process will take us about seven weeks before I can be "hands off."

"That sounds like a good plan. I'll look forward to showing you around."

As soon as Bill was on the other side of the door, Cynthia raced to the telephone to check her messages. Just as she thought, it was Mary. Quickly dialing, the phone rang two times when Mary picked up saying, "Hello there."

"Hey you, how's it going?"

"All is well. I just wanted to touch base with you before you checked out. Interested in staying for the weekend?"

*What the hell have I done? What the hell will I be doing if I stay? As much as I think it's the right thing to leave and leave well enough alone, I am really excited about staying and spending more time with her. I have always done the right thing, but for what? I've gotten the short end of the stick in every relationship. I'm doing what makes me happy for the moment. That bastard Jordan is gone, and I have a chance to live. I'm going to do whatever the hell I feel like, when I feel like it.*

"Can't stay for the entire weekend, but I'd be willing to stay until Saturday evening, provided I can get a flight out then, and that the hotel isn't booked."

"The hotel being booked isn't a problem, I have two guest rooms. Check the flights and let me know. I'll come over, pick you up and bring you here with me."

"I'll ring you back shortly."

At one o'clock p.m., there was a knock at the door.

"Oh, I thought you were the bellman."

"Are you ready to go?"

"Yes, I'm just waiting for them to pick up my luggage."

Silence filled the room for several minutes, which to the both of them seemed like hours. They stood at the doorway with the door cracked until the bellman showed up. Mary gave instructions to take the things to the front door. Her car was parked right out front. *Hmmm an SUV. Should have known she'd drive something that said powerful. A Cadillac Escalade, black with light gray, leather interior. A beautiful piece of machinery.*

They rode about twenty-five minutes to a "happening" night club. Mirrors and lights were everywhere. Three levels of music; the upper level jazz, the main level, R&B, but mostly 70's stuff and the lower level hip-hop. Why they had hip-hop was a bit mystifying, when the minimum age was thirty. People over thirty don't have the energy to dance all night to hip-hop. That seemed to be the place to hang if you wanted to get away from the crowd. This particular night, there was a jazz band playing. You could really get into the mood in that atmosphere. Drinks kept being filled. Before one could be completely emptied, there was another put in front of them. Cynthia's head started to buzz. Knowing she was not a drinker, she should have put on the breaks three drinks ago. Needless to say, Mary loved it. Cynthia gets even sexier when she's been drinking, in the way she dances, and the way she talks. She even smiles like the devil when she's got alcohol in her system. All of a sudden, a Marvin Gaye cut came on, and up to the dance floor Cynthia went. Raising her hands in the air, she slowly moved to the beat of the music. She moved her hips from side to side, holding herself with one hand at the waist and the other held high in the air, snapping her fingers to the movement of her hips. She closed her eyes and started singing along as if she were on stage with Marvin. "Ooh, mm, mm, mm," she lightly moaned as her energy drew the crowd to the dance floor.

Mary was so in awe of Cynthia's dancing she sat and watched with a sly grin on her face. The guys sitting at the bar next to Mary commented that the lady on the dance floor sure was hot! Mary nodded her head in agreement.

After several records, Cynthia finally sat down.

"Whew! It's been a long, long time since I've danced like that! I didn't know how much I missed dancing."

"How long has it been?"

"Many, many years."

"What kept you from getting out and letting your hair down?"

"Well, on top of my career and my child, I was married to an ASSHOLE that had a fit anytime I wanted to go somewhere without him."

"You were married?"

"Yes, until just recently."

# Deadly Choices

"Finally divorced, huh?"

"Actually, no. As fate would have it, the bastard died."

"I'm sorry."

"Please don't be. I feel so relieved. I don't have to be afraid of dealing with him and his bullshit anymore."

"Honey, I've been in those shoes. That's why I won't be bothered with a man and his shit ever again."

"It doesn't matter to me whether it's a man or a woman, I've been through so much, I won't take shit off of anyone."

"I didn't mean to imply…"

"Don't worry about it. I am at a stage in my life right now that it's all about what I want. If it feels right, I'm doing it. If I want it, I'm getting it, whether it's for the moment or a lifetime. No hang-ups and no strings."

The two both looked at each other and burst into laughter.

"Cynthia, are you thinking about last night?"

"Yep. How did that shit happen?"

"We both got into the moment. Are you trying to tell me you've never been with a woman before?"

"Never. Never even thought about it."

"Get outta here! You didn't miss a beat. I would have never thought…………hmm."

"Don't go getting all analytical, and over thinking the whole thing. Let's just have a good time."

Cynthia jumped up again from her seat, but this time grabbing Mary by the arm.

"Come dance with me."

"I don't do much dancing."

"Then just stand there, I'll dance around you. I bet I can make you move to the beat of the music."

Cynthia had a devilish look in her eyes, her half-cocked smile sending chills down Mary's spine. The guys sitting at the bar nudged Mary on, so she slowly glided to the dance floor. Cynthia held Mary by the waist and began moving Mary's hips from side to side. She whispered in her ear. "Pretend you're having sex. Move just like you did last night."

She winked at her and backed off. Backing only a few feet away she started swaying her hips from side to side. Once she noticed Mary getting into the swing of things, she moved closer. She got so close, Mary backed away.

"Shy, are you?"

"Not really, but a little less bold in public."

"Do you know any of these people? Are you a regular here or something?"

"No, but you never know who sees you, and I don't need a bad reputation. I have business to take care of in this city."

"That's right, you live here, I don't!"

Cynthia took Mary by the hand and danced her back to her seat. She grabbed her drink, quickly finished it, and took the hand of one of the guys sitting at the bar.

"Dance with me?"

"Gladly!"

Cynthia caught the attention of almost everyone in the club. Her energy was high, she was dressed sexily and when she walked the soft fragrance of her perfume lingered in the air. She wasn't a regular, so a new face in the place was refreshing. Although she was professional and classy, she was flashy. The way she walked even drew attention. She thought *Shoot, for the first time in a very long time I am free to be*

## Deadly Choices

*impulsive. I'm going to have fun on this trip.*

After another dance or two, they returned to the bar. Cynthia thanked him, and asked Mary if she was ready to go. Mary paused a bit before responding then nodded her head up and down, indicating yes.

The entire way back to Mary's place, not a word was said. Cynthia could feel the tension coming from Mary, so she figured she'd let Mary open the door to any conversation. She damn sure didn't want to get into a confrontation with this person she really didn't know. *Okay Cynthia, what the hell are you trying to prove? You have never been like this. All of a sudden not only do you sleep with a woman, but also the woman is a complete stranger. You've agreed to spend the weekend with this person you don't know. Do you need to see a shrink? Did Jordan's death have more of an effect on you than you think?*

She let the window down on her side to get some fresh air. Her conscience starting to rear its head, she didn't want to deal with the ugly truth, not tonight anyway. At that very moment she was feeling liberated, yet ashamed and confused. She didn't know whether to be glad that she no longer had to deal with Jordan and his watchful eye, or whether this is how she "really" is and never explored her feelings, or what. All she knew was that the last two days had not only been an experience of a lifetime, but one she'd enjoyed. She couldn't quite put her finger on how things would be in the days, weeks or years to come, but she did know that she had control. As in her professional career, she could do whatever she wanted and make the best of it. She and Mary managed to muster up small talk for the remainder of her stay, but the remaining hours weren't very comfortable.

Back home again, Cynthia continued with her normal way of living. Friday night rolled around, and instead of the usual time she spent with her daughter, she was itching to go to a night club. She had always enjoyed the time she spent with Chris, and nothing ever interfered with that, but after her little escapade with Mary, she wanted more fun in her life. *Am I wrong for feeling this way? Is it too much to ask to have a life filled with some fun instead of all responsibility? If it's okay, then why am I feeling guilty?*

"Mother, Mother can you hear me?"

"Oh, Honey, I'm sorry. Mom's mind was somewhere else. What is it?"

"I want to spend the night with one of my friends from school. May I?"

"Who is it?"

"Pat. You know her mother, Kathy."

"Kathy Hale?"

"Her name is Patty Hale, so I guess her mom's last name is Hale."

"Let me give her a call and we'll see."

*How perfect I know I can trust Kathy with my child. Chris is a teenager, that's when you need to watch them the most.*

"Hey Kathy, this is Cynthia Evans. How the heck are you?"

"Girl, I'm great! So it looks like our lives have come together once again, huh?"

"Yes, girl, our children have managed to make that happen."

"But remember how the good old days were for us?"

"We'll have to get together and catch up sometime."

"Definitely, so I gather the girls already have this spend the night thing planned and worked out?"

"Sounds like it. You know I don't have a problem with her coming over and I would hope that you're comfortable with it."

"Please, that goes without saying."

## Deadly Choices

"So I'll see you soon?"

"We'll be there in about an hour. Chris!......Chris! Come down here for a second!

"Yes, Mom."

"It seems as though you and Pat had this all worked out. You just baited me right into your plans, huh?"

"Not exactly like you're putting it, but we did discuss it. She asked her mom and I asked you. Isn't that what we were supposed to do?"

"Never mind, little girl. You are your mother's child. Are your things ready?"

"Packed, and in my overnight bag sitting at my bedroom door," she responded with this huge grin on her face.

"Well, I need to jump in the shower and change. I'll be ready in just a bit. Go listen to some of that music you like until I'm ready." *Ah ha! She thinks she baited me, but I'm the master of the game in this house! OOOOOH, I can go out on the town, without having to feel guilty! Now......what to wear? Something simple but tasteful, classy but sexy, and most of all, COMFORTABLE. Had enough of suits all week. Perfect. Black is always appropriate. The fabric doesn't wrinkle much, it's sexy, yet not too revealing, and it's comfortable.]*

Once Cynthia was out of the shower, the process went pretty quickly. A little blush, pressed powder, mascara, lipstick, deodorant, lotion and perfume. She slipped on the pants, the top, a silver necklace and silver earrings. Her hair was long and straight.

"Chris! Let's go!" Chris came trampling down the stairs like a herd of cattle.

"Girl, you can't be that excited."

"Ma', you and Dad never let me stay overnight, ever! Yeah, I'm

75

a little excited."

"We always thought it best for you to be at home. You never know what people do in their homes. I don't really care, but if it affects my family, then I have an issue with it. I am 100% comfortable with you staying at the Hales."

Cynthia's eyes were dancing with laughter, as she thought about the way she'd acted the last few days. *How could I be so judgmental? That's not being judgmental when what I did was behind closed doors, and not in front of minors.*

"Ma? Ma? What are you thinking about that has you smiling like that? And why did you get all dolled up? You never go anywhere except work."

"Well, I'm going to a night club, just to have a drink and socialize, since my child doesn't want to be at home with me."

"Awe, Ma, I just want to kick it with my girlfriend. I'm almost sixteen years old!"

"I'm okay with it. I know you're at that age, so have fun."

Cynthia called as they arrived, "Kathy, I'm pulling in your driveway, but I won't be coming in. I'm going out myself this evening, so I'm going to get going. Chris is headed up to the door right now."

"Fine. We'll talk to you tomorrow. Have a good time."

"I sure hope to."

# 8

*H*mmm, *looks like a nice crowd. That looks like Frank's car.*
Mixed in with the crowd, Cynthia made her way to her favorite spot at the bar. The bar gives you a chance to see everyone. After Jordan's death, Cynthia was truly in the "I want to let my hair down" mode. She sees this fine specimen of a man, two people away at the bar. Of course, she has to play it cool. She turned her barstool around slightly, enough to keep an eye on him with her peripheral vision, and thought, *Where the hell is he going? I can't turn around too quickly it would be too obvious that I'm looking.*

A minute or two later, she slowly turned her bar stool in the opposite direction, thinking maybe "Mr. Fine" was on the other side.

"Boy, what a pretty smile!"

*Damn! It's Mr. Fine right here in my reach. That's a damn shame. This chocolate should melt in your mouth not in your hand!*

"Why, thank you," she managed to say.

"I noticed you when you walked through the door. May I buy you a drink?"

"I've already ordered and paid for one, but thanks just the same."

"Then I'll get the next one. Sam, make sure her next drink is on me. Better yet, hers are on the house all night."

"Sure, James, no problem," the bartender responded.

"Would you care to join me at a table for some conversation?"

"Sounds like a good idea, but it's so crowded. Would there be any empty tables?"

"Follow me."

Over in the far corner of the club stood a glass booth with five tables set for four. There was one couple in the booth having conversation. James whipped keys out of his pocket and unlocked the door. *He must work here. The way he's built, he could be a bouncer. Maybe he's a co-owner or something. Who the hell cares, he's so fine he could be the toilet cleaner for all I care.*

The two sat in the very back of the booth. The man already in the booth spoke to James, and the lady nodded her head as they passed.

"I haven't even asked what your name is. What is it?"

"Cynthia. Cynthia Evans, and yours?"

"James Mayfield. So where do we start?"

"Tell me about yourself."

"Are you from here? What do you do for a living? What's your marital status? Stuff like that."

"Well, I'm from Atlanta, moved here about twenty years ago. I am single. I'm a realtor and I own this club."

"Really now. Let me ask this. Where did you get the name Spuratiks for the name of this club?"

"That's a lengthy story. I'll tell you another time."

"It's really catchy."

"So, enough about me. Tell me a little about you."

"I have lived here all my life. I'm an architect, just made partner at my firm, and a widow."

"A widow at such an early age?"

"Yes, and would prefer not to discuss it."

"No problem."

The night continued and the drinks kept coming, but Cynthia was starting to become bored. She didn't want to sit and make small talk, having had enough of being tied down. She wanted to have fun. She stood to her feet, took James by the hand, and asked him to dance.

"I usually don't dance. I'm not much of a dancer, but I'll give it a shot."

Cynthia broke into her sex pot dancing. James couldn't take his eyes off her. She danced all around him, as he stood moving his feet back and forth. *I see why he doesn't dance much. Shit, if he calls shuffling his feet back and forth dancing, wonder how he moves when he calls himself having sex,* she thought.

She moved closer to him, and started gyrating the lower part of her body against his. When another record started to play, she backed off and stopped dancing. James pulled her back against him, his eyes begging for more. She could tell how badly he wanted her next to him, so she made up an excuse that she didn't care too much for that song and she couldn't really get into it. He looked like a pitiful little boy, but followed her back to the room anyway. They sat at the table and Cynthia began to fan herself with her hands then pulled all her hair up above her head to get air to her neck.

"Boy that was quite a workout! I really love to dance!"

"I can tell. You do it well, too."

"Thanks, but I just move to the music. When it hits me, it's like the music takes over my body."

"So, Ms. Cynthia, would you like to have a bite to eat with me?"

"When?"

"We can leave now if you'd like."

"Actually, that sounds like a pretty good idea. Believe it or not, I'm not much of a drinker, and I've had more than my usual limit, so food on my stomach would be a good thing."

"Let's go then."

In the parking lot, Cynthia decided she'd follow James.

"James, I think I will follow you, so we won't have to come back here after we eat."

"Coming back here isn't a problem for me."

"Just the same, I think if I follow you, it'll save time on my drive home."

"Whatever makes you happy. I'm parked right up front. Get in your car and drive up to the front door. Here.... let me open your door."

They drove about fifteen minutes away to a really nice restaurant. Cynthia had lived in the area all her life, but never knew this restaurant existed. The waiter knew James by name, so naturally they got the royal treatment. The night grew on and they were having a good time. They laughed about everything. Cynthia couldn't remember laughing so much.

"So, James, it's late, are you ready to go?"

"You're ready to end the night already?"

"It's three-thirty in the morning, what do you mean already?"

## Deadly Choices

"It's still early for me. I usually don't leave the club until four or five a.m."

"I've been going all day. I just want to kick up my feet and relax."

"I don't live far from here. Would you like to come to my place and relax?"

"No thanks, I don't live far from here either. You're welcome at my place. That way, if my daughter calls I'll be there."

"I think I can do that. I would love to visit your place."

"Let's go."

At Cynthia's place, she invited James to get comfortable in the den while she changed clothes. When she returned to the den, James was stretched out on the sofa watching television. He reached up for her to join him on the sofa. He'd covered up with a bear skin rug, and invited her under it with him. She accepted the offer, snuggled next to him, and nestled her head in the fold of his neck.

"Um, you smell good."

"Thanks."

He reached up and began stroking her hair. She loved a man to stroke her hair. It was like a sedative to her. She got really relaxed. James didn't have a chance to make a move on her. She slowly turned around to face him, and gently kissed his lips. Their kisses got more and more passionate, and before they knew it, they were wrapped up in each other like twine. James and Cynthia made passionate love to each other. They connected like they'd been together for years. After the last climax, she laid in his arms and they fell asleep.

The phone rang about nine o'clock a.m.

"Mom?"

"Hmm"

With a high-pitched, excited voice, Chris asked her Mom if she could hang out with Pat for the day.

"Mom, we're having such a good time, I really want to stay for a while today. Can I?"

"Yes, Chris. What time should I plan to pick you up?"

"Her mom said she would bring me home."

"Fine, I'll see you this evening."

When Cynthia hung up the phone and turned over, James was looking directly at her.

*Hmm, he even looks good first thing in the morning. I could stand some more of what he gave me last night.*

Before the thought could leave her mind, James pulled her close and began making love to her over and over again. How quickly the hours seemed to pass. She finally explained to him that he needed to go so that she could get herself together before Chris came home. After they showered and dressed, Cynthia walked him to the door and thanked him for a really good night.

"Might I see you again, Cynthia?"

"That may be possible. I just have such a busy schedule, I can't tell you right now when."

"Can I call you?"

Getting one of her cards, she explained that all of her reach numbers were there, including work, home, cell phone and e-mail address.

"Great. I'll talk to you soon."

She stood at the door deep in thought. *I'm not interested in a relationship. I just want to have fun, when I feel like it, and with whomever I feel like. I hope he doesn't pressure me for a freakn' one-on-one relationship. Not interested.*

## Deadly Choices

Moments later the phone rang. Cynthia was surprised to hear Mary's voice.

"Mary, what makes you call?"

"I was thinking about you, so I came to Chicago. I'll be here for a week."

"Really?"

"Yes, I can't seem to get you off my mind."

"Mary, that's not a good thing."

"Why not?"

"Well, for one, what happened between us was a one time thing. Second, I'm not interested, in a one-on-one thing with anyone."

"I'm not trying to pressure you into a relationship. I merely thought that we could spend some time together."

"That's fine, but to just show up without warning seems a bit presumptuous, don't you think?"

"Maybe so, I just acted on impulse. Just as we did the night we were together."

"Mary..........."

"Before you say another word........can I see you?"

"My daughter will be home in a few hours and I really need to spend some time with her before the weekend ends."

"Oh you can make time for that man who just left, but you won't make time for me?"

"What did you just say?!! I know you're not watching me!!"

"Actually, it's not the way it seems I......................"

Cynthia hung up before she could think about it.

*She's watching me. Is she obsessed with me? One night together couldn't have provoked this. What have I gotten myself into?* Minutes later the doorbell rang. Cynthia trotted to the door, thinking

83

it was her daughter and her old friend, Kathy. Mary stood at the door with tears in her eyes.

"Cynthia, just hear me out. Please let me in."

"How did you know where I lived, and why would you just show up on my doorstep?"

"You're listed in the phone book, and the Internet gave me the directions. I was sitting outside when your company left. I wasn't spying; I was sitting there trying to find the words to say, and just happened to see him leave. Please, please listen to what I have to say."

"Come on in, only for a little bit."

"Cynthia, the time we spent together in Denver was the best time I'd had in a very long time. I can't get you off my mind. After my husband and I split up many years ago, I turned to a girlfriend who helped me get over him. We fell in love with each other and that's when I realized I was gay. She passed away two years ago and I hadn't found anyone who made me feel like that until I met you. I just wanted a chance for us to share the joy I was feeling."

"I just lost my husband a short time ago and I'm not interested in a relationship with anyone. I am just getting the chance to live and enjoy my life. Although I was intimate with you, I don't think I'm gay. I really don't think I'm ready to start a relationship with a woman. I don't think I can handle that."

"Could we just hang out as friends and see where it goes?"

"That's possible, but to just show up and pressure me, won't work. It can't be that way."

"Okay, maybe I was too aggressive. How do we get back on track?"

"For starters, you need to go back to Denver and let's

# Deadly Choices

communicate by phone until I come back to visit Denver, or until we've planned for you to come here. We can plan time to have dinner or go out or something."

"So I'm to just pack up and go back to Denver without spending any time with you?"

"You can't expect me to put my child on hold, or any plans I may have already made to accommodate your existence, do you?"

"Maybe not on that level, but be considerate that I'm here, and make some time for dinner or something. Couldn't you do that for me?"

"I'm sure I could later in the week, but I can't make any promises with my busy schedule. I made a pact with myself when my husband passed away, that I wouldn't do anything that wasn't good for me ever again. I'm going to stick to that. My child and I come first. I won't be held captive by and for anyone. Doing what I don't want to just to make someone else happy is not good for me, and I won't do it."

"I get the message. I'll back off."

"Do whatever you feel is good for you. I can only respect that."

Cynthia opened the front door, smiled and said, "Let's keep in touch."

Mary walked out the door and started on her way back to her hotel.

# 9

The weekend finally ended and the work week began. Cynthia, in her usual 'bout business mode, took a deep breath as she sat in her high back leather office chair, just closing another contract and feeling really good about herself and her career. She propped her elbows on her desk with her chin balanced in the palms of her hands, drifting off into distant thoughts. Her thoughts were painful, and full of memories.

*Mommy and Daddy, I sure do miss you. Here comes Uncle Bobby to my bedroom again! Hiding in the closet, shaking like a leaf to avoid the sexual abuse and beatings made me sick to my stomach. Uncle Bobby and Aunt Lucille took me in when my mother passed away. I was only 11 years old when my mother died, and I had no place to go. My dad died when I was born, and my mother was all I had. My Aunt and Uncle only took me in to get the social security check, which made me a free meal ticket for them. They never spent a dime on me. I wore hand-me-down clothes and run over shoes, ate hotdogs and bologna sandwiches, while they ate steaks and pork chops. Sitting at the same table they ate their meals and had no problem with me eating hotdogs and cold cuts. I can't remember eating a well-balanced hot meal from the time I moved in with them until I moved out. I decided at the age of twelve to make something of myself, and never let my children have to deal with the horrible stuff I did as a child. I thought I had the perfect plan to make a good life for my children and me. I was going to have the perfect man and perfect children. Well, Cynthia, you definitely didn't choose the perfect man. He was just like Uncle Bobby. He forced himself on me sexually whenever he felt like it and beat me whenever he had a bad day. Now, I'm becoming a slut just like my Aunt Lucille. This can't be in the cards. I thought I'd come a long way. I thought I had made it. With Jordan gone, I seem to be following the same pattern of the life I thought I'd escaped from."*

Closing her eyes and shaking her head, she came out of the thought, pressed the button on the intercom, and asked Sharon to come into her office.

"Sharon, we've just landed another contract and I want to talk to you about your position."

"Please don't tell me I won't be your secretary any longer."

"Actually, that's exactly what I have to tell you."

"What? Why, Cynthia?"

"I've been thinking about it since the Denver project when we had to hire so many people so quickly, and you weren't able to make the trip with me. So, I honestly believe that you would be better suited............"

"Better suited where, Cynthia? Not only have I been your secretary for many years, but I thought we were friends!"

"Take a deep breath and listen to what I have to say. Our friendship means a great deal to me, far more than our working relationship. I was thinking that we need to expand our division of the

business. I'd like for you to get in touch with the recruiter and start interviewing others for your secretary position. I want you to do the initial interviews, and when you've narrowed it down to the final two, I'll interview them and we will make the decision together. Once we have the person in place, and you have fully trained them, I want you to start shadowing me. Although you won't be a partner, I need an assistant. Are you up for the challenge?"
Silence filled the air for a brief moment.

"Cynthia, not only am I up for the challenge, I am so grateful that you chose me for the position. I'm so sorry for taking off on you earlier."

"Don't give it a second thought. We have a lot to do in the next few months, so get ready for early mornings, late nights, spur of the moment weekend hours and travel."

"You know none of that is a problem for me, with no husband and no children. I guess I'd better get the recruiter on the line and get this started. I am really thrilled!"

"Sharon, we also need to negotiate additional office space for the new architects. I'm sure the digs they are currently using aren't adequate. Will you get on that as soon as you can?"

Cynthia headed down the hallway to Maurice's office to inform him of the changes she would be making. They spent about an hour together, with Maurice in full agreement.

Cynthia returned to her office to find her message light lit up. Two of the seven messages were from Mary. Cynthia sat quietly contemplating whether to call her back or not. She raised the receiver, put it down then raised it again. She dialed and heard the phone begin to ring. Before she could hang up, Mary answered.

"Hey Mary, this is Cynthia, returning your call."

"Well, hello there. Glad you called me back. I was wondering if you would be interested in accompanying me to a concert in a few weeks?"

"Where?"

"Here in Denver."

"Who's coming?"

"There are several jazz artists on the tour. I can't remember all of the details. I just happened to hear it on the radio this morning and considered going. I figured I'd get more details after I spoke with you. Should I check into it?"

"I really love jazz, so, yeah, check into it. I have to tell you though I have a really full plate, so my time won't be my own for a while. I just signed another client, and will be making some organizational changes that will require a lot of my time. I hope when you give me the date and time, I'll be able to make it."

"I'll check and get back with you later in the day. I'll pay for your airfare."

"That won't be necessary. I'll be there if it doesn't conflict with my schedule."

"Great, I'll speak to you soon."

*What am I doing again? This woman won't let up. I'm going to have to hurt her feelings to get rid of her.*

When the phone rang again, she answered using her full name. "Cynthia Evans."

"Cynthia, James Mayfield,"

"Hi, James. What a pleasant surprise."

"I've been thinking about you for a few days, and thought I'd reach out to you and say hey."

"Glad you did. It's nice to hear your voice. I've thought about you a time or two over the past few days, as well."

"So what are your plans for the evening?"

"My daughter and I are having dinner."

"Well... could I get on your schedule for sometime this week?"

"The later in the week the better. Let me check my planner. Friday looks good. Would Friday work for you?"

"Fridays are the worst, but if there's no wiggle room in your schedule, I'm sure we could see each other Friday. Why don't you meet me here at the club Friday at your convenience? We could plan the rest of the evening from there?"

"I could probably do that. Let me speak to my daughter and see if she has plans. In the meantime, I'll put it in my planner."

"So Yum Yum, what else is new?"

Cynthia raised her eyebrows and burst into laughter.

"Yum Yum! Where did you get that from?"

"I just thought about the night we met, and that was the first thing to come to mind. Thought that was funny, did you?"

"Yes and no. I think it caught me off guard more than anything."

After a few seconds of silence, they both burst into laughter.

"Whew, I needed that. It took the edge off of my day. As much as I love what I do, I am feeling so overwhelmed. I could use some down time to laugh and kick up my heels."

"How high do you want your feet up?"

"Stop it. You're just being nasty."

"And you love it, don't you?"

"I'll answer that when I see you. How's that?"

"I'm going to hold you to that, too, so don't try to pretend that

## Deadly Choices

you don't recall what I'm talking about."

"I won't. I'd better get going. I have a meeting in thirty minutes. I'll talk to you soon."

"The sooner the better. Take care."

Cynthia's meeting with her new architects lasted about three hours. Although long and exhausting, it was very productive. They mapped out the plan for the new client and polished it to perfection for Cynthia's review with the client the following week.

Cynthia began tidying up her office to leave for the day. Ring, ring, ring. "This damn phone rings too much!" she remarked aloud, as she curtly answered, "Hello, Cynthia Evans."

"Cynthia, I have the information on the jazz concert."

*Damn. She didn't waste any time.*

"Okay. What is it?"

"Kenny G, Al Jarreau and Boney James. Two weeks from this Friday. Are you free?"

"That's one hell of a concert. How in the world did a promoter get those three all at once? I sure hope my schedule will allow for it. I just put everything in my briefcase. Let me dig it out. Hang on, I'm checking. YES! YES! I'm free. Get the tickets. I'll make travel arrangements later in the week."

"Then I guess I'll hear from you when you know what your flight plans are?"

"Yes, I'll call you as soon as they've been made. This sounds great. Thanks for thinking of me."

"My pleasure. I'll speak to you later."

On her way out of the office, she stopped at Sharon's desk and asked her to make travel plans to Denver, leaving two weeks from Friday. "Make it an a.m. flight."

"You never have out of town meetings on a Friday. Should I make it on your personal or corporate credit card?"

"Actually, it's business and pleasure. Put it on the corporate account."

"What are you up to?"

"We'll talk. Let's do lunch tomorrow."

"I'm going to hold you to that. Something's up, and you're going to tell me."

"Goodnight girl."

When Cynthia pulled into her driveway Frank was out in his yard. He struck up a conversation as soon as she stepped out of her car. After about ten minutes of conversation, she raised one foot slightly off the ground behind her pulling off her shoe, then the other, just the same.

"Your feet hurt?"

"Yes. A really long day."

"Well, I won't hold you. I can massage your feet if you'd like."

"No thanks Frank, but thanks for the offer. A long hot bath and a good night's sleep will do the trick."

As she turned toward her front door, Chris flung the door open shouting out the door.

"Mom! Telephone."

*Whew, saved by the bell. Frank was never going to stop talking.*

"Hello."

"Hi, Cynthia. This is Don Minnis. One of your new architects."

"Hey, Don. What's going on?"

## Deadly Choices

"Actually, I know that I'm way out of line for calling you at home, but I felt the office wasn't the appropriate place, either."

"Appropriate for what?"

"I just wanted to know if I could take you out to dinner sometime?"

"Don, I don't think that would be a good idea. It's really not my practice to go out with my colleagues other than for office functions."

"I was so drawn to you that I couldn't help myself. Actually, I thought it would be okay since I saw you in Denver out dancing with one of the clients. Don't get me wrong, I don't see anything wrong with it. I'm originally from Denver and I happened to be there the same weekend you went up for the meeting with the Mayor's office. I know Mary from High School, and knew she worked for the Mayor's office."

*Hmmm, now I see what Mary meant.*

"That's a different scenario than you and I. We work closely at the office in the same city, and I'm your boss. I don't think that's a good mix."

"I can appreciate your viewpoint, but know that if you change your mind I'm very interested. I hope this won't affect our working relationship?"

"It won't be a problem for me unless it affects your performance. Will it?"

"I definitely know how to separate business from personal. Not a problem."

"See you tomorrow."

*Do I have a sign on my back that says tramp? Where are all these people coming from? I've never been pursued like this before. Big dummy...you're not wearing a wedding ring any longer, either.*

"Mom, I fixed dinner. You hungry?"

"Very. What'd you cook?"

"Shrimp stir fry."

*The last time we ate together in this kitchen was the night my S.O.B of a dad hit my mom. The night that S.O.B. died!*

"So Chris, what made you fix dinner? What is it you're going to ask for or where do you want to go?"

"Nowhere."

"Sure, and I'm the new sheriff in town."

"Actually mom, I want to travel with you this summer. I was thinking, since you travel all the time, I could go with you when school is out."

Cynthia thought, *Oh SHIT. That puts a stop to my fun. She's not accustomed to being without me. How do I juggle the two?*

"Mom, I was thinking if one of my girlfriends went with me, we could shop and stuff while you work. I'm not a little girl anymore so you wouldn't have to baby sit me."

"That could work if you have a girlfriend with you. But you know I often work late. Would that be a problem for you being away from home?"

"I'd go out on the town. Some states have non-alcoholic clubs that my age group can go to without a chaperone."

"A Club! I don't know if I'm ready for that."

"It's just dancing. What's the big deal?"

"The big deal is that there are people who prey on young people in places like that. They know they are too old to be in there, and their only reason for being there is to pick up young, innocent boys and girls like you."

"Mom, there are people like that everywhere. You've gotta

# Deadly Choices

trust me sooner or later."

"It's not that I don't trust you, I'm concerned about your welfare."

"I know. You're doing the Mom thang, but I can handle myself better than you think."

"Oh really? How'd you learn to do that?"

"When I was little and those times Dad would hit you, when you were in your room he would..."

"He would what?!"

"Nothing Mom. Don't worry about it."

"What the hell do you mean don't worry about it? Tell me Chris!"

"There's really nothing to tell since he never did anything. He would try to touch me, but I would kick him. There were times that I think he hit you, because I had kicked him for trying to bother me."

"Why didn't you ever tell me this?"

"I figured since nothing ever happened, there was nothing to tell."

"But if something had happened, it would've been too late."

"Let's just forget about it. He's gone and I'm fine. Moving on...back to what we were talking about. When is your next trip?"

"Actually, I'm planning to leave two weeks from Friday, but Sharon is already making my reservations."

*"Shit...she doesn't need to go on this trip. How would I explain Mary?"*

"Mom! If I could get Patty to go with me, you wouldn't have to sweat it. She and I could take a separate flight and meet you there."

*Okay brain. Wiggle your way out of this one.*

After a moment of silence, Chris started her pitch again, but before she could get started good the phone rang. She jumped up from the table and ran to answer it.

"Mom, it's for you. It's Patty's Mom Mrs. Hale."

The two exchanged pleasantries and even struck up old times. After about fifteen minutes, but before Kathy ended the call she added;

"Girl, I got so caught up, I nearly forgot what I called for. Joe has to go out of town in a couple of weeks and I am scheduled to work that entire weekend. I really need for Patty to stay over for the weekend, if you wouldn't mind."

"Not a problem at all. What weekend?"

"Two weeks from Friday."

"I'm going to Denver that weekend, but Chris and I were just discussing the final details. My secretary probably already has my flight booked. The girls could take a separate flight and I'd meet them at the airport. I'll get them a separate room, hopefully adjoining to mine, or at the very least, on the same floor. Would you have a problem with that?"

"Not at all. When do you plan to make their reservations?"

"I guess tomorrow. I'll have Sharon make travel plans. I'll have her call you so that she can get your credit card information while she has the travel agent on the line. What's the best time to have her call?"

"I'll be here all day. Morning would be best, though."

"Fine. I'll talk to you later."

"Well Chris, looks like you and Patty will be joining me in Denver."

"Yes!" She balled her fists, and kicked her legs with excitement. She raced up the steps and called Patty.

## Deadly Choices

"HEY! Did you hear the news?"

"YES! My mom just told me."

"Girl, what are we going to wear?"

"Let's not take a lot. Then we could go shopping. We could use my credit card. I have a Visa which is actually my Mom's, but I have a card, with my name on it."

"You won't get in trouble?"

"That depends on how much we spend. As much as my mom shops she probably won't even notice. We just can't get crazy."

"I'll have some cash too. So we can use some cash and put some on the credit card. Guess what, there's a teen club there we could go to. Will your Mom let us go?"

"I don't know. We were just talking about that before your mom called. We can work on her when we get there."

"I am so excited...I'll talk to you later."

As the night grew on, Cynthia and Chris started their nightly routine. Chris was so hyped she could barely unwind.

The next morning Chris was up before the crack of dawn. The two went their separate ways and the hectic day began.

# 10

The days whooshed by like a whirlwind. Cynthia and Chris crossed paths in the evenings, but barely had the energy to talk. Chris came into Cynthia's bedroom and stretched out across her bed just to chat.

"Mom, only a few more days until our trip!"

"I know. You sound like you're excited."

"Patty and I both are excited."

Their chat lasted long enough for Cynthia to finish her nails, then they both retired for the night.

When morning came, the two headed out the door, going their separate ways. Once Cynthia arrived at the office, she found one of Jordan's sisters waiting for her. Linda, also known as "the bitch." Linda was very close to her brother, and now that he was gone, she was making life miserable for everyone around her. She's a really tall, slender woman, with a sharp haircut. Most women couldn't wear their hair that short and get away with it, but she wore it well. As a matter of fact, she was quite stunning, but her nasty attitude outshined her beauty.

"Linda? What brings you here?"

"I needed to talk to you about my brother's death. Some things just don't add up, and I wanted to ask you about the night he died."

"I can't really tell you anymore than I already told the police."

"Well, the police could give a shit one way or the other what really happened to my brother. My brother's file is collecting dust on someone's desk down there. I have called and dropped by the precinct more times than I can count, but to no avail."

"Let's go into my office. I don't have a lot of time to give you but I'll make an effort to help."

Sharon gave Linda a sharp glance then looked worriedly at Cynthia.

"Cynthia, do I need to get the two of you coffee or something?"

"That won't be necessary. She won't be here that long."

Linda looked Cynthia up and down as if she'd said something wrong. She glanced over at Sharon and sharply replied, "I'll have a cup of coffee, black with one sugar."

Sharon looked to Cynthia for approval. Cynthia nodded her approval, and Sharon winked in acknowledgment. While Sharon prepared coffee, Cynthia prepared her laptop to boot up then opened her blinds while they awaited Sharon's return.

Sharon walked into the room with a smug, but devilish look on her face. She handed Linda her cup first.

"Here you go. Black, and not too sweet." *Just like you bitch.* Sharon couldn't help thinking to herself. "Cynthia, here's yours, just the way you like it."

"Thanks, Sharon."

As Sharon exited the room, she gave Linda the once over, just to let her know she had her eye on her.

"So, Linda, what's on your mind?"

"I already told you what was on my mind. What I want to know is what took place at your house the night my brother died?"

"He came over about seven p.m., we had dinner, he hit on me like he always did, I fixed him a drink and we went to sleep. When I woke up, I couldn't wake him. I called 911, and that's all I know. I received a call from the hospital a few hours later informing me he was dead. That's all there is to it. There's nothing more to tell."

"Why didn't you go with him to the hospital?"

"Help me to understand why you think I should have. We were separated for a reason. He was in my bed against my wishes, AND he had hit me the night before. Our daughter was asleep and I wasn't waking her to ride to the hospital. Shit, he never went with me after he'd beaten the shit out of me. Where was he when he broke my jaw? Where were any of you for that matter? I wasn't feeling like the dutiful wife. I had no idea how serious it was until I got the call from the hospital."

"You weren't able to awaken him, but you didn't think it was serious?"

"I really wasn't thinking about the severity, I did call 911 to get help."

"Oh, right, you were real concerned."

"You know Linda, I'm not going to sit here and be interrogated by you. The police don't seem to be concerned and at this point, I really don't give a fuck!"

Cynthia stood from behind her desk and slowly approached the

## Deadly Choices

door, but before she could reach it, Sharon came in with more coffee on a tray. She winked at Cynthia and walked toward the chair where Linda was sitting.

"Linda, I thought you might want more coffee."

Linda shot a look at Sharon as if she could kill her. She knew Sharon was fucking with her, so she decided to fuck with them both.

"Sure, I'll have another cup," slyly grinning at Cynthia, as if to say, I'm not leaving just yet.

Sharon worked for Cynthia for many years and knew her well. She was not only the gatekeeper to her office, but more importantly, she was her friend. Her entrance with the coffee was perfectly timed and premeditated. As she reached the chair where Linda was sitting, she held the tray on one arm and reached for the coffee cup with the other hand. As she balanced the tray on her arm, the tray managed to slip and fall into Linda's lap.

"Oh, my God! I am so sorry. I guess a waitress job isn't in my career plan, huh?"

"You did that on purpose! How dare you, this is raw silk. Do you know how difficult it will be to get this stain out?"

"It wasn't intentional, Linda. Maybe you'd better leave and get this to the cleaners, before the stain sets in."

Linda stormed out of the office, swearing every step of the way. Cynthia and Sharon cracked up laughing as she got into the elevator. At the sudden ring of the phone, Sharon stepped out into the reception area to grab her phone. She rang Cynthia on the intercom and informed her that another sister was on the phone.

"I'm not in the mood for this shit so early in the morning. Tell her I'm tied up."

"Cynthia is tied up at the moment. May I take a message?"

"Yeah, tell that bitch I want to talk to her about my brother's death."

"She's already had that conversation with your sister just moments ago. She's extremely stressed and she doesn't need this right now."

"Look bitch, we're stressed too, trying to find out about our brother's death. Can you understand that?"

"I do, but Cynthia didn't have anything to do with it, so just leave her alone."

Sharon hung up buzzing the intercom to alert Cynthia of Mr. Franklin's arrival.

"Cynthia, Mr. Franklin is here to see you."

"Send him in."

Terry Franklin was one of the architects on the new project. They had a brief meeting, and Cynthia asked Terry to take the lead and meet with the client at the next meeting.

"This is quite an honor to meet with the client in your place. I'd heard you control all the projects and never let anyone meet with the client without you."

"In other words, you heard I was a controlling bitch?"

"In so many words, yes."

"It's not so much that I'm controlling as I am a perfectionist. I like things done right the first time, and generally no one seems to get it like I like it. For some odd reason, I feel a comfort level with you that you can handle this. Don't make me regret my decision."

"I'll do my very best to make you proud."

The hours passed quickly. It was already lunchtime and Cynthia hadn't accomplished nearly what she'd planned for the morning. Linda's interruption really cut into her day. Cynthia rose and

## Deadly Choices

walked to Sharon's desk.

"Cynthia, are we still having lunch today?"

"You would ask me that when I have so much to do."

"You always have a lot to do. If we wait until you're not busy we'll never have lunch. I really need some quality time with you to discuss my new role, where I am with my replacement and we still need to catch up on personal stuff like that business/personal trip to Denver. I told you I wasn't going to let you off the hook."

"All right fine, let me freshen up and we'll go."

They walked about two blocks away to a nearby restaurant. Before they could be seated, Sharon was drilling Cynthia about her trip to Denver. While Sharon was talking, Cynthia drifted deep into thought, mostly going over her past.

*I simply must get a handle on my life. I have done things that I normally would not have done. Even though I'm a bit ashamed, it's so adventurous that I'm having fun. It's like living a secret, double life. What do I do to stop this runaway train? Do I really want to stop it? I've always been so serious that I haven't had much fun. My abusive childhood wouldn't allow me to have fun. I was so withdrawn I wouldn't let myself have fun. Then Jordan came into my life and stifled me. He kept me from enjoying my life. I don't think I want to stop. I'm loving this. My Uncle Bobby sexually abused me as a child and I couldn't enjoy sex much. At one point he was going to leave Aunt Lucille for another woman, but the social security check kept him from leaving. I wish he'd taken his perverted ass to that ugly woman he had dated for years. He could have gone over there and molested the woman's son, instead of me. I guess the threats Aunt Lucille made that he wouldn't get anymore money for me made him stay. I know he was taken off his feet when I ran away at sixteen and a half, and anonymously contacted the state to stop the checks. He wasn't going to get paid for abusing me.*

"Cynthia? Where did you go? You haven't heard a word I've said, have you?"

"No. Sorry, I was just thinking about something."

"What's going on with you? You haven't been the same since you came back from Denver. Did Jordan's death affect you more than you're letting on?"

"I think Jordan's death may have had a profound effect on me. I don't miss him at all. I feel so free without him monitoring my every move, and I am happy for the first time in my life."

"So, what happened in Denver to make you act the way you've been acting?"

"How have I been acting?"

"Don't answer my question with a question. You've been acting differently and I've noticed."

"What have I done so differently?"

"Cynthia, quit it. Just answer. Stop questioning me. You're the one to answer the questions. You're the one who's changed."

"Okay, okay. What I'm about to tell you can't go any further than here with us, okay?"

"Fine, fine, just tell me."

"I met someone in Denver."

"What? Who? Where?"

"Would you let me talk? This is hard enough to tell."

"Hard? Why?"

"If you don't shut the hell up I'm not going to tell you anything."

Sharon took her hand and pretended to zip her lips.

# Deadly Choices

"When I met with the staff in the Mayor's office, there was a situation with one of their spouses. He had to leave and go to the hospital, which left me with one of them, who came to my hotel room to finish their portion of the plan. We worked many hours, and at the end of the evening we became intimate. It took me off my feet and I couldn't believe I'd slept with someone I'd just met. I stayed a night or two and we went dancing, out to eat, and just had fun. When I returned home I wanted to feel like that again, so I went out one Friday night by myself and met someone else. I took him home and we were intimate. The reason I'm going back to Denver is that my friend invited me to a Kenny G, Boney James, Al Jarreau concert."

"I see. So tell me about him?"

"Tell you about who? The Denver person or the one here?"

"Both. Start with Denver."

"I think I'd better start with the one here. Once I tell you about Denver you'll fall out of your chair."

"What? You have peaked my curiosity. Now I don't want to hear about the one here."

"Shut up, and listen. I really need to share this with someone. I am going out of my mind holding all this stuff inside. The one I met here was at a club called Spuratiks."

"Yeah, I know that place. I've been a few times and the owner is fine as hell."

Silence filled their space. Cynthia looked directly at Sharon and told her if she interrupted one more time, she wasn't going to tell her another thing.

"Anyway, Mr. Fine is who I met and was intimate with. He was really nice at the club. We went to dinner and then to my place. He's been calling, but we haven't gotten together again. We have plans to meet up in a week or so. My escapade in Denver is far more unbelievable. When we got together I expected it to be the one time and no more than that. Now, she's pressuring me."

With her glass to her lips, when Sharon heard "she" she spit her drink across the table.

"She? What the hell did you just say?!!"

"Let me finish, would you? Her name is Mary, and she truly caught me off guard. We worked long hours together, and when the evening ended she gave me a massage. At first I didn't think anything of it. It was like you or Ardelia giving me a massage, as we'd done many times before. She got me so relaxed, when she started kissing me it seemed so natural and it really felt good. I got caught up in the moment and just went with the flow. Again, I didn't think it would go any further, but since then she's shown up on my doorstep, and she calls me constantly. When she called about the concert I wasn't going to go, but when she said Kenny G, Boney James and Al Jarreau, I couldn't resist. You know I'm a jazz fanatic and I didn't give a shit who I was going with to see them. Now there's a slight glitch in my plans. Chris asked about traveling with me while she's out of school, and I tried to wiggle out of it, but one of her girlfriends needed to stay with us that weekend, so they are both going on the trip. I guess I forgot to mention that this morning, with all that was going on. I need you to book a flight for the both of them and get a room adjoining mine or one very near by."

Sharon sat there looking at Cynthia like she was a ghost. She didn't know what to say or do. A tear dropped from the corner of her eye then she abruptly excused herself from the table. She went to the restroom to regain her composure. After ten minutes or so, Cynthia entered the ladies room to check on her. She reached to put her arms around her, but Sharon jerked away. They stood there glaring at each other like strangers.

"Sharon, do you care to tell me what this is all about?"

"You really don't know?"

"No. Are you ashamed of me, because I slept with a woman?"

"Far from it! You don't know how much I care for you, and how long I've wanted to be with you?"

A puzzled look swept across Cynthia's face.

"What do you mean? We've cared for each other like sisters for many, many years."

"You may have seen me as a sister, but I've been in love with you for a long time."

"I had no idea that you loved me that way. We've never really discussed your feelings and I swear I didn't know you were gay."

"I go both ways."

"You never date at all. I just thought you were afraid of a relationship or commitment. I know that feeling well because of what I experienced as a child. I didn't question it, because sometimes people don't want to wear their emotions on their sleeve. I figured if you wanted to discuss it, you would bring it up."

"I could kick myself for not letting you know how I felt. Now another woman has gotten to enjoy you the way I have always wanted to."

"That's not necessarily true. I'm not looking to be intimate with Mary again, nor will I get into a relationship with her. I was with her one time, and I have no intentions of ever doing that again. I don't think I'm gay. I just experienced an intimate moment with someone who happened to be a woman. I'm not attracted to her as I would be a man, and I surely don't plan to have a relationship with her, or any other woman, for that matter. Mary and I can only be friends. I've made it very clear to her that I'm not interested in her that way."

"Don't you think going to this concert with her will be misleading?"

"Maybe, but she asked even after I made my position clear to her. She'll have to deal with that."

"Cynthia, I think you're misleading yourself, if you think she'll give up that easily."

"No, that's not true. I realize the position I'm placing myself in, but from now on, I'm doing what makes me happy. I'm having fun."

"Even at the expense of someone else?"

"Not necessarily that crass, but in a nutshell I'm doing what's good for me. I learned by being with Jordan that I won't put myself on hold for someone else ever again."

"What about your daughter? Where does she fit into this web?"

"She's still my priority. I won't do anything to bring her harm. I don't want her to feel like I did as a child. I want her to experience the joys of life, but I don't want her in a bubble thinking that life is nothing but joy. She'll have to deal with the reality life brings and I want her to know how to deal with it without falling apart."

"How much reality should she have to bear? Dealing with the fact that her mother slept with another woman, but 'really isn't gay' should go over nicely."

"She never has to know about that, unless you plan to tell her."

"Don't be silly. I won't be the cause of her crashing and

## Deadly Choices

burning. Sounds like you're doing a pretty good job of it yourself."

"You're being awfully nasty, Sharon. How can we get through this?"

"We will. It just hurts right now and I have to get a grip on my feelings. I still love you as I always have, and nothing will change that. Just give me some time to absorb it all and I'll be fine."

"I'm going back to the table. The waiter probably thinks we skipped out on him."

Sharon stood there gazing into the mirror.

*Why didn't I tell her a long time ago how I felt? I could have been the woman she experimented with instead of Mary. I want to meet this cow, and soon.*

Sharon wiped her face, straightened her clothes and returned to the table.

"Cynthia, I was thinking...why don't I go on the trip to Denver and accompany the girls? This way you wouldn't be pressured to be with them while Mary's around."

"You know that Chris is very independent and since her girlfriend will be with her, she probably won't want to be baby sat."

"I don't have a problem with that. I want to make sure that you and the girls get through this without there being any issues. I'll make reservations for myself as well as for the girls."

*This way I can get a look at Mary and check her out. There's more to this than Cynthia believes. Mary is not going to go away just because Cynthia says so. She's luring her with this concert bullshit, and Cynthia can't even see it.*

"I never said it was okay for you to go. You're just going to go without my permission?"

"Yep. I'm going. Like it or not."

They paid for their meals, and returned to the office.

# 11

The day finally came for the trip. Cynthia's flight departed at nine forty-five a.m., but the other three didn't depart until four-forty p.m. When they arrived at the hotel and got checked in, they called Cynthia's room.

"Hey, Mom. We're here!"

"How was your flight? What's your room number?"

"We're in room 305, just a few doors from you. You're in 301, right?"

"Yes, 301. I'm getting dressed for the concert."

"You're going to a concert?"

"I thought I told you. It's a jazz concert with one of my colleagues."

Chris thought, *So if we can get rid of Sharon, we could go to that teen club,* but said, "No, you didn't, but that's cool. Patty and I can find something to do tonight. Will you take us shopping tomorrow?"

"We could probably do that. Let's see what tomorrow brings. Come down so I can see you before I leave to go out."

Chris placed the receiver down. "Sharon and Patty, my Mom

wants us to come to her room to see her before she goes out."

As they started down the hallway, Chris tugged at the bottom of Patty's shirt to get her to fall behind Sharon's steps. She whispered that they could go to the club if they could get rid of Sharon. "What can we say to get her to leave us alone? If she won't buy anything, we'll sneak out when she goes to sleep."

Inside Cynthia's room, they gabbed about the outfits Cynthia laid out to wear. After thirty minutes of debate, they decided on a cute little number that was a soft pink, silk, two-piece pants suit, trimmed in rhinestones around the collar and around the legs of the pants. She wore clear sandals that looked like Cinderella slippers on her pedicured feet. Just as she put on her earrings, there was a knock at the door. Sharon raised a brow and went to greet Mary at the door.

"Hi, I'm Mary Collins, here to pick up Cynthia Evans. Do I have the right room?"

"Yes, you do. I'm Sharon, Cynthia's secretary and long-time friend."

The girls came running out of the room just to see who Cynthia was going out with. Chris nudged Patty, and they both looked suspiciously at Mary. Cynthia shouted from the bedroom. "I'll be out in just a second!"

When Cynthia entered the room, all eyes except Sharon's were on her. Sharon's eyes were glued to Mary, watching her reaction. She was very drawn to Cynthia and Sharon could see it. How the hell could Cynthia think that Mary wouldn't try to win her over, since clearly she was attracted to her. As Mary and Cynthia turned to leave, Chris asked, what time the concert was over and what time they would return.

"I'm not sure, why? Planning on doing something that you need to know my whereabouts?"

# Deadly Choices

"No, Mother. I was just doing what you do to me."

"But I'm the mom. I ask the questions, not you. By the way... that conversation we had about the teen club...don't even think about it."

Patty's head jerked towards Chris. The look on her face told it all. She looked guilty enough for the both of them.

"Mom. It's only down the street. It's walking distance from here. They even have a shuttle from the hotel to the club. If the club were that bad, the hotel wouldn't participate in getting people to and from there, right?"

"Wrong. I don't want you to go. Let me find out."

Chris looked like the air had been let out of a tire. Patty lost her posture, her shoulders slumped, then she looked to the floor. Sharon said she would keep an eye on them both. All five of them left the room together. Sharon, Chris and Patty returned to their room as Cynthia and Mary entered the elevator.

Chris and Patty went into the living room area of the suite and sat quietly. Chris looked over at Patty, then flopped her feet on the coffee table.

*How can we get out of here and to the club? Wonder if Sharon would let us go out of the room at all now? This is going to be a boring trip if we can't do something fun.*

Chris yelled to Sharon in the other room.

"Sharon! Could we at least go out shopping?"

Sharon entered the room with an attitude. "Don't yell at me young lady. If I let you, where do you plan to go, and what time do you plan to come back?"

"Just into downtown. It's not that far, so we'll only be gone a few hours."

"All right, go ahead."

Both Chris and Patty, snapping out of their funk, jumped up, gathered their purses and ran out the door. They asked the concierge how to get into town, and proceeded out the door in the direction they'd been given.

"Girl, we are out! Let's at least walk down to where the club is and check out what we'll be missing. It's right in the direction we're going."

"Okay, but don't try to get me to go in. I don't want your mother to kill us. And I sure don't want her to tell my mom."

"Fine... you chicken."

The girls went from store to store, buying something in every store they visited.

"Chris don't you think we have enough stuff? We don't need to put another thing on your mom's credit card."

"Yeah, I guess you're right, but I have to get a top and some jewelry. Are we going to use some of your cash now?"

"Yeah, we can do that."

"Let's go in here."

"Wow. This store is too cool. Check out this outfit."

"Check out the price."

"Whoa. If the rest of the stuff is this expensive, my cash won't buy us much."

"There's a sale rack. And look, there's a sale on the jewelry."

They had enough money to get a top for Chris and they both purchased some jewelry. Walking back to the hotel, they spotted a few good looking boys. The boys noticed them as well.
About a block later, they noticed the boys had stopped. They waited for the girls to get closer, then approached them with conversation.

# Deadly Choices

"Hey, what's up?"

"Nothing." The girls replied simultaneously.

"What's your name?"

"I'm Chris, and this is Patty."

"Where you going?"

"Back to our hotel."

"Hotel? You're not from here?"

The three boys looked at each other with a gleam in their eyes. Two of them started to speak at the same time. One backed off, and let the other one speak.

"So, where are you from?"

"We're from Chicago."

"Chi-town, huh?"

"Yep, that's right."

"You must check out the teen club right down the street. We're going tonight. Want to meet us there?"

"Maybe. My mom is so overprotective. She may not allow us to go."

"Come on. Sneak out after she goes to sleep. We do it all the time."

"Yeah, but this is your hometown. We're in a strange place, and sneaking out might not be a good thing while on vacation. We'll talk it over when we get back and see what we can do. It was nice meeting you, in case we don't see you tonight."

As soon as they got out of the boys' sight, Patty slapped Chris on the arm.

"Girl, what was that for?"

"We have to get to that club tonight! Ooh...the one in the middle is all mine."

115

"Oh no...not you, miss, don't try to talk me into going."

"Look, don't give me that bull. Let's just try to figure out how to get there."

"The only choice we have is to sneak out; wait until Sharon is sound asleep, put on one of these fly outfits, then bounce. You know we're going to get busted, yo?"

"Well, those "fine ass" boys are worth a punishment. I'll take it with a smile."

"Let's stop here at the Concierge desk and see what time the shuttle leaves."

"We have a pick up and drop off every hour on the hour. However, we have to have a permission form filled out by your parent, if you're under eighteen."

"We are under eighteen, but my mom is gone out for the evening."

"Sorry, we wouldn't be able to take you on the shuttle."

They gathered their packages and went up to the room. On the way up, Patty instructed Chris "This is the way we'll do this. We go in excited about our stuff, showing Sharon everything. While we're laying it all out, we decide what to wear, without Sharon knowing that's what we're doing. Hang everything up with the selected outfit in reach for getting dressed in the dark. Put your accessories in the pocket of the outfit. We can take our showers and pretend that we're going to sit up and watch movies. We can sleep on the pull out bed in the living room. Let Sharon have the bedroom, and after she's asleep we can get dressed and walk right out the door."

"There's a hole in your plan. If we hang our things in the closet, we'd have to go the bedroom to get them. We could wake Sharon getting our stuff out of the closet."

## Deadly Choices

"You're right."

"Let's show her everything in the living room then leave everything laid across the back of the lounge chair. Leave what we're going to wear on top so all we have to do is slip them on. Get the shoes you're going to wear out of the closet when we take our showers and bring them to the living room wrapped in a towel so that she won't question why we need shoes after taking a shower."

"Yeah, yeah. While we're watching movies we could do each other's hair. She'll think we're just playing around."

"Okay, that's the plan. Don't get nervous and give up the plan."

Finally, inside the room they started putting their plan into place. They talked up a storm. Chris nudged Patty at one point to remind Patty she was talking much too much, much more than she normally would. Sharon even had a look on her face indicating she too wondered what had gotten into Patty. Patty, seeing the look, explained, "We had so much fun today. I'm so glad to be here."

Chris jumped in and excused herself to take her shower, the clue for Patty to keep Sharon in the living room so that Chris could get her shoes into the bathroom without being noticed. Since Chris knew what Patty was going to wear she got her shoes too. This way, if Sharon came into the bedroom, Chris already had Patty's shoes. When Chris got out of the shower, dried off and opened the adjoining door to the bedroom, Sharon lay there in bed watching T.V. *Ooh, I'm glad I got Patty's shoes when I did.*

"We're going to watch movies and do each other's hair. Wanna watch 'em with us?"

"No, thanks. This has been a really long day and I'm exhausted."

*Good. Hurry up and take your ass to sleep.*

"Patty, you can go in the bathroom now."

"I couldn't keep Sharon in here long enough. She said she was so tired that she really needed to get some rest. If I pushed for her to stay in here she would have gotten suspicious. Damn, I didn't have a chance to get my shoes."

Chris dumped the two pair of shoes on the sofa, showing Patty she had her back. Patty grabbed and squeezed her tight, trying not to make too much noise. When Patty finished showering, she returned to the living room. Chris had already let out the bed and called for room service. Moments later, there was a knock at the door, and a voice announcing "Room Service" prompting Sharon to come into the living room to see who had knocked.

"It's only room service, Sharon. Are you hungry?"

"No, I was almost asleep until I heard the knock at the door. I'm going back to sleep."

"Okay. Sleep tight."

"This food is good! I've been so excited, that I hadn't even thought about food. I'm glad you ordered this."

They finished eating, and Chris opened the door to put the trays in the hallway, which brought Sharon back into the living room, when she heard the door close.

"Sharon, I was just putting the tray in the hallway. You can go to sleep, we'll be fine. I thought you were sleep anyway."

"Okay, I'll go to sleep. I see you don't really need me."

*Maybe now, with two false alarms she'll keep her ass asleep. We should be able to get out without a problem now.*

"Chris. Ordering the food was better than I thought. Now, even if Sharon hears the door, she'll think it's nothing and won't get up again."

"I was just thinking that. Looks like our plan is going to work, and we'll get to see those 'hotties' tonight."

"Come on, do my hair first."

They did each others hair, played with eye-shadow and lip gloss for a while then realized it was ten fifteen p.m.

"Check Sharon's room, Patty, and see if it's safe to get out of here."

"She is out like a light! Let's hurry up."

They were completely dressed in a matter of minutes, tiptoed to the door, eased the door open quietly, and slipped out. Chris put her foot at the base of the door to keep it from closing hard and eased it closed as quietly as she'd opened it. They were home free!

# 12

Mary and Cynthia were having a great time at the concert, which was held at a very large dinner club. White linen tablecloths and a small candle centerpiece adorned every table. Each table was set for four. Two empty places at the table meant that either the other two tickets at their table weren't sold, or, the other two were just running late. Mary was glad to have Cynthia all to herself. Cynthia noticed this really good-looking man at the next table who had been looking at her since they had arrived. His table was filled, but since there were three men and one woman at the table, she assumed that he didn't have a date. They flirted back and forth with each other throughout the second set of the concert. Mary was getting more and more jealous as they continued. He probably assumed Mary and Cynthia were just girlfriends hanging out. It was obvious he didn't view Cynthia as a lesbian. Mary, on the other hand, wasn't ladylike, but didn't look too butch, either.

Mary became furious that Cynthia was giving her attention to this man. She reached over, took Cynthia by the back of the head, and kissed her. Right then and there on the spot, Cynthia slapped her. She slapped her so hard that Mary's drink tipped over. It spilled all over the white, linen tablecloth and dripped into Mary's lap. Mary was so angry she stormed out to the ladies room. Cynthia, upset, put her head into her hand, elbows on the table, and shook her head. When she raised her head, all eyes were on her. The gentleman from the other table, stood to come to her aid, only to be waved off from approaching her. Cynthia, embarrassed, didn't want to stay, but didn't want to walk out either. If she walked out, she thought everyone would think she was going after Mary. Even though she was concerned, she thought Mary brought the situation on herself. The flirt at the next table decided to join Cynthia anyway. He sat next to her and ordered another round of drinks. He didn't say anything at first and neither did Cynthia. After a few moments of silence, Cynthia looked over at him and motioned her lips, "Thank you." He responded by nodding then winked to let her know that everything would be fine.

In the meantime, Mary was still in the ladies room trying to get the stains out of her clothes. Once the second set ended, Cynthia decided to go check on Mary. Before leaving the table she explained to her male companion that things weren't the way they appeared to be. She rose from the table and proceeded to the ladies room which was extremely crowded. She made her way past the crowd and into the lounge area, where she found Mary sitting on a sofa, stewing in anger. When she approached her, Mary didn't even acknowledge her presence.

"Mary, can we talk?" Mary still showed no acknowledgment. Cynthia didn't want to create a scene, so after a few more moments of silence, she went back to the table. When she sat down she introduced herself to the man who had joined her.

"Glad to meet you, Cynthia. I'm Derrick Peace."

Before they could get into serious conversation, the last artist came on stage. When Boney started to play, heads started to bob, fingers began to snap and bodies started rock'n. Cynthia really felt the music and was beginning to enjoy the rest of the night. Derrick and Cynthia were having a ball. Unbeknownst to either of them, Mary was standing in the doorway watching their every move. She became more and more agitated by their fun. She swiftly walked to the table and told Cynthia she was ready to go.

"Go ahead, I'll get back to my hotel just fine," Cynthia replied.

Mary didn't expect that. She assumed since Cynthia was not in her hometown, she would be intimidated by being alone. She didn't know Cynthia half as well as she thought she did. She failed at trying to get the upper hand. Cynthia wasn't about to let anyone do that. She'd had to deal with that stupid ass husband of hers for many, many years, and she learned to stay on top of any situation. Hell, her childhood with her Aunt and Uncle made her as strong as she was. As Mary turned to walk out, she gave Derrick the once over, picked up her pace and got the hell out of there. Cynthia drifted off for a minute wondering if Mary was okay, wondering if she'd done the right thing by letting her leave her alone.

Mary sat in her car with the motor running but couldn't seem to put it in drive. She sat quietly trying to figure out what to do. She knew she'd made a mess of things with Cynthia and saw no way of recovering.

*So now what? I will not let her make a fool out of me this way. I'm going to pay her back for this. She humiliated me in my hometown. How dare she come all the way here to be with me then let me leave alone. I bought the fucking tickets and she's enjoying the concert with someone else. Cynthia Evans you have to pay for this.*

She put her car in gear and sped off. She cruised up one street, then down another. No real destination, she just drove until something to do, or somewhere to go came to mind.

*That's it! She's got a gorgeous daughter. I'll get next to her. She won't know what hit her, and Cynthia will feel the same humiliation she made me feel tonight. I'll teach that bitch not to fuck with me again.*

She turned her SUV around and moved toward the hotel. She stood at the door and debated how to handle the situation. What reason would she give for showing up to see Chris, without Cynthia? As she stood there pondering her thoughts, the door suddenly flung open!

"Whoa, Mary what are you doing here?"

Mary stumbled and stammered over her words until a decent sentence finally came out.

"Cynthia and I had a little riff, and I thought I'd come by and wait until she came home, just to talk to her."

Sharon gave her a questioning look, but didn't have time to dissect what she'd just heard.

"Look, I don't know or understand what's going on with you and Cynthia and right now I don't care. The girls are gone!"

"What? Gone where?"

"I have no idea. I got up to use the bathroom, went into the living room to turn off the TV, and found them gone. I was on my way out to try and find them."

"Listen, you don't know the city, and someone needs to be here in case they call. I'll go look for them."

"Thank you so much. Do you have this number handy so that you can call me as soon as you know something?"

"Yeah. Yeah. I have it."

Mary couldn't get her words out very well, 'cause her mind was racing, plotting on what to do once she found them.

*This may work out better than I'd planned. I don't want to hurt her, but I want to humiliate Cynthia. How better to get back at her than with her daughter?*

Mary had driven about six blocks before she remembered the conversation Cynthia had with her daughter just before they left for the concert. She whipped a u-turn and drove four blocks to the teen club. Once inside, she waded her way through all these "hot" young girls and sweaty boys. There stood Chris and Patty, engaged in conversation with two, handsome young men. Mary stood there for a few minutes gathering her thoughts. Chris and Patty had no idea Mary was anywhere around and probably wouldn't remember who she was anyway without recalling their introduction at the hotel.

*So do I get them and take them right back to the hotel, like a responsible adult, or do I get them to trust me and convince them to go back to my place? I think I'll gain their trust and take them with me.*

Mary touched Chris on the shoulder, and to Mary's surprise Chris recognized her right away. Patty broke out into a cold sweat, but Chris remained calm and cool like she belonged there and had permission to be there.

*Hum. This girl is a bitch just like her mother. Oh yeah, I'll get them to go home with me. She thinks she's the shit, so I'll show her how to be a big girl. This will be like taking candy from a baby. Chris will go just because she thinks she can make her own decisions. I'll let her think it was her idea.*

"Hi, Mary. This is Trey and Brandon. What are you doing here?"

## Deadly Choices

"Step over here for a second, Chris. I went to the hotel and Sharon knows you're gone."

"What? Oh my God, my mother is going to have a fit!!!"

"That's why I'm here. Let's figure out what to do, to keep you and Patty out of trouble. Say goodbye to your friends and you and Patty meet me out front. Right away, okay?"

"Okay, we'll be right there."

Of course, Chris couldn't let on to Trey and Brandon that they were busted, so she played it off.

"Patty, we have a ride home so we have to go with our ride."

They bid farewell to Trey and Brandon, then met Mary out front as promised. Once inside the SUV, Mary sat without turning on the engine while they jointly decided the best way to handle the situation. Just as Mary thought, Chris suggested they go with Mary. Chris knew how crazy her mother would act when she found out, so she wanted to prolong dealing with her.

"I really need to call Sharon and let her know the two of you are okay."

"No! She'll make you bring us back to the hotel!"

"No she won't. I'll let her know that you're going to be with me for a while, but at least she'll know you're safe. That's the least I can do. It's not fair for her to sit around worrying until you return. I won't call her until we're at my house."

With the exception of the radio playing softly in the background, there was silence all the way to Mary's place. Once inside, Mary made them comfortable in the living room then went to the bedroom to call Sharon.

"Sharon, this is Mary. The girls are okay. They were at that teen club a few blocks from the hotel. They begged me not to bring them there right away so I brought them here to my place, just long enough for them to gain their composure, and prepare to deal with their punishment."

"No, Mary, you need to bring them back now!"

"I'll bring them back in a few hours," Mary countered, and hung up.

Mary joined the girls in the living room and offered them a drink.

"You're in high school so I'm sure you've tried a drink or two before, haven't you?"

"No, we don't drink, but right now I could use a cooler or something like that."

"I think I have some coolers in the fridge. I don't drink them, but I had a party not long ago and I believe some were left over."

Patty looked over at Chris, "This is just going to make matters worse."

"Nothing could be any worse. We are in deep shit, and there's no telling what my mother is going to do to us."

"Whatever."

Mary returned with two coolers and two glasses. She poured their drinks, and sat on the sofa next to Chris.

The girls were so terrified of what Cynthia would do to them they sat and talked with Mary for hours, hoping they could build up the courage they needed to go back to the hotel. Chris crossed her legs and sat Indian style on the sofa with her head placed in the palms of her hands. When she raised her head, she glanced over at Patty. Patty was passed out on the love seat. Mary shot a quick glance at Chris, and Chris bowed her head again. Mary reached to put her arm around Chris, but before her arm could rest on her, there was a loud knock at the door. Cynthia and Sharon were screaming to let them in.

"Chris! Chris, honey, let us in!"

Mary calmly rose and approached the door. As soon as she opened it, Cynthia and Sharon forced their way past her and into the house. While Cynthia headed for the living room, Sharon stood toe-to-toe with Mary and stared directly into her eyes. She wanted to get a sense of what may or may not have happened before they arrived.

As Cynthia entered the living room, Chris raised her head to look at her mom. Tears began to stream down her face. Cynthia didn't know whether the tears were a result of her sneaking out of the hotel room, or if Mary had done something with Chris to make her ashamed. At this point, Cynthia only wanted to know that her daughter was okay. She figured she'd find out all she needed to know after they'd left Mary's. Cynthia hugged Chris and woke Patty. As they were leaving, Chris turned to Mary and said thanks. Mary nodded her head and slammed the door.

*Damn, Cynthia and Sharon ruined my plan. How will I get to Chris without her being on guard? I'll bet Cynthia and Sharon will fill Chris and Patty's heads full of reasons why they should never be around me, hmmm?*

# 13

In the car no one had anything to say, but as soon as they walked into the hotel room, all hell broke loose.

"Chris and Patty, what the hell were you two thinking? Why would you leave this room to go to that teen club, when the last thing I said was not to go? I thought you had more sense and I surely thought you respected me more than that. What the hell were you doing with Mary? Well answer me, damn it!"

"Every time I try, you keep asking me questions!"

"Quit being a smartass and answer the damn questions."

"We just wanted to get out and be able to say when we went home that we went to that club. It really was no big deal. I told you it was cool, and it was until Mary showed up and told us we should go with her."

Sharon chimed in and began explaining, "Mary showed up here and when I told her the girls were missing, she offered to go look for them and suggested I wait in case they called. She must have remembered that the girls wanted to go there, and that's how she found them so quickly."

## Deadly Choices

"Well, help me to understand, Chris and Patty, why you went to her house instead of coming back here?"

"Mrs. Evans, we just wanted to get our heads together before we were punished. We only sat there in the living room talking."

"Talking?! You smell like liquor!"

"We only had a couple of coolers, Mom."

"A couple of coolers? You are underage for one cooler, let alone a couple. You know what...? Just take your ass to bed. We'll deal with this tomorrow."

Sharon and Cynthia sat in the bedroom discussing the situation and trying to figure out Mary's motives. Cynthia went on to tell Sharon how Mary acted at the concert and about the good time she'd had with Derrick after Mary left. Little did they know Chris and Patty were listening on the other side of the door.

"But, Cynthia, I thought she was cool with the fact that you didn't want a relationship with her?"

"She claimed she was. I think she expected to wine and dine me to get me back in her bed."

Chris and Patty jerked their necks and looked at each other, their eyes bugged out of their heads. They both put their hands over their mouth to keep from being heard, and tiptoed back into the living room. Under the covers, attempting not to be heard, they discussed the conversation they'd just overheard.

"Your mom slept with Mary? I didn't know your Mom was gay."

"She's not. I don't understand this, but I bet you that's why Mary came to get us. She wants to get back at my Mom. We better go to sleep. You know the hammer is going to come down tomorrow and we need to be rested."

About eleven fifteen a.m., the phone rang. Cynthia was not happy with the person on the other end.

"How dare you! You have a lot of nerve calling me. There is really nothing for us to discuss. You've made it very clear what your intentions are, and I'm not playing that game with you! Stay the fuck away from me."

When Chris and Patty heard the receiver slam down, they looked at each other, puzzled.

"I wonder if that was Mary?"

"Probably. My mom doesn't usually talk like that, so whoever it was really pissed her off."

Cynthia walked into the living room, stood in the middle of the floor and stared at the two girls. She made them very uncomfortable by not speaking. Chris knew when her mother was angry she could get out of control. She didn't know whether her mom was going to start shouting, or if she was going to beat the hell out of them both. Actually, she wasn't as angry with the girls as she was with Mary, but they didn't know that. She was pondering over how to deal with them without allowing her anger with Mary to cloud the situation. She decided, while standing there, that their actions were pretty normal for teenaged girls. What she'd been doing for the past few weeks, was far more severe and deserved more punishment than what the girls had done. Therefore, she decided to have a firm conversation with them about the dangers and consequences of their actions.

"Chris, from now on, when I'm traveling on business, you will be with me without the company of your friends. You will have to stay in the hotel room by yourself while I'm out on business. You can only have a companion when I'm traveling on personal time.

"Cynthia, I can't believe that there's no punishment for what

## Deadly Choices

they did. I was a nervous wreck worrying about them!"

"Sharon, it's my call, and that's how I choose to deal with it."

"Fine, I'll not say another word, but when she's out of control and you can't do anything about it, remember this day."

They got dressed and left the hotel to spend time in the city. While Cynthia and Sharon looked around the designer section of the store, the girls went into the junior section, where Patty looked up and saw Trey and his boys. They walked over to have a conversation with the girls. Chris was very uncomfortable, knowing that if her mother saw them she might go nuts. She walked them toward the dressing room where the racks were crowded and not visible to Cynthia and Sharon. The boys tried to convince them to meet again at the teen club. The girls knew that Cynthia wouldn't let them out of her sight tonight, so they passed without an explanation, even as Trey gave them his number and told them to keep in touch.

Once back at the hotel, they started packing for their flight the next morning. They ordered room service and kicked back for the night.

The next morning there was a tap at the door. Chris heard it and answered.

"Mary, what are you doing here?"

"Not so loud, kid. I wanted to see how you are."

"I'm fine, but if my Mom sees you she's going to go ballistic."

"Mary, what the hell are you doing here? Move, Chris."

Mary stood there gazing at Cynthia with contempt. *"Yeah bitch, I'm going to turn your world upside down."*

"I just wanted to see you guys before you left."

"I told you yesterday to leave us the hell alone. Why can't you respect that?"

"I'm sorry, Cynthia. I care for you and your daughter and it's not that easy to just walk away."

"Yes it is. You really don't know us. You just met me a few weeks ago, so how hard can it be?"

"Well, unlike you, I have a compassion for people in my life."

"People in your life? I haven't been in your life, or you in mine long enough to be compassionate one way or another! Get over it and leave me the hell alone!"

Cynthia slammed the door in Mary's face. When she turned around, Chris, Patty and Sharon were standing there, stunned at Cynthia's behavior. Sharon thought it best not to say anything, for fear Cynthia would take off on her. Without any words being exchanged, they all gathered their things and waited for the bellman to pick up their bags. The silence was heavy in the cab ride to the airport. Cynthia was still fuming from Mary's visit. As they took the long walk down the ramp and through the tunnel to their gate, Chris decided to break the silence. She figured her mom wouldn't be any more angry than she already was, so she struck up a conversation.

"Ma' can we stop and get a bite to eat since we have over an hour before our flight leaves?"

In a very low, not wanting to talk volume she said, "Yes that'll be fine."

"Chris, here's a place. Remember we went to this place back home after you, my mom and I went shopping?"

"Yeah, the food was gooooooooodddd."

Chris pulled Cynthia by the arm into the restaurant Patty had just suggested. Sharon and Patty followed close behind. During the meal they all started to warm up a bit. They had small talk during their meal, but you could still feel the tension in the air. Once they boarded the aircraft, Chris and Patty made a point to sit together. They figured they could chat without feeling the vibe Cynthia was generating. Once the captain gave the okay that it was safe to move about the plane, Sharon moved across the isle to a set of three seats that were empty. At this point, she didn't want to be bothered with Cynthia or her funky ass mood.

After they landed, Sharon told Cynthia she would take a taxi home. She knew it would still be uncomfortable for everyone, and she didn't feel like the hassle. At the house, Patty called her mother as soon as they dropped their bags.

"Hey Mom, I'm home. Can you come get me now?"

"I'll be there shortly. Look out for me 'cause I won't be coming in."

"Ms. Cynthia, my mom is on her way to pick me up. Thank you for taking me along. I had a good time."
Chris pulled Patty by the arm and guided her up the steps to her bedroom.

"Girl, what you going to do? When my mom tells your mom about us sneaking off to the teen club?"

"I don't know. Right now, I ain't saying nothing. I'm going to take my chances and wait until your mom tells. I'm not telling on myself. Anyway, your mom said it was a dead issue. Maybe that means she's not going to tell her."

"Yeah right, my mom not tell your mom that you were defiant. Dream on."

"I'm still going to take my chances."

Thirty minutes later, there was a honk in front of the house. Chris and Patty raced down the steps to go out and meet Patty's mom. When they picked up the luggage to leave the house, Chris was expecting her mother to follow. But to her surprise, she didn't. She told Patty to tell her mother hello. Patty smiled, "Yes I will," nudged Chris with her elbow and nodded to go out the door. Hurriedly, they put the things in the car and Kathy and Patty pulled off. When Chris returned inside the house, she sat next to her mother.

"Mom, what's wrong?"

"I have a great deal on my mind, and that situation with Mary just really sent me over the edge. This was supposed to be a fun trip and between Mary, you and Patty I was more stressed than if I were on a business trip. I'm very disappointed in you, but I guess at your age some of what you do should be expected."

"Awe Ma' don't feel like that. Patty and I just wanted to have fun. You forget, I'm not a little girl anymore, and you keep treating me like a baby."

"There's more to it than that. That situation with Mary was far more serious than you realize. Eventually, you'll see what I mean. I can only imagine what she may do, so stay away from her."

Chris rose from the sofa and returned to her room. Cynthia sat on the sofa for hours thinking about Mary's crazy ass. The phone rang a couple of times before Cynthia realized it was ringing. When she picked up the receiver she heard this dry, deep voice coming from the other end.

"Hey, Girl. What's going on?"

Cynthia perked up when she heard his voice.

"Hey, James. It is so good to hear your voice. I've been thinking about you."

"Why haven't I heard from you?"

"I've been out of town, remember? I just got back."

"Oh that's right. So when can I see you?"

"Since I just got home, I should probably stay in with my daughter tonight. How about the weekend?"

"Friday night at the club around eight o'clock, like we planned?"

"That sounds good."

"Then I'll let you go and look forward to seeing you Friday. Goodnight."

"Night."

Cynthia seemed to get some energy once she spoke to James. She got up and started stirring around. She unpacked and prepared for the week. Chris prepared some dinner, which they ate together, then retired for the night.

The work week began, and Monday morning at the office was as hectic as usual. Cynthia had meetings back-to-back. Tuesday and Wednesday calmed down a bit but, Thursday was a bitch. Not only was Thursday crammed with clients, but when Mary called near the end of the day, Cynthia was sent over the edge. Cynthia cursed Mary out so badly, she knew Mary would leave her alone from that moment forward. Cynthia, her blood pressure at an all-time high, packed her things and left for the day.

On the drive home Cynthia, stressed out, wanted to have a drink. Since it was early she decided to stop at Spuratiks. As soon as she stepped in the door, the bouncer, Sam took her by the arm, struck up a conversation and led her to the bar.

"Ms. Evans, what brings you in here on a weeknight? Haven't seen you in a while, how's it going?"

"I'm good. I had a very stressful day and thought I'd chill with a drink before going home. Is James here?"

"He was here a little while ago. I'll see if I can find him. Sean, fix the lady a drink. It's on the house. Cynthia, I'll be right back."

A few moments later the phone rang behind the bar.

"Spuratiks, Sean speaking."

"Sean, this is Sam. Be cool, man, I need you to keep the lady at the bar occupied. She's here to see James, and he's in the private booth with another lady. Keep her engaged in conversation and keep her from turning in that direction. I'll get James and try to keep this thang from getting out of hand."

"Yes, fine. I'll see you later tonight."

Cynthia was not paying attention to the conversation that Sean and Sam were having. Actually, she was sitting there fantasizing about being with James. Sean struck up a conversation with her, but it didn't hold Cynthia's attention. Not only was she not paying attention, she was very discreetly scanning the room with her peripheral vision. Although Sam made it to the private room to alert James that Cynthia was there without Cynthia noticing him, he didn't make it back as invisibly. When she saw him coming, she figured she should keep her eye in that direction. When Sam returned to the bar, it was obvious he was up to something, which made her even more observant. Out of the corner of her eye, she saw two people leaving the back room and approaching the front door. Cynthia turned and waved at James. He pretended he didn't see her and didn't respond. Cynthia got up from the barstool and swiftly walked to catch up with them. She knew if she didn't approach him while he was with the other woman, he would deny that it was him. Outside, in front of the club, she calmly walked up to them and spoke. She introduced herself to the woman, patted James on the shoulder and went to her car.

# 14

Friday night came and went. James hadn't called her, nor she him. Early Saturday morning the phone rang. James spoke in his deep, dry voice.

"Good morning."

"Hello, what do you want?"

"I wanted to discuss the situation we were in the other day. Will you allow us to do that?"

"There's no need to explain anything. You're not obligated to me, nor I to you. Neither of us has to explain our actions to the other."

"I said discuss not explain. I have wanted a one-on-one relationship with you ever since we met, but you didn't want that. Therefore, yes I do see other people, don't you?"

"Yes I do, but whatever I do, no one else knows about."

"So because you're sneaky and secretive makes your way better?"

"Sneaky? I like to keep my life private, but I wouldn't call it sneaky. The only person I try to keep my personal relationships from is my daughter. Considering her dad is the only man she's ever had in her life, I don't put her in a situation to have to deal with anyone else."

"So, why didn't you show Friday night?"

"I just didn't feel like it, and I didn't feel a need to put forth any extra effort."

"So, from here on, should I not call or bother you anymore?"

"That's up to you. If you're feeling me and I'm feeling you at the same time, it's no problem. I don't expect you to make any special efforts, nor will I."

"Fine, I guess I'll see you when I see you, huh?"

"Yep."

"Have a good day."

Before Cynthia could respond, she heard the dial tone. She looked at the phone and started laughing. *Hmmm, so he couldn't really take it. He talked a good game, but he didn't expect me to handle it as well as I did. Men...they're such hypocrites. They can dish it out, but they can't take it.*

Meanwhile, Cynthia decided to get out of bed and begin her day. Chris awakened shortly after and made plans to go to the mall with some girlfriends. While Chris was away, Cynthia muddled around the house, cleaning, napping and relaxing. The phone hadn't rung all day since she hung up with James. About four-fifteen, the phone rang while she lay on the sofa watching a movie.

"Hello."

"Hi."

"Why are you calling here?"

"I can't get you off my mind. I really need to see you. Can I come by and talk?"

"Come by and talk? You live in another state."

## Deadly Choices

"I came to town last night. I'm at a hotel downtown."

"No, you can't come by. I told you I don't want to see you, Mary. What do I have to do to convince you to leave me alone?"

"Cynthia..." Abruptly, Cynthia ended the call.

Nearly an hour later Chris came home with her girlfriends. Cynthia was still relaxing on the sofa watching movies. The girls came in laughing as they usually did when they were all together. They came into the room with Cynthia to show her what they'd bought. Ashley nudged Chris to prompt her to ask her mother if she could go to a party.

"Ma' there's this party tonight one of our schoolmates is having. Can I go?"

Cynthia, drained in her own personal bullshit, didn't care whether or not Chris went to a party.

"I don't care. Where is it and who's giving it?"

"This girl in our class named Monica. You wouldn't know her 'cause she was new to our school last year. It's her birthday and it's going to be at the Westin, in a ballroom. Most of us from school were invited, and since we're not in school it doesn't end until one o'clock."

"How do you plan to get there? Am I going to have to take you people?"

"Nah. Dominique's mom got her a limo. Her birthday is in a few weeks and this is part of her birthday present."

"What time do you plan to leave?"

"We're going to all get dressed here and leave at seven thirty. The limo will pick us up here."

"All right, but I expect you home no later than two o'clock."

"That'll work. Thanks, Mom."

All in unison "Thank you, Ms. Evans."

The girls jetted off to Chris' room to doll themselves up for the festivities. They were all dressed by seven o'clock, and returned downstairs for Cynthia to approve.

*"Damn, these girls look far better than we did in high school. Shit, they look grown."*

Everyone sat quietly watching TV until they heard the doorbell ring. Each of the girls jumped up as soon as they heard it, and scurried to the door to see if it was the limo. But to their surprise, it was Mary. Chris' eyes became wide, and the look on Cynthia's face was hateful.

"Hi, Mary. These are my friends, Christian, Dominique, Lolly and Ashley."

"Hey girls, where are you going all dolled up?"

"To a party at the Westin downtown."

They weren't able to carry on much of a conversation. The limo pulled up, but before the driver could get out of the car, the girls were racing down the steps to the car.

"Bye, Ma.'"

"Bye, Ms. Evans."

Cynthia stood in the doorway watching them pile into the car. As the driver proceeded down the driveway, she turned her attention to Mary. They stood there for a few moments staring at each other. Cynthia was so furious she couldn't find the right words to say. Mary was nervous as hell, knowing she was out of line for showing up at her door. After a few minutes of silence, Mary spoke up.

"Cynthia, please talk to me."

"Step back out of my doorway. Give me some room, you're crowding my space."

As soon as Mary stepped back, Cynthia slammed the door in

## Deadly Choices

her face. Mary stood there for a moment, dropped her head, and turned to return to her car. Cynthia returned to her spot on the sofa and flicked through the channels to find another good movie. The longer she sat on the sofa, the more anxious she became. She decided to get dressed and go out on the town. She found herself at Spuratiks, sitting at the bar. Since this was one of the hot spots in town, she found no reason she couldn't go without James being notified. She'd hoped though that another woman wouldn't accompany James. After about an hour, James noticed Cynthia still sitting at the bar, and approached her. They made small talk, but there was tension in the air. As James sat next to her, he felt a tap on his shoulder. When he turned around, so did Cynthia.

"How dare you leave me sitting alone while you sit here with another woman."

"I didn't know she was here until I came out to go to the men's room. There was nothing going on but conversation. I'll be there shortly."

The woman turned and left the club. Cynthia sat peering at James with contempt. James sat without saying a word. He found himself in yet another awkward situation with Cynthia.

*"Why does this shit keep happening to me? Why can't everybody just fuck around in private like I do?"* Cynthia thought.

"James, I'm going to leave now and get out of your hair."

"Please don't go, Cynthia."

"Oh, one is better than none, huh?"

"No, that's not the case."

"Save it, James. I'll see you another time. I'm not feeling this tonight."

Cynthia drove around for a bit to get some air. She decided to go to the Westin and "spy" on Chris. As she entered the hotel lobby, there was a jazz band playing, so she thought she'd sit and enjoy the jazz for a while. *Well, I'll be damned. Why the hell is Mary sitting not far from me? What the hell is she doing here? She said she was staying downtown, but is it here?*

Before the thought could leave, Mary was approaching her. *"Shit, I can't curse her out in public in an open environment like this. I'll just have to deal with her for the moment."*

"Cynthia, what brings you out?"

"Not that it's any of your business, but I was out on the town and wanted to check up on my child. What the hell are you doing here?"

"This is where I'm staying. After I left your house, I came back here and they were setting up to play, so I thought I'd stick around and check out the music. My room is just two floors up."

They sat listening to the music in complete silence. While they sat, Mary continually ordered drinks and they both kept drinking them. Cynthia was getting wasted, as the drinks continued to come. She convinced Cynthia to come to her room and discuss their situation. It was pretty easy to do once Cynthia was high on liquor. However, Cynthia wasn't as intoxicated as Mary seemed to believe. Cynthia wanted to get her in private so that she could set her straight, once and for all. Once they were in the room, Cynthia immediately lit into her. "Help me to understand why you won't leave me alone. I don't know how much it will take to get you out of my life, but it has to stop. You simply must stay away from me. If you continue to act this way, I'll get a restraining order against you. I will make a claim to the police and have it on file that you are stalking me. Do you want that?"

"I may be extremely aggressive, but I'm not stalking you. Why

## Deadly Choices

do you play these head games?"

"Head games? How do you feel I'm playing head games?"

"You make out with me, fly to go to a concert with me, then you turn the tables on me just as quickly as you laid with me."

"That was something that just happened. There should have been no strings attached and I believe I told you that there was no commitment, didn't I?"

"Yeah, you said that, but your actions said something else."

"After you made the scene you did at the concert, I knew you would be a trip in a relationship. I made it very clear the other night that you should go on with your life without me. I have been very firm with asking you to stay away from me, but you continually insinuate yourself on me. I want it to stop!!"

Mary having nothing else to say, realizing she couldn't handle her liquor very well at all, turned, walked to the bedroom and passed out on the bed. Cynthia left the room and headed home. She decided not to "spy" on Chris after all. Two o'clock on the dot, Chris and the girls were coming through the door. Cynthia was in her bed as if she hadn't been anywhere. She figured the girls didn't need to know that she had been out, especially to the Westin, where they were. If Chris knew she would have had a fit. Cynthia sat and listened to the girls go on and on about how much fun they had.

"Ma' the party was the bomb! The music was hot, the food was good, and we all had a blast."

"Ms. Evans, I've never been to a party like that before. Everything was so perfect."

"I felt like Cinderella."

"Please...Cinderella? You could at least use a real person to compare yourself to Lolly."

"Shut up, Ashley. Who did you feel like at the party?"

"I felt like I was J-Lo."

All the girls started laughing.

"J-Lo. If you were J-Lo you would have given the party. Be for real."

"Whatever."

While all the girls went on and on about how much fun they had, Chris sat back, seeming to be in a world of her own. Cynthia noticed Chris wasn't talking and asked, "What's wrong?"

"Nothing, Ma, nothing."

"Chris, I'm ready to go to bed. Can I go on into your room?"

"We all can go. I'm tired, too."

When the girls left the room and retired for the night, Cynthia had trouble going to sleep, even though she'd had her sleeping pills. She eventually dosed off.

The next morning, she got her paper from the front porch, fixed her coffee, lit a cigarette and sat to peruse the news in the paper. She couldn't get past the front page. The caption read. "Out of town woman killed at the Westin"

*"I wonder who that could be. Did it happen while I was there?"* Cynthia pondered.

She went on to read the entire article. *Mary Collins of Denver, Colorado was found dead in her hotel room by the maid. The coroner has determined the time of death to be within two hours before or two hours after midnight. The cause of death has not yet been determined, but investigators suspect fowl play. Investigators are looking into why she was in Chicago, and who she may have been here to see. They will have to work with the Denver police since she's a resident of Denver, but so far there are no leads. "Oh my God! They'll be looking for me.*

## Deadly Choices

*Should I go to them and let them know that she was here to see me and that I was in her room? No, if I do that, I'm their prime suspect. I don't need that kind of publicity. But if I don't it'll be worse if they have to come looking for me, I should probably sit tight and when they come to see me I can pretend that I didn't know. They don't know if I've read the paper or not."*

Cynthia rested her head in her hand and sat quietly at the kitchen table. She'd been sitting there for about an hour when the girls entered the kitchen.

"What's wrong, Ma?"

She almost blurted out that Mary was killed, but she didn't.

"Nothing, just a little tired."

"Awe, will we be in the way if we fix us some breakfast?"

"I'll go to my bedroom and you can have the kitchen to yourselves."

The girls, getting stuff from the refrigerator, started preparing their breakfast. As Cynthia lay across her bed, she felt just as she did when Jordan died. Numb, yet vindicated that she didn't have to put up with Mary's shit any more. A few short moments later, the phone rang. It was Bill Garcia calling from Denver.

"Cynthia, have you heard the news?"

"What news?"

"Mary's dead!"

"Dead! What happened?"

"No one knows yet. The police said they don't have any leads but they called me since she had my business card in her wallet, and she had no family to contact. Did you know she was in Chicago?"

*"If I don't fess up it will look suspicious."*

"Yes, I knew she was here. I saw her last night."

"You did? When?"

"A couple of times. She came by the house early in the evening then I ran into her at the Westin where she was staying. I left the Westin around eleven thirty or so."

"Well, as soon as I get more details I'll let you know."

"Please do, this is so bizarre."

*"I cannot believe this is happening. Why are people around me dropping like flies?*

From her bedroom she heard the doorbell ring. Chris answered the door and yelled up to her mom.

"Mom! There's someone here to see you. Wait right here, she'll be down shortly."

As Cynthia approached the door, she saw a male standing on the porch. She could only see his profile so she wasn't sure who it was. A lump hit the pit of her stomach, thinking it may have been a detective to question her about Mary. When she got to the door, the man turned to face her.

"James! What brings you by?"

"I was thinking about you and the situations we've been in the last few times I've been with you. I really felt a need to see you and talk with you. Is it all right that I'm here?"

"Actually, I'm kind of glad to see you. I really need comforting right now."

From the kitchen, Chris, watching her mom with James, didn't like what she saw. He was holding her mom much too close. They left the hallway near the door to proceed to the family room. The family room was out of ear shot from the kitchen, so Chris cooked up a reason to go in there.

"Ma' would you like us to fix you and your company something

## Deadly Choices

to eat?"

Before Cynthia could answer, Chris took two steps toward James and extended her hand to him.

"Hi, I'm her daughter, Chris."

"I'm her friend, James," he responded, while shaking her hand.

Chris, forgetting she'd asked her Mom if she wanted something to eat, turned quickly and exited the room. Her goal was to find out who this man was, not really if they wanted something to eat. She returned to the kitchen with the girls, where they made plans to hang out at Dominique's house for the day. Chris informed Cynthia that they would be at Dominique's, and they left. When they got to the street, Chris noticed Frank leaning on the privacy fence, gazing onto the patio of their house. Chris looked at Ashley, raised her eyebrow, shrugged her shoulders and walked down the street.

As the girls walked to Dominique's, Chris drifted deep into thought. *Why is Frank always watching my mom? He's always around. Even though they didn't see me, I saw both of them at the Westin last night. Frank is really weird. I know my mom likes him 'cause she's known him since they were kids, but he is strange as they come. I need to keep an eye on him.*

"Chris! Chris! Girl, what is wrong with you? Did you see those honeys that just drove by? "You can smell a fine one from a mile away and you let them get by you without a holla."

"I'm really worried about my mom. Since my dad died, she's been so different. I don't know what to think, or what to do about it. I need my mom back the way she used to be. I don't like this 'new wave mom.'

"I would love it if my Mom were as cool as yours."

Ashley nudged Dominique and winked.

"Cool is one thing, but acting like a big sister or something she's not is another. One minute she's acting like the mom I know, then the next minute she's somebody else. I'd rather she be in my ass like she used to, instead of like this. She might as well get some books and go to school with us. She's acting like a big ole' tramp. I hate it!"

The three girls looked at Chris as though she were crazy. They all stopped dead in their tracks when she screamed "I hate it!" Lolly stepped near her and put her arms around Chris to comfort her. The other two followed suit. The girls stood on the sidewalk embracing, until Chris broke away.

"Let's stop this shit. I've come to realize that my life will never be the same until my Mom gets back to her old self. I can't force her to change, so I'll deal with it until she snaps back."

"All right then...where's the car with the honeys that went by a minute ago?"

As the girls approached the house, a silver Lexus came to a stop at the curb. Dominique nudged Chris to do the talking as she always did.

"Hey babe, what's up?"

"Nothing. Just going to my girl's house."

"Mind if we get out and holla for a minute?"

Chris glanced at Dominique to make sure it was cool. She didn't know how her parents might act if they saw them talking to the boys in front of the house. Dominique nodded her approval.

"Yeah, that's cool."

As the boys were exiting the car they were giving their "male signals" as to who would talk to which girl. Actually, it really didn't matter. All four of the girls were pretty, built like an hourglass, and all

## Deadly Choices

the guys were handsome and cut to perfection. Each guy approached one of the girls and struck up a conversation. The guys, Tracey, Charles, John and Eric, eventually, started talking to the girls as a group instead of one-on-one. They exchanged digits and the guys went on their way.

The girls, giggling and excited, proceeded up the walkway to the house and into the family room, where they sat discussing the guys they'd just met.

"Why do girls always seem to get excited when they meet new boys, but guys don't?"

"Who knows? Who cares?"

"They're probably riding around looking for more girls already."

"Maybe one day we'll meet someone who wants a serious relationship."

"Oh sure...in high school?"

"I doubt it. Guys in high school are looking for one thing...a piece of tail."

Dominique's mother stepped into the room to see if the girls were hungry.

"Would you like something to eat? I'm frying fish and making spaghetti."

"Ummm...yes, I'll have some."

"Me, too."

"And me."

"Chris, what about you?"

"Huh...?"

"Do you want fish and spaghetti?"

"Yes, I'll have some, thanks."

"Chris, what's wrong with you?"

"Nothing, Ms. Mitchell. I just have a lot on my mind. I'm cool."

"Come on to the kitchen and eat."

They all went to the kitchen to chow down on the food. In the middle of the meal, Chris got up from the table.

"I gotta go. I'll talk to you guys later."

"Chris, what's up? You want us to walk with you?"

"Naw. I'm good. I think I can walk a few blocks home by myself."

The girls looked at each other puzzled, wondering what could be wrong with Chris, who hadn't been herself for days?"

Chris saw James leaving when she rounded the corner to her house. Picking up her pace so that she could speak to him before he pulled off, she stopped at the car as he put it in gear. She stood there with her hands on her hips and attitude all over her face.

"Hi again. Sorry I didn't get a chance to have a conversation with you earlier. So how do you know my mom?"

"We met at a social gathering."

"Are you serious about her?"

"Whoa, hold on a minute. I think you're getting a bit too personal."

"Personal? That's my mom I'm asking about."

"Then you need to ask those questions of your mom, don't you think? You're way out of line with this questioning."

"I don't mean to be out of line. I am concerned about my mother and I don't want to see her hurt. She's been hurt enough and I don't want anyone to ever hurt her again."

"Again, you need to speak with your mother."

"I'll do that."

Chris rolled her eyes at James and sashayed up to the house. On the way up, she saw Frank again, watching her every move. *"Weirdo. Does he spend all his time watching us?"* She and Frank exchanged a wave as she entered the house.

"Mom! Where are you?"

"I'm upstairs. What's wrong?"

She answered as she climbed the stairs. "Nothing's wrong. I just wanted to talk to you."

"What's on your mind?"

"Can we sit down and have a heart to heart?"

"Sure. What's the matter?"

"I have really been concerned about you lately. You're acting so different."

"Different?"

"Yeah. You have started going out to clubs. You've been hanging out with people that I would never have dreamed you would be with, and I don't get it."

"Do you feel as though I've been neglecting you?"

"No. I'm almost grown now. I don't necessarily need you the way I used to, but I want the mom I'm accustomed to, not this 'new age,' 'hip hop' mom that goes out clubbing all the time. I've always been proud that all my friends envied my mom. They said you are the bomb. You were classy and a professional."

"You and your friends don't feel that way anymore?"

"It's not that we don't, it's just different. You don't see a difference in yourself?"

"Of course, I know there's a difference, but I never imagined that it showed so much that you and your peers would notice. Do you see me as a tramp or something?"

There was silence for a moment. Chris raised her head, and when she looked her mom in the eye, tears dropped from her eyes.

"Kind of."

"Really? From your viewpoint, how do you see me as a tramp?"

"Well...take Mary for example. Why would you be hanging out with a lesbian?"

"There is nothing wrong with befriending someone who has an alternate lifestyle. I have always taught you not to judge people like that."

"I'm not judging her for her decision. I just don't think it's too cool for you to be flying out of town to hang out with her. Patty and I figured out there was something going on between you that was more than friendship."

"How did you and Patty come to this conclusion?"

"We noticed how she looked at you, and why is she always begging you to spend time with her?"

"She wanted something more than what I was willing to give. You can't hold me accountable for her actions."

"As much as you want to keep me a little girl, I'm not a little girl anymore. I know more than you think I do."

"You don't know how unhappy I've been for so many years. The years with your dad drained the life out of me. All I want is to get some fun back into my life. I didn't realize this was affecting you this way."

"I know how unhappy you were. I used to cry myself to sleep when I would hear Daddy beating on you. I remember those nights like they were yesterday."

"Oh honey, I had no idea. I thought I was protecting you from all that."

"You did what you could, and what you thought was best, but I always knew."

"So what do you propose I do to make you happy?"

"Why can't you be in a one-on-one relationship with someone, instead of dating so many people? It just seems like that fits you better than dating around."

"That was a better fit for me once upon a time. It's not a good fit for me right now. I don't want to be tied to anyone right now. I just want to have a little fun in my life. I have never had a chance to have fun. My childhood wasn't that great then I married your dad."

"Mom I don't want you to feel like I'm knocking you down. I guess I just need to give it some time, and maybe I'll get use to the 'new you'."

"I think that's a good idea. Give me some time and I'll work it out for both of us."

Chris hugged her mom and went to sit on the front stoop to clear her head. Cynthia sat on her bed in shock that her daughter was on to her behavior. For the first time in her life she was really enjoying herself. *What changes need to be made to make them both happy? How do I break the news to her that Mary is dead?*

Cynthia joined Chris on the front stoop.

"Wanna go out to dinner? We could talk some more and work this out. I have something to tell you anyway."

"Yeah, sure, we can go out to eat."

They both went inside, collected their purses and left for the restaurant. The drive was quiet. Neither of them had much to say, so they waited until they got inside the restaurant to talk. Cynthia decided to tell her about Mary while they waited for their entree.

"Chris, you'll hear about this soon enough, so I wanted to break the news to you myself. Mary was found dead at the Westin last night."

"Dead? How did you hear that?"

"It was in the newspaper this morning."

"I'm sorry to hear that, but I really didn't know her, so it doesn't affect me. Are you okay?"

"Not really."

"Why not?"

"Well for one, I was the one she was in town to see. We were having issues because I wanted her to leave me alone. I was there last night, and may have been the last one to see her."

"Everybody seemed to be there last night."

"What do you mean everybody?"

"Frank was there, too. I saw him early in the evening."

"Why was Frank there?"

"I don't know. I didn't talk to him. I saw him when I was going to the restroom."

Chris still didn't let on to Cynthia that she already knew she was there. She remained really calm, considering what her mother had just told her.

"I'm really concerned that when the police start to investigate, they'll come see me. I don't know how this happened, but I'm sure they'll find out that we had been arguing, and I was one of the last people she saw."

"Do you think you're in trouble?"

"No, not in trouble, just going to have to deal with being investigated. That won't look too good for me, and I hope it doesn't affect my business."

"See, this is what I was talking about. If you were like you used to be, you would have never been associated with her."

"That's all hindsight, and I don't think that my behavior has been that questionable."

"So tell me about that man that just left the house. Where did you meet him?"

"He owns a night club that I go to. I met him the night that you stayed at Patty's."

"God, Mom. That wasn't that long ago. He acts like he's known you forever. AND, were you seeing him and Mary at the same time?"

"Yes. What's the problem?"

"That's how tramps act. They're not committed to anyone. They jump around."

"It's not what you do it's how you do it. I haven't flaunted my relationships in front of anyone. I've been very private about my business."

"Not too private. I picked up on some of it. Your whole way of being has been different, and I don't like it. Something really needs to change, Mom."

"What would make you happy? Would you rather I just muddle through my life unhappy and unfulfilled?"

"No, that's not what I'm saying. I really don't know what I want other than for you to be happy. I just don't like how you're getting your happiness. Maybe I'm jealous that you don't make a fuss over me anymore."

"Make a fuss over you! You pushed me away a few years ago. You made it very clear that you needed your space. I respected that, because I know at your age space is necessary. When I stopped hovering and doting over you, I realized just how lonely I was."

"So, back to Mr. Night club, what's the name of the club you go to? Where is it?"

"I'm not the daughter, why are you drilling me?"

"I'm just wanting to be as much a part of your life as I can be. I can't go out with you and I can't go on dates with you, but I want to know in case I ever have a need to know."

"I guess that's okay. The club is Spuratiks up in Woodland Hills. That's all you need to know. Here comes our meal, can we eat?"

As the two sat and attempted to enjoy their meal, there was no conversation. Chris' attitude clearly projected that she didn't want to talk. Cynthia was a bit uncomfortable that her daughter knew more about her private business than she wanted her to, but she knew she had to deal with it now.

They finished dining and went home.

# 15

Once again the work week began. Cynthia and Chris still hadn't talked much, but they made every attempt to strike up a conversation.

Cynthia dropped Chris off at school, but decided not to go straight to the office. She stopped at a nearby coffee shop where she could have a cup of coffee and a cigarette, in peace. She knew once she arrived at the office, it would be a crazy place. As she sat at the table gazing out the window, a man approached her table.

"Ma'am, are you Cynthia Evans?"

"Yes, I am."

"I'm detective Emanuel Shelton of the Chicago police department. May I sit and talk with you about Mary Collins?"

In a low, humble tone she invited him to join her. *Stay cool whatever you do. Don't get emotional, but don't be too cold.*

"What can I do for you?"

"The body of Ms. Mary Collins was found at the Westin, and we understand that she was in town to see you."

The detective became silent and gave Cynthia a cold stare,

while he awaited her response. Cynthia put her cigarette to her mouth and took a sip of coffee, then gave the detective a questioning look. For a few seconds, neither of them said a word. The detective, feeling a bit beaten at his own game, was forced to speak.

"So, Ms. Evans would you care to answer the question."

"I didn't hear a question. What was the question?"

"Why was Mary Collins here to see you?"

"Oh...I didn't hear that question a minute ago."

She gave a quick smile and began to answer.

"She was here to persuade me to be her mate."

"Her mate?"

"Her lover, she was gay."

"Oh, I see."

"Do you?"

"Yes, it was a lovers' quarrel."

"No, I wasn't her lover. She wanted me to be."

"So you argued, she didn't see things your way, and you killed her?"

"You have got to be kidding me!"

"Sounds like an open and shut case to me."

"How was I supposed to have killed her? How did she die?"

"I'm not at liberty to give you this information."

"Well, I guess if I killed her I should know, huh?"

"Maybe you're just not letting on. You seem to be quite in control. No emotion, seems a bit odd don't you think?"

"There's no emotion because we only met a few weeks ago. I'm concerned as to why this could have happened to her, but I don't usually break down over someone I don't really know."

"As I see it, you don't break down at all."

## Deadly Choices

"What is that supposed to mean?"

"I understand you recently lost your husband."

Once again there was a moment of silence.

"Well?"

"Well what?" Silly me, did I miss another question?"

"My you're picky. How did you react to the death of your husband?"

"I grieved in private. I was with the man all of my adult life, and we had a child together. How would you have reacted?"

"I've been with my wife since high school and we have several children together. I don't think I would be back to work yet, and especially with a lover on my heels, that quickly."

Cynthia didn't respond, flinch or blink. She gave an icy cold stare.

*How dare he judge me? Everyone handles situations differently. What makes his way better than mine?*

As they sat in silence, Cynthia lit another cigarette and ordered a large coffee. She turned to look out the window as if he wasn't there. A short time later her cell phone rang.

"Cynthia Evans."

"Girl, where are you?"

"Sharon?"

"Yes, it's me."

"What's wrong?"

"Did you forget about the meeting with the partners this morning?"

"Yes, I did. I'm only a few blocks away. I'll be there in ten minutes."

"Ten is fine. You're not late yet. I was just reminding you."

"You are the best. I'll be there shortly."

She turned from the window and looked directly at the detective.

"Have a good day. Here's my card should you need anything else."

"And here's mine in case you think of something you need to tell me."

They both gave each other a half-cocked smile, although Detective Emanuel Shelton was quite irritated, yet intrigued with her.

Cynthia had a walk that could knock you off your feet. When she really wanted to strut, one couldn't help but notice her. The detective stood at the table and watched her walk away. When she reached her car she turned toward the window, winked at him and got in the car.

Sharon saw her pull into the parking lot and was standing at the elevator with her leather portfolio, notes and a cup of coffee. When the elevator doors opened, she took Cynthia's purse and briefcase. She handed her the portfolio, notes and coffee, informing her that the meeting was starting in five minutes and everyone was present, except her.

She walked into the conference room exuding confidence and ready for whatever the meeting might bring. As usual, with the aggressive and high-strung people in the room, the meeting turned into a war room. The meetings among the partners were always crazy, but through all the madness, they managed to be productive.

As soon as the meeting adjourned, Cynthia returned to her office, flopped down in her chair, and let out a huge sigh. While Cynthia sat staring out the window, Sharon peered at her from the doorway. Moments later she walked in and approached Cynthia's desk. Cynthia was so deep in thought that Sharon's presence startled her.

# Deadly Choices

"You have been rattled since you got here. What's wrong, Cynthia?"

"I just have a lot on my mind. I'll deal with it."

"If you need to talk, let me know."

Without any acknowledgment, Cynthia turned back to window. Sharon stood there for a second, then decided to leave her alone. Ring...ring...ring...ring...Cynthia was able to catch the call before it went to voicemail. She wished she hadn't as soon as she heard the voice on the other end.

"Ms. Evans, this is Detective Shelton. We spoke this morning."

"Yes, what can I do for you?"

"I had a few more questions, do you have a minute?"

"Not really, but I'll give you one."

"I appreciate your cooperation."

"Whatever I can do to help the situation."

"Thanks. So tell me, when did Ms. Collins come to town?"

"Two or three days ago."

"Did you see her the first day she arrived?"

"No."

"When was the first time she made contact?"

"The day after she arrived."

"Then how did you know she was here the day before?"

"When she called, before coming to my house the other day, she told me she'd arrived the day before."

"What time did she come to your house, and what time did she leave?"

"I don't really recall the time. I didn't know I'd need to know, so I didn't check the clock. It was in the afternoon when she arrived, and she left shortly after."

"What time did you meet her at the hotel?"

"I went to the hotel around ten p.m. and left about eleven fifteen, eleven thirty."

"That should do it for now. Thanks for your time."

Cynthia's head started pounding. *What the hell could be happening to my life? I can't handle this pressure and perform well on my job. Something's got to give. What should I do about all this? How do I stop it?*

Sharon happened to open the newspaper and see an article on Mary's death. She immediately jumped up from her chair and went into Cynthia's office. This was the first she knew of Mary's death.

"Did you know about Mary being killed at the Westin?"

"Yeah, I heard."

"Yeah, you heard? Why didn't you say anything?"

"I have been dealing with so much shit lately I just didn't think to tell you. Plus, as you recall, when I arrived this morning I went straight to a meeting."

"When did you find out?"

"Sharon...don't question me like this. I'm not in the mood. I've been questioned by a detective twice today. I surely am not going to be badgered by you."

"Sorry to bother you. I just wanted to know what was going on."

"You can ask what's going on without drilling me. I can't take that kind of pressure from anyone else today."

"Fine, I'll leave it alone."

With attitude, Sharon swiftly turned and marched back to her desk. *What is really going on with Cynthia? She's been really different*

## Deadly Choices

*since Jordan died. What could I do to help her? I ain't helping her with anything. She's keeping me in the dark so why bother?*

Cynthia noticed the time, realized she hadn't eaten, grabbed her purse and headed to the elevator. When she walked out of her office, she walked past Sharon without saying a word. Sharon raised her head and watched Cynthia walk away. *Huh, she didn't bother to tell me where she was going. What the hell does she have an attitude with me for? I was just trying to give her support. Fuck her then. She can take care of it her damn self.*

When the elevator doors opened, several people got off on that floor, but Frank was standing in the back.

"Frank! What are you doing here?"

"I was in the building taking care of some personal business. I'm going to lunch now, would you like to join me?"

"No, thanks. I have a need to be alone right now."

"I saw in the paper that your friend from Denver was found dead at the Westin."

*Now how did he know she was my friend, by reading the paper? I've never introduced them. He may have seen her at the house, but her picture wasn't in the paper. Maybe I should go to lunch with him and see what I can learn.*

They continued to make small talk in the elevator. Once they approached the ground floor Cynthia informed him that she would go to lunch with him. She did however elect to follow him, so that she wasn't dependent upon him to bring her back. She could leave once she got any information from him about how he knew that Mary was her friend.

They drove about twelve blocks to Cynthia's favorite Italian restaurant and waited for the entree' to arrive, as Cynthia began to probe.

"I just can't believe my friend was killed while she was here."

"Yeah...that's pretty messed up."

"How did you know that I knew her?"

"I've seen her visit your house."

"But her picture wasn't in the paper. I don't think I've ever introduced you when she's come by have I?"

"No, you haven't. Actually, I was at the Westin the other night listening to the jazz set, and I saw the two of you together."

"That still doesn't explain how you knew her name. How did you relate her to the person I was with the other night?"

"When she was leaving your house once before, I introduced myself to her. She told me her name and where she was from. I put two and two together when I read the article."

"Do you make it a point to introduce yourself to all my visitors?"

"No."

"Frank, I have to tell you that I'm really not comfortable with this. Something doesn't feel right."

"There's nothing to worry about. I would never do anything to hurt you. I've been in love with you since high school."

"WHAT?"

"Don't get alarmed. I wouldn't impose myself on your life."

"I have to leave, Frank."

Cynthia turned to get the attention of their waiter.

"Will you please box my lunch to go? I need to leave earlier than I expected. Here's my card to pay for both meals."

"Cynthia, I can pay for our meals. Just box her lunch and I'll take care of the bill."

## Deadly Choices

They both sat in utter silence. Cynthia was trying to digest what Frank had just told her, and it wasn't settling very well. As soon as the waiter brought her food, she rose from the table, thanked Frank for paying, and walked out.

# 16

Back at the office, the phones were ringing non-stop and Cynthia couldn't seem to clear her head. About three-fifteen, she began collecting her things to leave for the day. She wasn't being productive, so what was the point in staying? Upon her exit, Sharon walked into her office to speak with her about her schedule the next few days. Both of them had attitudes, therefore the conversation didn't go well. The tension was thick and they both seemed to need space. Cynthia picked up her purse and briefcase then brushed by Sharon without uttering a word. Sharon locked up Cynthia's office and returned to her desk. She couldn't believe that they were at odds with each other. They had always been able to manage through their differences, but this time felt like the end of their friendship.

Cynthia drove to a park near her house. She walked to a park bench near a pond to feed the ducks. She sat back on the bench and looked up directly into the sunlight to catch the sunrays. She slumped down on the bench to rest her head on the back of it. She closed her eyes and drifted into a deep state of mind.

Meanwhile, back at the office, Sharon was stewing over their conflict. She snapped at everyone who approached her, and slammed things around on her desk.

After being made aware of her unprofessional and rude behavior Maurice approached her desk.

"Sharon, what seems to be the problem?"

"Sorry, Mr. Robinson. Cynthia and I had an issue that really disturbed me. I know I need to adjust my attitude, and I will."

"Make it quick. We can't have one of our most capable, front line people behaving like this."

"Yes, Sir."

Sharon was really pissed that one of the partners had to put her in check. She was furious with Cynthia. She spun around in her chair, took a deep breath, and gulped down her remaining bottled water. She turned back to face the reception area with a painted smile on her face.

Luckily, the remainder of the day was quiet. The phone barely rang, and the constant churn of people at her desk was next to none. When Sharon glanced up from her desk, she noticed the clock said five-twenty eight p.m.

*Damn, where did the time go?*

Sharon tidied up her work area, clicked off the lights, and left for the day. On the way home, she decided to stop for a drink. She pulled into the parking lot of Spuratiks, and as she entered the building she bumped into James. She and James spoke casually, and Sharon went to the bar. She ordered her drink, swirled around on the barstool, crossed her legs, and while sipping her drink, flirted with a man on the other side of the dance floor. As he stood to approach her, James sat next to her at the bar. Immediately, the other man calmly and coolly redirected his steps to the men's room.

"So pretty lady, what brings you here this evening?"

"I had a really bad day and thought I would stop here and unwind before going home."

"Well, I'm really glad you did."

"Why? You don't know me."

*If only you knew, I know you better than you know. I'll show Cynthia what a bitch really is. Fuck with me, will she?*

"I'd sure like to. Is it possible?"

"Well of course, handsome, what's your pleasure?"

"I'm a diabetic, but a little taste of brown sugar levels me out."

At that point, they both were showing all thirty-two's. They both had beautiful, white teeth that seemed to light up the room. Sharon was so taken by this pick up line that she just laughed her heart out. When she finished and regained her composure, she said softly, "So you substitute brown sugar for insulin?"

"Hey, it seems to work."

"Then if it works, we definitely need to keep you from going into a diabetic coma, don't we?"

"It's about time for my shot. I have to have one within the hour."

"So where do you keep your diabetic paraphernalia?"

"In my bathroom at home."

James rose from his barstool, nodded at the bartender, took her by the hand and led her to the parking lot. All the while she was walking behind him she couldn't stop thinking about Cynthia.

*It is really tacky to do this to Cynthia, but since she wants to be a bitch, I'll be one, too. Besides, he's so fine I'd be a fool not to get some. It ain't even about him getting over on me...I'm getting exactly what I want.*

## Deadly Choices

James walked Sharon to his car and told her he would bring her back to her car later.

*Sharon, what the hell are you doing? You cannot do this to your friend. Don't ruin a longtime friendship like this. Humph, I'm getting some of this...fuck the friendship. Plus, he's not someone she cares about. He was a piece of ass to her, just as he is to me. We'll get past this.*

The moment James opened the front door he was pulling Sharon by the arm, straight to the bathroom. He just barely got the keys out of the door and didn't bother to lock it. In the bathroom, he pinned her against the wall, pressing his body firmly against hers. With her hands spread over her head, he held her by the hands preventing her from being able to move. His manhood revealed itself inch by inch with every moan she made, as he gently kissed her from her mouth to her breasts. Still not able to move the upper portion of her body, she became more and more wet, as the kisses got wetter and hotter. He moved her hands over her head close enough together that he was able to hold them both with one of his. He used his finger to slide her thong to one side. He then entered her and it was on! From banging against the wall to riding him on the toilet, Sharon was in pure ecstasy. James was so smooth with his lovemaking he was able to move them to the tub without missing a stroke, turned on the water and continued to take her to heights of unimaginable pleasure. Although a bit awkward, neither missed a beat.

*No this motherfucker didn't get my hair wet. Hmmm...it's worth it, shake it off.*

They eventually made their way to the bedroom where they finished each other off. Sharon glanced over at the clock and realized she was ready to go.

"It's getting late and I have an early day. Will you take me to my car now?"

"Yeah, I need to get back to the club anyway."

They showered and headed back.

Unbeknownst to them, Chris, Lolly, Tracey and Charles were cruising the parking lot trying to decide if they were going to attempt to get in the club.

"Chris, why did you make us come here? You know we can't get in, and my dad would kill me if he knew I was driving his car to this club."

"Oh Tracey, chill! There are a million Lexus' around here. Who'll know?"

"Hey, my dad is known all around here. I know they know his car."

Lolly looked up and saw the face of the man in the vehicle that just pulled up next to them. She nudged Chris, but Chris didn't acknowledge her.

"Chris, Look! Ain't that the man that was at your house to see your Mom?"

"Yeah. OH MY GOD. Look who's in there with him."

"What's up? Who are they?"

"Just pull over there. Pull over!!"

"All right girl, damn."

"Duck, Lolly. Sharon can't see us. Turn off the lights so they won't notice us."

"Y'all better tell me what the fuck is up. Got me sittin' here like Columbo or some damn body, and I don't know what it's all about."

"Shut up and let me see what they're doing."

"Shut up? Girl, you better recognize."

"I'll tell you in a minute. Please let me see what's happening first, okay?"

Everyone in the car got quiet.

"Ah! He's kissing her! This bitch is kissing him. I *know* she knows that my mom was hanging out with him."

As soon as Sharon pulled out of the parking lot, Chris and her crew sat discussing what they'd just seen. Chris was furious. She was so angry she started to cry. Lolly leaned over to console her, and Tracey and Charles had the same thought at the same time, *Why do girls always have to cry?* They looked at each other, sighed, and looked out the window. For quite some time, no one said a word. They sat so long that the windows fogged up.

"Chris, you ready to go now?"

"Yeah, take me home."

"Chris, you can't tell your mom."

"Why not, Lolly?"

"That would hurt her. You need to figure out another way to deal with this, just don't tell her."

"Whatever, I'll see how I feel in the morning."

"We all better get home or we won't see morning. My pops will kill me for getting his car home too late."

"Ah ha. Your pops don't care if you get home late, just not his car."

"You know what I meant, man. Quit being an ass."

The boys dropped each girl at her home and ended the evening. Chris knew she couldn't face her mother. She knew her Mom would see something was wrong all over her face. When she entered the house, she went straight to her room. She showered and climbed into bed. She lay there with the lights out, unable to go to sleep. When

## Shelly L. Foster

Cynthia peeked in, Chris pretended to be asleep. She surely didn't want to have a conversation. For hours she could only think about seeing Sharon and James. The longer she thought about it, the angrier she got.

*How could she do this to my mom? They've been friends for a long, long time, and she just moved in on a man my mom was seeing. I can't get over this bitch. I wonder if my mom would even care. Since she just met the man, she may not have a problem with it. Nah...she ain't having that from a so called friend. She's cool, but she ain't no fool. I'll deal with Sharon in my own way. She's going to pay for this.*

Morning came too quickly for Chris. The sunlight came through her sheer curtains and rested on her face. Yawning and stretching, she slowly squirmed out of bed. As she was making her way to the bathroom, Cynthia walked in.

"Good morning. I didn't hear you come in last night."

*Don't start asking a bunch of damn questions. I can't deal with that shit this early in the morning.*

"Hey, Ma. I didn't want to bother you and I was tired."

"Okay, but what's the attitude about?"

"I don't have an attitude. I just got out of bed and I'm still sleepy."

"Guess that's what late nights will do to ya, huh?"

"I guess."

Chris walked into the bathroom, and Cynthia went downstairs to have her coffee, cigarette and read the morning paper. Chris got completely dressed before going downstairs, in case she needed to escape her mother quickly. Chris muddled around in the kitchen, gulping orange juice and nibbling on a bagel, while Cynthia silently read the paper. When Cynthia looked up over her glasses at Chris,

Deadly Choices

Chris knew the questions were about to start. Cutting it off before it could get started, she gathered her books. Before she could get out of the kitchen, the phone rang. Chris grabbed it off the hook before Cynthia could make a move.

"Chris, how long before you'll be leaving?"

"I'm walking out the door now. What's up?"

"Meet me at our half way spot. We can walk together, okay?"

"Cool. See you in a few."

"Who was that?"

"Lolly. We're walking to school together. I'll see you tonight."

When Chris closed the front door, Cynthia folded the paper, took off her glasses and let out a sigh. She knew something was going on with her child, but she couldn't quite put her finger on what it was. Of course, like any mother of a teenager, her first thoughts were sex, or drugs, or something she didn't want to have to deal with. She sat for a while pondering over what to do, then decided to dress for work.

When she walked into the office, Sharon wasn't at her desk. Cynthia glanced at her watch, noticing it was nine-twenty in the morning. As she passed Sharon's desk, she checked to see if the computer was on, but it wasn't. There was no sign that she had come in yet. As soon as she entered her office, the phone rang. Sharon was on the other end.

"Cynthia, I overslept. I'll be in shortly."

"Overslept? Forgot you had a job?"

*Don't fuck with me bitch. I may not come in at all and go fuck your man some more.*

"No, I didn't forget I had a job, or I wouldn't be on the phone right now, would I?"

Dial tone.

*Fuck you, Cynthia. I won't be in at all.* She couldn't believe Cynthia just hung up on her.

Before the thought could pass, Sharon started dialing the phone. She thought about hanging up, but before she could think twice, a deep, dry voice answered.

"Hello."

She got a lump in her throat, but began speaking anyway.

"Good morning, James."

"Who's this?"

"Brown Sugar."

"Hey, there. Good morning, how did you get my home number?"

*Out of Cynthia's electronic calendar that I have access to Motherfucker, why?*

"Do you have an issue with me having it?"

"Not necessarily. Not many people have my home number, so I was surprised. What made you call?"

"I decided to take the day off, and I wanted to know if you needed a taste of Brown Sugar this morning?"

"Hum...that sounds good. Come on over."

"See you in a bit."

She showered and put on cologne, reached in her drawer and pulled out a peach lace thong, slid it on, put on her peach colored three-inch pumps, and a peach colored trench coat. She then pulled her hair up, clipped it, grabbed her pre-packed "on the go" bag, and strutted out the door. Within an hour, she was ringing his doorbell. James stood in the doorway in nothing but boxers, and a wicked and tempting smile. Not one word was spoken as they slowly and passionately began to kiss.

## Deadly Choices

He gave the belt on her coat one tug, leaving the coat partially open. She was very shapely, so the lace thong peaking through her partially open coat was ever so sexy. James took a step back to admire her. She took several steps back and rested her shoulders against the wall. Her back was arched and she tilted her head slightly to the side. Sliding her pumps off with her toes, James' nature began to rise. Moving in slow motion, she removed her coat, dropping it to the floor. As James took a step toward her, she held out her hands to keep him at bay. She reached up and removed the clip from her hair, allowing it to drop past her shoulders. She then took her middle finger and slowly moved her thong to one side and inserted her finger inside herself. Once again, James attempted to approach her, but she continued to keep him at bay. He leaned against the arm of the sofa, resting only a portion of his buttocks. As he began to stroke himself, Sharon walked up to him and straddled him. She positioned her knees on each side of him on the arm of the sofa, placing one of her breasts directly into his mouth. As he sucked and massaged her breast, he penetrated her. She moaned and groaned until he couldn't control himself. He picked her up and whisked her off to the bedroom, but to his surprise, Sharon took total control in the bedroom. Right in the middle of a really good stroke the phone rang. Since James was on the bottom, Sharon reached over, picked up the receiver and handed it to him. She knew she had total control then. He couldn't make a sound, giving her a chance to take advantage of the opportunity. Still on top and in motion, she turned to face his feet. *Look at my ass while you talk to some other bitch.* A smile came over her face, as she rode him like a horse racing in the Kentucky Derby. She stretched forward and grabbed him by the ankles. The sensation made James' toes curl forward. She heard a thump on the floor. *Damn he dropped the phone.* Still in control, Sharon leaned to the side, to allow him to roll over. They did and he was now on top. He reached down and picked up the phone. "Sorry about that. Can I call you later?" He rested the receiver on the base and got right back into it. The day passed quickly, and Sharon was ready to go. *Mission accomplished.* When she turned to face him, she found him fast asleep. She showered, but before leaving, she left her business card on the night stand. As she reached her car, she noticed a silver Lexus parked across the street. *Wonder who that honey is?* The thought passed as she drove off.

# 17

Chris, Lolly, Tracey and Charles had met up and decided to skip school. As usual, Tracey had his father's car. Once Sharon came out of James' house, the car was filled with silence. Chris sat patting her foot in frustration. When Tracey attempted to talk to her, she snapped at him.

"Why are you so mad now? You knew she was here, hell, we followed her. You need to get a grip."

"Fuck you, Tracey. I'm concerned about what this is going to do to my Mom."

"What's following the woman around going to do? If you ain't going to do nothing but follow her around and make yourself crazy, what's the point?"

"I don't know. I'm trying to figure out what to do."

Tracey started the car and pulled off.

Meanwhile, Cynthia was really upset that Sharon still hadn't shown up for work. She called a temp agency to get someone to come in for the remainder of the day, and the next day, as well. Although there were the other secretaries that Sharon had hired when she took over the role to be Cynthia's assistant, they didn't know Cynthia's daily routine like Sharon did. They helped the new girl as best they could. Cynthia was so upset she was unable to function, so she decided to leave for the day.

Once in her car, she knew she needed to relax. Just as she approached the door to James' house, he opened it with a surprised look on his face. "What are you doing here?"

"I was having a really bad day and I needed some comfort."

*Oh shit. After this morning with Sharon, I can't comfort you.*

"I was on my way to the club."

"Couldn't you stay with me for just a little while?"

"Well...okay come on in. It really can't be for long, though."

"If I could just lie down and relax in your arms, I'll be satisfied."

James had forgotten that Sharon left her business card on the night stand, but just as he realized it, he noticed Cynthia was already sitting on the bed. At this point, James knew he needed to divert her attention away from the card. He sat next to her and turned slightly toward her with his back toward the headboard. Bad move! Cynthia raised her arms and wrapped them around him, giving him a hug. Just as she rested her head on his shoulder, she saw the card on the night stand. She slowly raised her head, leaned over and picked it up. She sat quietly for a few moments then let tears roll down her face.

"What's wrong?"

"Why is Sharon Waters' business card here?"

"You know her?"

"Know her? When did she give you this?"

"She stopped by this morning unannounced. I only met her a week or so ago."

"This morning?"

"Yeah, she came by about ten-thirty."

"This is it!"

"What? What are you talking about?"

"Don't worry about it. See you around."

Cynthia got in her car and sped off. *What is up with Sharon? Why in the world would she do this to me? I have to confront her. I'll be damned if I allow her to walk all over me.* Cynthia pulled up at Sharon's house and sat there pondering how to handle her. As she approached the door, Sharon was coming out. She stopped dead in her tracks when she saw Cynthia. Cynthia stepped right into her space and started talking.

"Help me to understand why you would pursue James?"

"What are you talking about?" *Admit to nothing until you have to.*

"I was just at James' place. I know you didn't bother to come to work, but you were at his house all morning."

"I don't owe you an explanation as to my whereabouts."

"You do when I pay your salary. You were on my time."

Sharon tried to brush past Cynthia, but Cynthia wasn't having it. She stepped in front of her and stood firm. They glared at each other with hate in their eyes. Both were expecting the other to speak first. Cynthia, deciding she had to speak first, said with force, "Sharon, I'm not going to play this game with you. If you feel that our friendship isn't important enough for you to keep my confidences and sneak around behind my back, then we aren't the friends I thought we were."

"Cynthia, you expect everyone to kiss your ass, and I don't

like the taste of it. I'm not going to keep bowing to you to make you happy."

"That's not true and you know it. Our working relationship is totally separate from our friendship. If you're not mature enough to know the difference, then we don't have a friendship."

"Not a problem for me. I didn't come to you, you came to my house."

"So be it. You're fired. Have a nice life."

Sharon stood in shock as Cynthia turned to go to her car. She really didn't think Cynthia would take it to this level. She underestimated Cynthia's position, but took her gentle nature for granted. Sharon turned, unlocked her door and went back into the house. She dropped to the floor in disbelief. She couldn't believe she no longer had a job. Especially, one paying the kind of money Cynthia paid her. She realized she'd made some very big mistakes. *This bitch is mine now. I will do everything in my power to bring her down from that damn soapbox she stands on. Fuck getting a job, my only mission will be to destroy her.*

Pulling into the driveway, Cynthia saw Frank pulling in behind her. He got out, and approached her car window.

"Girl, I've been trying to get your attention for miles. What in the world would make you drive the way you did?"

"Frank, I really don't want to discuss it. I've had a really bad day, and I need to go in my house and relax."

"I understand. I just hadn't had a chance to talk to you since we had lunch, and I wanted to catch up."

"Another time Frank. Today is not a good one for catching up."

Cynthia pulled closer to the house, and got out of her car.

## Deadly Choices

Frank was still standing in the same place, a bit annoyed that Cynthia just blew him off.

"So, Cynthia, do you need me to deal with Sharon for you?"

*Awe hell, he's taking this shit too far. He knows way too much about my business. Is he crazy or just stupid as hell?*

Without responding or breaking her stride, she went into the house. Frank, dropping his head, shuffled back to his car.

Shortly after Cynthia settled in, Chris came home. When she came upstairs, she went straight into her Mom's bedroom. She found Cynthia stretched across the bed crying.

"Mom, what's wrong?"

"I had a really bad day, honey. I'll be fine, don't worry about me."

"Please, talk to me, Mommy. I had a bad day too, and I still want to hear about yours. Come on Ma, talk to me."

"Sharon and I had it out. I fired her, and she is no longer my friend."

"So you found out, huh?"

"Found out? What are you talking about?"

"I saw her last night with that man James who was coming over to see you. She was with him again today." *Oops. Shouldn't have told her about today. Now she'll know I skipped school.*

"How do you know about today? And how would you have seen them last night?!!"

Anxious to get the focus back on Sharon, Chris said quickly, "Calm down mother. We were out cruisin' last night, and happened up on them together. They were kissing and stuff, so it made me curious and we followed her today. I wanted to know what she was up to, so I could tell you, but you found out before I got a chance to. Mom, I tried to protect you just like you protect me."

Cynthia grabbed Chris and gave her a big squeeze.

"Honey, it's not your job to protect me from anything. You need to spend your time being a child, and let me be the adult."

"Sorry for trying to help."

"No, don't be sorry. I'm not scolding you. I just want you to stay focused on school, and not on my mess. My life is pretty messy right now, and I don't want you in the middle of it."

"All right, whatever you say."

They sat on the bed holding each other for quite some time, until Cynthia sent Chris to her room. Hours later they met in the kitchen. Cynthia was preparing something to eat, as Chris entered the kitchen. They made small talk about everything except Sharon. Chris was dying to get more details about her, but she knew if she broached the subject, her Mom would shut her down. She'd already decided that she was going to get to the bottom of it anyway. She didn't care if her mom got mad at her.

The doorbell rang about eight o'clock, and Chris went running to the door. Sharon burst in walking past Chris as if she were invisible. *Bitch, I'll call my girls, and we will beat you down right here in front of my mom.*

"Cynthia, I needed to give you a piece of my mind and…"

"And my ass. You have a lot of nerve coming in my house to give me a piece of anything. I'm not interested in hearing a word you have to say. Get the fuck out of my house!"

As Cynthia hurled a number of venomous remarks, the two of them stood there, toe-to-toe, peering at each other like two pit bulls about to square off in a fight. When Chris walked in, the tension seemed to ease a bit. Cynthia shot Chris a look, motioning Chris to leave the room. Chris left the room, but only stood around the corner so that she could hear what was being said.

"Sharon, I'm going to be calm and ask you nicely one more time to leave my house."

"Cynthia..."

"First of all, you're not going to come into my house and scream at me like I'm a child. With that said, let me show you to the door."

Cynthia took Sharon by the arm to lead her to the door, but Sharon snatched it away. As she snatched her arm free, she mistakenly hit Cynthia in the face. Cynthia didn't flinch. She paused for a second or two then proceeded to slap Sharon across the face. It didn't stop with one slap though. After the slap, she kicked her in her kneecap bringing her to the floor. She punched her as hard as she could on the side of her face. Once Sharon was stabilized on the floor, Cynthia gave her a piece of her mind.

"Bitch, I had to fight my husband for years, and I'll be damned if I allow some bitch to walk into my home, uninvited, and walk all over me. Not only will I take you down, I will take you out. You of all people should know me well enough to know that when I walk out of the boardroom and out of the corporate tower, I can handle myself in any environment. Don't mess with me or your ass will come up missing."

Still on the floor but too angry to cry, Sharon didn't say a word.

"Now get the hell up, and get the fuck out of my house."

Sharon pulled herself up and slowly walked out of the house. Cynthia hadn't noticed Chris standing in the hallway, but when she turned from the door, there she stood.

"Chris why didn't you go to your room?"

"I wanted to make sure she wasn't going to do anything to you."

"How many times do I have to tell you that you don't need to protect me. I can take care of you and myself. I really hate that you had to witness that."

"I'm cool, Mom. But like it or not, I've got your back."

Cynthia went to her bedroom to collect herself. She couldn't believe that she was in yet another situation that brought out the worst in her. *So what I snapped at her. It has to be more than that. There has to be more going on with her. We've been friends for too many years for a minor disagreement to affect her this way.*

Chris decided to call her girl Lolly and tell her about what had just happened.

"Girl, quit it. Your mom had a fight?"

"Not really. Sharon didn't stand a chance. My mom Muhammad Ali'd her right there in the kitchen."

"Oh snap. Your mom can bang?"

"Can she? I couldn't believe it. Whenever my mom and dad got into it, they were always behind closed doors. I never saw old girl throw a punch. I wanted to laugh, but I didn't know what was coming next and I didn't want her punching me out. She didn't even know I was downstairs at the time. She was pissed when she realized I saw her in action."

"Girl, this is too unbelievable. All I can see is your mom in one of her bad ass suits with her briefcase."

"Yeah, yeah, but wait, that's what she told Sharon. In so many words she told her don't fuck with her outside the boardroom. I wanted to be her cheerleader and say...go mommy, go mommy."

# Deadly Choices

The girls were squealing with laughter as they discussed the altercation blow by blow. Actually, Chris was quite proud that her mom could handle herself like that. However, Chris was still very angry with Sharon. She turned her focus and the conversation to Sharon.

"You know what though, Lolly?"

"What?"

"Even though my mom made Swiss cheese out of Sharon, I am still not okay with her. I don't appreciate what she did to my mom. I know my mom is very hurt by what her so called friend did to her. After all I've seen her do the last few days she still needs to pay."

"What you mean pay?"

"I don't know. I just know she needs to hurt as badly as my mom does right now. My mom is hurting in her heart and I wish somebody could make Sharon feel like that. Sharon's bruised up face will heal in days. My mom's heart is going to hurt for a long time."

"Chris, just chill out and let your mom handle it her way."

"Ah, punk out when my mom needs me the most? Is that what you would do for your mom?"

"Probably. I don't get in my mom's mess. She has way too many issues. If I got in her mix, I wouldn't even have time for school."

They both burst into laughter.

"Yeah, your mom does have issues doesn't she?"

"Yep, and I ain't going to trip with her."

"Well hey, girl, I'm going to go check on my Mom. I'll talk to you later."

When Chris got to Cynthia's bedroom door, she heard her mother sobbing. Hearing her mother cry like that made her furious. She got herself together and walked into the room. She lay next to her on the bed and cuddled up to her as close as she could. Cynthia reached over, put her arm around her and kissed her on the top of her head. They ended up sleeping through the night.

The next morning Chris woke up first. She slid out of the bed, and scooted off to her bedroom to get dressed for school. Cynthia awakened shortly after Chris and went straight to the kitchen for her morning cup of coffee and cigarette.

When Chris came down to the kitchen, she and Cynthia talked for a little while, while Chris ate her breakfast and waited to leave. Chris ran out the door at the last minute as usual to meet up with Lolly, just in time to go to school together. All Chris could talk about was her anger with Sharon.

Meanwhile, Cynthia was still sitting at the kitchen table pondering her recent dilemmas. She picked up the phone and called her old friend, Kathy.

"Kathy, this is Cynthia. Do you have a minute to talk?"

"Sure, girl, what's up?"

"I am under a great deal of stress right now and I'm thinking about taking some time off and going away for a few weeks. I was wondering, since school is almost out, could Chris stay with you for a few weeks while I get my head together?"

"Not a problem at all. She's welcome anytime. You should know that."

"I really appreciate it. I'll let you know details as soon as I can get everything in place."

"Just let me know what's, what and in the meantime, I'll make space for Chris."

"Thanks a bunch. I'll talk to you in a day or two."

Cynthia prepared for her workday and left for the office.

## Deadly Choices

When she arrived, Marge, the new secretary, was at her desk. Cynthia acknowledged her as she approached her office. The reception area had a different feel now that Sharon was gone. Cynthia missed her friend and what they once had. Marge was old, gray and matronly. She felt as though her mother was sitting outside her office monitoring every move she made. At any rate, Marge was qualified to do the job, so Cynthia figured once they got to know each other better they'd have their own relationship. Shortly after Cynthia got settled in, Marge came in with coffee. She brought a small porcelain bowl set with sugar and cream and packets of Equal.

"Mrs. Evans, I wasn't sure how you liked your coffee so I brought everything you might need until I know just how you like it."

"Marge, this is great. Nice touch with the porcelain bowl set. I like my coffee light and sweet. You can't give me too much sugar or cream."

"Fine. I'll make sure it's the way you like it from now on."

"Actually, I like the sugar and cream set. Bring it to me just the way you did today, but I don't need the Equal."

"My mother taught me to serve this way. I bought this set just for you."

"Oh, you didn't need to do that. I'll make sure you get reimbursed."

"That's not necessary. It was my pleasure."

Marge winked at Cynthia and returned to her desk. Cynthia sat sipping coffee while her laptop booted up. As she gazed out the window, the sunrays came beating in as she fantasized about making love to her man. She held the coffee mug with both hands, preventing her from touching herself. She was feeling very sensual and felt the urge to touch herself. She crossed her legs and pressed them together as tightly as she could to make the urges stop. Thankfully the phone rang and she knew she had to focus on work.

"Hello, Cynthia. How are you?"

"I'm fine. To whom am I speaking?"

"This is Phil Swanson. Long time no talk to."

They talked briefly about getting together, and agreed on three o'clock as a meeting time.

A big smile came across Cynthia's face, as she swirled around in her chair and back to her fantasy. This time, there was a real person to include. She wasn't able to stay in her fantasy world too long, though. The phone started ringing and Marge was coming in and out of Cynthia's office with questions. *I am really not feeling this job. I need some time off.*

The sequence of events propelled her to get away for a while. Cynthia called Marge into her office and asked her to rework her calendar, allowing time off for three weeks.

"Push all of my appointments out three weeks, unless there's one that is marked critical. Let me know if there's a critical one and I'll make the call."

"I'll let you know what the changes are as soon as I've contacted everyone."

"Call Maurice and ask him if I can get time on his calendar today to meet with him and the other partners."

Cynthia turned to her computer and surfed the Internet for places to go. After about twenty minutes she decided on New York. *New York is perfect. Anything I want to do, I can do it there. No one will know me and I can do as I please.*

"Marge, will you come in here for a moment?"

As soon as Marge entered the room, Cynthia gave her detailed instructions of what she needed her to do. "I'd like to leave next Monday. This will allow me time to take care of some things before I leave. I want an early flight and I want to return on a Sunday. Make my hotel reservations in the heart of the city, preferably near Times Square. I want to be in the thick of all the excitement, somewhere that I can walk to nearby restaurants, and near the subway trains. I'd like to see a Broadway show while I'm there. Go on the Internet and see what shows are playing. I'll take care of everything else once I arrive."

"Mrs. Evans, while you are away, will I still be needed here?"

"Yes, of course Marge. I need you to run things while I'm away. You will have the number where I can be reached in case of an emergency."

Cynthia was getting excited about her adventure. While she was finishing up paperwork, Marge informed her that the partners could see her. She made her way to the boardroom and had a brief conversation with the partners. They were all in favor of her taking time off. Paulie let it be known that she suggested time off when Jordan died and thought it was long overdue. By the time she got back to her office, Phil Swanson was waiting in the reception area.

"Phil, you're a little earlier than I expected."

"Yes, I cleared my calendar and came over after my last meeting, before I got sucked into any more work."

"Come on in."

She turned to Marge and asked her to hold all her calls. "It's nearly four o'clock so if the calls are light, you can leave around four thirty, if you'd like." Marge nodded as the two went into Cynthia's office.

The conversation started off with work related issues that they discussed for about twenty minutes. Phil rose from his chair, walked over behind Cynthia's desk and peered out the window. Cynthia glanced at him as he stood there, one hand in his pants pocket causing his suit jacket to rise slightly above his rear end. *Hmmm, nice ass.* Cynthia finished notes on her computer regarding their conversation then turned her chair around to face Phil. She crossed her legs showing all but her panty line. During her first meeting with Phil, when she first landed his account, she was quite drawn to him, but wouldn't allow herself to weaken. Now that she'd been unleashed she wanted him badly. She was hoping he would ask her out and they could get together at the end of the night. He was as sexy as he could be. He was a little over six feet tall, muscular, bald and smelled really good. *Hmmm would I love to get busy with you.* Just as she had the thought, Phil turned and faced her. They looked at each other for a few seconds without saying a word. Phil could feel her vibe and reacted to it. He leaned over her chair, placing each hand on the armrest. He then tilted his head slightly to the side and planted a smooth kiss on her lips. As he raised his head and began to stand, she gave a tug to his tie, pulling him back close to her. The kiss got more and more passionate. All of a sudden her office went from a comfortable work atmosphere to a hot steamy den of sin. While holding his bald head with both hands, she gently pushed him back to allow herself to stand. As she stood, Phil placed one hand behind her head and the other around her waist. Eventually, the hand around her waist moved downward gripping her butt. Without separation, they walked over to the wall right behind her door where there was nothing hanging on the wall. Luckily, she had on stockings and he didn't have to be bothered with removing pantyhose. He pressed her against the wall and began to remove her panties. Once he unzipped his fly and entered her, she let out a big sigh. As they stroked against the wall, each stroke became more forceful than the one before. They were making

## Deadly Choices

noise that they hadn't realized. Marge heard a thump and made her way to the door. When she got to the door, she could vividly hear the moaning. Her wig became skewed as she pressed her ear closer to the door. She raised her hand over her mouth, gasping at what she believed was taking place behind those doors. At first she thought about going in to make sure Cynthia was okay, but her better judgment steered her from doing so. When she dropped a stack of papers she was holding, Cynthia and Phil knew she was standing outside the door. Instead of stopping and finishing at a more appropriate place, Cynthia guided him to the sofa. She mounted him and the sex got juicier, wetter and more delicious. Their adrenaline became more intense when they knew that Marge was aware of what they were doing, but she couldn't prove it. When Marge could no longer hear the sounds, she picked up the papers, straightened her wig and returned to her desk. She was a nosey, old prude and refused to leave until Cynthia showed her face. She wanted the opportunity to look at Cynthia to show her how ashamed she was of her.

When Phil and Cynthia let out the last sigh, they looked at each other and burst into laughter. They were so tickled with having been so impulsive. Phil told her that he had been fantasizing about being with her.

"This was better than my fantasy."

"How so?"

"Well for starters, I never imagined in my wildest dreams that I would get with you in your office."

"I never thought we would ever get together at all. I have to admit that I was curious about you the first day we met."

"Me, too. That's why I called. I couldn't take it any longer."

"We'd better get ourselves together, in case someone decides to come in without knocking. You know we didn't lock the door."

"I know. Wondering if we'd get busted made it more fun."

Marge couldn't stand the pressure any longer. She got up from her desk, knocked once, and marched right into Cynthia's office. Given the age gap, Marge viewed Cynthia as one of her children, and felt she could treat her just as she would one of her own. To her surprise, Cynthia was sitting behind her desk and Phil in a chair, having a pleasant conversation. Marge's face turned red as she got a whiff of sex that filled the room.

"Marge? I thought you were gone."

"No, I had some things to tend to before leaving. Here's the information I printed out for you for your trip. I'll be leaving now. I'll see you in the morning."

She gave Phil a quick glance of disgust as she turned to exit the room. As soon as she closed the door, Phil and Cynthia looked at each other and once again burst into laughter. Cynthia covered her mouth so that Marge wouldn't hear them laughing.

"So, you're leaving on a trip?"

"Yes, I'm going to take some time off for a week or two and clear my head. I've had a lot going on since you and I last spoke, and I really need some down time."

"Where are you going?"

"New York."

"Really? Want some company for a day or two?"

Cynthia hesitated for a moment. She was struggling with the answer, since this trip is supposed to be to get away from everyone. However, this would be an opportunity to get busy with him without Marge standing outside the door. A day or two couldn't hurt.

"A day or two would be fine. Why don't you meet me at my

house and we leave together?"

"Do you have your itinerary, so that I can make plans?"

"Yes, that's what Marge just handed me. I'll make you a copy."

"Let me make sure my calendar will support my being gone and I'll let you know."

They went to the parking garage together and went their separate ways.

# 18

All the way home, Cynthia had a smile on her face. She felt like skipping when she got out of her car. Frank was working in his yard when she arrived home. Her excitement exuded all around her, and it made Frank very curious. He approached her as she gathered her things from the car. When she turned to close the car door, Frank was standing so close they nearly kissed.

"Frank! Why did you sneak up on me like that?"

"I didn't sneak, you just didn't hear me."

"What is it, Frank?"

"I just noticed you seemed rather excited, and I wanted to share in your excitement. What's up?"

"Nothing much. I'm going to New York for a few days, and I'm excited about my trip."

"You travel all the time. Why would a trip excite you like this? It seems like more than a trip to make you smile like that."

"I just had a really good day, that's all."

"Sure, tell me anything."

"Stop it, Frank. You're making way too much out of me being

## Deadly Choices

happy. I need to go in and unwind. Talk to you later, okay?"

Cynthia went inside and left Frank standing in the driveway. Frank stood there for minutes, wondering what was up with her then made his way back to his yard. Chris greeted Cynthia at the door. Chris was doting over her too much for Cynthia's comfort.

"Chris, what are you up to?"

"Up to? What do you mean?"

"You are only this attentive when you want something. What is it?"

"Well, Patty called and told me that I was going to be staying with them for a few weeks, and I was wondering if I could stay with Lolly instead?"

"I would much rather you stay with Kathy and Patty, since I know Kathy much better than I know Lolly's mom."

"But I'm closer to home, and more comfortable at Lolly's. We can go to school from her house just like we always do. This way, I wouldn't feel like so much had changed. Please, Mom?"

"I really don't know Lolly's parents, and I wouldn't be comfortable with it. I will let Kathy know that you can go over there on the weekends."

"All right. How many weekends will it be?"

"Only one full weekend, then I came home the next Sunday. I can pick you up from Lolly's that Sunday. I'll call Kathy and let her know what we've discussed."

Chris had a sour attitude as she returned to her room. She and Patty were really cool, but Patty wasn't as much fun as Lolly. She and Lolly went everywhere together and shared all their secrets with each other. Patty, on the other hand, was prone to tell everything she knew. Chris figured she could let her hair down while her mother was away, and she didn't want Patty in the way. But she figured she'd roll with it until her mother was in New York.

Cynthia went to her room and started packing. Although she wasn't leaving for a couple of days, she wanted to make sure she didn't forget anything. This way, she had time to check, and re-check what she was taking. She made a few phone calls, and left voicemail messages for clients providing them the opportunity to touch base with her with any issues or concerns prior to her departure. When her stomach started growling, she realized she hadn't eaten. She yelled to Chris, asking if she was hungry too.

"Yes! Chinese sounds good."

They ordered Chinese which was delivered in forty-five minutes. The two sat in Cynthia's bedroom and pigged out. When Chris went to her bedroom, she called Lolly to tell her she wasn't going to be able to stay at her house, while her mother was away. They pondered over what to do on the weekends they were going to be together. Naturally, Chris included Tracey and Charles in the plan. Of course they needed them to have wheels to get around, since Tracey could always get his dad's car. They both were getting pretty psyched about hanging out while Cynthia was away. Chris was devilish, and Lolly managed to follow suit. The two didn't get into much trouble, even though they sure did enough. After they ended their conversation, Chris laid in bed staring at the ceiling, contemplating the next few days.

As the sun came up, Chris was still staring into space. She hadn't slept all night. Other than being excited about her freedom while her mom was in New York, she was also thinking about Sharon. The situation between Sharon and her mom had never stopped bugging her. A small part of her wanted them to make up, and be close like they use to be. The other part wanted nothing more than to get a group of her

## Deadly Choices

buddies together and beat the shit out of her. As usual, when Cynthia awakened, she came into Chris' room to say good morning. She'd said "Morning" more than once before Chris realized she was in the room.

"Girl, can't you hear?"

"Huh?"

"I said, can't you hear?"

"My mind was somewhere else. I guess I'm sleepy."

"Well, it's time to get up and get it in gear."

Chris rose from her bed, and Cynthia returned to her bedroom. Their daily routine was the same everyday. They each did the same thing, the exact same way, everyday of the week. They moved about like robots until they made their way to the kitchen. The kitchen was where they had their morning conversations and came to life.

"Ma, can I have some money?"

"Money, for what?"

"Just a few dollars for snacks."

"Look in my purse. And you better not get more than three dollars."

Chris folded the money, placed it in her pocket, grabbed her bagel, and out the door she went. Cynthia sat there smiling. *I'm so glad my child is happy and well adjusted. All I ever wanted was for her not to have an unhappy childhood like I did.*

Cynthia had her moment, gathered her purse and briefcase and started for the office. As she turned onto Lake Avenue, she noticed a black vehicle sitting at the corner. The vehicle looked familiar, but she couldn't quite put her finger on who it belonged to. She slowed up as she was passing it, but the windows were tinted so dark she couldn't see inside. She proceeded a few more feet and turned into the parking garage.

When she stepped off the elevator, Marge sat peering at her over her bifocals, as though she were the flavor of the month. The closer Cynthia got to Marge's desk the more uncomfortable she became. She said good morning, and Marge gestured with a nod. Inside her office, she dropped her things on her desk, and opened her blinds. The black vehicle was still parked in the same spot. *Who's vehicle is that? I know someone who has a vehicle like that, but who?*

Just as her mind was getting geared up to recall it, Marge came in with coffee. She was as cold as ice. She was "nice, nasty". She was pleasant enough to not be considered rude. Cynthia noticed that Marge had the nerve to sniff the air as she walked in the room. The room did seem a bit stale from the day before. Just the thought of sex with Phil in her office made her wail with laughter. She placed both hands over her mouth to contain her laughter. She got so tickled that she laid her head on her desk. After a few moments, she raised her head, threw her hands in the air and spun around in her chair. The moment was curtailed at the thought of the black vehicle again. She sat there questioning herself to figure it out, then, dismissing it, decided to get back to work.

Her schedule was jam packed the entire day. When she looked over her appointments, all she could do was take a deep breath and suck it up. She knew she wouldn't have time to fantasize or daydream. It was a must that she stay focused on the clients she had to see. Anyway, the only reason the schedule was so tight was that she moved appointments to accommodate her two-week holiday. Marge entered the room to inform her of the arrival of her first appointment.

"Shall I bring him in now?"

"Yes, Marge, you can show him in. Thanks."

Marge didn't respond, or acknowledge Cynthia at all. She turned slowly, the only way the old bat moved, then walked out of the office. When she escorted the client in, she closed the door, returning to her desk.

Cynthia stood and extended her hand to greet him. *Damn he's fine.* The two exchanged pleasantries and got right to the heart of their meeting. After an hour and a half, that seemed to go rather quickly, the meeting ended. As Andre the new client, reached the door, Cynthia blurted out, "Would you like to have dinner?"

Andre turned around with a smile as wide as the Mississippi.

"Sorry, I have to meet my wife."

*Damn, go figure. Why did I do that?*

The embarrassing moment was avoided as Cynthia smiled and extended her hand with grace.

"I'm sorry. I didn't see a ring, and thought we could have a bite to eat together. My apology, and regards to your wife."

They both smiled and acknowledged each other. He took two or three steps, and Cynthia spied Marge standing in the doorway. Andre must have blocked her view to Marge. Marge stood with a wicked grin on her face, as if to relish in Cynthia's embarrassment.

Cynthia bowed her head, looking at the paperwork on her desk to avoid Marge's presence. She ignored Cynthia, and marched right in. She quickly stated what she wanted, then returned to her desk as quickly as she appeared. When she left, Cynthia turned to her favorite spot, gazing out the window. The black vehicle was gone. Cynthia was intrigued by the vehicle. Who did it belong to and why was she bothered by it being there? Something wasn't right.

Moments later, Cynthia's next appointment arrived. They met for about an hour, and concluded another successful meeting. Cynthia was glad this client was a woman. She didn't have to look at a fine specimen of a man sitting across the desk from her and desire him. As

Vanessa stood to leave, she asked Cynthia if she'd like to have dinner.

"That would be great, but I have a little work to do before leaving."

"I can wait for you at the restaurant. There's a neat one about a block down."

"Amelia's?"

"Yes. I'll walk down and have a drink until you get there."

"Okay. I'll meet you there in about an hour."

Just as Vanessa left, the phone rang. *Ugh, I'm never going to get out of here in an hour if the phone keeps ringing.*

"Cynthia Evans."

"Cynthia. This is Phil Swanson, how are you?"

Relieved he'd called now, she answered, "I'm great, and you?"

"I'm hanging on. I wanted to touch base with you and let you know I've worked out my schedule, and I can make the trip with you Sunday. I have to leave Tuesday afternoon though."

"Sounds like a plan. Are you going to park at my place and the two of us take the limo together?"

"Yes, that will work. I'll have the limo bring me back to your place."

"Great, I'll see you Sunday about eight-fifteen."

"See you soon."

Cynthia hung up and started drifting off to Fantasy Island. She shook her head forcing herself to focus on work, so she could get out of there and have dinner with Vanessa.

As Cynthia was finishing up, Marge came in again.

"Mrs. Evans, I'd like to leave now, if that's okay?"

*Perfect opportunity to treat her like she's been treating me.*

## Deadly Choices

Cynthia nodded her head in approval without looking up from her work. Marge stood there for a moment, perturbed that Cynthia didn't acknowledge her in a respectful way. She decided it wasn't best to scold her, as she would one of her children. This was her boss and ultimately she knew Cynthia had the upper hand. Gathering her belongings, she left the office. Cynthia heard the elevator bell ring, and looked directly into Marge's face as the elevator doors closed. She smiled, feeling a victory over Marge, with her motherly, overbearing, disapproving way. She logged off of her computer, put her laptop in her briefcase and headed for the restaurant.

Cynthia walked with a slow steady pace, swinging her briefcase with every stride. It was rare that she walked anywhere. Usually, she would drive two blocks, but figured she'd walk since it was such a pretty day. She knew she looked good, and wanted the world to notice. The sun was bright, but there was a light breeze that blew through her hair with every step she took. Just as she reached the door to the restaurant, she looked to her right and noticed the black vehicle again. *This is too coincidental. Who the hell is in there?* She was looking too good for her own good. As she arrived at the restaurant, she flung the door open too hard, banging the outer wall and the door bounced back onto the heal of her foot as she entered, damn near causing her to fall. Vanessa waved her to the table.

"What are you drinking?"

"Whiskey neat. Want one?"

"Ooh, that's too rich for my blood. I'll have a glass of white wine."

Vanessa snapped for the waiter, and took the liberty to order Cynthia's drink. They sat in utter silence until Cynthia's drink arrived. Since they really didn't know each other, they really didn't have much to say. Vanessa struck up a conversation asking Cynthia what made her get into the architecture business, and how she made it where she was.

"It's a long story, but, in short, I'm creative. This job allows me to use my creativity to its fullest. My clients generally like my ideas, with minimal to no change to my proposals. I was offered a partnership with the firm just recently. All of the partners are much older and thought a fresh, new face would attract business. Not to mention, I have worked my tail off for the firm for many years. I would like to believe that it was my skill that got me the partnership. And what about you?"

"Well, I got dumped into the business, since my parents own it. They wanted me to follow in their footsteps and take over the business when they retired. I really didn't have much choice, given the pressure they put on me. As long as I can remember, my dad has been pounding in my head how he built this business for his children. Since I'm an only child, all the pressure and focus was on me. However, regardless how I got here, I really love my job, and I'm glad that I let my parents push me into it."

The two talked for quite some time. They found that they were very comfortable with each other, as if they'd known each other for years. Cynthia didn't usually let women get very close to her, since they always managed to create havoc in her life. Sharon and Ardelia were the closest women in her life, and now Sharon had shown that she really wasn't a friend after all.

Cynthia looked at her watch and realized she needed to be leaving. She pulled out her wallet to pay, but Vanessa insisted on picking up the tab. Since they both parked at the office, they walked back together. Cynthia was a bit tipsy from the alcohol, which resulted

## Deadly Choices

in her breaking down right there in the parking garage. She felt the overwhelming changes in her life come crashing down without warning. She was a little concerned and unsettled by who might be in the black vehicle, too. As she wept, Vanessa held her and told her everything would be just fine. She offered to follow her home, and Cynthia accepted.

When they arrived, Cynthia began looking around before getting out of her car, for fear the black vehicle had followed them. Vanessa pulled in right behind her and got out of the car first. She opened Cynthia's door and led her into the house.

"So, what do you plan to do? You can't just close yourself up in the house and be afraid to go out."

"I'll call my next door neighbor. Frank will keep an eye on things around here for me."

"Would you like for me to stay a while?"

"No, thanks. I've taken up enough of your time."

"I really don't mind. Are you going to be alone?"

"Come to think of it, yes I will. My daughter is at a girlfriend's tonight, so if you can stay for just a little bit, that would be great."

"Not a problem. What's to drink?"

"Girl, you sure can put down the alcohol, can't you?"

"I have been known to handle a few. Have one with me to unwind."

"Have a seat in the den, and I'll bring in the glasses."

*I sure will. This may be easier than Sharon thought it would be,* Vanessa thought.

Vanessa sat on the sofa and made herself comfortable. Cynthia entered with the glasses then poured them each a drink. She turned on the stereo with light jazz playing in the background. Vanessa polished her drink off quickly then started on number two before Cynthia finished her first. As soon as Cynthia took the last sip of her drink, Vanessa refilled the glass. After about the fourth drink, Vanessa asked to use the bathroom. Although Cynthia was puzzled as to why Vanessa would take her purse to the bathroom, she didn't give it a whole lot of thought.

Once inside, Vanessa reached into her purse and pulled out her cell phone.

"Hey girl, I'm at her house."

"At her house? How'd you move so fast?"

"Luckily, she had an emotional crisis, and I offered to come home with her, and she took the bait."

"This is perfect. Bed that bitch as soon as possible. Do you have the recorder?"

"Yep, in my purse. This recorder is so small, she won't notice a thing. She's on her fourth drink, and from what I can tell, ya girl can't drink too much."

"I want to have enough on her to embarrass her, and cost her her career. Can you get real down and dirty?"

"Please, honey, not only can I, but I will enjoy it."

"You want her taken off her high horse as much as I do, don't you?"

"Not hardly. Although I don't know her that well, I kind of like her. You're paying me to do something for your own gratification. We've been friends for a long time and I figure you must have a really good reason for wanting to destroy this woman. I will enjoy it simply because I'm attracted to her. I don't think she has a clue that I'm a lesbian."

"We'd better get off the phone before she gets suspicious."

## Deadly Choices

Vanessa returned to the den to find Cynthia stretched out on the sofa, looking ever so appealing. She knelt down beside her, and with her index finger, lightly glided it down Cynthia's breastbone. At first, there was no response. But, the second stroke seemed to light a small fire. She was lying on her back with one arm raised above her head. The other arm rested across her body, and with her hand she touched herself. Once the fire was lit, she began to stroke herself. Cynthia was so intoxicated she didn't even realize Vanessa was caressing her. She wasn't in a conscious state and Vanessa knew it. Vanessa figured she'd better get the recorder set up, but couldn't decide whether to do it there in the den, or upstairs in the bedroom. She knew she had to control the situation in order to get it on tape, so she decided to do it right there in the den. Once she set up the video recorder, she went to work on Cynthia. Although still a bit out of it, Cynthia was very responsive to Vanessa's soft and sensual touch. Just as Vanessa had her completely aroused, Cynthia snapped out of her unconscious state, realizing what was happening. The reality of it all didn't seem to stop her though. Since she'd already been with a woman before, she wasn't afraid of it. She embraced the moment, and went with the flow. Vanessa was more compassionate and giving than any man had ever been with her. She aroused feelings she didn't know she had. She felt like she was walking on air, floating above the clouds and ready to explode like a punctured, helium filled balloon. Although Vanessa was attracted to Cynthia, she knew she was on a mission. The thought of this underhanded, pre-meditated seduction being recorded, made her more aggressive, more passionate and much more seductive than she would normally be. *I'm keeping a copy of this for myself. I'll be damned if Sharon gets the only copy. I want this for nights when I'm alone. Once Cynthia finds out I played a part in her destruction, she'll never speak to me again.*

The act finally over, they went upstairs and showered together. Cynthia mentioned it was late, and she needed to get to bed. Vanessa tried to get to the den before Cynthia, but wasn't successful. Vanessa stood at the sofa contemplating how best to get the recorder without being noticed. But, just as she bent over to pick up her purse, there were three low beeps that seemed very loud in the silence of the room. *Damn, that must be the end of the tape.*

"What in the world was that?"

Vanessa stood there, looking like a thief caught in a bank vault. Her eyes grew wide and Cynthia knew something wasn't right. Cynthia raised a brow and started in the direction the beeps came from. There it goes again...beep, beep, beep. Cynthia reached up over the fireplace and found the recorder on the side of a picture frame.

"I wonder where this came from?"

Vanessa couldn't say a word. She was choked up, even though Cynthia hadn't pinned it on her yet. This was definitely the time to leave. *I can't leave without the evidence. Sharon has paid me for a job and I intend to collect. But if I stay, Cynthia and I will surely have it out, and I don't want that kind of scene. Shit, what should I do?*

"Maybe your daughter had it up there and forgot to turn it off."

"No, she doesn't have a recorder like this."

"Maybe it's one of her friend's."

"Could be. I want to see what's on the tape."

*This can't be happening. The plan worked out too perfectly to be jacked up now. If I snatch it from her and run out of the house, she'll know that it was me. If I let her watch it, she'll still know it was me. Since I'm fucked either way, would I rather snatch it, take the money*

## Deadly Choices

*from Sharon and run, or lie and tell her that I only did it because I wanted it for myself?*

As Cynthia fumbled around attempting to get the micro tape out of the recorder, Vanessa fidgeted with the strap on her purse. As soon as Cynthia plopped the tape out, Vanessa grabbed it and fled for the front door. Unbeknownst to her, the deadbolt was locked from the inside and she had to use the key to get out. Cynthia stopped at the table in the hallway and held up the keys.

"Can't get out without these, so give me the tape."

Vanessa clutched the tape tightly in the palm of her hand, frantically trying to figure a way out. All of a sudden, there was a rattle at the door, then the lock turned, and the door began to open.

"Chris, what are you and Lolly doing here? I thought you were spending the night at Lolly's."

Cynthia was desperately trying to divert Chris and Lolly's attention from the situation at hand. Once the two were completely inside, Chris recalled seeing Vanessa before.

"Hey, aren't you Sharon's friend? I saw you with her once."

"Sharon! You mean to tell me you and Sharon are friends? Get the hell out of my house," she demanded.

"Cynthia, let me tell you what's going on."

"Chris, you and Lolly go upstairs...I don't need to hear shit from you. Tell Sharon she got me good on this one, but she'll never be able to do it again. And you can consider our business dealings null and void."

Vanessa didn't know whether to come clean and try to save face, or to really jump on Sharon's bandwagon to destroy Cynthia. Vanessa dropped her head and faced the door. She really felt like shit, and wanted the night to be over.

Chris and Lolly came running down the steps and as they bolted out the door, they yelled they'd be right back. "Lolly forgot something at her house that she needs for the morning."

Vanessa stepped onto the porch, and Cynthia stepped outside, as well. She wanted to see Vanessa pull off and leave her property. Vanessa began to cry, but as she turned to speak to Cynthia, Cynthia held up her hand, palm facing forward in a stop position, to prevent her from continuing. Even though night had fallen, the block was very well lit. The two were visible for probably a half a block.

"Hey Cynthia," Frank yelled from his driveway.

Cynthia gave a motionless wave, hoping he would not come over to talk. Not only did he get the message that she didn't want to be bothered, but he also sensed that something was wrong. He watched as Vanessa drove off and Cynthia returned to the house. He'd seen Chris and Lolly leave and heard them say they'd be right back, so he hung around outside to see that they returned to the house safely. Although Cynthia viewed Frank as a pain in the ass, she regarded him as a good neighbor.

When he saw Chris and Lolly coming up the street, he decided to strike up a conversation to find out what had happened with Vanessa. Chris and Lolly were glad to be able to gossip about the situation. They told him that she was a friend of Sharon's and Cynthia was livid that she was there. They didn't know much else to tell. As the girls disappeared into the house, Frank wiped his hand over his face, confused about the person Cynthia had become. *What is up with her? She's not the lady I once knew. The woman I've always been in love with has gone from a classy, well- respected pillar of the community, to a sex crazed, unethical, bitch and a whore.*

The mere thought that the picture perfect Cynthia was a farce

## Deadly Choices

made Frank furious, and he kicked the tire of his car to relieve some of his frustration.

Meanwhile, Cynthia was in her bedroom viewing the tape. She became sick to her stomach, realizing what damage Sharon and Vanessa could have done with the tape. She took three sleeping pills, and shortly the tape was watching her, instead of her watching it. Chris tapped on the door poking her head in to check on her mom. She couldn't believe what she was seeing. She ran down the hall, grabbed Lolly by the arm and dragged her back to Cynthia's doorway.

"Look, Lolly. Can you believe that?"

Lolly turned to look at Chris and noticed tears streaming down Chris' face. She quietly closed the door, took Chris by the hand, and led her back to the bedroom. Lolly tried to console Chris to make her feel better, but nothing could erase what she'd just seen. Knowing that Sharon was primarily responsible for Vanessa being at their house made her hate Sharon more than ever.

Lolly talked to Chris until they both drifted off to sleep.

# 19

The next morning came much too fast for the Evans household. No one in the house had much to say as they prepared for their day. Lolly was scared to say anything. She didn't want Cynthia to know they'd seen the tape, and she didn't want Chris mad at her for addressing the subject. She figured she'd let Chris bring it up if she wanted to talk about it. After all, it was her mother that was going through all this drama. *I don't know what I would do, if that were my mom. I would be so ashamed of her. I don't know if I'd let any of my friends know the stuff Chris clues me in on.*

When Chris returned from the bathroom, she chatted nonstop about the tape.

"How'd my mom get herself so tangled up in this mess? She needs her butt whipped."

"Yeah, but by who? You ain't gonna be the one to do it."

"Right, right."

The two girls rolled all over the bed, laughing hard. They kept the laughter to a minimum to keep Cynthia from asking what they were laughing about. Neither of them wanted her to know, or to ask them a

## Deadly Choices

bunch of questions. They straightened up and started for the kitchen. On the way down the hallway, Cynthia stopped them and asked, "What was the giggling all about?"

*Damn, does she have ears like a dog or what?*

The girls gave each other a quick glance to see who would be the one to answer. Chris spoke up, "Nothing."

"Nothing? How the hell do you laugh at nothing?"

"Ma, it was some stuff about this girl at school, dang."

Cynthia gave that motherly look, and Chris immediately responded to it.

"I mean, it was just some girl stuff ma, no big deal, okay?"

Cynthia was clearly not in the mood for Chris and her smartass mouth. She knew if she continued with the discussion, she'd end up slapping the hell out of her, so she turned and walked down the stairs.

Chris and Lolly stood in the hallway, giving Cynthia enough space between them. Chris was mumbling under her breath, and Lolly pinched her arm to make her stop. Both Chris and Lolly knew that Cynthia hated that.

After dropping the girls at school, Cynthia went to her favorite little coffee shop down the street from the office. She really didn't want to face the day ahead, but there was no safe haven anymore. Marge was a pain in the ass, and there was no one other than Ardelia in whom she could confide. Ardelia would be upset at how she'd been conducting herself, and she was too ashamed to talk to her about all that was going on. Feeling alone and confused, she drifted off into a world of her own. Out of the blue there were two short taps on her shoulder.

"Mrs. Evans."

Cynthia turned and looked over her shoulder. *Oh sure, all I need is this fucking detective questioning me again.*

Clearly she was not in the mood to be questioned again. In a very dry, uninviting tone, she answered, "Yes."

"Detective Emanuel Shelt..."

She cut him off in mid sentence.

"Yeah, I remember who you are."

"I have a few more questions about the Mary Collins case." He pointed to the chair and asked, "May I?"

She sighed and turned to face the window without acknowledging him or answering his question. He pulled out the chair and took a seat anyway.

"So, Mrs. Evans, have you had your moment of grief for your husband yet?"

Cynthia knew he was being sarcastic, in an attempt to annoy her when she didn't respond to the question, so he fired off another one.

"So how long did you say you and Mary were seeing each other?"

"If you don't have any relevant questions to ask me, leave me the hell alone."

"If I didn't believe they were relevant, I wouldn't be asking them. We can do this downtown if you'd prefer."

"You won't get anymore downtown than you're getting here. These stupid ass questions are really getting on my nerves. Are you in a position to arrest me, or am I supposed to solve your case for you?"

"So you want to play hard ball, huh?"

"I want to be left alone. Can you manage that?"

The detective stood and took Cynthia by the arm to prompt her to rise. She looked him up and down with fire in her eyes. *If this fucker takes me down to the police station, I'm going to sue the shit out of the police department.*

Cynthia stood to keep from making a scene, her body language indicating her feeling of disgust.

"So, we're going downtown?"

"No, I was merely helping you get up."

"I have no intention of leaving. You can let go of my arm now."

"I do still reserve the right to question you when I feel it's warranted."

"Duly noted."

Detective Shelton knew if he took Cynthia down to the police station, his boss would have his head on a platter. He thought he could bluff her enough to make her sweat. He had no sufficient evidence to link Cynthia to Mary's death, and he knew it.

She turned her back to him, lit a cigarette, and went back to deal with the thoughts and emotions that he'd interrupted. She wondered aimlessly into a state of utter confusion, so into herself that she didn't notice him leave. Beep, beep, beep. The alarm on her cell phone indicated she had a meeting in fifteen minutes. *Oh shit. Where did the time go?*

She raced off to her office and passed Marge who snapped a quick "Morning". Cynthia had no response. She felt an icy cold stare as she entered her office. Placing her things on her desk, she grabbed her leather folder and darted off to the boardroom.

Maurice and Paulie were seated at the long oak table, awaiting Billie's arrival. When Billie entered the room, a tall, slender woman accompanied her. *Who the hell is that? What could this woman's purpose be?* Maurice and Paulie must have had the same thought, because they didn't move when she approached the table and Cynthia knew someone had to make a move so the woman didn't feel too uncomfortable, but before Cynthia could speak, Billie began introductions.

"This is Sheila Franklin. I'm considering hiring her as one of our consultants. She comes highly recommended, and I'd like for you to take some time to speak with her this morning. I'd also like for her to stay and be part of the meeting today to get a feel of our current projects. I think her skills will be a value to us as we move forward. Sheila, these are the partners of the firm…Maurice Robinson, Paulie Cavil and Cynthia Evans."

The partners welcomed Ms. Franklin and offered her a seat. They gave her the floor to talk about what she could offer the firm. She stood and began to speak. At the sound of her voice, Cynthia's face twisted and the corners of her mouth turned downward. This woman's voice needed a volume control. Cynthia noted that the guest was loud and had a bad nasal condition, preventing her from effectively enunciating her syllables. The volume was distracting. They concluded two hours later, and Billie escorted Sheila to the elevators. When Billie returned to the boardroom, the partners were discussing some of the issues at hand. Billie immediately interrupted and asked, "What the hell is wrong with all of you?" The other three looked quite baffled. Maurice spoke up, questioning the accusation.

"What are you talking about, Billie?"

"You all made Sheila very uncomfortable."

"Uncomfortable. How?"

"You continually stared at her, but you looked away when speaking to her. What was that all about?"

Cynthia couldn't wait to tell her that the woman's demeanor would steer business away instead of attracting business.

"It was very hard to have a conversation with her, Billie. She was hard on the ears. How can you believe that she would be an asset to us?"

"She knows her business and..."

Paulie interjected. "And nothing. There is no way we can put her in front of a customer."

"Why the hell not?"

"Come on, Billie. You cannot be that oblivious to how loud she is. Not to mention you could hardly understand her. I wanted to say... repeat after me, how now brown cow."

"No, I'm not. I realize she has some issues, but it's nothing we couldn't work on."

"Let's be quite frank, Billie. We're in the architectural business, which means we create and design artful, skillful creations of beauty. Sending her out to a customer says we don't know much about our business."

"That's ridiculous, Paulie. Do all of you feel this way?"

Maurice, Paulie and Cynthia nodded in agreement, and Billie was very annoyed, displaying it by her not so subtle exit. The remaining partners sat in silence for a few moments, then adjourned to their respective offices.

Later, on the way to her office, Cynthia began to feel a sense of relief. She knew she didn't have to deal with the responsibility of hiring, or making any big decisions in the weeks to come.

The next two days passed slowly, but the closer it got to Friday, the more excited she became about her trip to New York. Phil called Friday to confirm their departure from her house.

Four-forty-five Friday afternoon, she made her way to the partners' offices to bid a farewell, and bring them each up to speed on any deals they would need to know about. When she returned to her office area, she was met by the cold dark stare of Marge's black eyes of coal. Cynthia advised her that she did not want to be disturbed on her trip by anyone, unless it was an extreme emergency. The two were still icy cold in their communication to each other, but somehow they to communicated effectively enough to co-exist.

Cynthia walked around her office, filled with anxious, nervous adrenaline, she couldn't seem to control. She paced like a caged tiger who'd just been captured from the wild, her excitement slowly becoming fear. Fear that her life wouldn't be the same when she returned home, that this person she'd become would overtake her, and life as she knew it would never be the way it once was. She was struggling with wanting and needing her independence, coupled with her need for excitement and adventure. She recognized the fact that the combination could create an electrical charge that would generate like an overloaded outlet. Eventually, she managed to get her feelings under control and went home to unwind.

Chris greeted Cynthia at the front door with bags packed and in hand.

"Girl, you cannot be that excited. Let me get in the door and situated before I take you to Patty's."

Chris relaxed, placed her bags on the floor, and without getting into a confrontation with her mother, she went to the den to watch television.

About an hour later, when Cynthia told Chris to come along so she could take her to Patty's, Chris couldn't get to the car fast enough. Cynthia laughed to herself, watching Chris scurry out the door. *Teenage energy. I wish my teenage years had been so carefree.*

They caught up on conversation during their drive. Cynthia wanted to make the best of the time she spent with her daughter, since

## Deadly Choices

she'd be away from her for so long. She felt like she was leaving home for the first time, and knew the separation wasn't going to be easy. However, she knew she needed to do this for herself. She had issues to resolve and she wanted so badly to let her hair down.

Cynthia went in the house and chatted with Kathy for a while. Then she and Chris gave each other big hugs and kisses before she left. Chris stood in the doorway watching her mother walk to the car. The moment Cynthia was in the car, she broke into tears. For some odd reason, she didn't feel like this was a getaway vacation at all. There was a gnawing feeling in the pit of her stomach that kept overpowering her, taking the feeling of excitement away. She couldn't figure out why she kept feeling this way, but she knew something wasn't right. Instead of giving in to it, she started the car and went home.

She killed the engine as soon as she brought the car to rest in the driveway. As she sat pondering over what to do about this nagging feeling, Frank approached the car. She was so deep in thought, she hadn't seen him walk up.

"Hey, Cynthia. Are you all right?"

He tapped on the window with the tip of his key, when Cynthia didn't respond. Startled by his presence, she jumped, then opened the door.

"What?"

"You've been sitting here for a bit, so I thought I would check to see if you were okay."

"Yeah, I'm okay. Just tired and I have a lot on my mind."

"Do you need me to do anything for you?"

"No, thanks. I just need a long, hot bath and a good night's sleep."

She went in the house, made sure she had everything packed,

and took her bags downstairs and sat them by the door. She took a bubble bath by candlelight, and was sleep within the hour. Unfortunately, her restful sleep didn't last long. That uneasy feeling awakened her and she couldn't go back to sleep. She got out of bed about three-thirty and piddled around the house. Once dressed, she was downstairs having her usual morning coffee and cigarette, reading the morning paper, awaiting Phil's arrival.

Phil was a little early. He rang the doorbell about eight o'clock. They shared coffee and conversation waiting for the limousine, which arrived around eight thirty.

# 20

New York City in all it's greatness! The hustle and bustle of the tourists was amazing just to watch. This wasn't Cynthia or Phil's first time there, but they were still amazed at how fast everything and everybody moved. They sifted their way to the baggage claim area and were swiftly whisked off to their limousine. The traffic from LaGuardia airport was bumper to bumper for miles. There were horns honking, engines racing and people shouting and swearing out the window of almost every car on the road. It was difficult to carry on a conversation in the back seat of the car, for all the noise. Cynthia sat peering out the window on her side of the car, thinking about all the things she wanted to do while she was there. Phil, on the other hand was anxious to get her to the hotel room. He wanted to pick up where they left off the last time they were together.

Two hours later they arrived at their hotel. Phil frowned at the sight of it. Cynthia reassured him that the outside wasn't a true indication of the inside.

"One thing about New York City, things may look pretty shabby on the outside, but often you'll find luxury at the core. Don't sweat it...we're going to have a ball."

"As long as there's nothing crawling in the bed with me, I'll be fine."

"Oh, really? What if I want to crawl in the bed with you?"

"You're a welcomed creature. It's those other ones I'm talking about."

Phil gave her a sly wink and proceeded to check in. As Phil took care of the check-in, Cynthia stood, observing all the people coming in and out.

*Um, that's a bad ass Donna Karan suit she has on. I simply must shop Fifth or Madison Avenue before going home. I could use some new rags to uplift my spirits.*

"Cynthia, we're ready to go upstairs. Where did you go?"

"On a mental shopping spree. I just saw a Donna Karan suit that made me want one."

The bell captain was at their disposal even before they could reach for their bags. They followed him to their room, tipped him and he went on his way. Phil practically exploded when he entered the bathroom and saw Cynthia clad in nothing but a black lace thong. She was bent over the bathtub checking the water temperature before stepping in. Cynthia knew he was in the bathroom, and intentionally stayed in her bent position just to get a rise out of him, literally!

"What are you trying to do to me?"

"What? I was just getting ready to take a bath. What did I do?"

"You know what you're doing to me."

Phil adjusted his clothes and turned to walk out the bathroom. Cynthia sat on the edge of the bathtub and crossed her legs. With legs crossed, her bare skin was all that could be seen.

## Deadly Choices

"So if I do so much to you, why are you leaving?"

Cynthia had a devilish grin on her face that Phil couldn't seem to ignore. He stopped in the threshold of the door, turned and slowly unzipped his pants. He dropped his pants to the floor and joined her on the edge of the bathtub. They began to kiss, but before they could really get into the groove, there was a knock at the door. They both scurried around the bathroom making themselves presentable. Cynthia answered the door to find the desk clerk with a note for Phil. When Phil opened the note, he immediately made arrangements to leave.

"What's going on? What's the problem?"

Phil sat on the edge of the bed, with a mortified look on his face.

"Phil! What's wrong?"

With a sorrowful tone and eyes directed to the floor he announced: "The note was from my wife. One of our children is very ill."

"Your what?!"

"I'm married, with three children, but we've been separated for quite some time."

"Oh that was a detail that you conveniently forgot to tell me about?"

"I saw no need since we are separated."

"You know what? ...Oh just forget it."

"Cynthia, this doesn't have to be an issue...especially now."

"Just hurry up and get the hell out of here. You're an asshole like all the rest of the men in my life. How could you deceive me like this? Leave and don't bother to call me ever again."

Phil was not in the mood to go at it with her. He packed his bags and left.

Cynthia sat on the bed in a daze. She couldn't believe what had just happened. Her mind danced with a number of thoughts. She sat thinking, burst into tears, and screamed at the top of her voice, she asked herself; *"What the hell is going on with my life?! Why does this shit keep happening to me?!"*

She returned to the bathroom, bathed, dressed and struck out to get the lay of the land. She stopped at the concierge desk to get a city map, and directions to Fifth Avenue. It was a beautiful day. The sun was bright, but not too hot. A slight breeze blew frequently enough to keep the perspiration away. As she walked down thirty-fourth street she browsed in several different stores. She really wasn't in a shopping mood, but knew she had to get out of that stuffy, old hotel room. She was so deep in thought as she walked, she'd walked all the way to forty-second street without even realizing how far she'd gone. She stood at the curb and hailed a taxi. "Madison Ave and 50th, please."

As she stepped out of the taxi, she was faced with choices of the "upscale" shops she'd been looking for. She wanted and needed a facial and body massage. She walked around and window shopped for a while. As she stood on the sidewalk gazing about the city, it was obvious she was a tourist. A tall, handsome man was standing next to her, looking in a store window. He nodded and said hello, and struck up a conversation about why she was standing there alone. She explained that she wanted to get a massage and he directed her to the salon directly across the street. She thanked him and darted off for a relaxing massage. As she stepped into the salon, the receptionist that greeted her was the ugliest woman walking the face of the earth. As Cynthia was about to speak, the phone rang. The receptionist held up one finger to stop her from speaking. As she answered the phone, she said "House of Beauty, this is Cutie." *Why in the world would they*

## Deadly Choices

*let this ugly ass woman answer the phone like that?* The moment the thought passed, she looked down at her name tag. *Get out...her name tag says 'Cutie'. Nobody that fucking ugly goes by the name Cutie.* It took all Cynthia had to keep her composure. Everything in her wanted to ask this woman if she really believed in her mind that she was cute. Since Cynthia didn't have one of her girlfriends around to laugh with, she felt like her emotions were being held hostage. "Cutie" stayed on the phone for a few more minutes, so Cynthia walked outside and stood on the sidewalk, pulled her cell phone out of her purse and called Ardelia. Before Ardelia could get "Hello" out of her mouth, Cynthia blurted out..."Girl, I wish you were here. There is this ugly ass woman in this salon who just answered the phone, "House of Beauty, this is Cutie." I couldn't contain myself any longer, so I had to call you." The two were laughing so hard, Cynthia had to pee. As she was ending her conversation with Ardelia, "Cutie" came to the door and told her she could speak with her now. Cynthia quickly asked if she could use the restroom first. Tears were rolling from her eyes which caused "Cutie" to be concerned.

"Are you okay, Miss?"

"Yes, I'll be fine once I get to the restroom."

Cynthia took time to get herself together and returned to the reception desk. There was a cancellation and she was able to get right in. She was directed to a changing room where there was a closet to hang her clothes and a locker for her purse. She put on a thick, white terrycloth robe then proceeded to the massage room. The place was packed. Every room seemed to be occupied. She stepped into the room to get the massage of a lifetime. The masseuse was a big, burley gay black guy, as good looking as he could be. *Why did he want a man? Probably 'cause he was afraid of having a Cutie chasing him down. I can't imagine Cutie with anybody! She's so damn ugly you feel sorry for her. There's not one feature on her that's attractive. She has so many teeth she looks like a piranha. Her nose looks like a pig, her eyes are too close together, and her eyeballs sit in the far outer corners of each eye. However, girlfriend had an air of confidence that the average woman couldn't carry off. Why am I laying here thinking about Cutie? Let me daydream about something more pleasant, but what?*

Mr. Universe look-a-like was giving her the best massage she'd ever had. She slowly drifted off to sleep, into her own little fantasy island. After the constant pressures of work and her daughter's teenage issues, she thought about nothing but shopping and sex. Naturally, she wasn't lying there thinking about a suit while this man rubbed every inch of her body. Moments later he stopped. When she turned and opened her eyes, he softly stated he would be right back. She winked in acknowledgment then went right back to her thoughts. A few minutes later the massage continued. For some odd reason, he was more into it than he was before. Maybe he's winding down before completion. He was now applying gentle pressure to her neck and behind her ears. He was hitting some pretty sensitive spots that made her a bit uncomfortable in that environment. She attempted to rise up on her arms as if doing sit ups, but he gently pushed her back down to the table. He leaned over and whispered into her ear. "Feel good?" Well, that wasn't expected. She raised her eyebrow, but didn't respond. She opened her eyes and instantly knew that this wasn't Mr. Universe giving her massage. She turned her head upward to look directly into the eyes of the gentleman she'd met on the sidewalk. He smiled and continued to massage her neck. She relaxed and went with the moment, not caring what happened next.

Truly she got more than she was paying for. He massaged

## Deadly Choices

her for another half an hour. It was so relaxing, she was moaning. He whispered once again in her ear and told her that time was up. She rose from the table and their eyes connected. Neither of them said anything. She wrapped her towel tightly around herself and placed her robe over her shoulders. He stood in the doorway and watched her walk back to her dressing room. A grin swept across her face as she dressed, thinking about the pleasure she'd just experienced.

Cynthia, completely dressed, headed for Cutie's desk. As she approached, she noticed a glass enclosed office that she hadn't paid any attention to when she first got there. There was a "suit" sitting in the chair with his head seemingly buried in paperwork. Cutie's phone rang while the credit card was being processed. Once again, she raised her hand and held up one finger to pause Cynthia from speaking. When she hung up, she informed Cynthia that she was invited into the office across the hall.

"Why? There couldn't be anything wrong with my credit card."

"There's no problem. The owner would like to see you in his office."

"What ever for?"

"He didn't say. He just rang me and asked that you come into his office."

"Where the hell is..."

Cutie abruptly cut her off by pointing to the glass-enclosed office, and an irritated Cynthia headed in that direction. When she reached the threshold of the doorway, the man in the suit raised his head. Cynthia's irritation was overcome with a joyous smile. He smiled back as he rose from his chair to introduce himself. Cynthia is always quite confident and in control, but her palms began to sweat, and she really didn't want him to shake her hand. She kept her hand curled around her handbag, but he surprised her yet again by touching her on her shoulder, guiding her to the chair in front of his desk. They conversed for about ten to fifteen minutes, after which he asked her out. She graciously accepted and knew then she really needed to go shopping. He had tickets to dinner and a play. She asked about the attire and he replied, "Semi formal. Bergdorf Goodman has a great selection. Might I suggest you see if there's anything in there that meets your expectations?"

Thomas, who owned the name of the stranger she'd just met, winked as she turned to leave. She smiled, nodded and told him she'd see him at seven o'clock. Cynthia took a step back into the doorway and commented, "Your face sure is familiar. I've seen you before, but can't quite figure out from where. Have you been to Chicago recently?" "Yes, I was there on business a few weeks ago." Since she couldn't put her finger on it, she went back to Cutie, who handed her the card and told her there was no charge.

Bergdorf's was a few blocks up Fifth Avenue. As she strolled up the street, she was thrilled with excitement. Her thoughts were random. *I hope this bastard isn't married and deceitful. Whatever... if they don't want you to know, they lie anyway. I don't give a shit anymore.* The moment she stepped in the front door of Bergdorf's, a sales person greeted her. Before going to eveningwear to find the perfect dress, she took a look at the shoe selection. After finding a pair of clear "Cinderella" slippers, she was off to find a dress. She tried on a number of beautiful t-length dresses, but none that quite had the spark she wanted. The sales lady continually brought in dresses for her review. Finally, after about eleven different selections. She came in with "the one." A soft, teal, little number, with layers of chiffon trimmed in

## Deadly Choices

tiny little rhinestones, just the dress for those "Cinderella" slippers. She asked the sales clerk if she could have the shoes brought to her so she could purchase everything together. The clerk brought several handbag selections as well. The clerk bagged up the dress, shoes and handbag, and thanked her for coming in.

"Did you forget something? I haven't paid for them yet."

"They've already been paid for. Mr. Alexander already called and had any amount of purchase applied to his account. He described you and told me what you were wearing. I was more than happy to assist."

Cynthia left the store in a trance. She couldn't believe the class of this guy. He pulled out all the stops. *What's tonight going to be like? It's going to be hard to top this.* She then realized she needed a pair of earrings and a necklace. She waded her way through a clusterfuck of people on the sidewalk of Fifth Avenue, and was drawn to a necklace and earring ensemble displayed in the window of Saks. While standing there it dawned on her where she knew Thomas' face from. *That's the guy who helped me when I dropped my purse the day Chris and I went shopping. What a coincidence.* She went into the store and made her purchase, returned to her hotel and ordered room service. While waiting for her food, Cynthia laid her things out and lay across the bed to relax. After the incredible massage, she didn't feel tired, but wanted to rest up for a long night. Her food arrived about forty-five minutes later. She ate a light snack to satisfy her over until dinner.

At six forty-five there was a knock at the door. She knew she couldn't answer too quickly, but her insides were dancing. She opened the door draped in chiffon and dripping with diamond like trinkets. Her shoulders and chest were lightly touched with sparkling powder. However, Thomas was not at the door. Instead it was his driver. A tall, muscular woman with gorgeous legs, removed her chauffeurs' cap allowing her long thick blond ponytail to drop to the bend of her knees. Cynthia stood there in amazement. She didn't know whether she was more amazed that he had a chauffeur or that the chauffeur was a woman, a beautiful woman at that. She invited her in as she adjusted her clothes, gathered her handbag and wrap and left.

In the elevator, the chauffeur said nothing. She stood tall and erect with no expression. Cynthia felt like a schoolgirl on her first date. All eyes were on the two of them when they emerged in the lobby. Cynthia didn't know if the attention was directed at the chauffeur, as she glided through the lobby like a gazelle, or at her for she was most stunning. Cynthia left a scent of Hypnotic Poison lingering in the air as she passed through. When the chauffeur opened the door for Cynthia to enter the limousine, Thomas stepped out to admire her. When Cynthia was seated, Thomas joined her and the chauffeur returned to the drivers' seat. She took a minute to return the mounds of hair back into a bun under her cap then started the car. Thomas sat in awe of Cynthia's beauty. He complimented her on how pretty she looked, but he went on and on so much she asked him to stop. That was way too much attention for her to handle. She wasn't accustomed to a man doting over her so much therefore it put her out of her comfort zone. It was obvious he was very comfortable and confident with who he was. They drove for nearly forty minutes, but the chatter made the time pass rather quickly. At their destination the chauffeur killed the engine as she brought the car to rest in front of the restaurant. She walked around to the back of the vehicle, removed her cap then opened the door. As they exited the car, she looked straight ahead peering expressionless over the top of the car. Apparently, she was his personal chauffeur, for neither of them spoke as Cynthia and Thomas walked into the restaurant. They had a

## Deadly Choices

reservation in a booth in the corner near a window looking out into the city. The limo was parked and the chauffeur was standing outside of it smoking a cigarette. Cynthia turned her attention to Thomas, her thoughts focused on his motives. *Handsome, intelligent, well-mannered, classy, obviously financially well off and well groomed. What the hell is wrong with him? He must need Viagra. No way he's good in the bed with everything he's got going. There's always something wrong. Maybe he's a maniac who beats women. Shake it off and just enjoy being treated like a queen. This is what you've always wanted. Go with the flow.*

"Cynthia? Cynthia?"

"I'm sorry. My mind was wandering."

"Am I not enough to hold your attention?"

"Absolutely, you are. I was just absorbing all this. I'm having a fantastic time."

The waiter arrived with menus and a bottle of their finest wine that Thomas had pre-selected. Cynthia pondered over her selection as they sipped the wine. She'd made her choice by the time the waiter returned. The atmosphere was so romantic Cynthia was soaking it up like a sponge. She was falling willingly and gracefully into whatever trap he had set. Again, her thoughts led her to question his motive. *He doesn't necessarily have any traps set. Perhaps he's just the perfect gentleman and knows exactly how to treat a lady. Even though this is like a dream come true, it's possible that it's time for things to come together.* Periodically, he'd smile and wink at her across the table. She placed her napkin on the table and excused herself to go to the ladies' room. He rose as she exited the room, and again when she returned. *Damn the excuses. There's got to be something wrong with him. He has definitely read the gentleman's handbook. Hmmm...got to get him to walk with me down the street. I'll see then if he knows he's supposed to walk on the outside, nearest the curb. If he gets that right, then I guess I'll just quit questioning.*

"Cynthia? I keep losing you. What's going on with you?"

"Nothing, I think I'm just amazed at how attentive you are."

"Is that a bad thing?"

"No, not at all. I promise I'll be more attentive for the remainder of the evening."

"Just for the evening?"

What timing. The waiter showed up with their food, so Cynthia was off the hook from having to respond. Cynthia placed one hand over her face and chuckled. The waiter looked at her with a questioning look. Thomas waved him off with an indication that it was a private joke. They had great conversation over dinner. They were having such a good time Thomas hadn't realized it was time to leave for the play. Cynthia was quite impressed when they walked out of the restaurant to find the chauffeur with the motor running, and standing outside the car, ready to open the door. It was as if she had E.S.P. or he'd zapped her from inside the restaurant. At any rate, Cynthia was a little tipsy from the wine. Her arm was linked with Thomas' as she lay her head on his arm. The chauffeur opened the car door, but Cynthia nudged Thomas indicating she wanted to walk. She had to see if he really knew what a gentleman was supposed to do or if he was faking. When he patted her on the hand, they turned to the left on the sidewalk. This put Cynthia on the outside nearest the curb. *This will tell the story now.* Before they could take two steps, he pulled apart from her, stopped, took a step back and crossed over behind her to assume his place nearest the curb. This was the move that convinced her she had a winner. *Okay, you got me now. I surrender.*

## Deadly Choices

He re-linked their arms, took the other hand and guided her head back onto his arm. Cynthia held him close with both her arms linked to his. The night was perfect. The moon was full, the breeze was light and the lights in Manhattan seemed to light their path. After about five blocks, Cynthia realized they would have to walk back five blocks. She stopped and looked up at him. "As much as I'm enjoying this walk, I don't know if I want to walk back as many blocks as we've walked to get here." Thomas smiled down at her and nodded his head backward. Cynthia leaned over, peered around him and found the limousine following slowly behind them. All she could do was smile. She gave him a hug as they stood in the middle of the sidewalk. He asked if she wanted to continue to walk or get in the car. They got in the car and headed to the play.

As expected, they were in the midst of a New York traffic jam. The chauffeur announced on the intercom that more than likely they'd be late for the play. Thomas asked Cynthia if she would be too disappointed if they didn't go. After a brief discussion they decided not to go to the play. Cynthia fantasized about alternative plans.

"It's not a problem for me, as long as you're okay with it."

As the thoughts passed through her mind, Thomas leaned over and kissed her. It was subtle and charming, but enough to make her want more. He reached over and let the window up to get privacy from the driver. She must have known this was her cue, 'cause soft jazz began to play. He slid down in the seat just enough for Cynthia to rest her chest on his. He reached for her, pulling her head closer and closer to his face. The subtle, charming kiss was merely a prelude to the passion he wanted to unleash. He kissed her with much passion. Yeah, she'd been with men and had sex with them, but the passion wasn't this intense. He wanted her as badly as she wanted him. They both had been secretly flirting with the idea from the moment they met. Her pheromones were kicking off a strong scent that Thomas couldn't ignore. Now at the point of disrobing, Thomas buzzed the chauffeur, and directed her back to Cynthia's hotel. *I wonder why my hotel? Why not his place? Must be a wife he conveniently forgot to tell me about.*

"If we were to go to my place we would never make it. We're only a few blocks from your hotel so if you don't mind, I'd rather go there."

*Damn it's like he can read my mind.*

"No, I don't have a problem with that. I don't think we can withstand much more foreplay."

"We'll go to my place next time. Since you'll be here for a few days, that will give us time to do quite a bit."

Just as they pulled up in front of the hotel, he let the window down to speak with the chauffeur. He gave her instructions to call his cell at nine a.m. then told her he'd see her tomorrow, and they exited the car. Although he was being fresh all the way up to the room, he did it with such taste that it was hardly noticed. Unlike the scent of Hypnotic Poison she left lingering in the lobby when she left earlier, she left the scent of a woman this time. Inside the room, he became much more aggressive. After closing and locking the door, he pressed her up against the door with the lower half of his body. He moved in a slow steady pace arousing her and causing her vagina to pulsate. She was longing for him to kiss her, but he wanted her to really want it before he did. He pressed his chest against her breast. He placed one of his hard nipples directly onto one of hers, rubbing them around in circles, causing her knees to buckle. He placed his face in her cleavage and ran his tongue across her breast to the nipple. He sucked her breast with just enough pressure to make it hot, but not hurtful. The motions

## Deadly Choices

made Cynthia wonder about his ability to follow through.

He turned to look directly into her eyes. She was longing for a kiss and he knew it. She was salivating and breathing hard. He turned her around to face the door, he unzipped her dress, removed the spaghetti straps from her shoulders causing the dress to fall to the floor. He stroked her back with his wet tongue, making her want him more and more. As she attempted to turn to face him, he kept total control without allowing her to move. At this point, he held her upper and mid body captive. She wiggled her bottom, trying to get close enough to him to entice him into letting her go. Not a chance. He backed away just enough to keep her at bay. He continued to work his magic and she was overwhelmed with desire for this man. He reached down and began to unhook her stockings from the garter belt. Slowly, gently, he rolled her stockings down each leg. Now covered by only the string of her thong, Thomas released the forceful hold he had on her and allowed Cynthia to turn and face him. She reached out and grabbed his face with both of her hands, pulling him close enough to kiss. He kissed her with such desire, he made her body quiver. She backed him up to the edge of the bed gently pushing him. She ever so slowly undressed him with as much desire and passion as he'd given her. Just when she thought she could take control, he turned the tables. He mounted her and began making love to her. She loved every minute of him taking and keeping control. She wanted desperately to be submissive to him and his power. She was marveling at the fact that he was confident enough in his manhood to overpower her. He took her to a place that made her scream with excitement. All night long, he pleasured her in ways that she never thought anyone could. She cleaned him up with a washcloth as he slept then took a shower. She climbed in the bed next to him, ready to sleep what was left of the night. Morning came much too soon. As soon as she was into a deep sleep she was awakened.

"Is it nine o'clock already?"

"No, baby, I wanted to be with you once more before the day got started. It's six o'clock. Just lay back and relax."

They were already up, showered and dressed, when Thomas' cell phone rang promptly at nine a.m., causing them to look at each other with disappointed eyes. Their time together was much to brief and neither of them wanted it to end.

Thomas blew her a kiss and left the room. It was at that moment, Cynthia decided Thomas was "the one" and pondered how to make him hers exclusively.

Sitting on the edge of the bed, lifeless, motionless and deep in thought, Cynthia could think of nothing but Thomas. She tried desperately to focus her attention on something else, but every thought took her right back to thoughts of him.

Ring, ring, ring.

"Hello."

"Cynthia, you are needed back in Chicago immediately," Marge whaled from the other end of the phone.

"What? Why? What's going on?"

"There is an emergency and I cannot handle the situation."

"Can it be handled over the phone?"

"No, you need to be here in person."

"Tell me what is so critical."

"It's too complicated to get into over the phone. I just know that only you can deal with this. Get home now."

Before Cynthia could respond, Marge hung up the phone. Cynthia sat for a second and peered at the receiver. *Old, crooked wig wearing witch. She'd better start treating me like her boss instead of*

# Deadly Choices

*one of her kids.*

Cynthia hung up. While searching for the itinerary for the number to the airlines, the phone rang. *Hmmm, maybe this is the old hag realizing she should have been making my flight arrangements.*

"Yes." She answered with an irritated tone.

"Hey, Sugar. What's wrong?"

"Thomas! I just received a call from my secretary that there is an emergency back home that I have to deal with. I'm looking for my itinerary to call the airlines to make arrangements to leave."

"Home? You're leaving me already? Please, don't go. Let's try to get to the bottom of it and you might not have to leave."

"The old hag wouldn't even tell me what was wrong. I don't know if it's business or personal. I would think if it were personal, my girlfriend or my daughter would have called. I won't be right unless I go see what's happening."

"Don't do anything until I get there. I'll be there in a few hours."

# 21

Chicago, six-thirty p.m., Spuratiks happy hour. A full house. James was at the door, greeting patrons as they came in. Since his club was one of the hottest in town, most of the professionals went there for happy hour. James was in full swing with drippy lines for all the women. Of course they all felt as if they were the only ones he said that shit to. He filled their heads with as much bull as he could. He knew exactly how to keep the business going, keeping the women happy and the men buddies. Just like him, they were all full of shit and fine as hell so it was easy for them to get away with it.

Once the house was full, James picked his prey and took her to his private spot in the glass room. The dance floor was usually crowded and the bar so packed, that if you weren't a regular and well known, getting a drink was next to impossible.

There were two women standing near the bar, but after realizing they weren't going to get the bartenders attention, they quietly took up residency in the back, right outside the glass room. They stood and conversed as much as they could over the loud music. One of them happened to turn slightly toward the glass and noticed James. Her eyes were glued on him. She watched every move he made, ignoring her girlfriend. Her girlfriend tapped her on the shoulder but she didn't respond. She placed her purse on her shoulder..."Girl I've got a dance partner. See you in a bit. Hang on to my purse since you are in la-la land."

She waved her off and kept staring. James was so in awe of the women that he was entertaining, he did not notice he had another admirer.

As the night grew on, the crowd began to thin out. James and his companion finally emerged from the glass room. It was quite obvious that he intrigued her. She, on the other hand, was just another conquest. She just didn't know it. Because he was successful and attractive, he had no problem getting successful, powerful, pretty women. He was so smooth that even the most educated, sophisticated, worldly women didn't see the bullshit coming. James was engrossed in making sure he had the night all lined up. He still hadn't paid attention to the female who'd been gazing at him all night.

Now, with very few people left in the club, the two girlfriends found each other, and decided to leave. Just as they approached the door, a man walking a few feet behind them blurted out one of their names.

"Cynthia? Cynthia Evans?"

She nudged her girlfriend and picked up her pace, never turning around. In a whisper from the corner of her mouth she said, "That's Frank." The two arrived at their car, leaving a bewildered Frank behind. He stood on the curb wondering why she wouldn't speak. *Damn, she's my next door neighbor and we've known each other since high school and now she won't speak to me in public. What's up with her? Oh, that's right, she and James had a thing going on. Maybe she didn't want him to see us talking. I need to check him out.*

Inside the vehicle, the two pulled off their wigs and laughed hysterically.

"Girl, that was close. We got in 'cause we looked just like our mothers with their ID. Who would have thought somebody would mistake you for your mom?"

"I know. I'm so glad my Mom is in New York. I couldn't have done it with her home. You never know when she's going to show up somewhere, and everybody knows she doesn't have a twin."

Chris and Lolly were having the time of their lives. If they only knew Cynthia had been called to come home, they wouldn't have pulled that stunt. Chris slapped Lolly on the arm and told her to hurry up and start the car. "Let's get the hell out of here before somebody else sees us."

"Let's get the hell out of here and get my Mom's car home. We're dead if she finds out we took it."

"We didn't take the car. You did."

"Awe, you gonna leave me hanging out here to get in trouble all by myself?"

"Girl, you know I got ya back."

"You better have more than my back if we get caught."

They laughed most of the way back to Lolly's, until a block from the house when they became somber. Checking out everything moving around them, they rounded the corner to the house. Lolly cut the lights to inconspicuously creep into the driveway. They slid out of the car and slowly, quietly, closed the car doors.

They safely made their way to Lolly's bedroom. Lolly's mom was conked out. She didn't even know what day it was, so she definitely didn't know they'd left the house. The girls disrobed and laid down for

## Deadly Choices

the night. Lolly went straight to sleep, but Chris couldn't seem to drift off. Chris was plotting to leave again, without being caught by Lolly's mom.

About an hour or so later, Chris got up, dressed, and left the house. She crept out of the driveway then turned on the lights once she wasn't facing the house. She cruised around for a while and found herself outside of James' house. She glanced at the clock and was alarmed at how late it had gotten. She turned on the engine and sped away. She nervously thought about what could happen if she was stopped, since she didn't have a drivers' license.

She gripped the steering wheel tightly and let up off of the gas. Twenty minutes later she was pulling back into the driveway. *Oh damn, I forgot to turn off the lights.* Quickly killing the engine and quietly exiting the car, she made her way back to Lolly's bedroom. Lolly was sitting up in the bed...arms folded and pissed off.

In a whisper, but a forceful tone, Lolly questioned Chris.

"Why did you leave in my mom's car? How you gonna steal my mom's car without bothering to clue me in?"

"You were sleeping really sound and I couldn't sleep. I just went riding around. What made you wake from such a deep sleep?"

"The lights from the car, dummy."

"You think the lights woke your Mom?"

"I don't know, and I ain't about to go see."

Ms. Hill peeked into the room.

"What are you girls doing awake?"

"We were just talking, Mom."

"Did our talking wake you, Ms. Hill?"

"No. I saw lights through my window, but when I got up and looked out nobody was there. Maybe somebody was turning around in the driveway." She shrugged her shoulders as if unconcerned, and closed the door.

"Whew. That was a close call."

"Yeah, and what if she would have come in here while you were gone? What would I have said?"

"Lolly! I get the point. You don't have to keep driving me about it. I won't do it again! Damn, go back to sleep."

Chris turned her back to Lolly and pulled the covers over her head. They both quickly drifted off to sleep. Chris had no idea that Frank had seen her at James' place. If she'd known, she wouldn't have slept so soundly.

At nine-thirty a.m., the phone rang. From down the hall, Yvonne yelled for one of the girls to pick up the phone. Chris picked up immediately and heard her mother's voice, which perked her right up. "Mom?"

"Chris, I was just calling to check on you. Are you doing okay?"

"Yes I'm fine."

Cynthia never revealed to Chris whether she was in town or not, nor that she'd been called about a problem. They talked for about ten minutes then ended their conversation.

Yvonne sat at her kitchen table in shock. Front page news – NIGHTCLUB OWNER MURDERED!! James Mayfield, Owner of Spuratiks nightclub was murdered last night at his home, shortly after closing his nightclub for the night.

She didn't know James well, but she'd met him a few times. She also knew that Cynthia had a fling with him. When the girls came into the kitchen, Yvonne folded the paper, placing it face down on the table. The girls were talking so much they hadn't noticed that Yvonne

## Deadly Choices

was in a daze. She rose from the table and left the kitchen, without them noticing. Lying across the bed, she reached for the phone. She called Cynthia to make her aware of the news. Unfortunately, she got her voicemail. She left her a message to call, but didn't give any details. Returning to the kitchen, she asked the girls if they wanted to go hang out with her. The girls looked at each other and simultaneously shrugged their shoulders.

"Oh, is it that bad to be with me?"

They spoke in unison, "No."

"We kinda wanted to hang out around the house today, but if you really want us to go, we will."

*Hang around the house means they have something up their sleeves. Yeah, I'm going to make them go with me.*

"Yes, I'd like for you to go with me. I could really use the company."

Chris and Lolly glanced at each other, slouched their shoulders, and headed for Lolly's bedroom.

"Girl, yo moms is trippin'. Why does she need us to go?"

"Quit it Chris. I don't want to go either but, how many times have we hung out with yo mom? Shit, I don't always want to go with her, either."

*Yeah, but my mom ain't whack like yours. Your mom can't even dress. She always looks crazy. Her hair is all over her head and she wears run over shoes.*

Chris was so tickled with her thoughts she began to grin.

"What you smiling about?"

"Nothing girl. Since I don't have a choice, it really doesn't matter does it? Ain't no trip, we can get through this."

Lolly looked Chris up and down, rolled her eyes, went to the bathroom and slammed the door. Offended by Chris' comments, Lolly consoled herself by thinking bold, unkind thoughts about Cynthia. They dressed then left the house.

## 22

Back in New York, Cynthia and Thomas were about to embark on a trip into lower Manhattan. Thomas convinced Cynthia to find out why she was needed back in Chicago and they were able to handle the problem without Cynthia having to leave New York.

"Thomas, do we have to take the limo? I'd rather experience New York on the subway."

"That's an experience all right. I guess we can do that. I've been here so long, it's not exciting to me, but if that's what you want to do, we will."

"Okay, let me finish getting dressed and we can go."

"You might want to wear flat shoes instead of those high heels you usually wear."

Cynthia put on a pair of white jeans, a pink and white striped oxford blouse and a black blazer with an anchor crest on the upper pocket, white trouser socks and black loafers.
Thomas was smartly dressed in tan khakis, white heavily starched shirt and a black blazer as well. They were the perfect couple. They both complimented each other with style and flair. Cynthia grabbed her purse

and they headed out the door. In the lobby, Thomas stopped Cynthia at the door, then turned and approached the Concierge. He had a brief conversation with him, rejoined Cynthia, and headed for the subway. On their way up the steps, the stench in the air was unbelievable. The streets reeked with the unpleasant smells. The streets were packed with people haggling over prices with vendors anxious to make a sale. They peddled their imitation designer wear like hot cakes.

"My daughter would love this stuff. She won't care or know that it's not the real thing."

"Most teenagers love it here on Canal Street. I wouldn't wear this cheap shit, but it's fine for the youngsters."

Thomas took Cynthia by the hand and led her down the steps into the subway. They jumped on another train and went to another part of lower Manhattan to have lunch. There was a quaint little Italian restaurant where they sat outside on a small patio out front and dined.

"Thomas, let me ask you something that's really been bugging me."

"What's up?"

"Please don't take this wrong, but I'm just curious how you could hire a woman so ugly to be your receptionist. What's up with that?"

Thomas cracked a smile then responded, "She's family."

"I am so sorry. I ..."

"Don't sweat it. She's my stepsister. Although no blood relation, she's family just the same."

Grinning from ear to ear, Cynthia had to ask, "So who the hell named her Cutie?"

They both burst into laughter. Cynthia put her hand over her mouth to control the volume of her laugh. Thomas was just as tickled,

## Deadly Choices

although he tried to defend Cutie.

"Her Mom named her with hopes that it would boost her self esteem. She knew at birth how ugly she was and that she would never grow out of it. Cutie doesn't think by any stretch that she's ugly. She has the highest self-esteem of anyone I've ever seen. I guess the old saying beauty is from within holds true for her. She is a wonderful lady."

"She would have to be!"

Although still laughing, Cynthia waved her hands to cut the conversation. Since Cutie was family, Cynthia felt that she needed to be a bit more sensitive. Their attention was redirected to the sight on the street. There was a six-foot two, two hundred forty-pound something in a hot pink, spandex outfit, roller skating down the sidewalk.

"Wait a minute...I know my eyes are playing tricks on me, right?"

"Nope. And before you ask, yes that was a man."

"But..."

"A man. Blonde hair, purse and all...it was a man."

"There's no way he can stay under the radar. He has no shame and could care less what anybody thinks."

"That's the beauty of New York. Everyone does their own thing and people don't have any issues with it. After a while it becomes old hat and what you see is not surprising. Why don't you stay at my place for a couple of days? I'll take you some places that will really make you raise a brow."

"That sounds good. I'd love to come to your place."

They finished their food and ventured back out into the city. The subway rides revealed more bazaar and interesting behavior. As the doors opened at the next stop a group of five boys entered the train. One carried a boom box and each of them positioned themselves in a specific place in the car. The one with the boom box proceeded to turn on a popular rap song. They set up their own stage in the subway car, and began to dance. They flipped and turned throughout the car without falling, bumping into the poles or touching anyone. It was so amazing, Cynthia couldn't believe her eyes. She shuddered every time one of them turned a flip. By the time they'd reached the next stop, the boys had finished their routine and were passing a shoe box for donations. No one applauded or commented, but several people gave donations. The boys exited at the next stop, but Cynthia and Thomas proceeded on. As they were leaving the subway car, Thomas shifted into a playful mode. He took Cynthia by the hand and whisked her up the steps and onto the sidewalk. Cynthia jerked his hand to get him to stop. She pulled antibacterial wipes out of her purse and cleaned her hands. When she finished cleaning hers, she cleaned Thomas' as well. The grit and grime from the dusty, dirty, old subway made her uncomfortable. Thomas started laughing. Cynthia turned around to see what she was missing.

"I'm laughing at you. You sure can tell you're not a New Yorker. Disinfectant wipes? Girl you should just wear a sign on your back... 'I'm a tourist'."

Cynthia smacked him on the arm, smiling in good humor. He took her arm, linked it with his and began trotting down the sidewalk.

"Thomas, why are we running?"

"Just felt like it. Lighten up...nobody is paying any attention to us."

About a block down was an ice cream shop. Thomas stopped and sat Cynthia in the chair outside the door. He went in and purchased two cones. Once back outside, he shoved the cone so close to her face, there was ice cream on the tip of her nose. They licked ice cream cones

## Deadly Choices

as they strolled down the street sharing with each other. All of a sudden, Thomas leaned over and licked the ice cream from the tip of her nose. Cynthia reared back in surprise, with a puzzled look on her face.

"You have had ice cream on your nose since I gave you the cone. I just had the urge to lick it off." He smiled and winked. They happened upon a novelty shop and went in to browse. Cynthia made a purchase then went out front to wait for him. The moment he walked out of the store, she squirted him with water. She'd purchased a battery-operated fan that sprayed a mist of water, but she squirted him until all the water was gone. She had no idea he'd bought the same thing. As soon as he realized her water was gone, from behind his back he revealed two water filled fans. He'd bought one for her too, but decided to give her a double squirt, since she'd surprised him. Cynthia took off running down the sidewalk, giggling as she ran. Thomas was on her heels, spraying water with both hands. Cynthia suddenly stopped and turned, facing him. She'd worked a can of confetti spray from the bag. She shot a few gobs of confetti directly into his face, surprising him. She turned and took off running again. As she stopped for a breath, Thomas caught up to her, holding her so close she couldn't break free. His adrenaline was running high which prompted him to kiss her passionately, right there on the sidewalk. Though they were tightly hugged up and obviously heated, the people passing by didn't give them a second look. When they came up for air, Thomas suggested they return to her hotel. At that moment, she was definitely game.

    Several trains and a few blocks later, they finally arrived at the hotel. She noticed the concierge wink as they passed, which made her curious. She looked up at Thomas when they entered the elevator, but his expression revealed nothing. She turned the key to her room, and with a mere crack in the door, her nostrils filled with the scent of fresh roses. Her eyes grew wide when the door was completely opened. At least four dozen rose petals in a variety of colors were sprinkled all over the bed. There was a bouquet of roses in a vase on the table. A basket of fresh strawberries and chocolate were wrapped in red cellophane and positioned in the center of the bed. The bathroom had a basket of aroma therapy products and candles sitting on the ledge next to the bathtub. She turned and looked at Thomas in amazement. Her mouth dropped open, but nothing came out. She was speechless, to say the least. This man was so thoughtful he must be the real thing. Before she could begin to speak, Thomas asked her to remove her clothes. She turned to go to the bedroom, but he requested she stay there.

"Don't leave. I want to watch you undress." She stood for a moment without any movement. While she stood in shock, Thomas started running bath water. He sat on the side of the tub and carefully watched as she disrobed. Although her lace undergarments were a turn on for him, he resisted removing them for her and helped her into the bathtub. He lit the candles while she soaked in the relaxing, hot water. He left her to soak while he removed his clothes in the bedroom. When he emerged in the doorway of the bathroom, Cynthia was laid back, resting on the bath pillow with her eyes closed. She had no idea he was standing there naked. He sat on the edge of the tub and began to bathe her. She was so relaxed she still hadn't opened her eyes. She opened them quickly when she felt him sink into the water on top of her. He picked up where they'd left off, with a kiss that sent her into space. She stopped kissing to bathe him. They talked while she massaged his body. The water was getting cold, so they decided to get out. As he was drying her off, he slowly walked her to the bedroom. He placed a silk scarf over her eyes, blindfolding her, gently laid her on the bed, and returned to the bathroom. She lay there anxiously waiting whatever he had planned. The fragrance of the rose petals was soothing, which sent her imagination on a journey. In the midst of her imaginary journey, she felt a light touch on her toes. They became moist and so did she. As he sucked her toes, she felt more and more relaxed. The gentle touch turned into an intense desire, as he dropped candle wax onto her thighs. In a matter of seconds, the sensation went from an alarming shrill to a pleasant moan. During a brief pause of the hot wax, there was wonder mingled with anticipation of the next experience. There was the thrill of not knowing what to expect next that kept her excited. She was so caught up in it that she left the creativity up to him. It wasn't long before the tender, gentle experience had them tangled up in an electrifying moment of passion.

# 23

Another front page news story...FRANK CARTER ARRESTED FOR THE MURDER OF JORDAN EVANS. Mr. Carter had the motive, means and opportunity. He will be detained and questioned, while evidence is being investigated.

At the precinct, three ruthless, cocky detectives were questioning Frank. They had already made up their minds that Frank was guilty. However, the lead detective on the case, Emanuel Shelton, was not present during the interrogation. One of the detectives pounded his fist on the table, with the hope of intimidating Frank into spilling his guts.

"I keep telling you fools that I didn't do it!"

"You need to answer the questions, or we'll find a reason to keep you in lock up all night."

"I think this would be a good time for me to call an attorney. Can I make my call?"

Before either of the detectives could respond, there was a knock at the door. A long arm reached in and handed one of the detectives an envelope.

"Hmm...looks like you will need to make that call, Mr. Carter.

## Deadly Choices

Seems as though the evidence we have makes you our man."

"What? Yeah, give me the phone."

"Read him his rights let him make a call, then lock his ass up."

After Frank was led to a cell, the three detectives went to see Detective Shelton. The first detective led off with, "We have our man for the murder of Jordan Evan."

"How so?" replied Shelton.

"We have his fingerprints and we can place him at the scene within a three hour period of the victim's death."

"That's a little weak. Show me the proof, because I have another person in mind."

"Who?"

"Just show me what you got first."

They presented Detective Shelton with a glass from the Evans household, with Frank's fingerprints. His fingerprints were also on the bedpost of the bed where Evans was found dead. There were also fabric and hair fibers at the scene that matched his.

"Okay, let me show you what the defense will do to your evidence. He was the next door neighbor to the Evans. Could it be possible that his prints are on more than just one glass, all over the house for that matter?"

"Sir, that's reaching a bit, don't you think?"

"What was his motive? What did he have to gain? You should have let him go and put a tail on him before you arrested him. If he gets the right attorney, they'll get him off in no time with this weak shit."

"Well, we can't very well go tell him now, oops just kidding."

"You're right, you can't. Now you'll have to work double time to make sure this sticks. Find out more, but I think all three of you are way off track."

"Who do you think it is?"

"I'm not sure, but I don't think it was him. Cynthia Evans comes more to mind than Frank Carter."

"Cynthia, why her?"

"She had the most to gain, and personally, I believe she's connected to the other two, as well."

"Not true. She couldn't have been with Mayfield. She's in New York as we speak."

"Are you sure about that?"

"Yes, we already checked on that."

"Then how was she at the nightclub last night?"

The other three detectives were stunned. They were baffled that this information didn't turn up when they questioned people who knew Mayfield.

"That can't be. We checked her out and she was, in fact, in New York. Her secretary said she was called to come back for an emergency situation, but she was able to take care of it without returning to Chicago."

"My sources tell me that she was at Spuratiks last night."

"Maybe they thought it was her. The place is pretty big and dim."

"You know I don't operate on maybes. It was her."

"I am personally going to check into this. I will check the airlines and the hotel where I'm told she's staying."

"Go do whatever you need to for this arrest to stick to Frank Carter. There's something about this lady that worries me. I felt that the first time we spoke. She's too in control. It's like she has calculated every move and every question that will come her way."

## Deadly Choices

Detective Shelton sat at his desk contemplating a trip to New York. *Maybe I'll go see for myself what she's up to.* Without giving it too much thought, he picked up the phone and called the airlines, booked a flight and headed home to pack. He didn't bother to inform the other detectives he wanted to see what they turned up. Meanwhile, the detectives went about their business to get more concrete evidence against Frank. They were determined that Frank was guilty, so they were bound and determined to get him convicted.

Days passed...Detective Shelton had not been able to get anything substantial to tie Cynthia to the murders. He made it a point to steer clear of her. He didn't want her to be aware of his presence. He stayed in New York for four days, clocking her every move. She spent the majority of her time with Thomas, and when she was alone she shopped. Actually, he became more intrigued with her as he watched her from afar. As he observed her, he began to see her differently. He noticed her sex appeal, and he no longer wanted to believe that she was capable of murder. Cynthia had a way about her that you either loved or hated. There was no in between, which made it difficult for Detective Shelton, once he fell onto the "love her" side. Had he not spent so many days watching and observing her, he might have been able to be objective. However, he too had fallen under Cynthia's spell, as so many others had. She didn't even realize the power she had over so many people. She was well aware of her sex appeal and intelligence, but had no idea of the power of her presence.

Detective Shelton returned to Chicago with a dilemma as to what to do. Although his instincts said she was guilty, he liked her now and was unable to clearly see any wrongdoing on her part. At this point, he couldn't see arresting her. He was willing to convict anyone to protect Cynthia.

## Shelly L. Foster

Meanwhile, after spending so much time with Thomas, Cynthia found herself in love again. In love like a schoolgirl who wants to be with her man every waking moment. Although she felt their lifestyles would prevent them from spending a lot of time together, Thomas made every effort to give her as much of his time as possible. He, too, had fallen for her as much as she'd fallen for him. She was tired of sleeping with different men, with no relationship or commitment. She thought that she wanted to be free of any ties or commitment, for fear the relationship would end up like the one she'd had with Jordan. She sat with the patio doors open, gazing out into New York City. The phone rang and diverted her attention. It was Ardelia checking to see what time she was coming home.

"Girl, I'm sitting here looking out onto the patio at an enormous bee. I have never seen a bee this big before."

"That's the queen. She heads up the colony and lays all the eggs."

"You make me sick knowing this kind of shit. Who the hell cares about what the queen bee does?"

"Anyway, the males are called drones. They only have one function; to fertilize the eggs of the queen."

"Oh, just like a man, huh? That seems to be his only function, too. We have to do all the work, and they just provide the seed to keep the human race alive."

"Exactly. We are the queens of the universe. We have a lot more power than we give ourselves credit for."

"That really makes me think about how and why we act the way we do. Maybe subconsciously, men know we, as women, head up the colony and that's why they try so hard to control us."

"Yep. You got it."

# Deadly Choices

"Well, I have some really good news. I met a man that I really like."

"What? Not just a man to take to bed?"

"No, girl. I am so crazy about this man it hurts. We've spent everyday together since I got here, and I hope this will continue."

"I can't believe what I'm hearing, but I sure am glad to hear it."

"I am so happy I really don't want to come home. I miss my child, but other than that, I don't have to ever return."

"Well, it's good you're coming home soon. Shit is hitting the fan and going crazy around here."

"What has happened?"

"Girl, James Mayfield has been murdered and Frank Carter has been arrested for the murder of Jordan."

"WHAT THE HELL DID YOU SAY?"

"You heard me. Yep, the police believe that Frank killed your husband."

"I just can't believe that. Why?"

"Hell, I don't know. He's had such a thing for you that maybe he thought Jordan was keeping him from you."

Yelling at the top of her lungs..."NO, NO, NO. THIS CAN'T BE TRUE. WHERE IS HE?"

"Still locked up."

"I have got to go see him. I need to talk to him face to face. I'll come home tomorrow. I'll call you as soon as I get home. Bye."

Cynthia sat in utter amazement. She couldn't believe what she'd just heard. Although someone was at the door knocking, Cynthia heard only the last two knocks and approached the door. Tears were streaming down her face as she opened it. Thomas was standing there, and immediately reached out to hug her. They held each other as he walked into the room.

"What's wrong, honey?"

"I just got a call that my next door neighbor has been arrested for the murder of my husband. I'm devastated. I just can't believe it!"

"Do you want to go home now?"

"Not really, but I need to go see what's going on. I told my girlfriend I'd be home tomorrow."

"I'll have your arrangements made, and we'll go out to eat or something to try to get your mind off of things."

"I really don't have the energy to go anywhere. Could we just stay here? If you're hungry we could order room service."

Thomas nodded his approval, and Cynthia handed him the room service menu. While Thomas placed the order, Cynthia went to the bathroom to get comfortable. She returned in her bathrobe and flopped onto the bed. She sat there like a zombie, but her mind was moving quickly. Thomas wrapped her in his arms with hopes of bringing her comfort.

After they ate, Cynthia began to pack while Thomas lounged and watched television. Not much was said the rest of the evening. Cynthia couldn't quite get her thoughts together and Thomas didn't want to overstep, so he let her be. She drifted off to sleep, curled up tightly in the warmth of Thomas' muscular arms.

She tossed and turned for the better part of the night, but Thomas didn't seem to mind at all. As day broke, he wanted to make love to her before she left, but wasn't sure if he should cross that line. He didn't have to. Cynthia turned to face him and began to softly kiss him. He made love to her to give her something to think about while they were apart. They left for the airport several hours later.

## 24

Twenty-first precinct, Chicago police station...Cynthia was separated by glass, but face-to-face with Frank nonetheless.

"Cynthia, I did not kill Jordan. I don't know what led them to me, but I swear I didn't do it."

"I am so confused by all this. I don't want to believe you did it, but what made the police arrest you?"

"They claim they have evidence that puts me at the scene within a three-hour period of the time he was killed. Sure, I was at your house that night, but so were several others. How is that a determination that I killed him?"

"You were gone long before three hours before he died. But wait a minute...I gave you a key once when I was going away and come to think of it, you never gave it back. Where is my key?"

"At home in my kitchen drawer. I went in while you were gone just to check the house, but I haven't used it since."

"I didn't know you used it then. I merely asked you to keep an eye on things, and to use the key for emergencies. Why would you go into my house and not inform me that you were there?"

"Cynthia, I just didn't think about it. I haven't even thought about the key and neither have you, for that matter. Come on now, I don't need you to doubt me, too."

Cynthia stood to leave, but Frank asked her to sit for just another minute. He drew his face close to the glass and whispered through the holes.

"I think I know who did it, but I don't think you want to know."

Cynthia raised her brow, but sat in silence. Frank continued to tell her what he thought. Cynthia was pissed at his accusation, and stormed out without responding to him. Frank knew he was crossing the line by revealing what he'd learned, but his butt was on the line and he needed an out.

Cynthia sped to Yvonne's house to pick up Chris. Yvonne tried to make small talk with Cynthia, but she wasn't interested in talking with anyone. She just wanted to get her child home. All the way home, Chris sat staring at her mom. Cynthia, on the other hand, had nothing to say. Once home, Cynthia kept busy unpacking, then showered and prepared some dinner. She called for Chris to join her in the kitchen. They ate a quiet meal together, and Chris washed dishes before going back upstairs.

Chris went into her mother's room to talk about her trip. Although a little distant, Cynthia shared her experience in New York and asked Chris if she would like to move there. Chris was surprised that her mom was considering a move anywhere. She knew Chicago was home, and believed it always would be. Moving and leaving her friends was not top on her list, but she told Cynthia she could go anywhere as long as she was with her. Cynthia was really glad to hear that since she had fallen head over heals for Thomas, and was strongly considering his offer for her to move there. She realized she couldn't make the decision without considering her child, her partnership at the firm, and her family ties, but she wanted to go in the worst way.

They talked for a half hour or so, then turned in for the night.

The week moved at the slowest pace ever, but Thursday finally came. Cynthia was itching to go out Friday for happy hour, but thought she should stay home with Chris since she'd been gone for so long. Chris came in the house beaming with excitement to go to a party Friday night. Cynthia agreed to let her go, knowing that it worked out perfectly for her. Cynthia was starting to snap back from the bomb that Frank had dropped on her, but was still a bit in never-never-land. The two made a night of it, watching movies until eleven o'clock. They both were looking forward to Friday and the weekend, so morning couldn't come soon enough.

The Friday morning sunlight was shining through in the bedroom window, waking Cynthia before the alarm could sound. She stumbled her way into her bathroom, before going to wake Chris. As she made her way down the hallway to Chris' room, she saw the light on. She poked her head in, but Chris was apparently in the bathroom. As she turned to go to the kitchen, she noticed a wig on Chris' dresser. She opened the door and went in. She picked up the wig to examine it, just as Chris was coming out of the bathroom. Chris stopped dead in her tracks.

"Chris, what are you doing with my wig?"

"Oh, I was just playing around with it."

"When?"

"Uh."

"Uh? Did you have this with you at Lolly's?"

"Yes. Lolly and I were just fooling around."

"Stay out of my shit, Chris."

Cynthia took the wig with her, and tossed it on her bed, as she proceeded to the kitchen. *What is this girl up to? I think I need to watch her more closely.* Cynthia sat at the kitchen table, trying to figure out what her child could be up to, and was so deep in thought Chris startled her as she entered the kitchen. The look on Cynthia's face indicated that she was perturbed. Chris knew that look, and didn't dare say anything to make matters worse. Chris left the house saying goodbye in a very low tone of voice, after which, Cynthia finished getting dressed and headed for the office.

Fridays at the office were generally mild, but today was extremely hectic. Cynthia was flying from meeting to meeting, with very little time to collect herself in between. Marge seemed to be more irritating than Cynthia remembered. She had to pass Marge's desk before entering her office. She caught a whiff of an old familiar smell from her childhood. She stopped and stepped back to Marge's desk.

"Marge, what is that I smell?"

"Ben-Gay. My knees were aching a bit so I rubbed a little on them."

"I understand ailments Marge, but this is hardly the place for the smell of Ben-Gay. Go rub it off and spray some Lysol or something to get rid of the smell." Cynthia returned to her office without giving Marge an opportunity for rebuttal. Although Cynthia had issues with Marge, she would not disrespect her elder. She took her authority to the limit though. She would only think about the things that she wished she had the heart to tell her. *Take your old ass home and sit down and your knees won't hurt. Old long in the tooth, twisted wig wearing old fossil.*

It was clear that Marge was not happy with the directive, but

## Deadly Choices

she crept her old ass down the hallway, support hose draped around each ankle and washed off the Ben-Gay.

The day came to a crashing halt, with Cynthia packing up to leave. As she headed for the door, her phone rang.

"Cynthia Evans."

"Mom, can I go to the party from Lolly's house?"

"Are you going to wear the same outfit you wore to school?"

"No, I brought clothes with me."

"Sounds like you planned to go from there all along."

"I was hoping I could."

"Fine, girl. I don't care. I need all the specifics. Where is it, who's giving it, and what time is it over? Where do you plan to go after the party? I guess you've made plans for that too, huh?"

"It's at this teen club called Jump Start. A girl in our class is giving it, and it's over at one o'clock."

"What is the name of the girl in your class? What are her parents' names and where do they live?"

"Her name is Judy Alexander and her parents' names are Bennett and Samantha Alexander. They live three blocks from us at 1650 Parliament. Can I stay at Lolly's after the party?"

*She's up to something. I'm going to let her hang herself.*

"Yes, you can stay at Lolly's, but I will pick you up first thing in the morning. I'm going to go out for a drink myself. If you need me, call my cell phone."

They blew phone kisses as they hung up.

# 25

Cynthia sat at the bar during happy hour reflecting on her times with James. She was missing the happy hours and the personal attention she got at Spuratiks. Actually, she was missing Thomas more than anything. She longed to be in New York with him, but right now was not the time. It was clear that her daughter needed her. She couldn't put her finger on what it was, but something about her was different. She realized that she was becoming a young woman, but she wasn't ready for that. She seemed to have grown up much too fast, and Cynthia was having a hard time holding on to her. She knew she couldn't hold on too tight, or Chris would push away. On the other hand, she wondered if she'd given her too much freedom in her earlier years. She was no longer the innocent little girl that was always at her side. Cynthia sat with her head in her hands, on the verge of tears, when this deep voice came barreling over her shoulder.

"Hey, will you talk to me now?"

"Frank! What are you doing out of jail?"

## Deadly Choices

"Those bastards didn't have enough to hold me for more than seventy-two hours. I'm telling you, I didn't do it."

"Frank, I believe you didn't, but I don't want to hear that crazy shit you were telling me the other day."

"Cynthia, if you would just listen, I know we could fix this."

Cynthia shot him a fierce "if you fuck with me I'll kill you" glance, then rose from the barstool and left the club. He knew if he opened his mouth, she would cut him down like a lumberjack in the forest. He surely didn't need any more trouble, so he let her leave in peace.

Cynthia drove around the city with all the car windows open. She was filled with anger, frustration, loneliness and confusion. As much as she'd always been able to contain herself and never let her emotions show, she felt that she was starting to lose that edge. She pulled over near a park, got out, and paced like a caged tiger. The wind whisked through her hair and swept through her clothes, cooling down the perspiration that had built up on her chest and back. She returned to her car and sped off, still without a destination. At home she found Frank waiting outside. He attempted to approach her, but Cynthia still wanted nothing to do with him. Just as she reached the porch, Frank blurted from his yard..."I'm telling you, it is her."

Cynthia ignored him and went in the house.

She lay across her bed in her clothes, screaming to the top of her lungs, "LORD, WHAT IS HAPPENING? HELP ME PLEASE." She jumped up, searching for her sleeping pills. She took three then headed to the living room to fix a drink. She could care less that alcohol and sleeping pills were a bad combination, the pressure was way too much to deal with. As she lay staring at the ceiling and thinking about all the things that had been happening in her life lately, the phone rang. Two short rings, ring-ring, two short rings a second time, ring-ring. That meant someone was calling anonymously. The outgoing message on voicemail recited, the number of the caller trying to reach you is not available to our network. If you would like more information on this caller, press "1". Cynthia pressed "1" and a recorded voice announced his name. Thomas. After the name was announced the recording asked, If you would like to receive this call press "1". Cynthia couldn't press "1" fast enough. She was weeping uncontrollably, and Thomas couldn't make out a word she was saying. "Honey, I need for you to take a deep breath, collect yourself and tell me what's wrong." Unable to get it together, Cynthia told Thomas she would talk to him later. On top of the emotional roller coaster, the pills and alcohol were kicking in hard. She took the last few sips from her drink and drifted off to sleep.

As the sun beamed in on her face, she could hardly open her eyes. Since she had told Chris she would pick her up early, she knew she had to get started. She crawled out of the bed, reached for her cigarettes, and slowly made her way to the kitchen. Coffee and a cigarette were her cure for the morning blues. She managed to pull herself together, dress, and leave for Lolly's. Getting dolled up was not part of the plan for the day. A shower and clean underwear were the only requirements. She pulled a fleece-lined jogging suit out of a dresser drawer, plopped a baseball cap on her head and headed out the door.

Chris and Lolly were outside as she pulled into the driveway. She motioned for Chris to come to the car. "Get your things, thank Yvonne and let's go."

"What's wrong, Mom?"

"Just get your things. We'll talk later."

Cynthia waved at Lolly, but Lolly dared not approach the car.

## Deadly Choices

She returned into the house with Chris, but didn't come back out with her. Chris sat in the car, but didn't look at Cynthia. On the other hand, Cynthia sat staring a hole in the side of Chris' face. She'd never turned the car off, so she placed the gearshift in reverse and backed out the driveway. They drove straight home, neither striking up a conversation. As soon as they were inside the house, Cynthia questioned Chris and her whereabouts from the night before. Chris bowed her head, but didn't respond to the questions.

"Chris? I know you heard me. Where were you?"

"I went to Jump Start where I told you I was going."

She had the nerve to have an attitude when she knew her whereabouts were questionable.

"Were you there the entire time?"

Yet again, Chris bowed her head attempting to avoid cross-examination. Cynthia stood directly in front of her, grabbed a handful of hair, and pulled her head up. She gazed directly into her eyes, awaiting a response. A tear or two rolled down Chris' cheek. Without any provocation, the tears began to flow uncontrollably. Chris slid off the sofa to her knees. She placed her hands over her face, covering her mouth as well. As she began to speak, her hands muffled her words. Cynthia dropped to the floor beside her, wrapping her close in her arms. Her heart was breaking to see her child in so much pain.

"What is it, Chris?"

"Mom, why are so many things happening to us? I just don't understand why nothing is going right."

"What are you talking about?"

"Ever since Dad died, you've been different. You've had all these people in and out of our lives, and I don't like it."

"Who are you talking about? I haven't brought anyone into

your life."

"Yes you did. Mary, James, Sharon, that Vanessa woman, and who knows how many others."

"I didn't make them part of your life. Sharon had been my friend for many years, so why is she part of that mix?"

"Because I have watched you turn into what my friends would so affectionately call you, a whore, a tramp, a scalawag. You were never like that, and it is eating me up inside."

"Why didn't you talk to me about your feelings?"

"I tried. I have talked to you, but you always tell me not to worry about you, how you're the mom and I'm the child. I'm not a child anymore. I know more than you think I do."

"So tell me, what is going on with you now?"

"I will. I have to get this off my chest, but I just can't right now. May I go to my room and take a nap. I'm really tired."

"Yes, but as soon as you wake up, we need to talk."

Cynthia decided to nap, herself. She retired to her bedroom, but couldn't drift off to sleep. She lay there in utter silence, pondering what her child was going to tell her.

# 26

Chris woke up several hours later and went straight to her mother's room. She thought Cynthia was asleep, her eyes were still closed, and decided not to wake her. As Chris turned to leave the room, Cynthia let her know she wasn't sleeping. Chris turned around and joined Cynthia on the bed. As Chris sat down, Cynthia sat up in the bed. Once again Chris' eyes filled with tears. They streamed down her face as she began to express her heartache. Sobbing with every word, she started her story.

"Mom, I knew Dad beat and humiliated you, ever since I was a little girl. I would sit in my bedroom and cry all night when you fought. I knew you were trying to protect me from knowing what was going on, but I knew all along. Then when dad died, you seemed to shut me out. You were always gone for work or with someone else. I thought if I hung out with my friends that the hurt would go away. I was missing you more than you know. I know that I was acting up a lot, but that was to get your attention. I thought it would make you stay around me more, and hang out together like we used to, but it didn't work. You just seemed to be angry with me all the time and I didn't know what to do."

Cynthia started to speak when Chris took a breath, but Chris asked her to let her finish.

"At first, I thought it would be great once we left dad, but he still kept hurting you. I was beginning to hate him. Every time I saw him I wanted to puke. Then Mary came along. She was pressing you for time with her, and I know you slept with her. I didn't know what to feel anymore. My mom had slept with another woman. I was wondering if you were now gay and I had to face my friends having a gay mother."

Again, Cynthia tried to interrupt, "Mom, please let me finish. I need to get this out. Then you started spending time with that man, James. To top it all off, you had a fight with Sharon. My mother the executive, fighting like an alley cat. Even though I was glad you won, I was so embarrassed that my mother was fighting. My friends were laughing and giving me the blues all the time, 'cause you had become the kind of woman that we decided we never wanted to be. I thought since my dad was dead, we could be really happy for once. But I was wrong. You just pulled further and further away from me, without noticing that I needed you."

"I thought..."

"Mom, please."

Cynthia nodded and allowed Chris to go on. Chris abruptly blurted out...

"I WAS RAPED, MOMMY! I WAS RAPED!"

Chris was overwhelmed with grief, desperation and regret. All Cynthia could do was hold her. She had no answers for Chris, but she had many questions; Who was it, where did it happen and when did it happened? The situation was far too critical to entrust anyone with this

## Deadly Choices

information.

Cynthia just wanted to get her child get through this situation. She gave Chris some aspirin and told her to stay in bed. Cynthia went down the hall to the guest bathroom and broke down. She cried unmercifully for about twenty minutes, until she was able to collect herself. She washed her face, arched her back, and marched back to her bedroom, like a soldier preparing for war.

Chris lay in the bed sobbing, wishing this were only a dream. Unfortunately, it wasn't, so they needed a plan to escape from it all.

The day seemed to pass slower than ever, dusk finally settling in, bringing the day to an end. Neither of them had much of an appetite, so eating was out of the question. Cynthia decided they would both stay home the next day and figure out what to do. She called her office, changing her voicemail to indicate she would not be in the office for the day, then called Marge and directed her to hold down the fort. Cynthia and Chris showered, snuggled up in bed and lay in complete silence. After a short while, Cynthia felt compelled to open her heart to Chris. "Chris I am so sorry for what you've been going through. I guess I was so caught up in my own issues I neglected to see what was happening with you. I've never told you about my horrible childhood after my mother died. Although that's no excuse, I think I was fighting to make sure you never had a life like that. I failed to be the mother I should have been. Instead, I became the mother I was trying so hard not to be."

"Mom, I just want us both to be able to start all over again."

"We'll figure something out. Try to get some sleep. Tomorrow's probably going to be another long day."

Once the lights were out, Chris was asleep in no time. Cynthia, on the other hand, couldn't sleep if her life depended on it. Actually, since her child's life depended on her, her life did depend on it. Her mind spiraled in a million different directions.

In the midst of her thoughts, a calming force came over her. For some strange reason, her anxiety eased and the knots in her stomach loosened. She draped her arms across her daughter, hoping to provide some comfort and sense of togetherness. Peacefully, she drifted off to sleep.

# 27

Shortly before the dawn lit the sky, the loud chime of the doorbell awakened Cynthia. Startled by the bell, she tangled herself in the covers, trying to get out of the bed too quickly. Once her feet hit the floor, she was disoriented, turning in circles looking for her robe. She managed to get herself together, made her way downstairs, and tiptoed to the kitchen. The blinds were always closed with the veins pointed upward. This allowed her to see out, when no one else could see in. *Who could it be? It had better not be Frank this time of the morning.* Her heart was racing, but her body felt numb. She placed her hand on the doorknob, and turned it slowly, but swiftly jerked the door wide open. Surprisingly, Thomas was standing on the doorstep with bags in hand. Cynthia lunged toward him, wrapping her arms tightly around his neck. The sudden contact caused Thomas to drop his bags, and he embraced her with what a man should always give to his woman; a sense of strength and support. Once Cynthia released the embrace, she stood before him with her hand over her heart, amazed that he'd come to her rescue. He gave her a half-cocked smile, acknowledging how much his presence meant to her. Cynthia stepped back, holding the door for him to enter with his luggage. They sat in the den on the sofa. Cynthia curled up close to him, placing her head on his shoulder. He kissed her on the top of her head, then raised her head by slightly pushing up on her chin. As their eyes connected, Cynthia's tears began to flow. Kissing her tears away, he talked as he kissed.

"Tell me what's wrong. What can I do to make it better?"

The words just wouldn't come out right. The baby babble made no sense to Thomas at all. He reared back with a confused look on his face.

"Settle down for a minute. You have to get it together enough to tell me what's happening. Just sit here for a second, swallow hard, take a few deep breaths then fill me in."

Before Cynthia could gain her composure, Chris entered the room. She stood in the archway of the den shocked that her mother lay in yet another man's arms. She projected a displeasing attitude as she spoke.

"Morning, Mom."

"Hey, honey. Come on in. I want you to meet Thomas. "

Thomas stood to receive Chris, who continued to stand more than an arms length away. She resented his being there, and the fact that her mother was again sharing her attention.

"Chris, come sit here with us. Thomas is the gentleman I met in New York. He's here to help us."

"YOU TOLD HIM?"

"Not yet. I was about to though."

Chris rolled her eyes then flopped back down on the sofa, crossing her arms, obviously unhappy. Thomas asked if they needed some time alone. Cynthia told him yes, and pointed him to the kitchen.

## Deadly Choices

"The coffee should be ready. It starts automatically around this time, so help yourself."

Cynthia turned her attention back to Chris, clearly irritated.

"Why are you being nasty, Chris?"

"I just told you last night what was wrong with me, and here you are first thing this morning with someone else."

"He called yesterday and when I didn't tell him what was happening, he knew something was wrong then showed up unannounced. I didn't know he was coming, but I'm really glad he's here. If anyone could help us through this mess, he can. You're going to have to trust that I will get you through this. He has the means and the resources to help us start fresh. Will you at least give me a chance to talk to him, and see if he's even willing to help us? We can't pour Deer Park water into these muddy waters to clear up the situation."

Chris sat tightlipped for a few moments then responded.

"Yeah, I guess so. Whatever you think is best. I guess I can't be too picky. I want to get as far away from here as we can. I just want you all to myself 'cause I think he's going to get me again."

"I understand what you need, but you also have to know that I need a mate in my life as well. Can you understand that I can love you, be there for you, and have a companion, too?"

"If I have to share you, I only want to share you with one person, and that person has to be good to you. As you would so famously put it, 'help me to understand' why I should settle for less than that?"

Cynthia smiled, and they both burst into laughter.

"We can do this, Chris. Just give it a chance okay?"

Chris nodded, and as she turned toward the doorway, Thomas appeared.

"Come on back in, honey. We are ready to talk."

Chris laid everything out. She gave details about how, and when she was raped, making the hair on the back of Cynthia's neck stand straight up.

"Lolly and I went to Spuratiks a lot."

Cynthia interrupted by asking, "The club? A lot? How?"

"Well, that's another story. I would wear your wigs, and I looked just like you. Several times people spoke to me, thinking I was you."

"It really concerned me that you didn't have a normal reaction to your dad dying, but I just thought you were in shock."

"I was. I was still shocked about the rape, and I didn't know how to tell you. I was scared and humiliated."

Thomas sat in silence, assessing everything that had been said, until he was ready to share his thoughts.

"Ladies, may I interject here?"

They both nodded their approval, and Thomas proceeded.

"I propose as I did when you were in New York...come live in New York with me. Pack up everything and move."

Chris shot a quick glance at Cynthia, then at Thomas. Cynthia looked at Chris, then to Thomas for his seal of approval. Thomas stretched out his arms, inviting them both in close to him. Chris really believed she and her mother could finally be happy. She let out a sigh of relief as the tears began to flow. Cynthia and Chris were still wrapped in the safety and comfort of Thomas' arms when he squeezed them tightly, affirming his commitment to protect them.

The three of them dressed and went out for some entertainment, stopped at a nearby restaurant, then checked out a movie. During their outing they attempted to regain some sense of normalcy, but there was still a strained feeling between them. It was achingly apparent that

## Deadly Choices

it would be a tough road to happiness, but they were committed and determined to make it work.

Cynthia planned to go back into the office the next day, so they called it an early night. As they pulled into the driveway, Frank had just turned to leave Cynthia's porch. Apparently he was determined to reinforce his theory about the murders. Cynthia's maternal defense shifted into high gear. She needed to get Frank in check. Literally, before Thomas could get the gearshift in park, Cynthia was reaching for the door handle. Thomas released his grip from the gearshift, and lovingly, but firmly held her by the arm. He pulled her close, pecking a kiss on her cheek. While close enough to whisper in her ear, he said; "I'll handle it." Cynthia was so unaccustomed to having a man who could handle his business that her natural and immediate reaction was to take control. Chris was even impressed, so much so, that when Thomas got out of the car she said, "Oh boy, you scare me."

A brief discussion with Frank was all Thomas needed. There were no obscenities, loud voices or unnecessary roughness. Although Cynthia had never seen Thomas faced with confrontation, it was evident, as with every other aspect of his life, that he always took control. There was no doubt in her mind that he had handled it.

Frank didn't acknowledge Cynthia or Chris as he passed the car. *Pathetic, little, spineless bastard.* Cynthia chuckled to herself, as the thought passed through her mind. They stayed inside the car until he was in his own yard, and Thomas motioned for them to exit the vehicle.

Once inside, mental and emotional exhaustion crashed in on them. Chris started up the steps to her bedroom, but after the second or third step, she backed down the steps and reached to hug her mother. They embraced for a moment and as they began to separate, Chris thanked Cynthia for being there for her and told her how much she loved her. She then turned to Thomas, but before she could say anything, Thomas covered her lips with his index finger. "There's nothing you need to say to me. You two are a big part of my life now, and I'll take care of everything." Chris smiled and shook her head, acknowledging his words, and headed off to bed.

Cynthia and Thomas followed her up the steps to retire as well.

# 28

Lights were out throughout the Evans household. Everyone had showered and prepared for the next day. While the television played on low volume, the light reflecting on Thomas' partially nude body made Cynthia forget how tired she was, and the long day ahead. She rolled over and nibbled on Thomas' ear. He raised his head slightly off the pillow; "Girl, what are you doing?"

"I can't sleep with you next to me."

"I can."

Cynthia raised herself up on one elbow, staring at him. He closed his eyes, but had a smirk on his face that she noticed. Her face cracked like a hard boiled egg hitting the floor. *Awe, he's starting his shit already. Have I misjudged another crusty ass man?* She lay back, but before she could pull the covers up, Thomas was mounting her. Cynthia was pissed, so, of course, she pulled away from his advances. "Lighten up baby, I was just teasing. Come here." Even though he'd sparked her, she played hard to get since he had burst her bubble. Of course, he wouldn't let her stay angry with him, which caused him to be even more persistent. He kissed the right spot and she gave in with more than open arms. Their love making was electrifying as always, which gave Cynthia only a few hours of sleep before her day began.

Cynthia woke up with the thought that the sun was blinding, but she wouldn't have to worry about that much longer. She squirmed about the bed for a while before planting her feet on the floor. As she sat up on the side of the bed to place her feet in her slippers, Thomas pulled her back into the bed. "No, no, no mister. If I stay in this bed, I'll never make it to the office." *I sure could stay here all day with you too...nah, better not.*

She scooted to the edge of the bed and stood to her feet, before she got weak. Thomas threw one arm behind his head and watched her every move. She asked if he wanted coffee or breakfast, but he offered to fix breakfast while she dressed.

Chris appeared in the kitchen first. "Ooh, breakfast. We don't eat hot breakfast during the week around here." Thomas smiled and fixed her a plate. Cynthia came down and looked her usual business best. To look at her you'd never believe she had any troubles. She was a master at portraying the perfect image. Thomas fixed her plate, then his. They all sat and had a quiet breakfast. Thomas offered to drive them to school and work. This way he would have the car to make preparations for the move to New York. Cynthia invited him up to her office to meet everyone. He got a quick tour but no one was around for him to meet. He kissed her goodbye as he left her office. He closed her door then tossed a handkerchief on Marge's desk as he passed. Just as the elevator doors closed, Marge returned to her desk, immediately wondering who could have left the handkerchief.

Marge held it for a few short moments, trying to figure out where it came from. In the midst of her thoughts, Cynthia rang her on the intercom.

"Marge, would you come in here, please?"

Marge stood in front of Cynthia's desk like a soldier with her note pad in hand. "Are the partners available anytime today?"

"I'll check their calendars and let you know. Is there anything else?"

"Not right now, but make sure they have an available hour. I need to speak with them all at once, so work on that, please. Adjust my calendar, if necessary, to get us in one room at the same time."

After Marge left, Cynthia turned her attention to some contracts she needed to review. She hadn't noticed earlier, but her message light was on. She checked her voicemail and there was one message. *No he didn't* She hung up the receiver, placing her face in the palms of her hands. "MARGE! " she yelled.

When Marge raced into the room – racing as fast as an old woman in support hose and orthopedic shoes could, she asked, "Any luck with that meeting, yet?"

"It's only been ten minutes."

"So, your answer is no?"

"Yes, the answer is no. I haven't had time to get it together."

"I'm sorry, Marge, I just need to have this meeting today. Please do it quickly and let me know as soon as you can. Thanks."

Marge turned and hobbled back to her desk. Cynthia was getting very anxious. The message from Frank made her nervous and scared. She knew she had to get all her loose ends tied up – fast. She called the mail room and asked Hollander to bring her three boxes and mailing labels. Hollander was there in record time. He always took care of her. Whenever she called him, he was there on the spot. She began packing personal items and labeling them to her home address. She packed up her most important files with hopes that she would still be able to work with them.

"Hollander, will you come back and pick up these boxes?"

She wanted to be as discrete as possible, for the moment. Getting everything packed and prepared to mail before meeting with the partners was probably most prudent, since she couldn't predict the outcome. Marge was so involved in rearranging schedules she hadn't paid any attention to the fact that Hollander was there.

"Cynthia, I have the schedules worked out. I have you all scheduled for two o'clock."

"Thanks, Marge."

With the boxes removed from her office, Cynthia focused on the clients she had to deal with for the day. She made a few phone calls, attempting to resolve any issues that were left hanging. Her head began to ache as she realized she hadn't eaten. It was nearly two o'clock, so she really didn't want to leave for lunch. She opted to grab a hotdog from the street vendor in front of the building. After paying for the hotdog and drink, she strolled over to a bench in the courtyard. She ate her lunch, lit a cigarette and soaked in the sun. She was feeling a bit carefree, although she knew how drastically things were about to change for her. She was hopeful that the partners would be agreeable to either a leave of absence for a few months, or would allow her to run her division of the business from New York. Nonetheless, she had to have the conversation, and she was moving despite any decision. If necessary, she was prepared to be bought out of her partnership. She glanced at her watch, realizing that it was nearly time to meet with the partners. She returned to her office to collect herself and prepare a compelling argument to support her request. She gathered her portfolio and headed for the boardroom.

The partners straggled in within three to four minutes of each

## Deadly Choices

other. They displayed a level of concern for the impromptu meeting. Maurice was always about business, while Paulie and Billie were a little more personable. Cynthia got right down to business, presenting her case. Naturally, the partners were taken off their feet, given the fact that they had no idea of all the stuff that was going on in Cynthia's life. She played on the death of Jordan as part of the reason for a hiatus. She knew that would pull on Paulie and Billie's heartstrings since they had wanted her to take time off when he first passed anyway. But that ploy didn't work with Maurice. He was strictly business and wanted to know how this would impact business, and how she would handle clients that were located in the city. There was no way to soften the bottom line impact this would have on the company. Her absence could put the business in jeopardy and Maurice's position was either you're in or you're out. *I knew if there was any push back it would be from this crabby, dried up old geezer. This fucker is going to keep my plan from running smoothly.* Cynthia was getting frustrated and it showed all over her face. Billie could see this meeting was going to spiral out of control if someone didn't take over. She took the lead to level out the frustration. After they calmly and rationally talked it through, Cynthia made the call. She decided to dissolve the partnership and get out of the business. Although she was furious, she shook their hands, thanked them for the opportunity to partner with them, and returned to her office. Maurice immediately went into survival mode. "I'll have my secretary get the recruiters on the phone. We need to replace Cynthia immediately."

"We don't need another partner right now, Maurice," Paulie interjected.

"I'm not suggesting we hire a partner, but wouldn't you agree we need someone capable to handle her projects? Despite all that has gone on, Cynthia was able to close the Denver project. That project alone is going to take an enormous amount of time and dedication."

"Yes, capable. That's the key word here. If you weren't so pigheaded, we could have kept her on board to handle what she already had working, and found someone capable in the interim for projects going forward. Now we have to scramble to make sure we don't lose the ones she was working on."

While Billie sat back watching the tennis match between Maurice and Paulie, her wheels were turning. "We really have just shot ourselves in the foot by not allowing her to function remotely for a while. We all will need to step in and do double duty to keep from losing money. Tomorrow, I'll have my assistant gather her files and we'll need to work the weekend to get up to speed."

"Let Mr. "I won't budge an inch," Maurice work the weekend. He was the driving force that caused this to happen."

Maurice reared back in his chair and pulled rank. "I am the most senior partner and have the most control in what goes on around here. Do you want to leave, too?"

Paulie got a dose of reality, swallowed hard, slammed her note pad on the table and left. She knew it best not to argue with him.

Meanwhile, Cynthia prepared to leave. She called Marge into her office and informed her that she would be leaving the firm, effective today. This came out of left field for Marge and she had many questions, but Cynthia wouldn't consider answering them. She did tell Marge that her services would probably still be needed, since more than likely, she would be replaced. "I'd come on in the office until one of the partners tells you that you no longer have a job. That's about all I can tell you right now." Confused and concerned, Marge returned to her desk. Cynthia was sick, wondering how long her severance package

## Deadly Choices

would keep her afloat. She had grown very accustomed to the lifestyle she had. What would she do now, without the steady income she was accustomed to making? She damn sure didn't want to depend solely on Thomas, but for now she didn't have much choice. She gathered the few things that hadn't been boxed, and left. She didn't want Thomas to come up and help her with her things, but managing a box, a briefcase and her purse, the trip to the front door was a bit cumbersome. As she was repositioning her "stuff" to go through the revolving door, she was juggling the box, balancing it on one knee and resting her chin on the top, attempting to slide her purse strap back onto her shoulder and grip her briefcase by the handle. An arm reached out to help her. Two hands gripped the box, allowing her to place her foot back on the floor. As she got her balance, she looked up to see who was lending a hand. Her mouth dropped open, but at first nothing came out. Her eyes bulged, she got dizzy and a burning sensation came over her.

"Frank! What are you doing here?" she asked in an excited tone.

"I was coming to see you. What's up with the box?"

"What do you want?"

"I really need to talk to you about this situation I'm tangled up in. I'm still being considered a suspect and I didn't kill anyone. We need to talk, Cynthia."

"Why do we need to talk? I don't have anything to do with it."

"But you do, well, your daughter does."

Not giving any indication that she was the least bit concerned, she replied.

"I will not entertain your bullshit theory, Frank. There's nothing to discuss."

Thomas, watching from the car, hadn't realized who Cynthia was talking to, but became concerned with her body language. He exited the car and entered the building. It was clear that Cynthia was agitated, so without engaging in conversation with either of them, Thomas took the box from Frank and escorted Cynthia to the car. Frank stood and watched them drive away.

As they drove, silence kept them company. The radio wasn't even on. Thomas was giving Cynthia some quiet space, allowing her to think and sort through her emotions. He knew she would talk when she felt up to it, so they proceeded all the way to the house without uttering a word.

# 29

Chris was already home from school by the time Cynthia and Thomas arrived. Chris instantly could tell something was wrong, but didn't ask any questions. Cynthia went straight to her bedroom and stretched out on the bed. She laid there for a good while before going back downstairs. Thomas was lounging in the den, watching television. Chris was in her bedroom, listening to music. Cynthia joined Thomas on the sofa and rested her head on his shoulder, as he reached up and stroked her hair. While stoking her hair, he asked if she wanted to talk. She held up her index finger, indicating it was not a good time. When they finished watching the movie, Cynthia raised her head and turned towards him. As soon as their eyes met, tears started streaming down her face.

"Honey, what's wrong?"

Sniffling, snorting, sobbing and babbling, she attempted to tell him what Frank wanted to talk to her about. Through the garbled words, Thomas was able to surmise that Frank was trying to convince Cynthia that Chris was committing the murders.

"I've already made arrangements for the three of us to leave tomorrow night."

"Tomorrow night? That's too quick, don't you think?"

"No, I don't. While I was out today, I arranged for movers to come pack up the house and store your things. The airline tickets have been purchased, all the utilities have been paid in full and scheduled to be disconnected in a few weeks."

"You've thought of everything."

"All you need to do is box up anything you want to ship to New York and the parcel service will be here tomorrow to pick up the boxes."

"I don't have boxes to pack everything I want to take."

"Yes, you do. They're in the garage."

Cynthia grabbed him around the neck and hung on to him for dear life. He expressed his concern and his commitment to her. Chris came bursting into the room asking, "What's going on?"

"We're leaving for New York tomorrow."

"TOMORROW! I need to say bye to my friends and get stuff from school."

"I'll take you to school tomorrow to get your personal things, but you really don't need to say anything to your buddies. We need to leave quietly. You can come back and visit your friends. Do any of them know what happened to you?"

Chris shook her head from side to side, indicating no.

"Chris you need to go upstairs and get everything together that you want to have in New York. Thomas has arranged for our things to be shipped tomorrow."

"I'll go out and get the boxes. You two should start packing."

Chris headed up the steps and Thomas out the door. Cynthia sat quietly on the sofa. *I cannot believe my life, as I know it, is about to be over. I have to start a whole new life, with a whole new way of living. What the hell am I going to do? I really don't have a choice.*

Cynthia rose from the sofa and went to her bedroom. Meanwhile, Thomas was in the garage when Frank pulled into his driveway. Thomas stood back and waited for Frank to go into his house before coming out with the boxes.

After about an hour or so of packing, the doorbell rang. Cynthia opened the door to find Detective Shelton. He wasn't as cold and hard as he'd been the other times they'd spoken, but he obviously had a reason for being there. At the sight of him her heart started racing, her stomach tied in knots, and her face went flush. Other than the color that drained out of her face, she showed no sign that his being there had any affect on her.

"Detective. What brings you here?"

"I have a few questions to ask you."

"About what?"

"Where you were at the time James Mayfield was murdered. May I come in?"

"I'd rather you didn't. Do you expect to be here a while? I was in New York."

Even, though the detective wasn't grilling her as he had before, she shifted into her "bitch" mode, like a lioness protecting her young. He surely didn't need to be in the house and see signs of their leaving.

"Is there something else you need to know?"

He gazed at her for a few seconds and responded with, "No, but I do reserve the right to come back and ask more questions, though."

"Fine. Drop by anytime."

She smiled and closed the door before he could turn. *Come back anytime you son-of-a-bitch. We won't be here.*

When she returned upstairs, Chris and Thomas were waiting at the top of the steps.

"What was that all about?"

"That was the detective working the murder cases. He wanted to know where I was at the time of James' death."

"That's all he asked?"

"Yeah. He came all the way to my house to ask what he probably already knows."

"I think we should have your things shipped somewhere other than New York. You should not be tracked to New York. At least if we throw the trail off a bit it will bide us some time. I'm going to change our flight reservations, too. We'll fly into Philly or D.C. and I'll have someone meet us there and drive us to New York. This way the trail will stop in either of those places and you'll be like a needle in a haystack."

Cynthia sat down on the steps with her head in her hands. Chris joined her, wrapping her arm around her shoulders.

"Mom, I am so sorry I caused so much trouble."

"You didn't cause the trouble. The rape wasn't your fault. I just wish you had said something earlier. We could have done something about it then."

"I was scared, and if I hadn't been out late at night and dressed to look like you, it probably wouldn't have happened. Since I don't know who the man was, I'm afraid he's going to get me again."

Thomas could see the pain they both were in, so he stepped in and reassured them that he would see that they would be okay. Chris and Cynthia were glued to the spot on the steps. Cynthia felt all her energy drain from her body, making her lightheaded. Cynthia hadn't noticed the tears streaming from Chris' face, but when Chris sniffled, she caught her attention. She rubbed Chris' back, giving her a sense of security.

"Cynthia, I know neither of you have a lot of energy, but we are under the gun. We have to get things in order. Before you unhook the computer, I'll print up mailing labels."

Cynthia nodded and she and Chris mustered up enough energy to get going again. Cynthia's focus was on packing what they would be taking. The movers would pack everything else and ship it, so that stuff wasn't a concern.

"I'm finished printing up mailing labels and it dawned on me that you shouldn't take the computer. You should probably shut down your Internet service, too. Chris will be tracked in a heartbeat through the computer. Tomorrow you need to go to the bank and pull out all of your cash, rather than transfer any. Also, cut up the debit card. You'll need to use cash or my credit cards for a while. The biggest hurdle will be getting Chris into school. Her records have to be transferred so I haven't figured out how we get around that."

"I know you don't want me to tell anyone that we're leaving, but I have to at least tell Ardelia. I should do a change of address on my investment accounts and creditors. I will need to use her address to keep any of it from following me."

"Understood, but why don't you set up a post office box and give Ardelia the key? That may take some of the pressure off of her and it'll take a little while before anyone trying to locate you will realize that Ardelia is picking up your mail."

"Good idea. I'll have lunch with her tomorrow, but I won't tell her where we're going."

Three a.m. they were almost done. Chris crashed out on her bed about midnight. Thomas stuck with Cynthia until everything they needed to take was packed. They showered then crashed too.

## 30

**D**ry and unenthused, Cynthia opened her eyes to the morning sun shining through the window. She turned to find that Thomas wasn't in the bed. She walked down the hallway to Chris' room and she wasn't there, either. At this point she was beginning to feel nervous and anxious. She grasped the handrail on the stairway tightly, as she took short, slow steps down the stairs. Once at the bottom, she heard voices in the kitchen. She turned and crept in that direction. She was coming to the realization that she would be creeping around a lot in the days and months ahead. She really needed to get a grip on how to handle the transition, but this situation was even distressing for her. She rounded the corner to find Thomas and Chris sitting at the kitchen table talking.

"Good morning, you two."

"Hey, Mom. You sure slept a long time."

Thomas got up from the table and ushered her to his seat. He kissed her on the cheek and poured her a cup of coffee.

"Want some breakfast? I can scramble you an egg and fix you some French toast."

Her listless and lethargic body hadn't quite gotten into gear. She waved him off, indicating she didn't want anything to eat, lit a cigarette and took a big gulp of her coffee.

"I don't do morning well, but thanks for asking. How long have you guys been up?"

"I've been up about three hours and Chris came down about an hour ago."

"I have so much to do. Why did you let me sleep so long?"

"I know you needed the rest, so I let you sleep. I already have everything that we're taking stacked at the front door ready for pick up. All you have to do is take care of your financial business and take Chris to school."

"You are incredible. What didn't you think of?"

Thomas gave a quick wink and headed upstairs. Chris was already upstairs and in the shower. Cynthia finished her coffee and went upstairs to dress.

Cynthia and Chris left to take care of business. Thomas stayed behind to greet the parcel service. When Cynthia went to see Ardelia, it seemed to be one of the hardest talks they'd ever had. Ardelia couldn't understand why Cynthia would just pack up and leave. She had a number of questions, but Cynthia couldn't answer them without revealing the rape. Chris desperately wanted to keep it secret. Cynthia gave Ardelia the key to the post office box and the keys to her house. She needed her to be there when the movers arrived, and there was no one else who could do it. They hugged tightly, not wanting to let go. When they broke their embrace, Cynthia kissed Ardelia on the cheek, and turned to walk away without looking back. If she were to look at her friend for too long, she may not be able to leave. They had been friends for better than twenty years, and their bond was very strong. Having to break away was hard for both of them. Ardelia stood in a state of shock. She knew her friend well enough to know that something critical was going on, but she wasn't going to apply pressure to find out. She didn't move from the spot where she was standing until Cynthia and Chris were out of sight.

Three o'clock and time was ticking fast. Their flight was scheduled to leave at nine-forty, but they were less than an hour from the airport. Cynthia and Chris returned home to find the boxes gone and Thomas asleep on the sofa. While he was sleeping, Cynthia fixed a bite to eat, while Chris went to her room to catch a nap.

Cynthia was enjoying her quiet time while she cooked. In and out of the refrigerator, she started throwing unnecessary stuff in the trash. Cleaning the refrigerator was not one of her favorite chores, but it seemed to be therapeutic at this moment. The aroma of the fish and spaghetti awakened Thomas from his sleep. He entered the kitchen with a smile and a hearty appetite. Cynthia woke Chris and the three of them ate together.

The closer the time came for them to leave made each minute harder and harder to face. Their lives would never be the same, and Cynthia wondered if they would really be able to escape.

Six-thirty came so fast Cynthia didn't have time to think, and surely no time to change her mind. When the doorbell rang, she jumped like a jackrabbit. A look of concern swept across her face. Thomas put her at ease by letting her know it was probably the taxi. He opened the door and pointed to their bags. While the cabbie loaded the bags in the car, Cynthia gave the house a once over, making sure she had everything she planned to take. *Boy, just as I thought I had a new beginning here, it ended before it got started good. I hope this journey will end up better than this.*

"Cynthia, it's time to go, honey" Thomas yelled from the bottom of the steps. Chris stood at the foot of the steps looking up for her mom. Cynthia emerged with grace and dignity. She refused to drop her head and leave in shame. She held her head high and proceeded down the steps.

They loaded up in the taxi, and left for the airport.

# 31

The wind blew and the rain beat down on the windows. A ferocious storm at three a.m. in New York City was not very welcomed by Cynthia. It seemed as though every time it stormed, or rained hard, Cynthia had flashbacks of the night Jordan died. The sound of the rain pounding against the window caused her to snuggle up closely to Thomas. She asked him to peak in and see if Chris was okay. He returned, informing her that Chris was sleeping as sound as a bear. He wrapped her up next to him, giving her the comfort she needed. Although his embrace should have reassured her that everything was all right, she couldn't seem to find the peace she needed. Maybe the pressure of all the things going on in their lives was far more than she wanted to deal with. She really thought that the move to New York would be the cure for her blues. Not even a full day, and she didn't have a warm and fuzzy feeling about this new life.

Time ticked away and morning finally came. After the wicked storm, Cynthia welcomed the sunlight. As she wiped her eyes to focus, she awakened to an empty bed. Just as the day before, Cynthia found Thomas and Chris in the kitchen. Again, they allowed her the consideration to sleep late.

The housekeeper, Melissa, entering the kitchen, asked Cynthia if she'd like breakfast. Cynthia declined, wanting only coffee and a cigarette. Cynthia lit a cigarette and sipped her coffee while Chris and Thomas ate. Thomas struck up a conversation designed to make plans for the day.

"What do you two want to do today? I figured I could take you out shopping and get a few new things. How's that sound?"

Chris grinned from ear to ear. What teenager doesn't want to shop? Chris and Cynthia were the "Shopping Queens." Thomas didn't know what he was getting himself into, shopping with the two of them. Cynthia had impeccable taste, so what he would have to buy her would surely put a significant dent in his wallet. Chris on the other hand, just wanted "stuff" and didn't care what it cost. They agreed to go shopping for the day. By the time they made it back to their bedrooms, the beds were made, and the bedrooms nicely tidied up. They dressed and headed out to Manhattan.

"Chris, don't you have enough stuff yet? I think you should put a halt on any more spending."

"Ma just let me get some jewelry and I'll be set, all right?"

Cynthia looked at Thomas for his approval. Thomas told Chris to get whatever she wanted, which was fine with Cynthia who hadn't purchased anything, being considerate.

They found Chris some jewelry, then happened upon a quaint little furniture store, which Cynthia convinced Thomas he had to visit.

"My place is fully furnished. Why are you looking at furniture?"

"For just that reason. It's your place. There's nothing in there that has my touch."

"Honey, you've only been there for a day. You'll have plenty of time to add your touch to the place."

Somehow, Cynthia didn't feel that she'd ever get to add her touch. She was determined to make it happen quickly. Not only was she feeling like a fish out of water, but not being able to really call Thomas' place home was getting the best of her. He was trying in his own way to make her feel comfortable, but she felt more like a guest than a partner. Never mind the fact that she was a control freak, and not used to someone else calling the shots. She was itching to control the situation, but Thomas was much too in control to let her take the reigns. As soon as he told her that she'd have plenty of time to add her own touch, she believed in her mind that was his way of politely saying no. Although irritated, she affectionately squeezed his hand, looked about the store briefly, and left without making a purchase. They inched their way up and down the streets of Manhattan, Chris still tickled pink with what she had, and Thomas continually picking out garments for Cynthia. Everything he wanted to buy for her, she declined. She gave one of those half-cocked, "kiss my ass" kind of smiles, and muddled her way through the day.

Thomas was beginning to feel the strain of her attitude, and thought a bite to eat might ease some of the 'tude. That wasn't going to happen.

As Thomas ordered lunch, Cynthia abruptly excused herself. Thomas ordered for her anyway, as he and Chris sat and talked. When the food arrived, Cynthia hadn't returned, prompting Thomas to send Chris to the ladies' room to see why Cynthia was taking so long. Chris returned to the table, informing Thomas that her Mom wasn't in the ladies' room. Thomas was a bit concerned, but knew scouring

Manhattan to find her probably wasn't the most prudent thing to do. Chris, on the other hand, knew her mom was pissed, and realized she just needed time to herself. She wasn't the least bit concerned, and dived right into her food. Thomas sat picking at his, managing to eat some of it. When the waiter returned to the table, Thomas asked him to box up Cynthia's food. He returned to the table with the food and the check, as Cynthia was coming through the door. She strolled to the table with packages in hand. Even though she had her smile back, and her bounce was back in her step, she was only hiding her feelings. She needed to prove her independence. *Fucker. How dare he try to control me? I don't need his ass to buy my fucking clothes. I can still buy whatever the hell I want, without his approval.*

"What's all this?"

"I saw an outfit in the window of the store a few doors down, and I wanted to check it out. I tried it on, and loved it, so I bought it."

"There's more than one outfit in all those bags. Why didn't you get any of the things I was trying to buy for you?"

"Once I saw the outfit, I thought about it even as we came into the restaurant. While you were ordering, I had an urge to have it, so I bought it before I changed my mind." *Don't question me, motherfucker. I didn't ask you to buy it for me, asshole.*

"Oh, I see."

"Mom, what else did you get? Let me see."

"Girl, I'm not going to take my things out of the bag in here. I'll show you when we get to the house."

"I've paid the bill, so if you are ready to go, we can."

Cynthia reached down, picked up her bags and started for the door. Chris and Thomas followed a few steps behind. Once on the sidewalk, Thomas asked if they wanted to go anywhere else.

"I'm ready to go back to your place and relax."

Cynthia intentionally said, "your place" to irritate him. She was waiting to see what the response would be. He picked up on what she was doing, but decided not to feed into it.

"It's your place, too."

Cynthia grunted and walked on ahead.

When they entered the house, they found that Melissa had prepared dinner. The aroma of spaghetti and garlic bread filled the house. Food was the last thing on Chris' mind. She had to go to her room and lay out her new duds. She pulled on Cynthia to go with her, so she could see what she'd bought too. Cynthia laid across the bed, while Chris took everything out of the bags. Cynthia wasn't the least bit interested in looking at new clothes, but she knew Chris was excited, so she stayed. After Chris checked everything out, she lay next to Cynthia and the two of them fell asleep. An hour or so later, Thomas appeared in the doorway of Chris' room. He observed them as they slept, wondering how things were going to turn out. The attitude Cynthia had earlier triggered concern for him, but in spite of what she may have been thinking, he really wanted this situation to work out. Of course, Thomas wanted to be the one in control. Cynthia, peaking through one eye, noticed Thomas standing in the doorway. She pretended to be asleep to avoid a conversation with him. The gnawing feeling she had the first night there wouldn't let up. Her gut said something wasn't right, which ultimately played tricks with her thoughts. She'd learned from past experiences to pay close attention to gut feelings. Although Thomas had ridden in on his white horse and saved them, Cynthia had not settled in comfortably. Something within her said she had made a poor choice. Thomas left the doorway and returned to his study.

This left Cynthia to her own thoughts... *"What have I done?*

*Did I react too quickly to Thomas' offer? I really think I should have thought this through before packing up and leaving my life behind. Chris and I could have dealt with this alone. It was too damn convenient for him, and the relationship was too new, to start a new life with this man. Now that my daughter has been raped, I really don't want to trust a man around her, especially someone I barely know. Fine damn time for me to start thinking rationally. We're here now, and I need to make the best of it. Maybe I'll go out this week and see what the job market is like. I have enough money to live on for a while, but I need a steady income so that I don't drain myself of what I have put aside. I will not allow this man to control me. I damn sure won't sit back and put myself in a position to have to ask him for everything. I need to get out and learn the city. There's not enough time left in the school year to worry about enrolling Chris now. Her grades will carry her through the few weeks left in school. That gives us time to learn more about our surroundings.*

Cynthia's movement when she sat up on the edge of the bed caused Chris to wake up. They both sat for a few moments, getting their bearings before going downstairs. Chris went straight to the kitchen, following the aroma of the food that still lingered in the air. Cynthia had decided to make the best of this situation until things could change. She crept into the study with Thomas, sat on his lap and draped her arms around his neck.

"What's that for?"

"I was a little nasty earlier, and I just wanted to apologize for being such a bitch."

*I can deal with your ass until I can do something different. I'm going to be the sweetest, little lady, you've ever met.*

"I knew this would be challenging for you, but I didn't expect you to handle it so badly. I know you'll snap out of it in time, but please give it a chance."

"I can, and will. Just hang in there with me, okay?"
Thomas placed both of his hands on each side of her face and softly kissed her. Like most men, he believed that kissing, hugging and love making always made everything all right. The soft, sensual kiss was beginning to get rather heated, and as Chris entered the room, they had to relax a bit.

"Excuse me, are you guys going to eat?"

Slightly embarrassed, Cynthia replied, "Yes, we're going to join you."

Chris turned and left the room as quickly as she appeared. Thomas and Cynthia burst into laughter. "Busted", Cynthia whaled. They walked out of the room, slightly bent over, still laughing.

Melissa came in to clean up the kitchen, after everyone had eaten. Chris was dying to call Lolly, but knew her mother would have an issue with it, so she went to her room to watch a movie. She was really bored, not having her girls around to "kick it" with. She was hoping to meet someone she could hang out with, but if they didn't get out of the house she would never meet anybody. Even though she was from Chicago, she wasn't all that comfortable with going out to meet people in New York. New York was like being in the middle of a movie that was going too fast. She figured going out and sitting on the porch couldn't be too bad. She took a book and sat on the porch. It was still light enough not to be afraid, plus she knew Thomas, Cynthia and Melissa were right inside. As she sat reading, a couple of teenagers walked past the house. They looked up on the porch, but never acknowledged Chris. A few moments later, about four other teenagers joined the two that had passed the house earlier. They stopped in front of the house, but said nothing to Chris. They were carrying on a conversation amongst themselves. Chris curiously observed them then decided to speak.

"Hi." She threw up her hand and waved as she spoke.

The kids slowly turned to look at where the voice was coming from. There were four teen boys, and two girls. One of the girls spoke back, made several steps towards the house and the others followed. Chris stood to receive them. Up on the porch, they all struck up a conversation. They all were in the same age group, so they seemed to have the same interests. Of course, they had many questions for Chris, such as, where she was from? What school would she be going to? What made her move there? And so on. Chris was enjoying the company, but definitely didn't want to reveal why they had left Chicago. An hour or so had passed when Melissa appeared at the front door. Dusk had begun to fall, and she didn't want Chris outside when it became dark. She told Chris to come in the house within the hour. Chris gave her attitude, and hesitantly agreed. When the time came for her to go in, the others suggested they come by tomorrow and show her around the neighborhood. She was thrilled to have met some people her own age, to make the transition a little easier.

Once Chris was in the house, Melissa tried to coach her on how to best deal with the new kids from the neighborhood. Chris politely informed her she wasn't a baby, and didn't need her to tell her anything. Melissa was irritated that this child had such a smart mouth, but also knew that came with the territory. She knew that kids at that age were trying to find themselves. She had a grown daughter who had already taken her down that path. She grunted "Uh huh" and retired to her bedroom. Chris went to tell her mother and Thomas about meeting the other kids, but when she turned the doorknob to their bedroom, the door was locked, and the sounds coming from the room suggested she not interrupt. She went on to her bedroom to read. Several hours later, she still hadn't been able to fall asleep, picked up the phone, then returned the receiver to it's base. She picked it up again and began dialing. After the second ring, she decided that calling Lolly probably wasn't the best thing to do, so she hung up. Moments later, the phone rang and Chris answered.

"Chris?"

Silence filled the air as Chris was unable to speak. She wanted desperately to talk to her friend, but her mother would be upset to find out that she'd called her. The agreement was to wait a while until they got everything under control. Chris justified answering as she picked up the ringing phone.

"This is Chris."

"Girl, I'm so glad you called."

"You just called me."

"You called first, and I got the number from the caller ID."

"I wasn't supposed to call, so you can't tell anyone that we've spoken, all right?"

"All right. So how's it going?"

"I don't know yet. I haven't been here long enough to say. We went shopping, and I got some new gear, and I just met some new kids on the block, but it ain't Chicago."

"I really miss you. I wish you were here. When are you coming back?"

"I don't know."

"Why did you guys just pack up and leave so fast anyway?"

"My Mom wanted to be with this man, girl. They are kickin' it and she wanted a new start."

"Ah, so why couldn't you call me?"

"I hear someone coming down the hall. I gotta go. Don't call me, I'll call you. Bye."

*Whew...that was close. I want to tell my friend what's going on. I don't like living like a spy just 'cause I was raped. I'm the one who wanted to get away...only because I was afraid the rapist would get me again. I didn't think I'd have to live in seclusion and not be able to have a normal life. Damn, what have I asked for this time?*

She pulled the covers over her head then drifted off to sleep.

# 32

Ring, ring, ring…

"It's nine-thirty in the morning. Who the hell would be ringing the doorbell this early on a Saturday morning?"

"Huh?"

Cynthia punched Thomas in the arm to awaken him. He mumbled a word or two and drifted back to sleep.

"Thomas! Someone is at the door."

"Melissa will get it."

Moments later there were footsteps coming up the steps. After they reached the top, they proceeded passed their bedroom and down the hallway. A few minutes later, two sets of footsteps trailed back downstairs. Cynthia's curiosity caused her to get out of bed and see who was in the house. She went downstairs to find Chris and six teenagers chillin' in the family room. Moments later, Thomas came to check out the visitors.

"Hello. Who's this, Chris?"

"Hey, Mom. This is Olivia, Michelle, Drew, Joey, D.C. and 'T'." We met yesterday while I was out on the front porch reading.

They want to show me around the neighborhood. Can I go out with them for a while?"

Cynthia gave Chris a worried look, wondering if she was just asking to be polite, or if she really wanted to go. She figured she'd test the waters a bit before saying yes. Naturally Cynthia wasn't thrilled about her daughter, who'd just recently been raped, leaving with people Chris didn't really know.

"I had some plans for us today. Maybe you guys could go another day."

One of the girls looked over at Chris and shrugged her shoulders. D.C., the most extroverted of them all, chimed in, "I just live a few houses down. My mom and dad are home if you want to meet them."

This gave the others a comfort level to speak.

"Here's my telephone number. You can call my folks now. They're both at home," added Olivia.

"Boy, you guys are chomping at the bit to get Chris introduced to the neighborhood."

Chris still hadn't piped in to add her two cents. Cynthia still didn't know if Chris really wanted to go. Thomas caught on to what Cynthia was trying to do, so he called Chris to the other room, away from her peer group.

"Chris, do you want to go with them, or would you rather we keep you from going?"

"I'm a little uncomfortable, but I want to make new friends. If I don't go, they'll think I'm a baby and they might not want to hang out with me anymore. We're going to be within walking distance, so I guess I'm cool with going."

Thomas joined Chris as they returned to the living room.

## Deadly Choices

He and Cynthia on the same accord, he took the lead, and Cynthia followed. After Chris agreed to go, she raced upstairs to shower and dress. Thomas sat and entertained the kids, while Cynthia went to the kitchen for coffee and a cigarette. Melissa joined her at the table. The look on Melissa's face gave Cynthia reason for concern.

"What's that look for, Melissa?"

"I don't think much of those kids."

"They all come from pretty good homes around here, right?"

"Yes. What's your point? A nice house and decent parents don't guarantee you to be great teenagers."

"I guess you have a point. Teens will be teens."

"You should keep an eye on them, and so will I."

"Fair enough. I really need you to help me through this transition, Melissa. This is very difficult for me, so as much coaching as you can provide, I'd appreciate it."

Melissa began to tidy up the kitchen, while Cynthia puffed on cigarettes. Chris entered the kitchen to let Cynthia know she was leaving. Cynthia's eyes bugged when she saw Chris in the outfit she'd chosen to wear.

"Why are you showing your belly, legs and arms? You have left nothing to the imagination."

"Ma it's hot already, so you know it's going to get hotter. We're not going to be in a nice, air conditioned car. We'll be walking up and down the streets."

"Yep, and you look like a street walker. We need to talk."

Cynthia grabbed Chris by the arm and led her upstairs, using the back stairway.

"Chris, did you forget the primary reason we left Chicago?"

"No."

"Why! Why did we leave?"

"Cause I was raped. Do you have to keep reminding me?"

"Obviously, I do. The way you're dressed right now only causes someone else to think along those same lines."

"Awe, Ma, that's not true."

"I'm sorry. I just don't want anything else to happen to you. Forgive me for how I reacted, but please cover yourself just a little."

"All right Mom. Good looking out."

Chris changed her top and came down the other flight of stairs into the front room. Cynthia winked her approval, and all the kids rose to leave. Cynthia and Thomas stood in the doorway until the teens were no longer in sight. Cynthia stormed to the kitchen and paced like an anxious kid on Christmas Eve. Her life was filled with nothing but issues to contend with. At every turn, there was something significant to deal with. She honestly thought she was way past all the bullshit life had to offer. She truly believed that she had endured as much as any person could in a lifetime. The sheer fact that she'd gotten out of Uncle Bobby, and Aunt Lucille's wicked ass house with half her wits about her was amazing. She figured after escaping the nonsense of that household, everything else would be a downhill ride. Guess not.

Thomas walked up behind her and kissed her softly on the back of her neck. She wasn't responsive at all, obviously in never - never land. Thomas put his best move on her, but still no reaction. She couldn't quite grab hold of one situation, and work it through, before she was hit with another. Overwhelmed was a mild assessment when Cynthia added this to the turbulence going on in her life. She knew if she didn't gain control quickly, the turmoil would surely bring her to destruction. Sharon and Vanessa had already attempted to destroy her in Chicago. She was determined not to let anything or anyone bring

## Deadly Choices

her down. *I guess it's time to put on my best performance. I cannot crumble and have Thomas believe I am this weak, pitiful, powerless, needy little morsel who needs to be saved. I don't mind if he stands up and holds his place as the man, but I will not be dismissed as his little lady. I have worked too hard to allow myself to be reduced to an insignificant piece of ass. So far he's fucked me, taken me shopping and fed me. That's no more than he'd do for a call girl. Hell, he won't let me buy furniture for this fucking, overly masculine den of testosterone. I was so excited to have met someone who knew which fork to use at dinner. He was funny, classy and let's not forget he's damn good in bed. Huh, I guess I forgot to check out what would drive me crazy. He's a control freak, I'm a control freak and we're going to drive each other nuts! Nah, he'll drive me nuts 'cause as much as I hate that he's strong, that's what I love about him, too. I guess since Chris is out for awhile, I could hang out in the bed with Thomas. If I keep him sexually satisfied, he will believe I'm one hundred percent into this fucked up decision I made.*

"Cynthia. Cynthia, CYNTHIA!"

The volume of Thomas' voice brought her back to reality.

"Yes, honey. What are you screaming about?"

"Although you were standing right here, you clearly were somewhere else. I wanted to take advantage of having some alone time with you this morning."

"Wanted?" Cynthia responded, with a raised brow and a smirk on her face.

"I said wanted 'cause I couldn't seem to get next to you."

She took him by the hand, led him to the bedroom, pulled him close and began to seduce him. The seduction was her way of suckering him into her web. She needed to be able to manipulate the relationship, allowing him to believe he was in control. She pleasured him in ways he'd never been pleasured. Before it was all over, she had taken him to a place he didn't want to return from. Once she knew he was there, she turned it off, and left him alone. As he begged for more, she slid out of bed yearning for more herself, but very aware of what she'd done. Thomas was not fooled by any of this, and made a mental note to always stay ahead of her.

He rose from the bed and joined her in the shower. Cynthia jumped out as soon as he stepped in. She peeked around the shower curtain to grin at him. They both let our hearty laughs, only they each had a different reason for laughing. Cynthia slipped on a knit jogging suit to sit on the front porch. Not long after, one of Thomas' buddies came over to visit. Cynthia invited him to sit on the porch and asked Melissa to get Thomas, who came down about ten minutes later.

"Hey, Curt. Man, I haven't seen you in a long time. What brings you by?"

"I was in the neighborhood and thought I'd stop. I didn't know you had a little lady living with you now."

*Here it goes...little lady, little lady my ass. I am not his fucking little lady. You big fat, funky, onion head critter.*

Cynthia's thoughts made her laugh out loud. Thomas and Curt looked at her, each with a puzzled look on their face.

"Neither of us said anything funny, what are you laughing about?"

"I'm sorry I wasn't paying attention to you guys. I was thinking about something else."

Curt and Thomas continued to talk, reverting as far back as their childhood. After Curt mentioned where they lived growing up, Thomas immediately redirected the conversation. Although Cynthia

## Deadly Choices

wasn't totally engaged in their conversation, she noticed when Thomas changed the subject, which aroused her curiosity. She attempted to ask questions, but before Curt could answer, Thomas interrupted and redirected the conversation once again. Cynthia decided to observe, rather than talk. Her eyes shifted back and forth, watching every move. Thomas could feel her vibe, which made him slightly uncomfortable.

"Curt, wanna go out for a drink?"

"Yeah, man. It's been a long time since we've done that together."

Cynthia squirmed in her seat wondering if she'd be invited to go. Even though she didn't want to, she knew if he didn't ask, she would be offended. Thomas stood then walked into the house. She figured at that point that she wouldn't get invited. A few minutes later, Thomas returned to the porch in a sport jacket with his wallet in his hand. He leaned over, kissed her on the forehead and informed her he'd be home later. Curt shrugged his shoulders and bid her a pleasant farewell.

After the men were out of sight, Cynthia went inside to pick Melissa's brain. While Melissa cleaned the kitchen, Cynthia began her inquisition. She discovered that Melissa had worked for Thomas for better than fifteen years, and figured she would know as much about him as anyone. During the course of the conversation, she learned that Thomas grew up in Chicago. Melissa, thinking she'd said too much, became cautious. Although Cynthia thought it best to put on the breaks with her inquiry as well, Melissa was fully engaged and willing to tell everything she knew. She took Cynthia by the hand and led her to a storage room inside one of the guestroom closets. She pointed out a couple of boxes which stored some childhood memorabilia. Melissa winked at Cynthia as she left the closet. Cynthia sat on a stool in front of one of the boxes, a bit apprehensive and fearful of what she might discover. As she placed her hand on one of the boxes, she heard Melissa carrying on a conversation.

"Hello Chris! What brings you all back so soon?!"

The volume in Melissa's voice was at least four times her normal tone, an indication to Cynthia that they were no longer alone in the house. Cynthia scurried out of the closet and into her bedroom.

Olivia, Michelle, Drew, D.C. Joey and "T" had all come back with Chris, and decided to watch movies. Chris came upstairs to let her mom know they were going to hang out at the house. Chris noticed Cynthia was in a far off, distant mood. She was willing to tell her new buddies that they couldn't stay, but Cynthia encouraged her to go back downstairs and have fun. Although a bit hesitant, Chris returned downstairs. During the course of the movie, Chris, preoccupied with concern for her mom's mood, accidentally changed the channel on the T.V. The timing was perfect. The face on the television was her mom's favorite T.V. character. She jumped to her feet and yelled up to Cynthia, "Mom! Mom! Come down here quick."

Startled by the sound of Chris' voice, Cynthia scrambled to get out of her bedroom. As she approached the top of the steps, Chris yelled once again.

"MOM! Stringer Bell is on the T.V.!"

Cynthia's heart fluttered, as she desperately attempted to get to the television set. She was so flustered it hadn't dawned on her there was a television set in her bedroom. Just as she took her first step, her haste caused her socks to slip on the hardwood floor and...boom, boom, boom, boom, boom, bam. She got downstairs, but not quite the way she'd planned. The group of kids looked at each other for a split second, then dashed to the staircase, where they found Cynthia stretched out at the bottom of the steps. They all wanted to burst into laughter, but didn't think they should. Cynthia lightened the moment by asking, "Is Stringer Bell still on?" She cracked a smile and said, "He'd better be after all I went through to get down here." Quietly, everyone walked back to the family room.

"All right...he's still on!" She walked up and kissed the television set, turned to the kids and said, "You can laugh now." Since no one wanted to laugh first, Cynthia did, and she was laughing so hard, she almost wet her pants. She flopped onto the sofa, and the kids followed suit. They were all hysterical at that point. The noise aroused Melissa, so she came in to see what was going on. Cynthia told the story, and made her sit until another scene came on with Stringer.

"Oh, he's hot mama mia! I'd fall down the steps for him, too! What's this show about?"

"Hell, I don't watch it for the storyline. I just get a Stringer fix and I'm satisfied. Talk about eye candy. A glaucoma patient could save money...a glance of Stringer will clear up the vision for sure. She sang softly, with her foot dangling from the sofa...Um, um Um, um good, that's what Stringer Bell is, Um, um good. Damn!"

Melissa trailed closely behind Cynthia as they left the room. When Cynthia reached for the staircase handrail, Melissa tugged on the back of her top, and whispered informing her she'd left the light on in the storage room.

"You should make sure you never leave the light on in there, and always put everything back exactly the way you found it. The Mr. notices anything out of place."

"Does he go in there much?"

"He didn't before you moved in, but I know how protective he is of those things. He's very secretive, so be careful when you snoop."

Melissa pealed off towards the kitchen, as Cynthia made her way up the steps. Halfway up, she heard the front door open. As Thomas closed the door he noticed the kids in the family room. Unconsciously he shot them a stern look. As a long time bachelor, he wasn't accustomed to a house full of people. Cynthia, observing from the steps, found Thomas' demeanor unacceptable.

*I thought he was classy and polished, when in actuality he's an egotistical, controlling, closet gangster.*

Thomas, looking up, noticed Cynthia watching him. He assumed she'd put him on the shit list when he didn't invite her to go out with him and Curt. However, Cynthia had made it up in her mind to be the loving, attentive little lady he expected her to be. In the meantime, she couldn't let on in any way that she was suspecting of any ill will on his part. She sat on the steps, welcoming him into her arms, as he kneeled in front of her, softly kissing her lips. Olivia, Michelle, Drew, Joey, D.C. and "T", had decided to leave and stood in the hallway, watching Cynthia and Thomas kiss. Cynthia opened her eyes to an audience. She broke free of the kiss asking, "Why are you people looking at us?" Without a response, they turned and quickly made it to the door, shouting goodnight as they left. Chris locked up then followed the aroma coming from the kitchen. Thomas and Cynthia decided to eat as well. The three sat, ate and conversed for a while, then, shortly thereafter, turned in for the night.

Regardless of Cynthia's suspicions of Thomas, she couldn't get enough of him. She wanted him in the worst way. Fortunately, he was very receptive to her aggression. She took advantage of him, since he'd been out drinking most of the day. His ability to be in complete control was slightly impaired, so she did whatever she pleased. Actually, she

# Deadly Choices

got a kick out of watching him try to take control. At every attempt, she poured it on more and more, while observing his reactions. Usually, he sent her to the clouds, but tonight was her turn to return the favor. If he'd never allowed a woman to take over in the bedroom, he would now know the intensity that takes you to your highest peek. "Ummm," he moaned, as she watched his toes curl up. She grabbed hold of his ankles and rocked back and forth. A slap to her backside made her rock faster. Together they reached a point of no return, as they released a sigh of relief.

# 33

Back in Chicago, the partners at the firm were working incredibly long hours to maintain the client base Cynthia left behind. They still hadn't found anyone to replace her, and although they'd interviewed a number of qualified people, couldn't agree on one of them.

Marge was under a lot of pressure getting the interviews scheduled. She worked long hours, with the hope that someone would be hired soon. Although each partner had their own secretary, Marge was charged with the task of working with the employment agency. Without Cynthia, Marge expected her duties to be light. Ha! The old bag was working harder in her golden years, than she had in all her working days. No one wanted to admit it, especially Maurice, but they wanted, no needed Cynthia back in the fold.

Meanwhile, the detectives at the police station were still baffled by the murders. The detectives that arrested Frank were bumbling idiots. Together they couldn't solve their way out of a paper bag. The Dynamic Duo spent countless hours following up on leads and reassessing the evidence. No matter which way they turned it, nothing gave them conclusive evidence of who'd committed the crimes.

    Frank, still very disturbed by his arrest, had taken a leave of absence to get himself together. He visited the police station on a regular basis, to inquire about any progress. He was also on a mission to find Cynthia. Her sudden move made him further believe in his own theory. He was determined to find her and put the pieces to the puzzle together. Finding her wouldn't be as hard as convincing her of his thoughts. The only thing was that he didn't know the first place to look. Her phone records only showed that it had been disconnected, while the final bill was sent to her post office box. He figured Ardelia would know, but knew there was no chance in hell she would reveal Cynthia's whereabouts. He found himself in a maze of disbelief that he was ever accused in the first place, not to mention going through the ordeal of being arrested. Clearing his name and removing the stain on his reputation was top priority. He had no plan or remedy in place, but if motivation and raw nerve were ingredients to the recipe to clear himself, then he was cooking. Actually, Frank had more balls than Cynthia ever gave him credit for. His annoying, pestering ways would undoubtedly be key attributes in his quest. Hell, he was more persistent and fearless than the police seemed to be on this case. He spent every waking moment mapping out possible scenarios. Most of them had a significant flaw or two that would cause the theory to flop. Nonetheless, with every failed attempt to solve these murders, he became more relentless to solve the whole, sickening situation. His long time admiration for Cynthia was rapidly changing to contempt. Frank was on the brink of a meltdown. If he didn't get to her soon, and bring this to closure, the pressure could cause a tidal wave of fury.

    Frank nestled himself deep into his easy chair, hopeful that the answer to the crisis would miraculously fall into the midst of his thoughts. Failing to come up with any answers, he lay his head back to relax a bit. Minutes later it occurred to him that Marge might know how to locate Cynthia. Pondering over how best to approach her, he sat up, covering his face with both hands. He slipped on his shoes and headed for his car. As he stepped onto his porch, Ardelia pulled into Cynthia's driveway.

Unsuspecting Ardelia, didn't have a clue how complicated Cynthia's life had become, and Frank was just as clueless. He didn't know that Ardelia was in the dark. With it in his mind that Cynthia's oldest and dearest friend would be fully aware of everything in Cynthia's life, he approached her very carefully.

"Hey, Ardelia!"

"What's going on, Frank?"

"Missing my girl. Is she going to stay gone forever?"

"Don't know how long she'll be gone."

Frank didn't believe her. Still probing, he added, "Should I keep an eye on things for her? I'd like to touch bases with her. How can I reach her?"

"Don't know, Frank."

*Hmmm, wanna play games, do you?*

"You two know everything about each other. You expect me to believe that you of all people have no idea where she is?"

He struck a nerve with his accusations, but Ardelia didn't feed into it. She gave him a dirty look and repeated her response, "Don't know, Frank." Frank, deciding not to continue to press her, reverted back to his original plan...Marge.

During his half hour drive, he contemplated not going, figuring if he wasn't really prepared, he'd get nowhere with her, either. Instead of turning around, he played questions through his mind and mentally

# Deadly Choices

organized them.

When he approached the reception area, he found it empty, took a seat on the sofa and waited. Nearly fifteen minutes had passed and no one surfaced. As he stood to leave, Marge appeared in the hallway. Her wig was mangy and twisted as usual, but she didn't reek of Ben-Gay for once. She recognized Frank's face, but didn't know him by name. As they got closer, Frank extended his arm to shake her hand. Marge's eyebrows turned inward as her forehead wrinkled, wondering in her mind why he'd be approaching her. Reluctantly, and barely touching his hand, she shook it.

"Hey, Marge, I'm Frank Carter, Cynthia's next door neighbor."

"Yes, what can I do for you?"

"I have misplaced Cynthia's new address and phone number, and I was wondering if I could get it from you."

Marge squinted her eyes and gave him a suspicious look over the rim of her glasses.

"At least you had it to lose. She never gave it to me."

"What's so top secret? Why is it no one will divulge her information? Her best friend Ardelia claims not to know, either."

"I can't answer for her, but as I said, she never gave it to me."

"This is really bizarre, but I've been keeping an eye on her place and really need to touch base with her. Will you please get it from one of the partners?"

"They aren't her partners any longer?"

Frank thought it odd when Marge told him Cynthia was no longer a partner. *This is really getting creepy.*

"So none of you have a clue where she is?"

"If she gave you her reach number then you would know where

she is, yes?"

Frank was busted. The only way for him to save face was to leave, quickly.

"Forget it. Just forget it, Marge."

As she opened her mouth to speak, Frank rushed to the elevator. Marge was confused by Frank's intentions and wanted now, more than ever, to know what was going on with Cynthia.

Once she returned to her desk, she decided to call payroll to see if they'd give her any forwarding information. Since they knew she was Cynthia's secretary, she figured it would be simple.

To her surprise, payroll wouldn't divulge anything. Marge probed and pleaded, but wasn't successful. She briefly pondered over what to do then went back to work.

Frank, on the other hand, was more determined than ever to locate Cynthia. The wheels in his head brought his thoughts to a screeching halt, figuring Ardelia was probably more of a connection than she may have realized. Finding the connection was the problem. He logged on to his computer, hoping to locate Ardelia's address and telephone number. He was successful, so he played around attempting to zero in on Cynthia's forwarding information, efforts which were a complete waste of time. Cynthia and Thomas had closed up everything clean and tight, leaving no trail. The only link to Cynthia was her post office box, and Ardelia was instructed to pick up the mail, and keep it at her house. Frank wasn't certain what to do next.

# 34

Three days later...

"We have now landed in sunny Chicago. The temperature is ninety degrees and the time is four-fifteen. Thanks for flying with us, and we hope to serve you again," the pilot announced over the speaker.

Cynthia was seated in first class, and was the second person to leave the plane. She'd decided on a whim to fly home to Chicago to pick up her mail. She didn't pack a stitch since she was returning to New York that evening.

She hailed a taxi and headed to Ardelia's house, calling Ardelia on her cell phone to let her know she was in town. Ardelia wasn't home, but said she'd meet her there.

Approximately forty-five minutes later, they were locked in an embrace in Ardelia's driveway. After they made their way into the house, Ardelia was grilling Cynthia with questions. After discovering as much as she had about Thomas' past, Cynthia felt compelled to bring her friend into her confidence. They talked for several emotionally exhausting hours, leaving Ardelia blown away by all she'd been told.

She was most concerned about Chris and how she was coping with the rape and the move. Cynthia replied, "Chris has settled in fine, and never mentions the rape. It seems as though the rape was just the tip of the chaotic zone we've entered. My head feels discombobulated with all this unnecessary junk I'm dealing with. I really need your help. Will you help me sort through this?"

"I will do whatever I can."

Cynthia glanced at her watch, realizing she needed to leave for the airport. They grabbed their purses then went to Ardelia's car.

In the meantime, Frank had finally decided what to do. Keeping a watch on Ardelia led him to Cynthia. When he saw the two leaving the house, he couldn't believe he'd stumbled on Cynthia this very day. He hung back, but followed them to the airport. Ardelia dropped Cynthia curbside, and made sure she had all her reach information. Frank didn't want to lose sight of Cynthia, so he chanced a parking ticket and left his car parked at the curb. He trailed her inside to see what flight she'd take. As long as he at least had a destination, he'd be able to track her. The moment he saw her destination, he felt his hopes diminish.

*Shit. New York! She could vanish in New York among all those damn people. I'll have to stick with keeping a close eye on Ardelia.*

Cynthia sat in the waiting area until time to board the plane. She hadn't noticed Frank slinking around. She was more anxious to get back home and set her and Ardelia's plan into motion.

Thomas was lounging on the sofa in the family room. Chris and Melissa were in the kitchen, as usual. Cynthia strolled in as if she'd just been to the grocery store. She barely spoke to Thomas as she passed the family room. She was on a serious mission to bring Thomas' motives for entering her life to the forefront. She reached into her drawer and pulled out a small box that she'd found in Thomas' "secret closet." One of the items in the box was an old black and white picture. It was so old, it was cracked, and the edges had turned a brownish yellow. The picture displayed a man and woman in their late twenties or early thirties, and a young boy about five or six years old. The man and woman looked very familiar, but she couldn't quite put her finger on who they might be. She set the picture to the side while she fumbled through the box. She happened upon a few letters banded together. Slowly she opened one and began to read it. It was three small stationary pages filled with I love you, I miss you, I can't wait to be with you. As she made her way to the end, it was signed, M.W. She wondered about the full identity of M.W.

She read the next letter. This one was as mushy as the first one. It was signed, once again, by M. W. Just as she began to open the third letter she heard someone coming up the steps. She replaced the letters and the picture in the box then returned it to her drawer.

She stepped into the bathroom and turned on the water, washed her face, and when she returned to the bedroom, Thomas was undressing.

"Where have you been all day?" Thomas asked in a stern, dry tone.

"Oh, just out and about, why?"

"Because I wanted to know. Are you going to answer?"

"I just did," she replied in a very nasty tone.

Thomas didn't see any benefit in continuing to question her. By now Cynthia was sitting on the bed in a black lace thong. The sight of her in a thong gave him a hard on. He reached for her, and she immediately responded. They were so involved, no matter what the issues were, nothing ever kept them from having sex.

"Ahhh..." Cynthia sighed.

She wasn't the one in control this time. Thomas had her like putty in his hands. He knew he'd gotten next to her, as he did when they first got together. *Huh, I know how to control your independent ass,* he thought.

"Baby, where were you all day?"

*Yeah, you think 'cause you sexed me so good, I'm under your spell. I'll play. You can't know that I'm on to your deceiving ass, anyway.*

"I, I, I ugh..."

*Got your ass babbling like a baby. Yeah.*

"Go ahead, spit it out." Thomas chuckled.

"I went on a fishing expedition about town."

"A fishing expedition, fishing for what?"

"Oh, checking out my new world. I just wanted to know what I'm dealing with here in the Big Apple. You have to know how hard it was for me to make this move."

"I guess I assumed you would be fine, knowing I had your back."

*You would think that, you hubris, egotistical lunatic.*

"I'm okay with you having my back, but I need to be able to hold my own."

*Play nice. Fuck him again. Maybe he'll stop questioning me. I thought women were the ones who always wanted to talk after sex. Ugh...shut the fuck up!* Her thoughts passing, she rolled over to go another round. That one round turned into an all nighter. The next thing they knew, morning was on the horizon.

Thomas was first to awaken. He slipped on his robe to go get coffee. When he opened the bedroom door, Chris was standing there about to knock. Thomas' robe wasn't closed, so his tattooed chest was

## Deadly Choices

the first thing Chris saw. She swallowed hard, her eyes bulged then she dashed off to her room. Thomas closed his robe then went on to the kitchen. As soon as he was downstairs, Cynthia got out of bed to go check on her daughter.

Chris was curled up on her bed in a fetal position, crying and shaking. Cynthia softly approached asking, "What's wrong?"
Chris shook her head from side to side, indicating "Nothing." Cynthia's maternal instincts told her something else, but she didn't try to force the issue. She sat with Chris for a while to see if she would confess. At that point, Cynthia figured she'd keep a very close eye on her daughter for a while. She was concerned about Chris' emotional stability. She had been dealing with too much drama in the past few months, and it had to be getting to her.

While Thomas and Cynthia were having coffee, Chris entered the kitchen. At the sight of Thomas she dropped her head, and sat at the table close to her mom. Thomas struck up a conversation, but Chris wouldn't engage. Although Cynthia was keeping the conversation alive, she carefully observed Chris. Every time Chris looked up, she instantly looked right back down at the floor. Thomas reached over to push her head up by her chin, but as soon as his fingertip touched her chin, she jerked away and jumped up.

"Don't touch me! Don't touch me!" she yelled. Cynthia jumped up, and wrapped her arms around her.

"What's going on with you? Please talk to me."

Thomas sat calmly, waiting for Chris' response. Chris wasn't stupid and wanted nothing to do with him. She took off running back to her bedroom. Cynthia stood and glared at Thomas for a few moments, then followed Chris. She was able to calm Chris enough to get her to agree to go out for the day. She wanted to get her out of the house to see whether or not Thomas was the threat. From what she had just witnessed in the kitchen, she assessed that he was, but wanted to know exactly what he'd done. They dressed and left the house.

They were out all day. They took in a movie, had lunch, and window shopped. Cynthia tried repeatedly to get Chris to open up, but to no avail. While Chris looked around the store, Cynthia stood in the middle of the floor. She stared as if in a trance, at someone she believed was starring at her. Too stubborn to blink, she stared for quite some time. Chris walked up behind her asking, "What's wrong?" Cynthia went on and on about the rude person staring. Chris looked around, but didn't see who she was talking about. Puzzled and confused, she remarked, "Mom, are you losing it?"

"No, why the hell would you ask me that?"

Chris scrunched her nose, then sarcastically replied, "Cause there ain't nobody staring at you."

Cynthia extended her arm and pointed to the man. Chris looked at the man her mother had pointed to, put her arms around her mother and said, "Mom, you really should wear your glasses."

"Why?" Cynthia asked.

"Mom, it's not a real person staring at you. That's a life sized, cardboard cut out."

They burst into laughter, which they both really needed to do, and left the store, still laughing.
Cynthia had considered getting Chris therapy, but now considered it for both of them.

Now that she'd made a complete fool of herself, Chris seemed to be the stable one. Cynthia shifted her thoughts back to the box with the letters. All the way home, she racked her brain, trying to come up with the name associated with the initials signed on them.

## Deadly Choices

After a full day together Cynthia and Chris arrived home shortly before dark. The house was dark and empty. Neither Thomas nor Melissa was there. Chris went to her room, and Cynthia to hers.

Cynthia's first order of business was to read the remaining letters. The last letter wasn't signed "M. W.", as were the others. It was signed "Big B". That particular letter wasn't mushy at all. It was very matter-of-fact, but the intent was gingerly saying good-bye.

"M. W." and "Big B" were ending their relationship, but how did these two people connect with Thomas?

Cynthia picked through the box, hoping to find something... anything that would tie some of the pieces together. She looked carefully at all of the contents in the box, but nothing pointed anywhere. She tucked the letters and pictures in her purse so she could have copies made the next day. As she went to return the box to the "secret closet," she heard the front door open. She didn't want to chance getting caught in the closet, so without thinking, she slid the box under the bed in the guest room then hurried down the hallway to Chris' room. She and Chris were chatting as Thomas appeared in Chris' doorway.

Chris immediately clammed up. Her mood and demeanor shifted into an extremely, introverted state. Chris was far from being an introvert, so the shift definitely caused concern.

*What in the world could have happened so suddenly between these two, to make my child clam up like this?*

While Thomas stood there with an unbecoming grin on his face, Cynthia got up off the bed to leave the room. Chris trailed her to the door. At the threshold of the doorway Chris closed the door, and locked it so quickly Cynthia had to pull her blouse through the crack. Cynthia began questioning Thomas to better understand what had taken place within the last twenty-four hours. The only answer he was able to give was that Chris had seen him with his robe open that morning. Cynthia assumed that episode may have triggered something about the rape. By locking herself in her room, it was apparent Chris wanted solitude.

Thomas, on the other hand, was acting a bit shady. Cynthia couldn't prove anything, especially if Chris wouldn't open up, but she realized Thomas knew more than he was sharing.

This was one night she had no interest in being intimate with him. As a matter of fact, she didn't want to be in the same room with him. But she knew if she changed drastically, he'd surely know she suspected something.

She showered, found a corner at the edge of the bed, wrapped up tightly in the covers and closed her eyes.

# 35

The next day, Cynthia awakened to an empty bed. She shuffled down the hall to Chris' room, tried the doorknob, but was unable to turn it. She tapped on the door for Chris to unlock it.

Chris asked her to stay until she'd had her shower. Cynthia pulled her arm and pleaded with her to tell her what was going on. While pulling away, Chris quietly responded, "I can't."

Cynthia's heart was breaking and her brain felt like it was going to explode. She had once again gotten herself tangled up in an unhealthy relationship.

Once showered, Chris dressed in the bathroom. She came out completely clothed, causing Cynthia to comment, "What, you have something that you don't want me to see?"

"Naw. It was just quicker to dress in the bathroom."

"Whatever, can I go get my coffee now?"

Chris gave her thumbs up, but was on Cynthia's heels every step of the way.

Melissa cooked enough food for eight people, as always, but Cynthia wasn't interested in eating. Her body felt sluggish and lethargic, like a beat up, old Chevy. A jolt of caffeine, sugar and nicotine was the jumpstart she needed. However, Chris had piled her plate with potatoes, bacon and several pieces of French toast. Whatever was going on with her didn't affect her appetite.

Cynthia didn't ask Melissa about Thomas, but was wondering where he might be. The thought was still lingering when he came into the kitchen, the mere presence of him making Chris unable to swallow her food. Thomas announced that he was going out for the day, which brought a sense of relief to both Cynthia and Chris. Cynthia wanted the freedom to snoop a little more, and Chris just didn't want him anywhere around.

Once Thomas was gone, Cynthia showered and dressed. Chris stayed in the kitchen since she didn't have anything else to do. While she was still pigging out on her food, the doorbell rang. Melissa answered to find Olivia, Joey, D.C., "T", Michelle and Drew. Even though she didn't care much for them, she invited them in. Chris heard their voices and went to the door to greet them. She offered them breakfast before saying hello, since her mouth was stuffed with food. The group declined and invited her to hang out with them. She raced up the steps pleading with Cynthia for permission to go, which after getting, she hurried back downstairs and out the door.

Now that Chris and her crew were gone, Cynthia was free to roam about the house as she pleased. Melissa was too busy cleaning the kitchen, making beds, and tidying up the house to pay much attention to her. Plus, she was her partner in crime since she turned her on to the "secret closet" in the first place.

Cynthia dug into boxes and sifted through pockets of clothes, but still didn't find the meaning of M. W. or Big B. She was determined to make the most of the time she had without Thomas' watchful eye.

## Deadly Choices

She fumbled around in the closet for so long, lunchtime snuck up on her. She put everything back in place like Melissa coached her then went to the kitchen to have some lunch. Melissa was whipping up one of her Mexican specials and the aroma was calling her name. She helped herself to a plate with enough food to feed two people.

"Melissa, I am so stuffed I can hardly move."

"Eat, Mommy, eat it all."

Cynthia lovingly rolled her eyes, knowing if Melissa said eat one more time, she wouldn't be able to move enough to fix another plate. Stuffed like a Thanksgiving turkey, she lit her after dinner cigarette, and had another before heading back to the "secret closet."

She sat on a small wrought iron and satin cushioned bench, trying to decide what else needed to be searched. It was hard to remember what boxes she had already opened and which ones hadn't. *Shit, if I have to come back in here again, I need some sort of system. I can't keep wasting time looking in the same boxes more than once.*

She got up to find a pen or pencil in the guestroom so she could put an unnoticeable mark on the boxes she'd already looked through. She found a pen and returned to the closet. Once again time flew, but just as she was about to give up, the box she was just about to close had a jewelry box with a man's diamond ring that looked to be worth a lot. The jewelry box had three more pictures, as well. She slipped the ring and the pictures into her pocket, put everything back in place, and went to get some fresh air on the front porch. On the way out, she fixed herself a drink and grabbed her cigarettes.

As she enjoyed the evening breeze and watched the sun turn from yellow to orange, Chris and her buddies were coming up the block, causing Cynthia to delay the rest of her search.

*Damn, I won't be able to check out the ring and the pictures until later, now.*

The group of kids were laughing and talking loudly as they approached the porch. Once they were close, Cynthia placed her index finger over her lips to quiet them. Before they could make it onto the porch, Cynthia could smell something burning. Smoke was lingering from her cigarette, but the smell was burnt hair. While trying to quiet the kids, she singed her bangs. She started flapping her hands, fanning her hair, jumping up and down frantically. Chris and her buddies ran to her aid, but naturally there was nothing they could do.

Joey leaned over and whispered to "T". "Every time we come over here something happens to her Mom. She's either accident prone, drunk, or just plain stupid." "T" held in his laughter but, tears began to roll down his face uncontrollably. He bent over holding his stomach, jumped off the porch steps, and ran to the sidewalk. Joey, Drew and D. C. followed while Cynthia, Olivia and Michelle were concerned with what might be wrong. The fellas paced up and down the sidewalk while "T" got himself together. Just when he thought he was ready to return to the porch, Joey said, "She might be stupid, but she's fine as hell." He spoke in a high pitched tone, mocking Cynthia, saying, "Uh, duh, I'm so clumsy and stupid." All the boys started laughing and tears started flowing down "T's" face again. After a few minutes, they returned to the porch. Cynthia asked if everything was all right. The boys composed themselves then sat quietly on the opposite side of the porch.

Cynthia decided to go in and leave them to hang out by themselves. She stopped to fix another drink before going to her bedroom. Sitting on the porch with the ring and pictures in her pocket was driving her crazy. Just before she sat on the bed, she pulled them from her pocket. She examined the ring and found an inscription on

## Deadly Choices

the inside of the band. "Love you forever...M. W." The cut of the three diamonds was flawless. They sparkled so they nearly lit up the room. She placed the ring next to her on the bed as she brought one of the pictures up close to her face. The picture had to be twenty or twenty five years old, but the man in the picture couldn't have been anyone but her Uncle Bobby. Her eyes crossed and she felt light headed. She wiped her eyes with the back of her hand, thinking her vision must have been blurred. The focus on the man was still the same. It was Uncle Bobby! *If this is Uncle Bobby, then who is the woman? It's not Aunt Lucille, so who the hell is it? Better yet, what is Thomas doing with it?* She was more baffled than ever. She put on her glasses to better examine the snapshot. The ring the woman was wearing looked vaguely familiar. *Where have I seen this ring before? Someone I know wears this ring, but who the heck is it?*

In the midst of her thoughts she heard footsteps on the stairs. She scrambled about the room to hide the ring and pictures. As she closed the dresser drawer she turned around to find Thomas standing in the doorway. He seemed to be in a fabulous mood. He wasn't withdrawn and cold as he'd been earlier in the day. He glided into the bedroom, smooth as silk, took Cynthia by the waist, and began kissing her. His passion ran high as he whispered in her ear, "We're alone." Although slightly reluctant, she gave in to her physical desire. While she was physically active her mind was swirling, trying to figure out who the woman in the picture could have been. Before reaching their ultimate peak, Cynthia abruptly stopped moving. She gripped her forehead with palm of her hand. It suddenly became clear.

She pushed Thomas off of her, raced to the bathroom, dropped to her knees and vomited in the toilet. While Cynthia was busy dry heaving, Thomas stepped in the bathroom. As soon as she noticed him, she screamed for him to get out! He hesitated for a second, closed the door and returned to the bedroom.

Cynthia got into the shower, but couldn't stop the flow of tears. She was disillusioned, but more afraid than anything. She pulled herself together to return to the bedroom. She couldn't stomach the sight of Thomas, and had decided while in the shower to leave for a few days. She informed Thomas that she and Chris would be leaving and didn't know for sure when they'd return. Thomas' ego had been wounded by her shouting at him, so he wasn't interested in hearing anything she had to say. He merely sat and observed her moving feverishly about the room. She left the room, returning with her luggage.

After packing for herself, she went to Chris' room to pack her things, too. While she was in Chris' room, Chris came upstairs.

"What's going on, Mom?"

"We need to leave for a few days."

"Why? What's up?"

Cynthia was not in the mood to be questioned. She snapped back at Chris, "Just get your shit so we can get the hell outta here." Chris knew that tone far too well, and knew best not to push. She went to the bathroom to get her toiletries packed.

Their bags were packed and sitting at their bedroom doors while Cynthia made flight arrangements. Unfortunately, the next flight out wasn't until morning. She booked a seven a.m. flight, so they needed to be up and ready to go by four-thirty a.m. That wasn't too bad, since it gave them just a few hours to be in the house.

Thomas was still upset, so he went out drinking. While he was gone, Cynthia called Ardelia. She gave her the scoop and told her she'd be back in Chicago by morning. Ardelia let her know the partners were looking for her and wanted her to get in touch with them.

"I wonder what they want."

"I don't know, but it sounded important."

"Actually, going to the office to see them would be ideal."

"How so?"

"I will fill you in when I get there. Can you get us from the airport please?

"Yep, I'll be there when you land."

Chris and Cynthia hung out in the kitchen with Melissa. Cynthia didn't have much of an appetite, so she puffed on cigarettes while Chris pigged out. Melissa could tell something wasn't right, but didn't pry. She was hoping Cynthia would say something, but she never did.

Chris and Cynthia were returning to their bedrooms as Thomas came through the front door. He was so shit-faced he was stumbling and staggering, bobbing and swaggering his fine, psychotic ass up the steps.

By the time he made it to the bedroom, Chris was barricaded in her room behind a locked door. Cynthia was curled up in the bed, pretending to be asleep. Thomas stripped down to his boxers and flopped onto the bed. Cynthia didn't so much as flinch. They both drifted off to sleep.

# 36

Three-fifteen a.m. the alarm rang, incessantly. Cynthia hit the snooze until three-thirty. She managed to muster up enough energy to slide out of bed and make her way to Chris' room to wake her up.

Cynthia tiptoed around her bedroom to keep from waking Thomas. She and Chris got dressed and the limo driver was waiting in the foyer when they got downstairs. They were able to get out of the house and to the airport without Thomas waking up and interrupting their flow.

When the plane landed in Chicago, Ardelia was standing at the gate. They embraced and immediately started talking. Chris strolled ahead of them, pretending not to be excited, but overjoyed to be back home.

After they arrived at Ardelia's place, Cynthia called the firm. Marge was surprised to hear Cynthia's voice, and transferred her straight to Maurice's office, who made it very clear they wanted her back. They arranged to meet with the other partners to work out the details. Since Chris had gone to the guest room to nap, Ardelia was patiently waiting for Cynthia to hang up the phone. As soon as she did,

## Deadly Choices

Ardelia was all over her with questions.

Cynthia started her tale of woe in a calm, rational tone. As she got further into the dynamics of it all, she started to come unglued. By the time she got to what brought her back to Chicago, she was out of control. She covered her face with both hands, speaking into her palms. Her words were so muffled, Ardelia scooted closer and wrapped her arm around her shoulder. She bent over, attempting to make out what she was saying. Ardelia was getting frustrated by not understanding the drivel, but tried to be patient. She put her hands on each side of Cynthia's face, holding her head steady, and looked directly into her eyes.

"Calm down, Cynthia, so I can understand what you're telling me."

"CALM DOWN! CALM DOWN? I SAID THE PICTURE I FOUND WAS OF MY UNCLE BOBBY AND..."

"And what, Cynthia?" Ardelia pleaded with the utmost of concern.

"AND THE WOMAN IN THE PICTURE IS MARGE!"

"Marge who?"

"The old, Ben-Gay wearing woman I hired to replace Sharon!"

"How'd she know your Uncle?"

"Fuck, I don't know! What was Thomas doing with it, is what I want to know!"

"Are you absolutely sure it's her?"

"The picture is over twenty years old, and she looks a lot different, but the ring she has on in the picture is the same ring she still wears."

"Why don't I go with you to your meeting tomorrow and try to get the scoop from her while you meet with the partners?"

Cynthia and Ardelia had no idea that Chris was awake and roaming around the house until Cynthia said, "I believe that Thomas orchestrated most of the unfortunate bullshit that has been happening to me. I know I've made some bad decisions, but something in me says everything has been manufactured, and it leads back to him."
Chris chimed in.

"MOM, HE'S THE ONE WHO RAPED ME!"

Cynthia and Ardelia froze then Cynthia started gasping for air.

"WHAT... WHAT DID YOU SAY?"

At this point, Chris knew she had flipped the switch on the tracks and the trains were about to collide. She was too afraid to say anything else.

"Chris, talk to me. Why didn't you tell me this before we moved in with him?"
"I DIDN'T KNOW IT WAS HIM UNTIL THE OTHER DAY!"

"A few days ago when you stopped talking, and started locking your bedroom door?"

"Yeah."

"What made you know then?"

"When I came to see you that morning, he was leaving the bedroom and his robe was wide open. I saw the tattoo on his chest, and that's when I knew it was him. I couldn't see his face the night he raped me, but while he was on top of me, his shirt was open, and that's all I saw the whole time he was on me."

"Why didn't you tell me as soon as you realized it was him?"

"He told me the night of the rape that if I said anything, he'd hurt you. Since we were living in his house, I was sure he'd kill you, and I'd be without you, and stuck there with him."

All three of them burst into tears. Cynthia couldn't believe how she'd been fooled by him, and Ardelia was in a state of shock.

When the crying session ended, Cynthia wanted nothing short of castrating him. She knew that wasn't possible, so a kick-ass plan to counter and blow his agenda to high hell became her goal. She figured on forming an alliance with Frank to help pull it off. Ultimately, Frank's name could be cleared in the process, if her instincts were right.

"Chris, I promise you one thing...Thomas is as good as gone. He's history in the worst way."

By now, Cynthia was in a dangerous state of mind. The evening was still young, but neither of them had a desire to go anywhere or do anything. They hung around in the living room, trying to watch television, but it was watching them instead, eventually, going to bed for the night.

# 37

Morning couldn't come fast enough for Cynthia. She was up and dressed by the crack of dawn. She wanted to catch Frank before he left for work, not realizing Frank was on leave, and didn't have to go. Knowing Ardelia wouldn't mind, she took the keys to her car and struck out for Frank's house.

When she arrived, she noticed that no lights were on, assumed she'd missed him, and went into her empty house instead. She moped around, missing what was supposed to be the beginning of a great new life. Instead she'd gotten herself tangled up in what felt like the Twilight Zone." Something led her to her bedroom, where she found a monogrammed handkerchief. The initials were, T. W. A.

*Hmm. Thomas must have left this.* She thought to herself. She tucked it in her purse, and didn't give it another thought.

Moments later, the doorbell rang. Frank came over, expecting to find Ardelia. Before he could ask any questions, Cynthia gave him a brief synopsis of what was going on, and what she needed him to

## Deadly Choices

do. He was all for it, ready and willing to stick it to Thomas. Cynthia rushed to get back to Ardelia's before her meeting with the partners.

Chris and Ardelia were barely awake, and neither was in the mood to deal with the day. Ardelia had to go to drill Marge for answers. With Thomas out of the picture, Chris was fine with staying there alone.

Cynthia and Ardelia left for the office, arriving about twenty-five minutes later. Marge was at her desk when they got off the elevator. She sent Cynthia to the conference room and Ardelia sat in the reception area, about eight feet from Marge's desk. Ardelia didn't want to come across as overly anxious, but was so ready to pounce all over Marge. Instead, she waited and bided her time. Once she noticed a quiet period from the constant ringing of the phones, she began her inquisition.

Surprisingly, Marge spoke very freely, glad that someone had taken an interest in her personal life. She went on and on about where she was from and all the places she had lived. She tearfully mentioned an estranged son, but she hadn't had any contact with him in years. She reached in her desk drawer and pulled out a handkerchief to pat the tears away. When she finished patting her face, she tossed the hanky onto the upper corner of her desk, out of her way.

Now that Ardelia had pumped Marge and gotten all the information she wanted, she talked with Marge a little longer, just for courtesy sake. Ardelia couldn't wait for Cynthia to finish, so they could leave.

Marge's twisted, uncombed wig was driving Ardelia nuts. She had an urge to take it off of her head, comb it, and place it back on her head...straight. She only had to fight the urge for a little while. Cynthia came strutting down the hallway in full stride. Something told

Ardelia that the meeting had gone well, and she couldn't wait to get the details.

Cynthia approached Marge's desk and informed her she'd be rejoining the firm in a few weeks. She didn't stick around for small talk, but jerked Ardelia by the arm and stuck as close to her as a Siamese twin until they were on the elevator. On their way down, she asked Ardelia, "Did you see the handkerchief on Marge's desk?" Cynthia was digging in her purse as she waited for Ardelia's answer.

"Yeah, so?"

"So I found this in my house this morning, and the initials on the both of them are T. W. A."

"Okay, so?"

Getting a little frustrated and annoyed that Ardelia was acting like a mindless four year old, Cynthia snapped, "Thomas Walters Alexander? Does that ring any bells?"

The lightbulb went off in Ardelia's head, as her eyes sparkled with understanding.

"Oh shit! Marge told me she had a son, but said they'd been estranged for many years."

As they stood on the sidewalk in front of the building, Ardelia took the hanky from Cynthia and returned to Marge's desk.

She threw the hanky on Marge's desk, then verbally attacked.

"Marge, I thought you told me you were estranged from your son and hadn't had any contact with him in many years."

"That's correct," Marge replied very calmly.

"What is your son's name?"

"Thomas."

"Are these his initials on both of these hankies."

Marge held both of them in her hands, wondering how the one

# Deadly Choices

she had appeared on her desk weeks ago.

"Yes, they are. His middle name is my maiden name and I took my maiden name back when I got divorced, so we don't carry the same last name anymore."

"He's the man Cynthia left to live with, and we just learned that the sick son-of-a-bitch raped Cynthia's daughter."

Marge's mouth fell open, but before she could say anything, Ardelia stormed to the elevator.

*He swore he'd get Bobby for dumping me after I left my husband for him. Thomas always regretted not having a male role model in the house, but I never imagined he'd go to this extreme for revenge.*

Ardelia jerked Cynthia by the arm to hurry her to the car.

"Girl, Thomas is Marge's son!"

Cynthia's adrenaline ran high, and her heart started beating fast. She laid her head back on the headrest, reaching way back into her memory bank. They rode in silence while Cynthia tried to connect all the dots. Suddenly, it all came together.

"Ardelia! I remember Uncle Bobby and Aunt Lucille fighting about him leaving. She told him he wouldn't get a dime of the money they received to take care of me, and she would see to it that she drained him of everything if he left her. The woman he was leaving her for had to be Marge."

"When I talked to Marge, she said that she left her husband when her son was a young boy, and her son was very bitter and resented her for that."

"I'll bet Thomas is doing all this to get back at Uncle Bobby, but why did he target me and Chris? I'm going to try to reach Uncle Bobby and Aunt Lucille to see if I can get some answers."

They arrived back at the house and Cynthia went straight to

the telephone. The number she'd always had for them had changed and there was no new listing. She hadn't spoken to either of them in a long time, so she didn't know any other numbers to call. She booted up Ardelia's computer, hoping she could track them down on the Internet. After about twenty minutes, she found twelve different matches to the name search in Chicago. She printed them out and started making calls. On the fourth call, someone answered, "Yep." *That's how Uncle Bobby always answered. This man has to be Uncle Bobby.* Cynthia spoke right up, in a less than enthusiastic tone.

"Uncle Bobby?"

"Cynthia?"

"Yes. I can't believe I found you."

"What made you call?" He asked.

"I really need to talk to you and Aunt Lucille."

"What would you need from us after all these years?"

"Uncle Bobby, my daughter and I are in the midst of a horrible situation that seems to be swallowing us up."

"Tell me some details before you get here."

"People close to me have mysteriously died, my daughter was raped, we moved to New York with a man who I thought was going to make everything all right in our lives, only to find out that he's the one who raped my daughter."

"Who is this person?"

"That's what I wanted to talk to you about. His name is Thomas."

"Thomas who?"

"Uncle Bobby, can we just meet and talk this through?"

"Yeah, yeah we can do that. Just tell me his full name."

"Thomas Walters Alexander."

## Deadly Choices

Uncle Bobby damn near collapsed. He told Cynthia that he couldn't see her until later in the week."

"Uncle Bobby, it won't take that much of your time. Can I please come today?"

"No. Later in the week is the best I can do."

Uncle Bobby hung up before Cynthia could respond or confirm his address. She sat and listened to the dial tone for a few seconds before hanging up.

Ardelia came in the room when she heard the receiver slam onto the base of the telephone.

"What's going on?"

"Uncle Bobby won't see me today. He claims later in the week would be better for him."

"Let's just show up at his house tomorrow morning."

"That won't go over too well, but I'm game."

They piddled around the house for the remainder of the day, looking forward to meeting up with Uncle Bobby the next day.

# 38

Traveling down the interstate to Uncle Bobby's, the closer they got the more nervous Cynthia became. She figured by taking Chris along it would be easier for Uncle Bobby to accept their unannounced visit.

However, when they pulled up in front of the rickety, old, run down house, Cynthia couldn't believe her eyes. Even though they didn't treat her very well while she was growing up, they always kept a nice house.

The three slowly made their way to the front door. The wood on the front porch was splintered and rotten. With every step, they thought the floor would give way and they'd go crashing through. They looked for a doorbell, but naturally it wasn't working. They knocked several times, but there was no answer.

Disappointed, they started back to the car. Cynthia kept looking back, hoping someone would appear. As they were closing their car doors, Chris saw a reflection near the front door of the house.

## Deadly Choices

"Look, Mom!" Chris shouted as she pointed to the front door. They all scrambled to get out of the car and back onto the porch. Once there, Cynthia's mouth fell open in shock at what she saw. Aunt Lucille was in a wheelchair with tubes running from her nose and mouth. She motioned to Cynthia to open the door.

Nervous, yet anxious, she opened the door and they stepped inside. Cynthia immediately started talking. She had no idea that Aunt Lucille couldn't speak any longer. She went on and on, explaining her devastating situation, until she recognized Aunt Lucille's unresponsive gaze.

Cynthia dropped to her knees at the foot of the wheelchair. She rubbed Aunt Lucille's hands with an affectionate massage. She told her she'd ask yes or no questions, and to blink once for yes, and twice for no. Her last few questions made her know that Uncle Bobby was gone. He'd packed some bags and left the day before. Cynthia asked if she could look around the house and did so with Aunt Lucille's permission. All of his clothes were gone, but fortunately she found some papers that tied him to Thomas. She tucked them away in her purse and returned to the living room.

Cynthia still had bitter feelings toward Aunt Lucille and Uncle Bobby for how badly they'd treated her while she was growing up, but, feeling sorry for her in that condition, kissed her on the cheek, then left.

Once they drove off, Cynthia sifted through the papers she'd found. It was unbelievable how Uncle Bobby and Thomas had calculated every sick, twisted ploy to devastate Cynthia's life. She learned by reading through the papers that Thomas was responsible for Aunt Lucille being in a wheelchair, and Uncle Bobby's sorry ass sold Cynthia and Chris out to save his own hide.

## Shelly L. Foster

Cynthia was fuming with anger at the very thought of Uncle Bobby still interfering in her life. When they got back to Ardelia's house, she and Ardelia spread all the papers out on the dining room table, while Chris went to call Lolly. They pieced the papers together like a puzzle, hoping to make enough sense of it to file legal charges against them.

Surprisingly enough, the papers led them down an even more frightening path. It appeared as though they were linked to Jordan, Mary and James' deaths. They'd spent an enormous amount of time planning, calculating and orchestrating tactics that would bring Cynthia to her knees. Cynthia scooped up the papers and told Ardelia, "Let's get copies of everything."

Chris elected to stay and talk on the phone while they went to make copies. While they were on the road, Cynthia called Frank and asked him to meet them at the house. Once copies were made, they went straight back to the house to meet Frank.

Frank, Ardelia and Cynthia put everything together, then planned a strategy for the next day. The time had come for Thomas and Uncle Bobby to take the fall for all the havoc they had caused in Cynthia's life. They dropped Chris off at Lolly's, and Cynthia, Ardelia and Frank headed to the police precinct. They stormed into Detective Shelton's office, slamming papers on his desk and simultaneously telling him about the manufactured scheme.

Of course, Detective Shelton couldn't act solely on what they were telling him. He let them know that he and his team would look into it. Frank and Cynthia were livid that he was so damn cavalier about their findings. They left, but also decided not to leave it to the police to bring it to closure. The police had already proven that they were unreliable, ill-equipped, pitiful, pathetic excuses for law enforcement,

## Deadly Choices

anyway.

Cynthia was leaving for New York the next day, Frank was to go back to Aunt Lucille's, and Ardelia would man the phones at the house. Cynthia asked Chris if she wanted to stay at Lolly's for a day or two, and naturally she said yes.

Cynthia had no idea how this situation would spiral, or if it would become a dangerous situation for her or her child, so she wanted Chris safely tucked away. They dropped Frank off at his house, and Cynthia and Ardelia went back to Ardelia's. They went through the night without saying much to each other. They both were in a grey, dismal mood. The gloom was hanging low throughout the house.

Regardless of how concerned Ardelia was for Cynthia, she couldn't begin to understand her pain. Cynthia felt as though all her dreams, goals and accomplishments had evaporated into thin air. After all the abuse she'd endured growing up, and the years of hell Jordan had put her through, she wasn't expecting to go deeper into the hell hole.

Cynthia lay in bed, far from a good nights sleep. As much as she despised Uncle Bobby and Thomas for creating this much grief in her life, she knew she had to stay anchored and focused. If she weren't grounded, everything could blow up in her face.

Morning came without Cynthia getting any sleep. Ardelia dropped her off at the airport and wished her the best of luck.

The entire flight, all she could think of was crushing those two weasels, and watching them fry in the electric chair.

"Thank you for flying with us. The current temperature in New York City is eighty-eight degrees. Have a pleasant stay," the pilot announced.

There was no need to go to baggage claim since she had only a carry on bag. On her way out she was approached by a fine, charismatic man who talked to her all the way to the taxi.

*Oh hell no. This is not happening to me. The last thing I need is to hook up with another crazy motherfucker. He's fine, but he talks too damn much to have any social graces.* She hopped in the taxi and closed the door before he could say anything else. She put her hands over her ears and screamed before telling the taxi driver her destination.

She went straight from the airport to Thomas' house, turned the key, and discovered it didn't unlock. Disgusted, she realized Thomas apparently had the locks changed.

She walked around the house to see if there were any open windows where she could see inside. The blinds were up in the window near the kitchen on the side of the house. The rooms she could see into were empty, not a piece of furniture in sight. Completely baffled by Thomas' sudden move, she returned to the front of the house, thinking about what she must have left inside, and relieved she'd left most of her things in storage. As she sat on the front porch with her head gripped by the palms of her hands, Chris' buddies came walking down the block. She motioned for them to come up and talk to her. She questioned what, if anything, they might have seen going on since she and Chris had been gone.

Olivia was the first to speak. She'd seen a moving van there yesterday. Then Drew chimed in, "I saw the housekeeper lady crying when she left, but she left with a few suitcases in a taxi." After getting all the info she could from them, she decided to go back to where they'd met...House of Beauty, and see if Cutie might be able to steer her in Thomas' direction.

She arrived in town about an hour and a half later, shocked to find an abandoned business. Tears came streaming down her face, as

## Deadly Choices

she looked at the Commercial Real Estate sign that read, "For lease." *Damn it, he knows that I know. He's several steps ahead of me again. Shit, all the evidence I gave to the police won't do me any good if both Thomas and Uncle Bobby have disappeared.*

She could see her life crumbling right before her eyes and couldn't seem to do a damn thing to stop it. She leaned against the window, partially sitting in the window seat. She was fighting back the tears that were trying to force their way out, trapped with no hint of a possible solution. New York was too big and congested for her to play private eye, so she took a taxi to the airport and waited for her flight. The hours of sitting left her with only her thoughts. Her mind raced, rewound, paused and played...on, and on, and on. If it weren't for her daughter, suicide would have been an option, but she would rather wait for the opportunity to smell the aroma of their butts burning in the electric chair. She wondered all the way home if she'd ever get that opportunity since they'd vanished so quickly. Surely the bumbling, boys in blue squad wouldn't be of any help. She believed if the rain falling didn't feel wet like piss, they wouldn't have the wit to open an umbrella.

By the time the plane landed in Chicago, Cynthia was mentally and emotionally exhausted. As soon as she sat in Ardelias's car, she lapsed into a temporary emotional breakdown. She cried, screamed and pounded her fists on the dashboard. Ardelia sat patiently and let her get as much of the hurt out as possible. Unfortunately, traffic patrol wouldn't let her stay where she was parked, so she moved the car outside the terminal area, not quite making it past the parking lot. Luckily they were going slow. Cynthia opened the car door while the car was in motion and vomited onto the street.

Once she gained her composure, they continued to the house.

Cynthia's head was aching so badly her eye sockets burned. She took several pills to relieve the pressure in her head, placed a cold compress over her eyes, then drifted off to sleep.

Ardelia stayed downstairs, anticipating the details of the trip. Obviously, she could tell things didn't go well, but had no idea of the magnitude of the problems and how tangled up Cynthia had become. Ardelia snuggled up on the sofa and was napping when the doorbell rang.

Frank came charging through the door, ranting and raving about what he'd learned at Aunt Lucille's house. Ardelia ran upstairs to wake Cynthia.

Frank filled them in on his findings. He had gotten to the house when the nurse was there, and she told the whole, sordid story. He'd found out that Aunt Lucille was Thomas' first victim. He got to her first, so he'd have Uncle Bobby right where he wanted him. Knowing at that point how vicious and determined Thomas was, he became Thomas' puppet, dancing to every tug of his strings. A couple of days after Jordan was killed, the nurse overheard him discussing it with Thomas on the phone. That's when Uncle Bobby was instructed to follow Cynthia. Thomas bought Uncle Bobby a vehicle with dark, tinted windows, and he tracked her every move.

"So that black sport utility vehicle that I noticed was Uncle Bobby?"

"Apparently so. Thomas has enough money to make anything happen. Getting Uncle Bobby under his thumb was insurance."

"But, why me? Uncle Bobby was the one who dumped his mother, and left him without a father. No one Thomas has hurt had a damn thing to do with that."

"After the nurse overheard the conversation about Jordan's

## Deadly Choices

murder, she started taping the calls."

Frank pulled out a bag full of tapes and told her to listen. Ardelia left the room to find a portable recorder. When she returned with it, they sat for hours listening to the tapes.

The very last tape revealed the answer to her questions. Thomas and Cynthia went to the same high school, but she only knew him by his nickname, Butter. He was a couple of years older, very withdrawn, nerdy and always alone. Cynthia, on the other hand, had confidence and was very well known. One of her girlfriends, Candace, took a liking to Thomas, and the attention made him start to come out of his shell. He built up enough nerve to ask Candace out, and she accepted. But, when the time came to go out, not only did Cynthia convince Candace to stand him up and tell him she didn't want to go, but they humiliated him in public on top of it.

Cynthia had coerced several of their high school chums to go with Candace to meet Thomas on the date. They teased him about his clothes and joked that he didn't have a clue what to do with a girl. The last words he remembered stayed with him until this day. Those bitter words drove him to become educated, wealthy, a great lover, socially graced and powerful. He knew by achieving those things he could get and do whatever the hell he pleased.

Cynthia had told him that he was a spineless, limp noodle who was a carbon copy of his wimpy dad who couldn't get his woman. He lost her to a man who didn't want her or Thomas. He'd never amount to anything. Maybe one day when she was successful, he and his mom could come work for her.

Those words were etched into Thomas' brain, and it was her turn to suffer. He worked extremely hard to become the man he was. Everything he did, he did with the thought of Cynthia. Not only was he not the same withdrawn, nerdy boy he once was, he looked completely different than he did in high school.

Cynthia was really concerned that not only did Thomas have more money and resources, but he had all her things, and was now missing in action. Before now, she didn't realize he was dangerous, but she had become jittery and scared. She didn't have the energy left to spar with him, who behaved like a crazy son-of-a-bitch.

She was more willing to swallow her pride and let those blithering, blockhead boys in blue chase the ghosts.

They gathered up the tapes and took them to Detective Shelton. Cynthia was staid and demure while they talked to the detective. Frank and Ardelia sat quietly and listened to the detective explain to Cynthia what his squad was prepared to do. Neither of them believed a word he said. They rolled their eyes, and basically tuned him out until his words became nothing more than a mumble. They left his office feeling about as secure and safe as a goldfish in a tank filled with piranhas.

# 39

**W**eeks passed and the police hadn't made any progress, or so it seemed.

When she called the storage company they wouldn't discuss anything with her. Since Thomas made the arrangements, he was the only one they would talk to. They were probably on his payroll like everybody else. Cynthia was literally starting from scratch. She and Chris bought new furniture and moved back into the house. Thank goodness it wasn't sold. Ardelia wanted them to stay with her for a while, but Cynthia felt trapped, living in someone else's home. She needed her independence.

She swallowed hard and put it all in perspective. She was glad the partners had asked her to come back to work and she was so ready to go.

She didn't think Monday would ever come, but it did. She was sharp as a tack. She strolled in the office in a black silk suit. The skirt was long and straight. The jacket was long and cut perfectly to fit her curves. Her blouse was white and heavily starched. The cufflinks matched her earrings and necklace.

She stood outside her office door for a few moments before going in. Once inside, she looked around, taking it all in. Nestled into the Italian leather of her chair, she was feeling pretty damn good. When Marge arrived, she came in with coffee. It felt like old times again. She gathered her things for the Monday morning partner meeting. The partners gave her a warm welcome, then got right down to business.

Cynthia functioned as though she had never been gone. She was in her element, and loving every minute of it. The partners gave her back her client files, with the expectation that she would close any open issues, and keep from losing any business. In other words, she was to save the day.

Excited and ready to take on anything, Cynthia returned to her office to reach out to her clients. She called Marge into her office to talk about expectations. She thought it best to keep Marge around. She didn't think Marge knew all the details, but if Thomas were to come out of hiding, she wanted her near. There was always a chill in the air when they were together, but Cynthia wasn't about to let the only link to Thomas slip through her fingers.

Days went by, and each day Cynthia and Marge co-existed better and better. Chris and Cynthia hadn't forgotten or overcome all the madness in their lives, but they were slowly getting back some normalcy.

The phone rang.

"Cynthia Evans." She spoke into the phone.

"Mrs. Evan?"

"Yes."

"This is Detective Shelton."

Cynthia sat up in her chair. "Have you found them?" She

## Deadly Choices

asked.

"We have tracked them down, but unfortunately there's nothing we can do."

"Nothing you can do?" her confidence waned, despite the fact that she'd given them so much evidence.

"They're out of the country. We can't touch them now."

Cynthia slammed the phone down and swung her chair around to face the window.

*There is a reason and a season for the treason I spent under his terror. My eyes have expanded and I demand growth. I am the queen bee I noticed outside my window some time ago.*

After thinking about it long and hard, she refused to cave into the pressure. She decided to focus on her work and her child again. That was what was most important, anyway.

Thomas had disappeared from her life as quickly as he appeared, or so it seemed.

Check out a sample chapter of the upcoming sequel……………..Coming soon!

*"Deadly Consequences"*

# 1

"Run. Run Cynthia run!" Ardelia grabbed Cynthia by the arm, pulling her along the downtown streets of Chicago, fearing for their lives. They ducked into the doorway of a closed restaurant. They stood holding each other, shivering with fear. Moments later, they heard footsteps coming in their direction. They were paralyzed by the mere thought that they were in danger. As the rapid footsteps got closer, their embrace became more intense. They tightly shut their eyes, accepting that they would die in each other's arms. The footsteps stopped at the doorway, which made their adrenaline race, their hearts pound and their anticipation of death a reality in their minds. As they waited for their demise to come to fruition, a calm soothing voice asked, "Are you okay?"

A sigh of relief overwhelmed them both, and within a few seconds they opened their eyes and released their embrace, but they were unable to speak immediately. After collecting themselves, Cynthia spoke first.

"We were being followed by two men, so we hid in this

doorway."

Ardelia chimed right in, offering her two cents.

"We thought you were them, and we just knew we were about to die."

One of the men reached into his pocket pulling out a police shield, to identify who they were. The other one offered to take them home. They declined to be taken home, but did ask to be escorted to their car.

Once at the car, they hopped into Ardelia's Mercedes and peeled out fast, leaving the officers standing at the curb in their smoke. The two men glanced at each other then proceeded to their car.

Ardelia and Cynthia went straight to Cynthia's house, arriving in record time. They went inside and flopped down on the sofa, still amazed by their ordeal.

Cynthia was taken aback, since her life seemed to be getting back to normal. After Thomas and Uncle Bobby disappeared, she figured moving on would be fairly easy to do. For a while, normalcy had been a thing of the past. For months Cynthia had fought her way through an emotional battlefield, giving all she had to Chris, and her business. Chris was finally able to sleep alone, and in her own room again. Cynthia had her business relationships gripped in the palm of her hand. A sense of security and a road to recovery was in reach. Now this...*Who could that have been following us?* Cynthia thought. Her mind was on overload, ready to explode at any moment. She realized what was happening, and took control. There was no way she was going to allow Thomas to reek havoc on their lives again.

While they sat in silence, collecting their thoughts, the doorbell rang. They both jumped up from the sofa and crept to the door. After the ordeal they'd just experienced, neither was too eager to open the

## Deadly Consequences

door. Ardelia peeked out of the bottom corner of the window, but was only able to see one set of feet, a large pair of penny loafers with no indication who they belonged to. Cynthia cracked the door enough to get a full frontal view, and was relieved to see it was only Frank. Frank had a questioning look on his face, as he observed Cynthia's hesitation to open the door. Once over the threshold, he questioned what was wrong.

Cynthia and Ardelia each gave an account of their perilous day. Frank's demeanor was a bit alarming. He didn't seem to be surprised or up in arms by their story. Cynthia immediately noticed how unconcerned he appeared to be, and commented, "What's up with you Frank? You don't seem to be the least bit concerned."

"No, that's not it at all. I'm just taking it all in. I thought this mess was in the past, and didn't expect to hear what you'd just told me. Do you think the men you saw were Thomas and Uncle Bobby?"

"We don't know who they were. By the time they were close enough to see their faces, we were too busy running away," Cynthia responded.

Ardelia interjected, "At the time, we didn't care who it was. We knew we were in danger, and acted accordingly. What difference does it make who it was? Our lives were threatened and the bottom line is we escaped unscathed."

"It matters if it was a random situation, or if it's Thomas and Uncle Bobby. You should be prepared to deal with whatever fallout may come later. Either way, you're still scared and panicked so..."

Ardelia cut him off in mid sentence, "Of course we are still scared, but you act as though we shouldn't be."

"That's not it at all. I just think that if it's an isolated situation, and Thomas and Uncle Bobby aren't in the picture, there's nothing to fear."

Cynthia raised a brow, irritated by his blasé attitude. It was apparent that his company was no longer She decided Frank's presence was no longer welcome, so she stood and walked to the door.

"Thanks for stopping by, Frank." she announced as she opened the front door.

Frank rose from his seat and left without saying a word. Cynthia slammed the door as he exited, and returned to the den with Ardelia.

"Can you believe how nonchalant he was?"

Ardelia shook her head in agreement, then drifted into her own thoughts. Frank's statements made her replay the events, searching for more details in her mind. She figured if she thought about it more methodically, she would recall something that her emotions had allowed her to omit. Ardelia rested her head onto the back of the sofa, propped her feet on the coffee table and closed her eyes. Cynthia moved to the recliner and curled up in a fetal position. Soon they were both asleep.

Meanwhile, Frank was next door at his place feeling sorry for himself. He had always been weak for Cynthia, but she'd been humiliating him ever since he was mistakenly arrested for the murders, and tried to pin them on Chris. At any rate, he was not riding on her bandwagon anymore. He only stuck as close to her as he did to help get the stink of the murders off his back. Actually, he'd begun to loathe her. In his eyes she was wicked, and needed to be brought down a peg or two. He pondered his thoughts for a while then turned his energy to a movie that had been watching him, instead of him watching it. Eventually, he was snoring on the sofa.

Several hours passed, and Cynthia and Ardelia were stirring about the house. Cynthia decided to fix them something to eat, so she went to the kitchen to prepare a meal. Ardelia joined her in the kitchen, striking up a light conversation. Neither of them wanted to think about what had happened earlier, much less talk about it. Before long they were laughing about the outfit Cynthia's secretary, Marge had worn to the office.

"The fashion police wouldn't have written her a ticket; they would have taken her ass straight to jail in that get-up."

Ardelia was laughing hysterically, when Cynthia made the comment, but managed to make her own silly remark as well.

"They would have stripped her, burned her clothes then took her to jail butt naked. Those clothes didn't deserve a ride to the police station."

"Do you think I should make her get a makeover? Maybe I could give her a bonus, strictly for shopping purposes."

"Hell, she would spend the whole wad on a closet full of floral, striped and polka-dot mistakes. You need to take her to a fashion consultant."

"I don't want to be seen with her. Even with twenty-first century clothes, she still reeks of Ben-Gay."

"And don't forget the stockings that fall and drape over her shoes."

Cynthia covered her mouth with her hand, gasping, and on the verge of tears. She waved her other hand in the air, in an attempt to stop Ardelia from commenting, but it didn't work. Ardelia came back with more.

"What about the wig? Don't forget the mangy wig that smells like old cooking oil."

Choking and sniffing, Cynthia bent over holding her side then ran out of the kitchen. Ardelia ran behind her laughing, and joking more about Marge. Cynthia ran into the bathroom and locked Ardelia on the other side. Ardelia was pounding on the door and shouting jokes at the same time.

"Maybe if she took a bath, more often than once a week on Saturday nights, her odor might not linger, and the stench wouldn't hit you in the face before you enter your office!"

Cynthia jerked the bathroom door open, with eyes as big as golf balls.

"Girl! Are you telling me you can smell her, when you enter my office?"

"You can't smell it? I never said anything 'cause I thought you knew."

"I must have become immune to the smell. Oh my God, my clients smell that stinky odor when they come in my office!"

"Yep, I would imagine so. I smell it every time I come to see you."

Cynthia went back into the kitchen and Ardelia followed. Cynthia sat at the kitchen table, and placed her head in her hand. Ardelia could tell Cynthia was embarrassed, so she let up on teasing her. Cynthia raised her head, and naturally the embarrassment showed all over her face. Ardelia smelling the odor didn't embarrass Cynthia, but she was definitely embarrassed about the clients who must have smelled her.

"I had a client come see me today that I was a little taken with, and he was interested in me as well. I hope he doesn't think I'm the stinky one. Maybe that's why he got the hell out of my office so fast."

"Anyone that comes in your office knows it's Marge that's stinking. The smell leaves your nostrils three feet into your office. He

## Deadly Consequences

knows it's not you, so don't sweat it."

"That's easy for you to say. You're not the one who people think smell like a sour pickle closed up in a jar for a long period of time."

Ardelia pointed at Cynthia and shook her head. They both fell out laughing again.

"That was wrong. She doesn't smell that bad."

"The hell she doesn't. She is F U N K Y. I'm going to have building services come down and fumigate tomorrow. Then I'm going to have a heart to heart with ole' girl about her personal hygiene. And then...she simply must go to a fashion consultant. Her nineteen sixty nine wardrobe can no longer be worn at my place of business."

Cynthia was irritated with the thought of her clients having to smell that terrible odor when coming into her office.

"Let's not spend anymore time talking about stinky old Marge. Let me tell you about this guy I met today."

"I don't want to burst your bubble, but the last thing you need is to get involved with anyone right now."

"Why not? It's been months since all that mess with Thomas. Am I expected to be a hermit?"

"No, you're not expected to be a hermit, but I would think that with all you went through, you wouldn't want to be bothered. I thought you were going to focus on your daughter and your work?"

"Well, Ms. smart ass, we talked about a business venture. He's good looking, but that's not the focus of the relationship."

"I'm sorry, but you didn't say it was for work."

"You didn't give me a chance to say much of anything before you lit into me. It's not about work with the firm. It's about a new business venture for me to consider."

"What kind of business?"

"Real estate investments."

"How will you be able to juggle your current business, your child and real estate investments?"

"There won't be much leg work. I will only be investing as a financial partner."

A concerned look swept across Ardelia's face, and she tightly closed her lips. She knew if she spoke, Cynthia wouldn't like what she had to say, so she said nothing.

"What? What is it, Ardelia?"

Silence filled the room, but Ardelia wouldn't say a word.

"Come on, spit it out Ardelia."

"I'm sure you don't want to hear what I have to say."

"Yes I do. Tell me."

"I don't think you should get involved with anyone you don't know, especially investing your money. Why would you take a chance with your money with a stranger?"

"There are five investors to purchase a mall that is drowning. We're going to revitalize the mall, and the community. There's not a lot of risk."

"Not a lot of risk? Not a lot of risk? Giving your money to someone you don't know is a risk, Cynthia."

"I feel good about it, and it's going to make me a lot of money."

"How did you come to know this guy? What made him ask you in on the deal?"

"We met a few weeks ago by chance, while I was having lunch. We talked for hours, and then we scheduled time to meet today."

"So, like I said, you don't know him."

## Deadly Consequences

"Right, Ardelia. I don't really know him, but I'm going to invest anyway. What's the worst thing that could happen? I could loose a few thousand dollars, but I stand to gain several million. The higher the risk, the higher the reward."

"Whatever. I'll be right here when you need a shoulder to cry on."

"Why are you putting your pessimism in my space? I can do without your negative energy."

Ardelia pushed away from the table, grabbed her purse and car keys, and left.

All the way home, she thought of nothing but how Cynthia was making a big mistake. She didn't understand how Cynthia could be so careless and trusting, after all she'd been through. Part of her wanted to turn her car around and go back and shake some sense into her, but she knew Cynthia would only dig her heals in if she felt pressured to change her mind. She felt a pang in her gut that said Cynthia was headed for trouble. Nonetheless, she was hopeful things would work out as Cynthia believed they would.

Back at Cynthia's house, Cynthia was loafing around, unable to eat. She kicked up her feet, stretching out on the sofa to relax. Although she believed in her friend, and valued her opinion, she had never gone to Ardelia about business decisions before, and her decisions had always worked out fine. She was ready to make more money, and the investment required minimal dollars up front. She didn't feel any amount of apprehension, so she decided to go with her instincts. She picked up the phone and called Anthony D'Amato to set up a time for them to finalize their deal. They agreed on Friday at three o'clock. After finishing their conversation, Cynthia wrapped up in a blanket, and drifted off to sleep.

# Shelly L. Foster

*Deadly Choices*
**By Shelly L. Foster**

Book Club Discussion Questions

❖ The book starts with Cynthia taking a beating from her husband Jordan, but shortly after she successfully evades him, she gives him permission to come to her new home. Why is the behavior so common in women living in abusive situations?

❖ When speaking to James, Cynthia tells him that she's not looking for a relationship and that she just wants to have a fun when she feels like it with whomever she feels like. Why do you think she went from desperate housewife, to mourning widow, to all around party girl in such a short period of time?

❖ It's clear what Mary's intentions were toward Cynthia. What do you think Cynthia's intentions for her relationship with Mary were?

❖ When Chris expresses her opinions of her mother's new behavior when she and Cynthia have their "heart to heart", Cynthia tells her "it's not what you do, but how you do it". In your opinion, is this an adequate way to address a teenager's concerns?

❖ Without knowing him very well, Cynthia almost immediately tells Thomas about the rape of her daughter, to Chris' total embarrassment. Do you think this gave Thomas a knowledge base he needed to further manipulate Cynthia? Do you think people can give up "too much" personal info when meeting someone that can lead to future manipulation in the relationship?

❖ Considering Cynthia's prior behavior and decisions, do you think her response to her daughter's rape was par for the course? What about her reaction to finding out who actually raped her daughter?

❖ If you had to choose one, which do you think people lean more towards when making choices in general, values (how a person was raised) or personal desires?

# Deadly Choices

## Book Club Survey

1. **Do you consider yourself an**:
   _____ Avid reader (more than 3 books per month)
   _____ Moderate Reader (2 – books per month)
   _____ Light Reader (1 book per month, sometimes not finishing the book)

2. **Types of books you usually enjoy reading**:
   _____ Fiction
   _____ Non-Fiction

3. **Title/Cover:**
   Intriguing -
   (would make me pick this up in a bookstore)
   Interesting -
   (fits story would not make me pick up in a store)

   **Storyline:** Please circle one
   Page turning     Typical
   Moderately Interesting   Not Interesting

   **Writing Style:** (verbiage, flow of reading)
   1= agree, 2=somewhat agree, 3=disagree

   Easy to read and follow           1  2  3
   Indicative of first time author   1  2  3
   Difficult to follow the story     1  2  3
   Verbiage made it easy to picture
   characters/places                 1  2  3

**Ending**: Did the ending make you want to read the second book?   Yes/No

## BOOK AVAILABLE BY CONTACTING
### Royal Peacock Publications
*Deadly Choices* - $17.95
### ORDER FORM
PO Box 931
Dayton, NJ 08810-0931
732 274 9494 Fax
www.Royal-Peacock-Publications.com

Name _____

Address _____

City _____ State _____ Zip _____

Contact Telephone # _____

Book Title _____ Qty _____

Total Due                           $ _____

Sales Tax                           $ _____

Shipping & Handling per book Add    $   6.00

Total Amount Due                    $ _____

Form of payment
o        Master Card    Card # _____
                Exp . Date _____

o        Visa           Card # _____
                Exp. Date _____
Driver's License No. _____

Signature _____

o        Money Order

# Deadly Choices

## NOTES

Shelly L. Foster

NOTES